THE SINFUL SON

THE SINFUL SON

VINCE P. HENNESSY

Charleston, SC
www.PalmettoPublishing.com

The Sinful Son
Copyright © 2021 by Vince P. Hennessy

All rights reserved
No portion of this book may be reproduced, stored in a retrieval system, or transmitted in any form by any means–electronic, mechanical, photocopy, recording, or other–except for brief quotations in printed reviews, without prior permission of the author.

First Edition

Paperback ISBN: 978-1-63837-153-3
Hardcover ISBN: 978-1-63837-154-0
eBook ISBN: 978-1-63837-155-7

TABLE OF CONTENTS

Chapter 1: A Troubled Relationship — 1
Chapter 2: The Sinful Son — 31
Chapter 3: The Torturer, Sweet But Psychotic — 48
Chapter 4: Internal Insights — 72
Chapter 5: A Demonic Dream — 97
Chapter 6: The Illusions Of Time — 105
Chapter 7: Mr. Monatomic — 143
Chapter 8: Future And Past Decisions — 181
Chapter 9: The Dark Future Ahead — 194
Chapter 10: Departure: Cape Cod Killer — 205
Chapter 11: The Darkness Within All — 223

CHAPTER 1

A TROUBLED RELATIONSHIP
(Somewhere off the coast of Florida. April 16, 2022)

Jolting straight up in his bed with the throat-scratching growl of a defensive animal, Damon's heart beated rapidly as he tried to get a hold of his surroundings. With a bang of his lethal fist, he turned off the loud alarm clock that was next to his bed.

"You annoying bi-" Physically biting his tongue with his sharp teeth, Damon stopped himself from cursing. It had been decades since he had last cursed. After realizing that he was above everyone else, he had vowed to never curse, as he was meant to be a savior, and unholy words would soil his reputation. Still, he could not stop his mind from thinking of vulgar and crude expressions, and given his past memories, he had difficulty not cursing, as it was almost natural to do so.

Damon squinted at the glowing red numbers on the clock, the only things visible in the pitch-black and windowless room. *Why do I have an alarm set for nine in the morning? What a waste of recovery time that my temple-of-a-body requires. My heart's enraged with a thousand fires. I've probably lost a day or two of life from waking up so early.* Aggravated, he thought for a moment, half-asleep as he was. *Oh... I know why*, he mentally grumbled.

Placing his hands on the edge of the bed, Damon pushed off of the musty mattress whose half-rusted springs cried out in response. Although he had woken up earlier than usual, his morning routine was almost always the same, and so he had no need to turn the lights on to know what he was doing. To him, the darkness was far more comforting. Carefully sensing his surroundings and using his memory, Damon grabbed a tall glass of lemon-water from his nightstand and drank it all in order to properly function. Placing it down, he shuffled across the dark room to a corner across from the door.

There in the corner was where his day truly started, and where he became his true self. Grabbing his costume, or uniform as he called it, and scientific gear from a display rack, Damon swiftly became what Kronos had nicknamed The Dark Depressor. He exited the room into the bright and bland hallway, dressed as if he were the Grim Reaper himself, but far worse.

The building in which he resided was almost a horrific labyrinth, and Damon passed through several medicinal-like hallways that were in poor condition, some with flickering lights and others stained with blood. The sights had grown old and routine, but the musty and moldy smell of the place still bothered him when he was not dressed as Florida Phantom, for, in his uniform, he was safe from the cancerous odors.

Knowing the labyrinth-of-a-building from years of navigating it's almost identical hallways, Damon swiftly arrived at his destination, a fast-walker by birth. He turned into a small kitchen which was dimly lit, ducking down to fit under the doorway, as his masculine physique was too tall. He quickly scanned the room, his eyes stopping on a woman who was leaning against an old fridge, eating a durian fruit. She gently rubbed her fingers across the spikes of the fruit, tenderly sipping the blood of one purposefully cut finger before throwing the skin into a small garbage can beside her. She glanced up at him inattentively before returning her attention back to the fruit.

"Morning, Damon," the woman said emotionlessly. "Glad to see you're up bright and early as I had told you to be." It was silent for a moment except for the ticking of a clock that was off-beat, the battery half-dead as the hands of the clock moved monotonously. "You're not *still* mad at me, are you? That would be foolish, of course, but I can only speak for myself. Besides, you're always angry, so it wouldn't surprise me. You hold grudges over the smallest and stupidest things."

Damon leaned against the wall opposite from the woman, all of his features hidden beneath the darkness of the black cloak except for a pair of fear-inducing red eyes that would send Satan himself back to Hell out of terror. His height was staggering and made mountains look small, and while not wide, his body seemed to be giant and unstoppable, capable of grabbing the planet itself and pushing it into the sun if possible. His darkness was all-consuming like space, and the presence he brought seem just as hostile and lethal. No life could exist where he went. If death had a physical form, Damon was the existing embodiment of such a terrifying figure. His aura of rage and destruction was preceded by an eerie and unsettled calm like the feeling creatures get before a major storm came, and animals fled when they sensed him approaching. His footsteps made the ground tremble slightly with each step, and he walked so fast that the land beneath him was never still. His breaths seemed to be contained hurricanes that could easily break free, and Damon's heart constantly pounded so quickly and powerfully that it could be mistaken for the sound of distant thunder, another warning of the aura of utter natural destruction that he exuded without effort.

Damon reached into the deathly darkness of the black hood and disabled the mask around his mouth and nose that filtered his naturally horrific voice into a monstrous one of unimaginable terror. Damon cleared his throat, the sound alone an echo of thunder, before speaking, his words emitting a mixed tone of half raging beast, and the other half the pondering tone of a profound philosopher. He was an unnatural combination of the most inhumane darkness of death and the holiest pureness of life.

"It's hard to stay mad at the only thing you have besides yourself, even when the burning hatred and rage is justified." Damon looked at the woman, who stood frozen like a statue, her wavy ginger hair and white dress only moving ever so slightly with the light wind that was created by a ceiling fan overhead that was missing a blade and spinning so slowly that it might as well have not been moving at all. "*Even* if that thing is a woman, and one who cares more about herself and inflicting pain on others than sharing her love with me. One who is a deceitful manipulator of weak-hearted men who have nothing else. The truth is that all you care about is yourself. As grateful as I am, I've known that since you first saved me, for even that was done in the interest of yourself."

The woman softly sighed and looked up at the tall shadowy figure just a few feet away, locking her grey eyes into the red artificial ones higher up that stared down at her with pure contempt. Her face shifted between hurt and frustrated, but whether or not it was earnest or fake was undeterminable. "Damon... you know that's not true. I-"

"As expected of a manipulator and liar, who has been one ever since her unholy birth. You would dare to claim that it's not true, just as any accused person would, but it is undeniably true, whether justified or not. As long as I can remember, which goes back to when I first met you, you have always been a sadistic sociopath and psychopath. The worst of both worlds."

"*That's* such-"

"Yet... that's never stopped me from loving you, and none of the other horrible things have either. Even though you constantly manipulate me and take advantage of me and lie to me, I stay loyal and in love because I care about you so deeply that I would rather be hurt and with you than alone and emotionally healthy. I *never* judged you like everyone else did, for I can see what they cannot. My heart is pure, and my eyes are divine, and I know the true you, but I cannot deny the negative qualities that so viciously possess you. Until recently, they have been forgivable and tolerable despite how unholy they were, but your drive to torture has only gotten worse, and it will continue to get worse. It is an addiction that will grow exponentially until the level of torture and pain required to satisfy you is impossible to achieve, and if it is, enacting on it will result in consequences too large for us to handle. Your addiction will physically, mentally, and emotionally consume you, or you'll consume everyone else instead. You must cleanse your tainted soul of torture thoroughly by detoxing, and I am here to help you. I hold a grudge and am upset because I care about you, and I'm the only person who does. The closer you get to being unnaturally satisfied, the further away you push *me*, like we are but drifting boats upon a rocky *sea*."

"Now you're taking the rhyming talk and poetry out on me? That hurts. It hurts to hear you treat me like some addict who has lost her marbles. A manipulator and liar? Ouch." The woman walked away from the brown fridge and leaned against the end of a worn-down island in the center of the small kitchen. "Damon, think about the past. You love to do that for yourself, so why don't you do it for me for once. Who has provided for you for all these years? Who has loved you like a mother but also like a girlfriend? Who saved you from the streets and allowed you to uncage the version of yourself that was locked away inside? Who is the only person you're not angry around? Who let loose the true you that was an outcast of society because his views weren't accepted?"

"You did, but-"

"But *what*, Damon? Why would I do that?"

"Don't you *dare* try to guilt-trip me or use loving actions to make me think that I'm being too harsh. Those used to work on me, but that was a *long* time ago. You want me to answer that you did it out of love, that you saw something in me, and that you're not crazy, and I'm the one who's being a terrible person. Those are all false. They're lies that worked perfectly at the time, and for the past few decades that I've been by your side. I know the truth, though: ***you just needed someone to be your little henchman!***" Damon thundered powerfully, almost shaking the whole room as he pointed at her with a swift and violent motion, all the air around him dispelling from the force as his black cloak move like its own entity with him. "You only saved me because you needed someone to gather people for you to torture and have your way with! It was *never* about me. Upon your person, you shoulder many wicked sins, but manipulation is by far your gravest."

"Stop acting all macho around me. I'm not selfish or a manipulator, and if you truly believe that I have been all this time, then you would have left decades ago. If I *truly* needed a henchman, then why choose *you?*" the woman asked as she stopped leaning against the island and stood erect, her tone no longer hurt but rather that of a manipulative psychiatrist who was fond of mind-games. "Why save *you* of all people? After all, you were just a scrawny boy on the verge of death with a broken life and no future, or *any* potential, as far as anyone else was concerned. No one was coming for you, and you knew that. There are *billions* of people in this world, Damon," the woman exclaimed as she gestured to everything. "Do you honestly think that I didn't see *something* in *you?*" She stopped and stood still again, staring directly up into the burning artificial eyes that glared at her from across the room. "But then again, I guess that *anyone* could be **The Sinful Son**," the woman hissed, her eyes almost smirking. "Is that what you're saying?"

"*No!*" Damon shouted out devastatingly like Satan himself in a rage as his fiendish voice echoed throughout the empty building. Damon clenched his deadly hands into killer fists as his whole body instantly tensed up with uncontrollable rage. His chest heaved with hatred, and the weight of the air in the room grew heavy with his ominous aura of absolute destruction. He appeared to be even taller than before. "**Only I can be The Sinful Son**," Damon stated with a forceful point at himself. "He's not just any person, nor any broken person! It's not just about enduring emotional and verbal abuse or the terrible trials of a relentlessly unsurvivable life. **The Sinful Son** is a mindset, a belief, and an alter-ego of only one person, and that's me. You knew that when you saw me in the hospital!" Damon bellowed, his voice enraged as he pointed at the woman again. "You knew that only *I* was powerful enough and truly fated in unholy intertwined paths to become the servant you needed."

"You're *wrong*, Damon," the woman replied coldly. "What you're implying is self-conceited and delusionally fictional. I didn't know *that* when I found you. How could I have known that? No one except you knew what you could become. I saw *something* in you... yes... but I could have never imagined how great you would become. You've far exceeded my expectations, even while holding back and only using a small portion of your unholy power."

Damon, who was constantly angry as if it were his natural state, was shaking with rage as he stood up straight, no longer leaning against the cracked wall, his head almost touching the damp ceiling. His chest and arms rose with each heavy breath as he held back from rushing across the room and killing the woman he loved in an unforgivable outburst of wrath. The beating of his heart was thunderous, and his veins and arteries were railways for rushing trains of molten blood. "Is that so? Among the unexplored concepts of this universe, it's quite possible that such a truth exists, even in the heart of she who lies and manipulates instinctively as was coded into her very person upon conception. It would be false for me to deny such an existence. If that truth does, indeed, line up with you standing here before me, then *what* exactly did you see?"

The woman left her position at the head of the island and walked around the corner of it, sitting down on a tall stool with a stained cushion. She stared at the doorway from which Damon had entered, her elbows on the island, and propped up to hold her head as she dared not look at him, her mind flashing back to the past. "At first glance, I just saw an idiot who had tried to kill himself, or who *had* killed himself to be more accurate. Then, I saw a teenage boy who was lost in the world. No... scrap that. Not lost, but misguided by others, and even himself. I could see that you were mentally and emotionally abused, and that's putting it kindly. Your heart was shattered to the point that the glass shards of it may as well have been grains of sharp sand. You can tell when someone's been mentally and emotionally broken, or at least I could. I had been studying psychology for years to try and understand my own twisted mind, but in the end, I could never figure out this mental drive to inflict pain," she said with a tap on her head. "I'm sadistic through my genetics, and that's all I think I'll ever be."

"An unfortunate truth for many suffering souls, but alas, it is not so cemented in our lifetime that such a deeply embedded quality can never be changed or removed. Though I lack holy faith or heroic hope, the grains of sand comprised of the glass shards of my once whole heart do fill an hourglass that turns with each day, knowing that progressively, as each grain passes through, we are closer to a better version of ourselves."

"If you lacked hope, then you wouldn't have been able to say that, and besides that, you're wrong, Damon. The only way to stop something natural from happening is to destroy its source. My death is the only way to end my addiction, and ironically or fittingly enough, my addiction will probably lead to my death. That's kind of beautiful, isn't it?" She did not require a response from him to know that he disagreed. "I was never able to find out why I was basically psychotic or why I was so different from the other girls at school. I thought that if I could fix you, and help you be who you were meant to be, then maybe all hope for me wasn't lost. You were beyond repair both physically and mentally, but I saved you, so for a short while, I believed that could be applied to everyone."

"So, selfishness was indeed a part of the larger puzzle of your actions and mental thoughts of insanity, just as I boldly stated it was. Not that I, **The Sinful Son**, would lie or state an unholy untruth, but I had blinding love, so infectious as it is, convince me that perhaps you had acted out of selflessness. If that is indeed so, then I assume you believe wholeheartedly that you have fixed me?" Damon asked with a voice of dark emotions. "Did you do what was best for me, or what was best for you?" The woman did not move or even make the slightest noise as she just sat there, frozen in place, her gaze still on the doorway. "Look at me with eyes that pierce through flesh and fill every vacant region of a soul and travel along every sharp edge of a broken heart, and then take a mental recollection of secularity and the rest of the world. From those two drastic comparisons, create a truthful answer to the question I have asked you: is it with a wholly pure heart and only truth that you think you fixed me?"

The woman hesitantly turned in her stool to face Damon. She studied the silhouette of his large frame, which, despite its biologically humanoid form, was more like a monster's than it was a human's. She looked up at the terrifying red eyes that burned in a constant state of utter despise and violence, powered by the undying hatred that filled his hot veins. Almost hidden in the dimly lit kitchen filled with patches of shadows along the walls, the woman could only partially see the black cloak of modern science, whose dark sleeves covered Damon's arms and whose midnight colors draped his sides and back, and whose large hood shrouded his head in a cloud of eternal darkness from which there was no escape. Her eyes followed down the split between the two sides of the cloak, and she could see nothing but black beyond the parting of the cloak except for a grey metal band wrapped around Damon's abdomen and connected to the exoskeleton that covered his person underneath the cloak. She noticed his hands, which were covered in large metal gloves with three short spikes along the top of his knuckles, and how his hands invariably moved between closed fists and open hands. She lowered her head and inspected the metal boots that he wore around his feet, which also featured spikes. He was a monster inside of a human inside of a machine covered by a fictionalized idol. The truth was as he stated it: he was far different than the rest of society.

"Paradoxical as it may be to the untrained mind, which unfortunately fails to grasp the deeper concepts of philosophy and the unholy truths of this universe, silence can be more deafening than any noise, and it can say more than any list of well-written words could ever hope to accomplish, even if the albatross' feather is dipped in blood to form the cursive that stains the page that will be added to a library of tragic truths. Your speechlessness is evidence, though I do not believe in patterns amongst humans, of your feelings of regret and shame, as well as untimely defeat. Admit it, and I will forgive all, as though I lack a heart due the severing of it into atoms and then beyond that, I am still with emotions, though they are only negative ones by the standards of society, and I am more than capable of forgiving the woman I love for what she has done to me. Starting anew is not impossible, and while any sane and regular man would abandon so despicable and vile a woman as you are, I am here, by your side right now, hoping to continue to be with you for all of eternity, should you be able to apologize and change from your wickedness."

The woman remained speechless for a moment before chuckling with a bit of insanity in each piercing note. She looked at him, power and manipulation convulsing in her eyes. "I'm *laughing* because I've just figured out what's going on here… and the irony of it all is rather fascinating. You're calling me a liar, manipulator, and selfish, when, really, *you're* the one who is all of those things," she stated with a point not of accusation but of what she completely believed to be a true fact.

The dark power exuding from Damon shot out like a wave of instant-death, but he did not say anything, nor did he move despite seeming to be ready to flash across the room like a shadow and snap the woman's spine as easily as an alligator could crunch down on a snake that tried to threaten it. He was entirely speechless.

"**The Sinful Son**? You love being him because you are him, and that has nothing to do with me, and you've never cared about what anyone else thinks. Society can burn down and perish for all you care, and we both know that's true. You're trying to use **The Sinful Son** to guilt-trip me! He's certainly an outcast from society, and I did encourage the idea, but that's not my fault. You know that you can't help me overcome my addiction, and it tortures you because you're in love with me and don't want to abandon me or kill me. How touching," she remarked with a smirk. "The only person who can truly help me or stop me is, ironically, myself. So, you think that by villainizing me, I'll realize that I have to stop myself. Oh, Damon, how *cuuuuute*!"

"How utterly impudent of you to speak to me so condescendingly just because you believe you're accusations are true, undeniable, and justify your sense of power, which is, truthfully, a false power granted to you by the hideous lies you feed both yourself and I! Unfortunately, the events and actions of both myself and you have most certainly created a situation in which only you can defeat yourself, but it is not my intention to villainize you in order to achieve that victory and defeat."

"Really? Is that so, Damon?"

"Undoubtedly so. To villainize you so that you would defeat yourself would inevitably result in consequential chaos that could lead to your unfortunate demise, further insanity, or a rebellious attack against me, and I can assure you that none of those vile results are what I desire or would ever desire."

"Hmm." The woman almost smiled mischievously. "Then what exactly are you trying to get at, Damon? If you're not trying to villainize me, then why are you saying all of these awful things about the woman you love and have loved for years. Why would you speak so harshly about the woman who has taken such good care of you for so long."

"The point I wish to make is one of convincing you to stop by opening your mental eyes up to how far from the world we have journeyed together. Though the memories are fond ones, the wicked deeds honorable ones, the murders righteous ones, the rescues heroic ones, and the message of salvation that **The Sinful Son** offers an enlightening one, the unholy path we journey on, paved by misfortune, torture, and pain, has reached its untimely but inevitable end. For us, at least, for beyond that is a void of inescapable blackness or madness, if not both combined into a most nightmarish mental beast that would possess us, and the only other option is to turn back or take a different path. The societies across our small world are vast and complicated, covered with a system of paths with more trails and paths every few feet that have their own ways and parts, but that only grants us a greater chance of success, *Francesca*. We must return from the brink of eternal condemnation now or else our souls will be so blackened, our hearts so cursed, and our minds so broken, that there will be absolutely nowhere to go except further into the consuming void or to our deaths, though the darkness and suffering of the two will become indistinguishable. Therefore, from my monstrous entity, I extend my severed arm, held by my remaining one, almost detached as it is from my decaying body, as the rope that will tug upon your back and pull your being backward from the edge of spiritual death and physical death, and lead you to where beings like you and I might find some sort of restful peace after all that we have been through. I've started turning around, and I don't have the strength to do it, but I'm offering to help you, who is even further than I am, to turn back as well."

A deathly silence filled the heavy air of the room, made only all the more intimidating and dangerous by the ominous figure and deep words of **The Sinful Son**.

Francesca's evil eyes calmed down, and there was clarity in them. She frowned, and her face contorted as if this were the first time she had ever truly looked at Damon. There was actually sanity in her. "I don't understand it, and I don't mean all of your complicated philosophical talk or anything." She paused a moment, looking at the humanoid across from her, hidden in the darkness both of his choosing and that of what was already there. "There's something really wrong with you if you love such a foul creature such as I am. I've acted in unforgivable ways and said unforgivable things. Actually, everything I do is inhumane. I've always been crazy, and when I used that helmet I created to manipulate my brainwaves and nerves through electricity, I only grew more psychotic, yet you've stayed by my side despite how awful I've been to you. That's so insane that it makes me temporarily sane. *Why* do you love me, Damon? Better yet, *how* do you love me?"

"For years that turned into decades, I have been by your side, so the list of reasons pertaining to my love for you is as endless as the unexplored expanses of space beyond our world. To list all your good qualities and all that attracts me would be taxing, repetitive, and rather pointless, for words cannot properly capture some emotions, nor can they apply to beings such as you and me. I am an individual broken by others, but you are an individual broken by your own self. I wish to help you."

"But help doesn't equal love!"

"It can, but that's only part of it. There's also the fact that you saved me. I don't just mean from the brink of self-induced death or the hospital that day but from *everything*. You saved me from the corrupted society that we live in and from the people who did me wrong and who would do me wrong. You saved me from my despicable family, dare I even call them that. You saved me from the two people I had become, and from the war they had started fighting. You merged them both into one. Then, on top of all of that, you gave me the freedom to do whatever I want. ***I am free.*** If I had gone back home that day and ended up becoming a criminal in life as inevitable as that would have been due to how society breaks many individuals, I would have been arrested or killed a long time ago. But with you and your technology, I'm free to be **The Sinful Son**. I'm no longer a would-be criminal. I'm a savior because of that. I represent the mentally and emotionally abused and broken through the verbal thrashings and actions of others. A few months ago, you had me do that prison raid, remember?"

"Everything we've done blends together, but yes, I remember. You ripped the prison bars off of a cell and beat a man to death. He was a serial rapist or something, and you lectured him about the sins of lust. Later on, you told me all about your concept of villains. You also killed five guards through other violent means, which made me quite happy to hear. You brought a dozen of the worst prisoners here for me to torture and have my way with. From that, I managed to release some dopamine in my system, the world lost some truly evil people, we helped lower the overly-high population, which resulted in more food, air, space, and money for everyone else, and you got to vent some anger out while preaching and saving. It was a victory for everyone." Francesca was silent for a moment as she thought. "However, I have a feeling you're not concerned with any of that. You came back a different man that day, Damon, and that's what this is about. What happened?"

"You and I, our bodies have aged along with our minds as the years have passed by, and so we know that it has been a long time since we started. I killed people when I was a teenager, and I've been living in the shadows ever since, and only jumping out into the light to get revenge. That is what would eventually lead to **The Sinful Son** being born. Well, he was always a being, but his potential was never unlocked on purpose until the. I was just a once-man with no one and nowhere to go, along with you, who was a mentally unstable woman with a brain that released dopamine when inflicting pain on others or experiencing it on its host's own body. That is how our journey began, and for many years, decades which passed by swifter than any child could imagine, we went from place to place, killing, torturing, all while enforcing justice that the morally righteous are unable to do. We've been stationed down here for a few years now, doing the same thing."

"If you have regrets... I'm afraid that it's too late now, Damon."

"A man who knows the truths that I know, and who has been through the most unbearable tortures of the mind, spirit, and heart, have no regrets. Regret is indeed an unstoppable virus that affects us all one day, but I have iron veins and an iron spine, so forged from the strongest battles of a childhood unlike any other, that I am an antibody-carrying patient who is immune to that horrible disease. **The Sinful Son** was an idea I had when I was a young man, but I never brought him forth into reality until a few months ago. He is meant to be utilized by a teenager or a young adult. I'm far too old for this now, or at least I'm not at my prime despite how powerful and dangerous I am, just as most older people secretly are. Now, I realize that I should have done so much sooner, for now, I understand his powers, and they are far greater than I could have imagined."

"Well, that suit I made is pretty impressive, and you are-"

"Not my superhuman strength, Francesca, nor am I referring to my speed or manipulation of chemistry and biology. The intense heat and aura of death I create are of no concern to me in reality. I mean my message. What ***The Sinful Son*** represents, and how I am helping those who are me but younger or older or not in as much pain. He originally emerged for revenge, backed by my undying rage and hatred, but times have changed. As Damon, the created purity of this world, merges more and more with him, I become different, and I shall continue to do so until I reach either death or my final form. Either way, I am the man I always dreamed would come to my rescue. Never for my life was ***The Sinful Son*** meant to be... no... he was meant to be the first, and I had not realized that."

"What are you talking about?"

"After I killed the first two guards who had attacked me, I entered the main hallway, which was lined with old-fashioned iron bars and cement cells. I had the black smoke trailing around me but not with the microbiome-killing gas. I didn't want everyone getting sick, for most of the people there were worthy. It went dead silent as soon as I stepped foot into that hallway, for a sight as unholy and gravely intimidating as myself is enough to almost kill a healthy human being through fright alone. That was when it happened: the prisoners began to worship me as if I were some sort of prophet descending down from a stage that I had created for others like me to watch. All of them worshipped me, and it shocked me so much that I was speechless compared to the usual poetry I lecture. They called me ***The Sinful Son*** as they shouted out to me in praise and faith. I suppose my reputation was bigger than I had thought. Some of them bowed down, and others got onto their knees, but most of them reached their arms through the bars and tried to get a touch of me as if I might heal them. That image of walking down the hallway with all of those arms reaching through for me... I'll never forget that."

"I... didn't know about all of that. Still, what's the point of your story? You like attention? You have a large ego? What are you trying to say?"

"Such pointless questions are part of the many chains holding back our society, along with such impudent interjections. You lack respect.

From seeing those people, or at least the ones who were in prison because they had been turned into monsters through the words and actions of others, made me realize how many more of us there are, Francesca. The broken are growing more abundant, which is the exact opposite of what I had always hoped, growing up so horribly as I had. They deserve another chance. Everything that has happened to them has been beyond their control, just as it had been beyond mine. The mentally and emotionally broken are not responsible for their actions or how they respond to what has happened to them. People say you are in control of your mindset, but an unholier untruth has never been so infectiously spread amongst people. The broken are a better version of people, for they know what life can truly be like, but I hope to prevent everyone from being broken one day. That time will not be during my lifetime, for my constant state of hate and rage tolls my body beyond the decaying rate of survivability for even the healthiest of men, and so I shall die young because of the emotional, mental, and verbal abuse I have suffered. Before I go so dramatically and despicably into the unknown beyond death, however, I shall serve the broken people as much as I can by being ***The Sinful Son***, just as I have been for the past few months now. It's not just about revenge anymore, but now it's also about rescuing."

"You… want to be a hero? Damon, that's not who you are! You were born a villain and made an even worse one by your rotten family, and there's no changing that."

"I am well aware of that, for my death will undoubtedly follow soon enough after these next few days. I know not why, but a sense has gone off throughout my unholy figure, warning me that my death is imminent and inevitable. Granted, I am a paranoid man whose habits of protection and safety go far beyond normality and seem to be preventing unlikely situations, but this is a different feeling. Whether born from my natural instincts, my experience as a man who has claimed many lives, or hints from the most merciful side of a cruel fate, I know it is coming. Before that happens, however, I want to

give the remaining broken ones on this world the chance that I never had, and such unordinary and seemingly random feelings and such a sense of purpose is no joke nor mistake, for I can feel the power of such ideas flowing through me as much as my undying rage and hate do. As a young man, before I allowed **The Sinful Son** to release some of his unholy powers through me, I wore a ring that symbolized the ability and purpose to change rage into creativity and life. That belief is returning to me after all this time. I shall be a savior of the mentally, emotionally, and verbally abused. Although, I already am that, and I have been for the past few months now, given my recent actions and thoughts as Florida Phantom, as the news has so disgustingly named me. Neither of us realized it because you're in your own world of pain, and I am a walking man of molten emotions, but I am a representative of the broken, who is meant to be a founding father and lay down the path that the first leader shall have them journey down. Perhaps generations will come and go, worse or better than the last and the next, before the end of that path is reached. It's quite possible that the path itself loops around in an unbreakable cycle or has a complicated system of alternative routes creating a spider's web, but the path must be made regardless of the unknown future."

With a frustrated sigh, Francesca massaged her pale temples, which each featured a thin vein. "Listening to you talk is torture far worse than any of the physically painful things I do to people, which includes ripping off each nail and plucking each eyelash off of their body. Granted, those are some of the more merciful things I do, but still. Every time you talk, I feel like I'm sitting through an advanced university-level English class on steroids while I'm on drugs." Francesca sighed, and for a while, she was silent as she thought over everything Damon had said. "Honestly, I don't like what you said or where this path will leave you, but I know exactly what you mean."

"Regarding what?"

"I guess everything you said. You were broken by others, and now, you want to help others who are like you. The first step in that goal, which you didn't even have in mind yet, was killing your abusers and seeking revenge on awful people. I won't stop *The Sinful Son* from being a representative of the broken if that's what you truly desire. As long as you get people for me to torture, then I'll be happy. Even if its near the second half of your life, at least you found a purpose and a place. At least you have others to blame everything on. My own mind is what tore itself apart. *Nothing* is worse than that. I was born to be a killer, and it's just awful. To not be able to control how you feel, to be forced to live a certain way… it's worse than anything else, honestly."

"Although I, myself, have never been a victim of excruciatingly agonizing mental torture that came about at my own unstable mind's hazardous thoughts and plaguing questions, I am more than capable of understanding how awful such an existence is. That's one of the main reasons why I forgive you." Francesca looked up at him. "You asked me how I could forgive you for what you've done, and what you've just stated is actually the answer. I know you don't mean to hurt me or push me away, for it is far beyond your control. Most of the time, at least."

"Thank y-"

"**Excitement and gratitude are not yet welcomed, for I am not quite finished yet,**" Damon stated coldly in a loud voice, all air around him expelling away in fear as he almost took a step forward. "There is still one inevitable question that *cannot* be ignored, for it has appeared, been thrown around, and disappeared every few weeks for the past few decades. *Now* is the time that we finally answer that question so that it might find peace, with us finding peace along with it. Time and again, we have had the same old question asked from my mouth to your ear, and like an abstract artwork painted by a brilliant craftsman on acid, your answers are always vague and up to interpretation. I want an exact answer today. No more indecisive answers or excuses, nor shall I tolerate such troublesome mind games or neutral answers. Neither of us can change, nor can I just change, until this question is answered, for it shall impact a great many things." Damon took a deep breath as he calmed himself down. Powering off the artificial red eyes of contempt,

Damon looked at the woman who stared back at the lifeless aura of darkness that lay within the hood. "Do you love me, Francesca?"

"First of all, stop saying my name so much. You know that I don't even like that fake name, so *stop* it. Secondly, you know I hate that question," Francesca replied as she turned away from Damon and stared back out into the hallway. "Still, you're not wrong. It has been years of us having the same conversation. Times are changing, and so are you, apparently. I guess you deserve an answer, or at least whatever idea of love my brain has to offer. Plus, if you truly believe that you're going to die soon, then there's no harm in having this conversation regardless of the outcome."

"Then speak freely and honestly for once."

"I've always admired you, Damon. You truly are broken. I don't think anyone will ever understand that. Even if you wrote an entire book about it like you probably would, the readers would never get what you've been through because the memories are too buried and painful to retell, and there's so much emotion that you can't capture with words. I doubt your poems help people understand. You speak like a madman who is also a literary expert, which makes it difficult to understand you, but through our conversations, I've begun to understand you and how truly horrible your life was. They say that everyone's life sucks, but yours goes far beyond that. The mental and emotional abuse that you suffered would have destroyed anyone. But *you*... you endured it somehow. Granted, you were driven to suicide just as anyone else would have been, but you're a unique survivor, not just physically because of what happened, but also as a human being internally in the soul and heart. You are strong, both mentally and emotionally, and there is a difference. Even with bottling everything inside, even with absolutely no one... you've still kept your sanity and even a pure heart. You've used the wickedness forced upon you as a force for the greater good by teaching those who are rich and lazy and those who are happy and popular what life is truly like. You eradicate those who were never meant to have children or be parents. You free frightened, angry, and sad children from alcoholics, drug-addicted, and abusive parents. And I love that you are so strong in resisting everything that has happened to you, but-"

"But, unfortunately, as the truth and past cause to be so, I've been mentally and emotionally abused and broken," Damon said softly with a voice intertwined with regret and bitterness as the red eyes appeared again. "I've been tormented through talk, demonically deceived, and monstrously manipulated, to a point far beyond death and desiring the absence of life, and my mental and emotional resurrection has cost me my humanity and a normal life in order to continue my existence. Therefore, unfortunate as it is, I can never be loved, nor can I ever love. Nobody will ever love me, and I'll never know what love is because I've never actually felt it before in my whole life, and I can't truly experience it ever, for that is the curse that was placed upon me when I was just a young man."

"Damon, I di-"

"My ideas about love are all fantasized versions of it from the romantic dreams and words of profound poets and wonderful writers. I ravenously crave the affection of women because I was never loved by my mother. My father and siblings were my enemies as well, and from that, I hate almost everyone. I never had the love of family, nor did I have any friends or mentors. Society is and always has been my enemy because I was never properly introduced to it. Everything was always ruined for me, to put it in a merciful and kind way."

Francesca got up from her stool, and Damon stared into her eyes, which were a mixture of broken and insanity, with a slight warmth of sympathy. She wanted to stop him from talking so negatively, but she knew not to interrupt him.

"I'll never be able to know what life is truly like because I'll always have a consuming feeling of loneliness lurking within me, covered by untamable rage and hatred. Yet, that's only the mere beginning of it all." Damon began to breathe more uncontrollably, and his hands constantly clenched and unclenched. "The truth is I've had chronic depression for all these years, but not the crying and moping kind. I have the aggressive side of it, where I'm filled with hatred and a longing for revenge. Nothing can ever make me happy because the past haunts me constantly, or at least what's left of it after that foolish helmet. In fact, I never even experienced happiness when growing up. I don't have a single joyful memory from my childhood, and the first time I was happy was the first time I got revenge by killing. How pitifully unholy."

Francesca started walking over to Damon. Despite the large hood and darkness that hid his figure and face, she knew that he was on the verge of tears. They were not tears of pain or sadness, however. He was the kind of man who would cry the angrier he was because his body began to get physically worked-up, and he was trying to hold everything together to prevent an unstoppable rampage from happening. As a child, a lot of people insulted and shamed Damon for crying, but they did not realize that the tears had shed were in the place of devastating punches that he was holding back. He cried because the good side of him was losing and struggling to hold back the monstrous calamity that was beginning to break free from the mental prison inside of him. When he cried like that, his tears were not only salty, but they were physically hot. It was almost unnatural how high the temperature of the water droplets was, but they were physically and mentally heated by a blazing fire of hatred and rage that burned within him like the sun burning within the blackness of hostile outer space.

"I can't be satisfied because my heart is entirely shattered and broken, and even if real love is poured into it, the liquid force, which is most certainly a necessity of life, merely leaks out of the half-healed cracks. All I am able to capture are a few droplets that are eventually evaporated by the heat of my anger. My veins are filled with undying rage and vengeance because I had always hidden my emotions and true feelings, to say the least. I always held back because I tried to be a hero, which meant no revenge and no fighting. Purity was something I valued and something that I still value. I let everyone who did me wrong get away with it. I tried to do what society, school, and my family saw as right. Except I'm not a hero at heart, and the falsehoods I tried to live only made my life worse. I am blessed with the unholy power of ultimate knowledge and truth, but thrust into a world of liars and backstabbers, along with those who were in denial, such a blessing was more so a curse because-"

Damon was cut off short as Francesca wrapped her arms around his torso, signaling to him that he could stop. "I know," she whispered. "I can't and won't deny any of that because it's all true. I know you're all of that, and I can't love you because of it, but what we have works, so why is there a need to enhance it to true love? We have sex, we care for each other, we live together, we work together… I mean… what *more* do you want? Marriage? You know that can't happen. Just be grateful for what you have." She stood as high up as she could on her tippy-toes, but she could only reach the chest of Damon, despite being almost six-foot-tall herself. He leaned down, and removing his mask from within his hood, he allowed his cheek to be kissed by her. She pulled back after a moment. "I know that you can't love, and neither can I. We're doing the best we can, Damon, and I know you can say you love me, but I'm never going to say I love you. It's not that I don't care for you. I do want this to work, and we should talk about it in detail," she glanced over at the clock, "but-"

"***But you need me to do something today, and it's a timely matter with minutes passed that can't be retrieved back, so this connection will have to wait as it always does, year after year,***" Damon spat out in retort as he shook his head in frustration and disbelief. There was no doubt in his mind that she had done that on purpose. He fixed his mask and then crossed his arms as he leaned back against the aging wall, almost invisible except for his artificial red eyes, which seemed to be burning with even more hatred than earlier. "How convenient. I see that you happen to need something as if right on ***cue***. What exactly do you want me to ***do***?"

Francesca threw her hands up in the air. "And *there's* the rhyming talk again. Could you save it for your online poetry, Damon of Darkness, or whatever your social media name is? I promise you… this will be the last thing for a while, and, in my defense, I had you wake up early for the mission, not to talk about our feelings. And *actually*, today is more for you than me. Sure, you'll be getting some people for me to torture, but you'll be saving some hurt souls as well."

"Is that *so*? Then forth, I'll *go*, prepared to fight and ***die***... bringing with me... a blackened ***sky***. How did you find these targets?"

"I was out for a stroll the other day, an umbrella over my shoulder to protect my pale skin when a little girl bumped into me. Instinctively, I went to grab my knife and kill her, but I was freshly happy from torturing some people, so I calmed down rather easily. Besides, it was too public. Turns out, she had run away from home, and with tears in her eyes, she begged me to help her. She actually needs **The Sinful Son**, and so I promised to send a man of dark power to save her."

"Though my heart is filled with ***hate***, I believe this encounter to be that of ***fate***. What exactly is the situation?"

"It's relatively simple," Francesca replied with a yawn as she walked over to the kitchen and poured herself a cup of tea. "Quite heartbreaking to hear, actually. Not to me, but I'm sure you'll find it sad. Honestly, I can't believe how fast kids seem to be growing up mentally nowadays. Even just their circumstances seem to be maturer situations or more complicated than when we were kids. It's really odd, and I honestly don't know if it's better or worse for them to have childhoods like that. Does losing innocence younger make you smarter and more capable of handling life? Even if it does, is the cost worth it? I don't know, but I honestly don't care."

"That's certainly a noticeable change amongst our society and the new generations, and what you have spoken is indeed true. Undoubtedly, it has both positive and negative consequences, depending on the people and situations, and I too, like many others aged as old as we are, ponder the causes and effects of such perplexing scenarios that did not occur as frequently when we were young."

Francesca raised her hand in a gesture to stop. "Alright... that's more than enough, Damon. Not everything you say has to be a thousand-page novel. Anyway, the little girl is only ten years old. She's the daughter of a wealthy couple whose marriage was arranged years and years ago to keep money in both of the families. They grew to love each other, I suppose. I'm sure they did, given how much money they both ended up with."

"How utterly despicable. Such an arrangement seems unethical, especially when attempted among such a reformed and free society as ours, but I suppose everyone can always get away with something if they truly desire to. That and money is far stronger than any substance when it comes to sealing lips or melting iron spines. However, you know that I believe in love and life over money and fitting in with society."

Francesca went to sip at the tea but burnt her lips, grinning in reaction to the hot sensation of pain. "*Anyway*, her older brother, who is a complete brat, verbally abuses her, and he hates her. Her young parents are neglectful to her, spending all of their time enjoying themselves since they were spoiled ever since they were young and still have more disposable income than several families combined. Their parents, her grandparents, were rich as can be and left all of the money to their children, who have done nothing but wasted it. In fact, she was told that she was only born to appease her grandparents even more because they wanted a granddaughter besides jut a grandson. Her parents favor the brother, but they ignore her and constantly insult her. Again, they didn't want kids really, but Mr. 'macho' likes having a son, so that's the story. She ranted to me for a while, and she claims that God set everything up so that she would see us and get help before it got worse. I honestly didn't think children really believed in God."

"That is awful, to say the least, and what you've told me, just like my stories of pain and terror, is probably just a thin layer of snow atop the iceberg whose large body is deep below the dark waters, hidden from those who do not dive deeper into matters but only stop to see the small piece of ice floating above the water. I'm guessing you want me to bring the parents and brother back here for a painful **lesson** on what happens when you serve ***oppression*?**" Damon lethally punched his metal fists together, the cold and lifeless sound echoing throughout the kitchen with reverberations of death.

"I'm surprised you want to hurt them so badly. Well, not really, but there's always the possibility that they're innocent, and she's lying or exaggerating. Are you sure that you don't want to investigate first to make sure you're not hurting innocent people? I'll kill anyone and everyone, but you're more of a righteous guy who makes the tough decisions that other ethical people can't, so it's up to you."

"Your concern is quite surprising, but I assure you that there's no need for an investigation into the true personalities of these people. What I've heard so far is more than enough to make it all believable. Kids are the only ones to state the truth about adults, or at least their own parents. Especially when they are hurting more than they are loving or being loved, as negative emotions are what cause the survival instinct that humans have lost and buried to fully reemerge. Should it so happen that my arrival there and the evidence I gather from my expert senses concludes that the girl was indeed lying or exaggerating, then, as it right to do so, I shall leave them to their own lives. However, the probability of such a scenario occurring are small for even the optimistic statistician, and I truly believe that girl is telling the truth. Therefore, I'll capture them for you so that she might be saved, and so you can fulfill the unholy requirements your body demands for happiness."

Francesca nodded her head, and her lips curled into a wicked smile as she looked at Damon before sipping at her tea. "More than half of that was unnecessary, but I like the way you're thinking. It's not quite enough, though. I actually had something *bigger* in mind, because you're not going to be attacking their home."

"Oh? That's rather ***unexpected***. So, then, where *am* I ***headed?***"

"Ew," Francesca cringed, "I hate it when you use slant rhyme. You know that's a pet peeve of mine. I love chaos and hate organization, but slant rhyme is so ugly." She shook her head. "Whatever! Except for the rich people who don't like to show off that they have money, what do most people with a lot of money do to show off?"

Damon shrugged his broad shoulders. "Unfortunately, I have never experienced what it is like to be wealthy, and the fictitious characters of literature I've read about have usually been proper gentleman, reserved in their impulse to show off. Given my knowledge of society and its people, which is rather biased and limited, I assume that they like to buy fancy cars and watches and overly-expensive clothes. Perhaps, some even get a couple of purebred dogs or renovate their house."

Annoyed, Francesca rolled her eyes and threw her hands up in half-playful frustration. "Pfft. Well, you were supposed to get it on the first try. So much for you being super smart. I mean, I'm sure those are all right, but more importantly, they like to host…?"

Damon let out a small menacing chuckle of realization. "That's right, and a perfect opportunity to arrive and preach. I should have guessed such an occasion on my first try, but I tend to associate such events with juvenile punks who drink or dance. They like to host parties," Damon said as he nodded his head, cunning and mischievous thoughts beginning to muck about in his skull. "Big parties to be precise, with tons of booze and food. Roasted pigs and lobsters are often served, as far as I know… along with fancy wines and chocolates. More importantly, that means there'll be plenty of people there. The roster is probably full of other horrible people, though I shall not assume the morals and personalities of all the guests attending. I could make a grand entrance, and there might even be a few fights against some privately hired guards, which would be most vital to growing the influence of ***The Sinful Son*** even more. Then, the police will try and stop me, of course, but hopefully, I'll be out of there before things get too serious. I'm more than capable of handling dangerous situations with figures of authority, but I'd prefer not to. So this is why you had me set my alarm clock early, isn't it? The party is today, and ***soon***? Perhaps just after the sun peaks at ***noon***?"

"That's exactly right. They're supposed to be hosting a fancy brunch at the Hall of Homestead building that was just built last year. The girl told me everything, and if you want to show **The Sinful Son** to the world in the best way possible, this is the perfect time and place to do so. Well, it's a good start, at least, and far better than your previous appearances. No news channel will be there since it's not a big public event, but there'll most likely be a photographer, and with so many people there, a few are bound to escape and tell everyone what happened."

"True as that is, I'll still be able to get enough publicity to announce that I am **The Sinful Son**. Then, all shall know who I am and what I stand for. ***I'm sick of hearing people call me Florida Phantom***! The news has disgraced me with that tasteless name. They make me sound like some washed-up ghost story that people tell young children to prevent them from roaming around Florida at night. It is ***unforgivable***! I am so much more than that!"

"*Easy* now, Damon. You said that the past and present have condemned you to an untimely death caused by your own hateful heart and boiling blood, but there's no need to speed the inevitable process up. The world and I still need you, at least for a few more years. After today, everything will be in our favor, and it'll only get better from here. The brunch is some kind of private gathering for celebrating spring or some crap, so everyone there will either be other rich people or close friends and family. She heard that they ordered an ice sculpture, so I'm sure you could get creative with that if you want. She said her father is reckless, but he is paranoid and always has a personal guard with him, so he's bound to have several hired for the party."

"I stand at the pinnacle of survival, my physical body forged by the unstoppable power of my mind, which has endured years of verbal, emotional, mental, and social torturing and suffering unlike any other horrible combination of lives. Therefore, I am equal to many **men**... perhaps more than a hundred and **ten**. A few guards are nothing in comparison to **me**, and their bodies shall be delivered to the Florida **sea**. To avoid getting wet, the perimeter guard will probably just wait at the main door once the storm comes, making him an easy target.

It's supposed to rain quite terribly today, though that is essentially the weather here every day. The perfect elements for my fiendish **plot** and righteous goal. That matters ***not***, however, and I am more concerned about what the building is like."

"Are you rhyming more and more? Jesus Christ, have mercy on me!" Francesca shook her head and laughed to herself. "He would never. Anyway, you'll be able to tell which building it is. It's in the middle of a few acres of townland that's not allowed to be built on anymore, and they didn't spare any expense when making it. There's a giant gate in the front with the name on it. As far as the inside goes, she told me that it has several rooms, but they'll be in the center one, which is the biggest room meant for events. It's a large open space with golden floors and some tables or whatever she told me. I wasn't paying that much attention. Oh, and apparently, there have been reports of wild gators on the property, so keep an eye out. Not that they could hurt you, but just warning ya."

"Alligators?" Damon let out a fiendish laugh that was intertwined with animal-like sounds. "They're actually one of my favorite kinds of animals, which is just another fact that most failed to inquire about, as I grew up" Damon muttered to himself. "This'll be more entertaining than I had originally thought, and though I am incapable of experiencing positive emotions, I believe this will be fun."

Francesca eyed Damon skeptically. "*What* are you thinking about?"

"Do not be alarmed or intrigued, for it is just something I plan on doing at the **brunch** to disturb their appetites for breakfast or **lunch**. There's something that I've always wanted to ***do*** that I think I'll finally be able ***to***. Forget about that, ***though***," Damon said as he shook his head. "There's one last detail I must ***know*** before I prepare myself then ***go***."

"The girl's name," Francesca assumed as she fidgeted with her fingers. Damon nodded his head. "I suppose that would help you find her in case there are other girls there. Her name is Lilith, and she made it clear that she hates the nickname Lily because that's what her 'mom' calls her. So, don't call her Lily." She took a large gulp of her tea before throwing the cup into the sink, allowing it to shatter. "That was fucking disgusting! I hate cold tea. It tastes horrible!" Francesca gagged and stuck her long tongue out. "Ugh! That ruined my morning. Anyway, I looked it up, and the name Lilith actually means night monster or ghost." A psychotic smile stretched across the woman's pale face. "I love it when everything lines up perfectly, don't you? Her name is almost who you are. Perhaps she can become your disciple."

"My disciple? What do you mean by suggesting that I forge such a relationship with the young girl? It's true that I mentioned being the founding father but not the first leader of the path I hope to create, but to have her be the first leader would most certainly be a cruel thing to do. There's no doubt that this young girl will quickly win over the fatherly pieces of my heart that never got to live or thrive, and that will only further convince me to lead her away from the life I have chosen."

"No rhyming that time? Suit yourself, then, but you can't spare everyone you rescue if you truly wish to save the future world. One of them must become your disciple of darkness and death so they can take over when you die. Apparently, you believe you're going to die soon, so you better find a replacement before it's too late."

"Unfortunately, what you speak is indeed the truth of my unholy *fate*, and soon it will eventually be too *late*. I shall find someone worthy and do so before my untimely death does *arrive*, and I'll make sure that the broken ones *survive*. What time is the brunch at?"

"Around eleven or so. I wanted you up early because I wanted you to have time to get over there. Look at how much time we've already wasted chatting. Anyway, I want you to wait until ten or fifteen minutes have passed, that way everyone is there and listening to her father, who is supposedly going to give some kind of speech. Then you can make whatever lecture you want about being fashionably late."

"Understood, and my apologies, but you and I come first in life, and that you should *know*. It is time to save Lilith, *though*. Seeing as the time is swiftly approaching the beginning of the party, I'll head out *soon* and hope to arrive just before *noon*. I'm assuming this building's location, like everything in life, is inconvenient for me?"

Francesca chuckled a bit, though the emotion of the chaotic noise was indeterminable. "Well, it's not along the coast if that's what you mean. The Hall of Homestead is a few miles inland, and it'll take a while to get there. Take the boat to the coast, get off at the special dock, and then you'll have to walk to the building. It's an overcast and rainy day, so you should have no problem getting there if you really wanted to go in your costume. Especially since you're a master at stealth operations, but I would suggest you just go as you and then bring the costume and put it on there. The cops will probably be on the lookout for you, and I don't want you to be intercepted before you get to the party."

"*It's not a costume!*" Damon boomed with a sudden impulse of anger as he stomped his foot, cracking the tiled floor and shaking the ground. "Your lack of respect and care about my feelings is truly appalling and despicable! *The Sinful Son* is a man! A personality! An identity! To refer to the glorious creations you have made and combined with my life, forged from the depths that exist beyond the deepest layer of Hell, is downgrading and-"

"*Fine!*" Francesca rolled her eyes and let out a heavy sigh. "Take your villainous garments of an alter ego in a bag or something and transform into him when you get to the Hall of Homestead. Just take the boat and go," Francesca commanded in frustration. "You're so fucking annoying."

"Annoying? It's annoying to have to politely request time and again that we have mutual respect for each other and then get angry when time and again you refuse to do so through your neglectful words? I never call you Ma-"

"Say that I'll kill you!"

"You get angry enough to wish to kill me when I dare to think about saying your true name? How amusing! Then you know exactly how I feel regarding *The Sinful Son*, *Francesca*," Damon spat out with contempt. With the artificial red eyes burning brighter and hotter and the floor shaking underneath each step, he stormed out of the room, mumbling under his breath as his heart thunderously beat.

CHAPTER 2

THE SINFUL SON

(Homestead, Florida. The Same Day: April 16, 2022)

Still enraged, despite having vented aloud to himself on the boat drive over, Damon arrived at the Florida coastline just as a devastating hurricane would. He docked the boat at a secret port Francesca had arranged for them, and the wooden dock creaked as he landed after leaping over the edge of the boat. He glanced around, but no one was out other than a fisherman or two. Dressed in an oversized black hoodie that hid every detail of his face, Damon began his mission.

After his long walk from the beach, which was nothing compared to the many miles he had swiftly walked during his lifetime, Damon arrived at an alleyway. The grey storm clouds overhead had darkened with natural overwhelmingness, and trickling rain had begun to escape from the clouds, making the darkened atmosphere all the less visible to most people. It provided the perfect cover for Damon as he changed behind a dumpster into his uniform. He arose from behind the graffitied and over-stuffed dumpster as **The Sinful Son**, and it was eerily quiet out except for the wind and the rain. He was the only person braving the nasty weather, which was bound to get tremendously worse.

Cautiously looking right and left to make sure that no one was around, Damon exited the alleyway cloaked in the unholy garments of

The Sinful Son, both externally and internally. He crossed the slightly flooded street with swift and phantom-like movements as the rain began to trickle down even harder. No cars drove by, nor did he hear any in the distance. The wind and a few birds were the only noises drifting amongst the rain, but the birds quickly flew off as if they knew that two storms were coming.

Arriving at the other side of the street without being seen, Damon pushed through a wall of hedges that surrounded the perimeter of the land the town had purchased, and he trampled decorative grasses and flowers before looking up at the Hall of Homestead, which loomed before him like a grand palace.

"Created by the people for the people, just as this blessed country was, this building is most certainly an impressive display of human architecture and Florida funds," Damon muttered to himself as he looked at the large building just a distance away across a field of grass and neatly swept paths. The paint that covered the walls of the building was a mixture of orange and gold, lined with neat trimming of white marble. It was three stories tall and perhaps as wide as an acre of land in order to fit the various rooms meant to be used by the public.

Surveying the property, Damon eyed plastic balls of white light that were strung up between the palm trees decorating the property of the building. The wires and leaves shook up and down in the wind as the rain continued to fall. He was angered by the sight, and he could not help but talk to himself as always, mumbling to maintain his cover.

"How unforgivably despicable, not just of Florida, but of every place that allows and commits such atrocities! Such unintentional heinous crimes are not limited to the simple creation of buildings such as this wondrous Hall of Homestead, but also include the other luxuries of countless towns. They spent more money on this building than fixing all of the potholes in the roads. The orphans starve, the homeless rot, the roads break, the bridges crumble, the animals suffer alone, and the forests are chopped down… all while these people create buildings for the rich and the few." Wicked bolts of lightning began to break out across the sky, and Damon looked up at the unstable dark grey clouds overhead, which were starting to cry more torrential tears than before. "*It's time*," he stated aloud with his monstrous voice filtered into one of a demonic killer through the mask he wore. "It is finally time to-"

Damon was cut off by an aggressive and deep growl. He looked around alertly, his eyes stopping on a giant alligator that was in front of him, about twelve feet long. It opened its large mouth filled with crooked teeth and let out another threatening growl that echoed like the thunder overhead, the alligator's dark green scales reflecting the light from the bolts of the storm.

"So *masked* within the *grass* that lay before me, you are the lurking *beast* of which Francesca did *speak*. A terrific terror of nature, which I most certainly *admire* with prideful competitiveness that burns like a *fire*. My entire life of pain and terror, I have always dreamed of my bare body against your scaly *skin* in a wrestling match both on land and in the water, which I would *win*. Had my thermal vision been turned *on*, I would have seen you hiding amongst the *lawn*."

In response to Damon's poetic statements, the alligator simply let out another growl, more powerful than the last, as it moved forward a bit. While most animals were afraid of **The Sinful Son**, the territorial creature seemed to not be intimidated.

Damon chuckled menacingly. "You dare to challenge me yet *again*, then so be it and meet your *end*. It's my turn," he muttered as he smashed his right fist into his left palm, the metallic pound emitting a threatening sound of death. With a stomp of his foot on the ground, which caused the moist dirt to tremor and break, Damon, a being of eternal hatred and rage, let loose a screaming roar that powerfully outmatched the thunder overhead and almost shook both the Earth and sky. It echoed throughout the empty streets. It was an unstoppable sonic boom of imminent destruction and death.

The alligator quickly turned around and, hastening with its four scaley limbs, tried to escape the wrath of the inhumane being it had instinctively challenged. In a natural instinct of survival, the alligator attempted to dig its claws into the ground as it felt Damon grip its tail and begin to pull the creature back toward him, hand over hand. He yanked the reptile straight to him, and it fell to the ground below him. A metal boot on each of the animal's front shoulders, Damon grabbed the top snout and pulled up, breaking the alligator's jaw before slamming the limp top back onto the bottom jaw. He stomped on the head to crush its skull, ensuring that it was truly dead.

Damon looked up as he saw a ray of golden light shoot out from the front of the building. *Just as I, with my vast intellect and theoretical predictions of the future, combined with my own paranoid traits, had predicted earlier, the perimeter guard had gone inside to protect the entrance once the rain had started. Now, he's sticking his head through the front door. He must have heard my thunderous roar.* He watched as the guard turned on a flashlight and stepped out with an umbrella. Damon crouched down as the beam of light passed by his direction, though he knew that he was too far away for the guard to see through the rain. *I'll show him that **The Sinful Son** and his rescue mission have **begun***, Damon thought to himself with a wicked smile inside the darkness that masked his face.

The guard, unaware of Damon's presence, took a few steps away from the building, scanning the area. He looked around observantly, using the beam of light to slice through the daytime darkness caused by the clouds. Failing to see anything, he turned around to head back in. Then, he stopped. He perked up his left ear, thinking he had heard something moving in the grass.

Approaching the guard, who was now more suspicious, Damon was dragging the alligator behind him with one hand wrapped around the creature's long tail. Cloaked in his own darkness and the rain, he continued toward the guard, lurching controllably forward like a monster from a video game with each fatal step.

The guard slowly spun around, checking the perimeter one final time, failing to spot Damon, whose red eyes were currently turned off. He turned around to head back inside but put the flashlight away as he pulled out a walkie-talkie. "False alarm," he radioed to someone on the other end. "It must have been the storm... nope... nothing out here as far as I can see... yes... of course, I checked the whole perimeter... really... no... and why are you breathing so loudly... what do you mean, that's not yo-"

The guard was knocked down as his right side was slammed by the heavy corpse of the alligator, which Damon, one hand around its tail, had swung directly into him. "Hell!" The guard fell to the ground by the forceful impact. "What was that? Who's there?" The guard rolled over, his side flaring with pain, and he saw the dangerous silhouette of Damon looming over him. Instantly, two blazing red eyes appeared above the guard, and he screamed. "Florida Phantom!"

"*No!*" Damon boomed as he gestured to the world as if he were the ruler of it as he towered over the little man. "*I am THE SINFUL SON, and my reign of salvation has just begun. Listen to my unholy voice and choose now, while you still have the choice! Death now or torture later?*"

The guard was an unresponsive mess, terrified by the unholy entity looming over him. His right side was in agonizing pain, and he suspected that at least two or three of his ribs had been broken by the impact of the alligator. His walkie-talkie had been knocked out of his hand and was out of his reach as it sunk into the wet grass. Calling for backup would be impossible. Knowing he had no other choice, the guard reached for a gun.

"*Since my hateful heart does care, your life, I shall choose to spare.*" With earthquake-causing force, Damon brought his muscular leg, combined with the exosuit strength, down on the guard's face, the metal boot crushing everything. "*Though most would consider death unmerciful, it is nothing compared to the torture you would have to undergo,*" Damon said in consolation to the corpse on the ground below him. The guard's skull was shattered into uneven pieces, and the rest of his face an amorphous blob of flesh, muscle, and blood. One of the eyes had popped out of the socket, and it was hanging on to the blob by an organic thread. "*Actually, you had no choice, as you were always meant to end up dead, as I, unfortunately, need your head.*"

Although his powerful stomp had left it looking like an old shrunken head sold in gift shops, Damon planned on making a grand entrance with the head of the guard, as cliche as it seemed to him. Grabbing the deformed head by its base, Damon twisted the guard's neck around a few times before pulling up, his one foot on the chest of the dead guard. The grotesque sounds of the bones cracking and breaking, and the flesh tearing apart were masked by the heavy rain and battle of thunder and clouds overhead.

Looking at the severed zombie-like head in his hand and the horrified expression on the distorted face, Damon froze. He grunted in anger at himself as he clenched his hands into fists. He took a deep breath. *You can't afford to stop now*, he thought to himself. *A true gentleman and caring guy like myself, as well as one who is emotional and vulnerable, is easily guilted and filled with regret, but I mustn't allow that. I'm sorry, guard. Truly, this is not what I want. I know that. However, there's a little girl in there who needs my help, and there are, unfortunately, thousands of people like her in this world who also need my help. It is, indeed, true that I am more human than anyone else, which is ironic given how monstrous I am, but I have to sacrifice my humanity in order to save everyone else from the sins of others. Therefore, I shall remember it all. I am a machine whose fuel consists of negative emotions of anger, rage, hatred, and revenge, to name a few, and I have turned my mind into a perpetual motion device that infinitely generates such necessary emotions. I am always angry, and so, I'm pissed at you as well. I have to be.* Damon looked up at the clouds as an uncontrollable bolt of lightning broke out across the sky.

Tightening his grip on the piece of neck bone sticking out of the bodiless head, Damon stood up from the corpse and continued forward to the Hall of Homestead. He stealthily opened the entrance door before perfectly closing it once inside. Before him was a short corridor, and he followed it until he got to a lobby-like area that had hallways on either side that wrapped around the entire building and met on the other side. In these hallways were doors to each of the various areas of the building, but Damon assumed the large doors in front of him had to open into the room where the brunch was being hosted.

Scanning the area, Damon saw no guards. Creeping forward, he went right to the side of the large doors, ensuring that no one would accidentally open the doors into him if they decided to leave. Against the wall, he could hear music playing and people talking. The brunch was undoubtedly just beyond those two doors.

Now curious, Damon crept toward the door, making sure his footsteps were light. He opened the one door just wide enough that he could see into the room, and with his red eyes turned off and the vantablack cloak, no one could even tell that a person was there. He quickly scanned the room. The walls were gold-colored, and they curved to a high ceiling that had an expensive crystal chandelier hanging from its center. Throughout the room were people seated at circular tables clothed in white. Damon looked over to his left at a line of rectangular tables, which were covered with a variety of breakfast and lunch foods. A man fueled by mainly high amounts of vegetables and protein, Damon looked over at all of the fancy pastries at the far end of the line of tables, repulsed by the temptations that sat there like a trap for him. He had been on an extreme-sugar-cut diet for decades and was mainly powered by celery and grapefruit. The deserts almost seemed to be a trap, as if the people inside knew he would be distracted and tempted. Separating the tables with the alluring pastries from the tables with the regular food was a giant ice sculpture of several flowers reaching upward, two of which had closed heads.

Turning away from the food, Damon looked over to his right, where there was a string of tables lined with blue and white gift bags for the guests. *Hmm. Gift bags? Based on the horrific description Lilith gave Francesca regarding her unholy parents, I had assumed they weren't the kind of people to give anything away, including gift bags. Perhaps, it's merely for maintaining their status among these snobs. I doubt their hearts would be so kind and caring. It's just to maintain their social ranking. Where are the hosts, actually?* Damon scanned the room, his eyes stopping on a stage against the back wall directly across the room. A young man dressed up in a white dress shirt decked with a red bow tie and black suspenders, which featured a flower on each side, was standing in the center of the stage with a microphone. *That's the ugliest outfit I have ever seen.* To the man's left was a young woman who was dressed in a loose floral dress. Then to either side of them was a chair. A teenage boy, who seemed to be only thirteen or fourteen, sat in the chair to the right of the young woman, a smug expression on his face. In the other chair, which was to the man's left, sat a small blonde girl in a light green dress, who seemed upset as she held up her head by propping her chin into her hands. *That has to be them... the father, mother, rotten brother, and Lilith.* Damon nodded his head in satisfaction to himself.

The young man on stage signaled to a person in the back of the room, and the music stopped playing. *Didn't she mention a speech,* Damon thought to himself. *Perfect timing, as always.* He turned his attention to the man on stage as the microphone emitted a metal screech, which caused everyone there to cringe, including Damon.

The young man laughed. "Sorry about that, everyone. Technical difficulties like every microphone tends to cause." He quickly adjusted his red bow tie as he looked at everyone seated at the fancy tables. "Before I begin, I'd like to thank all of you for attending this annual party. As always, I'm Mr. Siolla, your devilishly charming and handsome host." Everyone chuckled, and he let out a sigh of relief. "I know that we normally host a dinner, but I felt like brunch would be nicer, so we're trying it this year. Now, I know you're all anxious to get to the food, so I'll keep the speech short. When I founded our club, it was originally for pure fun. The idea was to get a couple of rich people together to waste money on booze, food, maybe hook-ups, and perhaps some gambling. For a short time, us rich guys and gals did exactly that. But then I was married to my lovely wife, Sierra," the man said as he pulled his wife closer to him. She waved at everyone with a condescending smile. "She became Sierra Siolla, and I became a married man. I realized that I wanted our gatherings to be more than just a party. That was when I-"

There was an outburst of screams among the crowd as something went soaring through the air like a rocket and landed on the stage at the feet of Mr. Siolla. His wife screamed before throwing up. Mr. Siolla gulped and trembled as he beheld the severed head of his hired perimeter guard at his feet, blood still dripping out of it.

In an instant, everyone turned and looked to the entrance to see where the head had come from, and several people gasped and screamed as they saw the towering villainous entity standing there, his red eyes ablaze. They all trembled in their seats and those who did not were utterly frozen in fear. A few fainted from sheer fright. Among the crowd, there was the whispered name "Florida Phantom" from those who were brave enough to share the information. Other than that, it was silent, and no one moved.

The door closed eerily behind Damon as he took another menacing step into the room. "*That was when you realized what? That deep within your heart's core, you wanted something more than a social class war?*" Damon yelled sarcastically with contempt, his voice demonically echoing throughout the large room. "*You have known nothing about the true terrors or life, though your abundance of wealth is not the only factor in causing that. You would dare say that you wanted to do more than just enjoy life, all because of your arranged-marriage-wife? What blasphemous lies you spout to all these people who are about. I know that is not at all true, and it is exactly why I have come for you,*" Damon boomed as he pointed up to Mr. Siolla on the stage, who was absolutely terrified, his knees quivering. In fact, a stain of dark urine was visible in the front of his pants.

Damon carefully observed several guards getting into positions and communicating with each other. They were waiting.

Mr. Siolla dropped the microphone in fear as black smoke began to pour out of Damon. "What d-d-do you m-m-mean? I... I haven't done anything wrong! You want our money? Take it! We all have plenty?"

"*Your money? I have no need of it, for I am wealthy in anger and rage. I've come to tear you from that stage and avenge your daughter's pain.*" Damon pointed to Lilith, who had bunched herself together in an attempt to shrink away from everyone, her feet on the chair and her knees in her face. "*You've grown up knowing nothing about working hard or enduring the torment of others, nor were you ever broken by lovers. You've been nothing but spoiled since your first year, and it's true, which is why I can sense your fear. Money is what the government and the I.R.S. collect, but I am a collector of sinners who'll break your neck. I am THE SINFUL SON! Spoiled as you are, you knew not how to raise a daughter, and now I have no choice but to exact justice and slaughter.*"

Mr. Siolla looked over at his daughter before stepping in front of her. Her mother and brother had joined Mr. Siolla in blocking her. "I don't know what you're ta-ta-talking about. What pain? I would never hurt my daughter. I've treated her right for her whole life! Who are you to judge me? How would you know anything?"

"Because I summoned him," Lilith stated coldly for everyone to hear as she stood up from her chair and stepped away from her family. There was a wave of shock that exploded throughout the guests of the brunch, who were utterly silent other than a few gasps. Damon made no comment, but he eyed Lilith's brother, who clenched his hands into tight fists, his arms bulging out of his light green polo. Her father and mother were more shocked than anyone, but it was comprised of more angry emotions than sad ones. Lilith was shaking, but she was slowly getting confidence from Damon's presence, believing that he would help her no matter what happened. "I got help that day I ran away from you all."

Mr. Siolla's face shifted between several emotions all at the same time. "*What?* You summoned him? I don't understand. How? Why? What are you talking about, Lilith? We've been nothing but good to you for your whole life, and this is how you repay us?"

"No, you haven't, dad! You're lying! You and mom make fun of me all the time. You're always calling me a useless child and saying that I was a mistake. I listen to everything around the house. You only had me because grandma wanted a granddaughter, but then she died anyway, so what was the point of having me?" All color drained away from Mr. Siolla's face, and his whole body grew stiff. "That's right, I heard what you and mom said! You always curse at me and talk about how you're too busy for me! Busy doing what? You sit around the pool, sipping at drinks, and eating fancy fruits! You *are* spoiled. He's right," Lilith said with a point to Damon. "You've never worked a day in your life. Everything you've ever done is either for yourself or for him!" Lilith pointed to her brother, whose face was almost as enraged as Damon's artificial combination of darkness and technology. "You think he," she pointed at Damon, "is a demon, well, *you're* the Devil! *Both* of you are," Lilith said as she gestured to both her father and her mother before running off of stage crying.

"That was undoubtedly a heartfelt and truthful confession. Now, you all know of the hidden oppression that has been plaguing Lilith and causing her depression." Damon pointed at the Siollas, who were huddled together and backing up. They truly feared for their lives. ***"Mr. Siolla and his wife are neglectful people who care about only themselves, and I have been sent to send them to Hell. She could not stand or tolerate such atrocities any longer, so she summoned me because, though broken, together we're stronger!"*** With pride, power, and intimidation, Damon chuckled as everyone stood up and backed away as he took another menacing step forward, shaking the floor as black smoke leaked out of his terrifying figure.

"*Ahhhhhh*! Let go of me," Lilith cried out as her father forcefully picked her up. She looked across the room at Damon, her eyes screaming as much as she was, her one arm outstretched. "Help me, *please*! Don't let him take me away," she begged through tears. "It'll be so much worse, now if I'm stuck with them!"

"I'll give exactly fifty grand to whoever kills that manipulative monster," Mr. Siolla shouted desperately as he grabbed his wife by the hand and ran off of the stage with his family. "Try beating those hired guards! You'll never make it out of here alive!"

Damon went to go chase after Lilith, but he stopped when he saw three guards closing in on him. Two males and one female. He smirked menacingly in his personal darkness, and a small laugh reverberated inside of him. "*I am **THE SINFUL SON!** I represent the broken ones*," Damon bellowed with a point to himself. "*I am the fiendish phantom of the dark and night. I am here to fight for what is just and right! The only human powerful enough to defeat me is myself! I shall be killed by no one else!*" Damon quickly flipped over and grabbed the closest table, using it as a shield. He charged forward with the table held up in front of him. The guards attempted to shoot at him through the table, but he rammed them like a triceratops, knocking all of them down.

Chaos broke loose as everyone went running for their lives as the black smoke spread everywhere. A few brave men hesitated a moment, the reward of fifty grand on their mind as they glanced over at Damon. Understanding that they stood no chance, having seen how easily he knocked down the guards, they joined the others in scrambling for an exit other than the doors behind Damon, which happened to be the only ones except for two in the far corners.

One of the male guards jumped onto his feet, using only abdominal and leg strength. A gun in hand, he tried to charge at Damon to ensure a close and fatal shot since the cloak made it hard to tell exactly where Damon's organs were, but the man was too slow, as Damon had already wrapped his right hand around the man's throat and lifted him off of the ground. The female guard, seeing that Damon was temporarily distracted, rushed forward with a taser. With brutal strength, Damon crushed the man's windpipe and threw him into the woman, who went tumbling back and was shocked by her own taser. Damon did not like to directly kill women, as he had great respect and love for almost all women. However, he did take ones he found evil to Francesca.

The last guard attempted to get in close as well to provide back-up, but Damon swiftly countered him with a leg sweep that sent the man to the floor before he punched the man's face with so much force that his skull caved in on itself. Now, the Hall of Homestead had two shrunken heads for decoration.

Damon looked through the ever-swarming crowd of panicking people in an attempt to locate Lilith among the chaos. To his right, in the back corner of the room, he spotted the Siollas attempting to escape. He took off running, bursting forward like a bullet. With remarkable speed and a powerful leap, he traveled like a vicious hurricane, landing between them and the door within a few seconds. His landing shook the ground like an eighteen-wheeler would shake the road as it passed by small houses, cracking the polished floor below him for a few feet in all directions. Standing erect and looking down at them condescendingly with his artificial red eyes ablaze, Damon towered over them like an unstoppable tornado of black smoke and dangerous debris.

The woman cried out in fear. "She's my baby! I birthed her!"

"I'm not going to let you take my daughter," Mr. Siolla stated in a shaky voice, attempting to be bold. "We've bought her plenty of food and taken her on vacations. I don't know what's wrong with her or why you're here, but it's not true. You kill me, and *everyone* will be looking for you. I have a large payment with my will to hire a private investigator since I'm a paranoid man. They'll find you!"

"*Really, is that so? That's critical information to know, but that's not how things will go.*" Damon took a menacing step forward, cracking the floor again, and the Siollas backed up, terrified. Lilith was still trapped in her father's grip as he held her against him with one hand. They all seemed utterly powerless before the unstoppable being of death approaching them. "*I am THE SINFUL SON, and I'm here to save a broken one. She speaks the truth, and I know it all. All your riches, yet your empire will fall. Release Lilith, and allow her to come to me. Otherwise, we'll have to journey across the sea, where you'll meet a woman who is far worse than me.*"

Mr. Siolla shook his head in defiance, but he screamed as Damon grabbed his arm, which was holding Lilith. Damon broke Mr. Siolla's arm with unstoppable force, bending and twisting it in an unnatural direction that resulted in grotesque noises that made his wife wince and scream. He broke his arm as if it were just a twig. Lilith fell gently to the floor. Her brother charged at Damon and kicked him in the shin, stubbing all of his toes against the exosuit. The boy cried out in pain and then screamed as Damon completely lifted him up into the air, holding the boy by the torso over his hooded head. With a powerful thrust of his arms over his own head, Damon threw Lilith's brother across the room, and the boy went ripping through the air before powerfully smashing through the ice sculpture. *My apologies, Francesca, but I couldn't think of anything creative or ice- get it- to do with the ice sculpture.* Damon grabbed Mrs. Siolla by the back of her neck as she attempted to run away, and he threw her to the ground. Her body hit the back of Mr. Siolla's legs, and he fell to the ground on his broken arm, crying out in even more pain. Slowly squirming on the floor like worms, the Siollas were all defeated.

Damon cautiously looked down when he felt a gentle tug on his cloak. His artificial red eyes met a brown pair of eyes staring up at him with hope and fear, tears dripping from each of the glistening orbs. It was Lilith. She spoke softly, her voice shaking as she did. "Are you really the fallen angel sent to save me? Are you the one that Ms. Francesca promised to send?"

Bending down onto one knee, Damon still towered over Lilith, but he figured it would make her feel safer. "*I am*," he replied softly, although his voice was still deep and monstrous. "***A mountain of apologies that you had to witness such nightmarish acts of violence on top of all that you have had to endure. However, it is the end of the war. I assure you that you're saved now, and I shall take you away from here. There is no need to be afraid or fear.***"

"Thank you," Lilith said as she hugged Damon's one leg, which had its knee up, sobbing as she did. Damon looked down at Lilith, and something convulsed inside of him. Something he had not felt in a long time but had always longed for. "You don't have to apologize. My parents and brother should pay for what they've done," Lilith said as she stomped her foot and cried. "It's not right! I'm not a mistake, right? They're wrong... aren't they?"

Damon slowly nodded his head. "*Indeed. They are most certainly wrong. You are not a mistake. Your soul is not theirs to take. Perhaps, throughout history, the present, and even the future, there are a few rare examples of truly evil people, but there is a difference because some are misguided. No one is ever born a mistake, An accident is different than a mistake, and you'll do well to learn that. We were not born to be treated this way, such as you and I have been treated. There are wicked people in the world, and some are especially cruel. Parents raise their children, but that doesn't mean they always raise them the right way.*"

"But why?"

"*You are still young, so perhaps you have not yet figured out what I once learned when I was a young man but old enough to observe, analyze, and determine information that would forever ruin a child. The unholy truth of the world is that some people simply aren't meant to be parents, and I mean that in two different ways.*"

"Two... different ways?"

Damon nodded his head again. "*The first is that some people are so horrific that to combine their genes to create a child would result in an uncontrollable beast of unimaginable horror that could then go on to make even worse beings. They aren't meant to be parents because vile beings should not reproduce. The second reason is more important, and it is the lesson I learned that I shall now pass on to you. Some parents are simply never meant to be parents just because they aren't compatible with others, including their own children. They'll complain about doing regular parent duties, they'll hate their own children, they'll never understand what to do, and that seems awful, but it is the truth. Whether due to their genes, culture,* teachings, past, or personalities, I'm afraid that some people are never meant to be parents."

"You mean that some parents don't like being parents?"

"*It is much deeper and complicated than that, but I suppose that is a simple way to sum it all up. Such was the case with yours, Lilith. I apologize for that. Being the child of parents who should have never been parents is one of the most fatal and nightmarish situations that can occur in our world. Oftentimes, it is one of the few situations where there is little we can do to change it without such drastic consequences or changes to our lifestyles.*"

Lilith half-smiled. "You talk a lot and use fancy words, but I think I understand. So, my parents were never meant to be parents just because that's how the world works sometimes?"

"*That is most certainly one way to summarize it simply. However, it matters not, for you no longer need to worry about your awful parents. One day, I'm sure that you will understand it all. You're free to do whatever you want now, but I feel responsible for whatever happens to you next. Therefore, I shall take you with me until we figure out what to do with you. You don't have to be what they raised you to be, nor what they had called you or labeled you as. It's, unfortunately, far too late for me, but there's still hope for you.*" Damon stood up, all of the black smoke gone from the room. He looked down at Lilith and extended his right pinkie finger. "*I pinkie-promise you that today they will indeed pay, and your life will forever be bettered.*"

Lilith accepted the large metal finger with hers, and she shook up and down, a bitter-sweet smile on her face. "Okay! I don't mind staying with you for a while. You seem nice. Are we leaving now?"

"*Surely, we shall depart rather soon, for it is almost past noon. First, we must gather up your family and the fallen guards, but that is a task that won't be hard,*" Damon stated as he pulled out a long metal chain from inside his cloak. "*We'll tie them up, and after I get the keys to your car from your former-father, I'll drive us over to the*

dock, and I assure you that we won't be stopped. From there, we'll take my boat over to the island," Damon said as he stood up.

"An island?" Lilith giggled.

CHAPTER 3

THE TORTURER, SWEET BUT PSYCHOTIC
(Somewhere off the coast of Florida. The Same Day: April 16, 2022)

Francesca, a mental mess, made far worse by the frustration that now swirled about her chaotic mind, waited until she heard the echo of a heavy door slam on the far side of the building travel along the barren hallways. Sticking her head through the kitchen doorway and peering down the hall, she made sure that Damon was truly gone. He was a self-trained spy, so often times he stealthily stayed back after purposefully closing the door to hear her complain aloud to herself about him. That alone had led to countless arguments between the two. By now, however, she knew to bite her tongue until she knew he was truly gone.

"That takes care of that," Francesca muttered as she shook her head in frustration, returning to the kitchen. "Years and years, and it's only getting worse." She began to pace around the kitchen, muttering to herself so quickly that her words were more like conglomerations of sounds that made no audible sense. "My mind may be deteriorating faster and faster, but I know I'm right. Perhaps this vigilante crap or whatever he thinks he's doing will lead him away from here. But I *need* him," she hissed in anger and frustration. "Unfortunately, we need each other even though this isn't working." She sighed. "Now, what to do? My morning has been completely ruined by all this emotional garbage.

Feelings? Years of studying psychology to find that it has no answers for me? It's all lies." She started fidgeting with her fingers. "What can cheer me up? All my victims are gone. No. Wait! I'm a genius," Francesca said with a twisted grin as she skipped down the hallway and entered into a large room that had no lights on, her hands twitching.

After groping the cold wall of the large room and finding a switch and flicking it, Francesca added a bland sense of light to the pitch-black room, dimly illuminating a torture chamber whose walls and floors were lined with various body fluids and a few decomposing body parts. The nauseating smell, however, made the looks of the room rather pleasant in comparison to the air of the room, which was solely comprised of a variety of bacteria and deathly odors dispelling themselves from the stains and decaying traces of once-life.

Taking a deep breath in through her nose, Francesca smiled to herself before walking over to where a man was suspended in the air and tied up on the other side of the room, each of his limbs pulled to a corner by a tightly bound rope.

"Morning, sleepyhead!" Francesca shouted as she approached the man. "Sorry for the wait, I had to deal with Damon, and he is an absolute *pain* in the ass. I mean, I can fake it for a while, but there comes a certain point where I can't stand him anymore. The problem is that he's like the perfect guy and super caring, which just annoys me. It ruined my morning, but then I remembered that I had spared your life *yesterday* so that I would have someone to torture *today*. How genius of me!"

The man groggily opened his eyes and squinted against the light as he adjusted to it. He blinked a few times before peering at the sadistic smile before him. He moved his head lethargically, struggling to keep his eyes fully open. "What? Where am I?" The man looked around and then pulled against the ropes but stopped as his arms swelled with pain. He noticed that he was suspended a few inches above the floor. "What's going on? Who's Damon?"

"So many questions, and so many answers. That's basically life summed up, actually. You don't remember how you got here? You poor thing," Francesca commented as she caressed his face, which turned away in response. She let his head drop as she backed up a step, looking at the large frame of the man.

"Did you drug me?"

"Yes, but that's the best of it. I don't blame you for forgetting. I mean, you and your buddies were pretty drunk when we got all of you. A couple of college kids celebrating the lacrosse season. You know, I used to play, but I was kicked off of the team for purposely launching the ball at people's faces. Also got kicked off of the fencing team for violent behavior, but that's a whole different story."

"What?" The man asked, still not fully awake. "My friends?" He groaned in pain as he raised his head and looked to his left, all hope fleeing from his face as it distorted into one of horror. He wanted to scream, but his throat muscles clenched up instinctively, fearing that if he screamed, the woman before him would kill him. A man was tied up just as he was, but the skin of the victim was wholly removed, the corpse nothing but a muscular disfiguration of what was once a man. Clenching his fists, the man could not help but cry.

Francesca smiled wickedly as she looked at the expression of horror across the man's face. "Now you're awake," she said with a growing grin and a demented laugh. "I see you're admiring my work of art," she commented as she walked over to where the skinless man was hung up. Francesca looked over the corpse, almost laughing proudly to herself. "I figured that if a peeler could work on a potato or an apple, then it would do just as well on human flesh. And *boy...* did it *peeeeeel*," Francesca remarked wickedly as she rubbed her hands along the muscular strands and tissues of the torso of the hung-up body, which were stained red.

"That's... that's absolutely horrible and disgusting," the man cried out in a choking voice. "This is a nightmare, right? I doubt even I could or would imagine something so grotesque, though. You'd peel the flesh off of a human being? What's wrong with you?"

"He was still conscious too. For a while, anyway. At first, the blood was spilling all over the floor, but I fixed that," Francesca said with a gesture to four buckets underneath the skinless man, which were all filled with a dark red liquid. She laughed again at the expression across the man's face as he frantically tried to break the ropes. "Don't look so disturbed! I promise I'm not crazy enough to drink blood. Despite my paleness, I'm not a vampire," she said with a lick of her lips and a stroke by her mouth with her one finger. "The reality is just that I didn't want to slip if the floor got all wet. This room needs to be cleaned. Usually, this torture chamber is spotless, but I've gotten lazier and crazier lately. I'll have to find somewhere to dump those buckets of blood, but the ocean is no good. I don't know where else, though. We *are* on a private island, so I guess it doesn't really matter if I bury them."

The man was speechless and hyperventilating as he looked over the stained strands of muscles and tissues, which were the only layers left across the skeleton of what used to be a man. The blonde hair of the victim was still intact on top of his head as the man studied the shoes that were still around the hanging corpse's feet. "Oh my God," the man muttered gravely through sobs. "I couldn't even recognize him, but now I know who that was." He locked eyes with the frozen orbs within the skull of the peeled face. "Jason? What... what did you do to him?"

"*I peeled* almost all of his flesh off using a kitchen peeler," Francesca replied, almost taken-back by the man's question. "Was it not obvious? I could've sworn it was pretty obvious. I mean, I basically just told you that. Unless it was a rhetorical question?" She laughed demonically. "Oh. My bad. It must've been rhetorical and you're suffering from denial. Look, at least I kept his underwear on and spared his pride. Shows how merciful I am, and-" Francesca jumped back as vomit began to drip out of the man's mouth as he coughed, unable to lean forward to properly throw up. "Ahh! Oh, that's disgusting!" Francesca yelled as she grew uneasy looking at the mixture of putrid colors. Her eyes shook uncontrollably. "You stop that, or I'll kill you, you gross son of a bitch!"

Whether a holy act of God or an intense force of mind-over-body, the man stopped throwing up instantly as the woman stormed toward him. She reached into a pocket in the side of her white dress and pulled out a handkerchief. She dabbed the cloth at the man's mouth before throwing the dirty handkerchief into one of the buckets of blood.

"That's what grosses you out? After you peeled all of the flesh off of my friend while he was still alive… you're disturbed by vomit? How hypocritical," the man mumbled.

"Shut up! I hate when people mumble or mutter stuff. It's either cowardly or condescending, and I hate both of those." Noticing a grossly discolored drop of vomit on the white sleeve of her dress, Francesca stormed out of the room without saying a word.

The man watched as Francesca left, his mind trying to understand what was going on. He tensed his arms as he pulled against the ropes again, and this time, they seemed to weaken a bit. The man tried to force his legs forward to break the rope, but it was a useless effort. He glanced back over at his friend, a tear leaking out of his eye. "Did I die last night? Is this Hell?" Hesitantly, the man looked over to his right, immediately regretting the decision. The man was emotionless as utter disbelief filled him. "Anna? What did she do to you? That's awful. God, please… where are you?" The man sobbed as he looked at a girl who was strung up like the other victims. The girl's waist was sliced open, the intestines pulled out and constricted around the girl's body before tightening around her neck. "Did she choke you to death with your own intestines?" He began hyperventilating again, the fear inside him growing more uncontrollable. "Where am I? Please tell me that this is all just a horrible nightmare," the man cried out, his voice echoing throughout the vast and barren room.

"I'm afraid not," Francesca shouted from across the room as she descended a cement staircase. "This place is very much the real world. It's quite nice, isn't it? Almost a dream come true. Well, at least for me it is," she said with a gesture to herself with a psychotic smile. "I'm sure that you don't feel the same way as I do. Nobody can feel the way I do, and it's both a blessing and a curse. Rather than have you all strapped down to chairs or tables, I string you up. After all, I'm neither a doctor nor an interrogator. I'm The Torturer."

The man's half-teary eyes widened as he looked at Francesca, who had changed her outfit. She was dressed in black jazz pants and a tight white tank top, her wavy ginger hair resting just past her shoulders. What caught his attention the most were the hundreds of scars which decked the arms of the woman and which ran across her shoulders and medium chest, stopping at the base of her neck. "What.. what happened to you?" The man asked, sympathetic, and empathetic by birth. He looked at the scars which were slightly darker than the pale skin, which they were engraved into, all of them different sizes, shapes, and depths. "Who did such horrible things to you?"

"I did," Francesca replied emotionlessly but with a sadistic smile and a gleam of insanity in her grey eyes. The man was speechless and horrified. "Don't look so horrified, but be mystified! These beautiful scars are my own doing," she said softly as she rubbed her right hand along the scars on her left arm. "They are my own wondrous creations of art made from pain and dedication, along with an unbreakable determination and an addictive desire. One might say I am a being, constantly struck by my own hand, but I suppose that's everyone in their own ways."

"How come your hands and face are untouched? Is your whole body scarred?"

"Only one man, or a monster as he is better known, has ever seen all of my scars if you must know. But the answer is yes, almost my whole body is scarred-over. Even my softest and most delicate parts are. As far as this goes," Francesca gestured to her face, "I'm crazy, but not enough to damage my pretty face. I'm quite the beauty, and it'd be a shame to ruin that. Besides, it'd draw public attention if my hands and face were scarred, which is something I'd rather avoid. But, I suppose you'll die anyway, and you're the first to see my scars and inquire, so I guess you can see my best scars." Francesca turned around and lifted the white tank top up so that it rested around her shoulders. The man looked at her smooth back, intrigued at what he saw. Long scars followed the curves and frame of her back, all separate, yet they formed an abstract outline of two thin angel wings on each side of her back. The woman pulled the white tank top back down as she turned around. "Look at that expression! Well, you're a little perverted, aren't you?" She teased as she giggled.

"No. It's not *that*." The man looked into her eyes, unsure of what to think. "The scars on your back, they... they form angel wings. Was that intentional? Did you carve those?"

Something convulsed inside of Francesca's chest. She gulped. *Why is his voice so full of concern and care? It goes beyond just curiosity. It's like Damon's tone, in a way. What's this feeling I have?* She shook her head energetically and then spun it around to straighten herself out. "Yes and no," Francesca replied as she folded her arms across her chest. "Do you believe in God?"

"Can't say that I'm not losing faith in this moment here, but I believe in the big man in the sky. He's just busy right now, I guess, or it's all part of His plan. Who knows? My prayers are usually selfish ones, but I don't think He'd ever abandon me at a place like this."

"Well, your faith must be stronger than you think because you're talking rather calmly for a man strung up in a torture chamber."

"That's because there's nothing else I can really do except talk. Panicking will literally do nothing. Based off of what you've got going on here, I assume you're not religious?"

"Why do you say that? Thou shall not kill? I suppose I've broken that particular Commandment, but that doesn't mean I'm not forgiven or religious. I *was* raised in an atheistic household, but I converted when I was a teenager. My brain chemistry began to change during those years. I had always been sadistic by birth and nature, but that was when it all started to grow stronger. I do believe in God," she stated as she pushed her hair aside to reveal two small scars on the left side of her neck, which formed the basic shape of a cross. "I'm not entirely sure why He gave me a mental drive to torture people or a brain that releases dopamine when experiencing or inflicting pain, but He did make me a redhead," she commented as she curled a few ginger strands around her fingers. "That's all I need to be satisfied with believing in Him. Otherwise, none of it would make any sense, and I prefer to understand all things on at least a basic level."

The man shifted his eyebrows as he watched the woman move her hair back into place, covering the cross-scar. "What? I'm not entirely following what you're trying to say. What does your hair color have to do with your faith and belief in God?"

"I won't blame you for your unintelligence. Most people don't know this, and those who do probably wouldn't be able to draw the connection that I have, for it's nearly impossible. Everything lining up perfectly can only be explained by religion." Francesca began to pace back and forth in front of the man. "Not many people know this, but people with ginger hair are more sensitive to stuff, such as cold weather or spices. Not too much of a big deal, but we're also more sensitive to pain and pleasure. *Imagine* that: a woman who is mentally satisfied by pain and inflicting it happens to also have ginger hair." Francesca made a circle through the air with her hands as if highlighting something grand. "The Lord has blessed me so that I can be truly delighted in what He gifted me with. He gave me not only a mental drive to torture people and myself... but He *also* gave me the best body to do so. What more proof do I need than that? It's not a coincidence at all. It's a wicked blessing from God!"

"That's... insane, to say the least. Certainly interesting and a good theory, but probably not true or good reasons either. You're really giving believers a bad reputation, in all honesty. I mean, I'm supposed to support my fellow Christians and Catholics, but I can't really support what you just said."

Francesca tilted her head and let her mouth fall open in shock, her eyes wide and gleaming. "Why not? It doesn't get any more perfect that what I just said! You're such a sourpuss," she remarked with a shake of her head, one hand on her hips.

"I'm glad you believe, but those reasons are psychotic ones. What you said doesn't line up with the teachings of the Bible at all, and why would God even do that?"

"Well, I certainly can't speak for Him, but I'm afraid that you and I are in disagreement," Francesca said with a twisted smile and a wave of her finger. "They're pretty valid reasons. I mean... I torture people... and I have the best body to enjoy it the most. So, doesn't that all line up perfectly? Well, cutting myself, that is. I don't enjoy abusing people more because I'm a redhead. *That'd* be insane. I just feel more pain and pleasure when I inflict pain on myself, which is almost what Damon would call a paradox or something. Except pain brings me pleasure, so really, I feel double pleasure, in a sense. You see, when my drive to torture and inflict pain first came about, I didn't want to hurt other people. I knew that was wrong. So, I tortured animals, but they can't experience pain like we do. They don't have the screams or words to properly express how much it hurts, which is the best part sometimes. After a while, I started cutting myself in safe ways. Then, eventually, I killed my two brothers, two sisters, and my mom and dad, but that's a whole story of its own."

"How did you go so undetected? I mean the animals you can hide or blame on childhood ignorance, but there's no doubt that they got concerned once they began to see the scars. I mean, it's hard to hide so many scars, and to do so would arouse a lot of suspicion."

"Despite how many children were in my family, I did get equal attention from my parents. At first. When I was a little girl, I would hurt animals a lot, as I mentioned, but that quickly turned into a secret hobby of mine. They were more concerned about the fact that I got into a lot of fights at school. I would beat the crap out of other girls. My parents were always supportive of me, though. But things changed as I grew more sadistic and mentally unstable. I moved on from animals to myself and then to other people. One day, my brothers pissed me off like all older brothers do, and when combined with my mental drive to inflict pain, I killed them," Francesca said with a twisted look of satisfaction. She laughed. "They are the only victims who were granted instant deaths of mercy, rather than the torture I usually inflict. Either way, I killed them. What fools they were to mess with me, The Torturer. Of course, they were unaware of how close I was to mentally snapping, but all siblings usually are."

"How," the man gulped, almost afraid to ask, "did you do it?"

"How did I kill them and get away with it? Oh, darling, please… such questions have answers far worse than you could ever hope to imagine, and you've seen things in this room that are terribly horrific, so don't delve any deeper. It just so happened that both of my parents were out that day. Then, my little sisters got on my nerves as well, and after torturing and killing them, I was on a kick! I felt so good after disposing of them that I was instantly addicted. After all, I had been suppressing my unholy feelings for years." Francesca quickly clutched her chest as if her heart were in physical pain. "Damn it!"

"What is it? Are you okay?"

"I used the word 'unholy' in that last sentence. Damon uses that word a lot, and I fucking hate it," Francesca yelled as she stomped her foot against the ground. "Anyway, I killed my two brothers and two sisters," she began to count her kills on her fingers, "and then my mom, my dad, and a few neighbors, but by that time, I was detached from death." Francesca zoned out and looked at the floor for a bit, her mind somewhere else. "Detached from death and life," she whispered to herself as she started counting on her fingers again and muttering to herself, counting over and over again on her fingers, faster and faster. "Never… never normal. Always, something was wrong. They ignored me. I tried warning them. They said it was a phase. I would grow out of it, but I didn't. Now, all must suffer because of their mistakes. I was born… no, created to inflict pain and kill. Who am I to fight nature's purposes?"

The man was quiet for a moment as he looked at Francesca, who he, with his sympathetic and empathetic heart, thought needed help. Her arms and hands were twitching, and she was shaking her head in disbelief and denial. Her face shifted and twisted between several various emotions, each one more intense than the last. As forgiving and as kind as he was, however, his heart was already crowded with fear and confusion. He looked at Francesca again, hesitant to disturb her, but he wanted answers, and that powered his anger. "And *that's* what this building is: a place to torture people?" he asked as he looked around the large empty room, which was nothing but dark grey cement and dim lights. "Is *that* why you killed my friends? Just for the *fun* of it? They were innocent people! They don't deserve this, and neither do I! Why did you choose us? How did we even get here? Who exactly are you? Please, let me go. I think you just need help. Your parents may have ignored your cries for help, but that doesn't mean everyone else will as well."

"Stop! Stop it, stop it, stop it!" Francesca yelled while stomping her foot into the ground. She squeezed her eyes shut in pain and put a hand to her head. "You're giving me a *headache* with all of your questions." She looked up at the man, tear in her eyes. "Do you honestly think I'm the kind of person who can answer so many questions at once? I'm a genius, it's true, but not like that. An inventor, yes, but I can't process my own thoughts or words." Francesca took a deep breath, steadying her shaking arms. "However, I do have a soft spot for you due to how calm you are. I suppose that you do deserve the truth, so ask your questions one at a time. Luckily for you, I could use a distracting conversation right now in my life." Francesca straightened her face and put on a smile, but the man could not tell whether it was real or fake.

"Who exactly are you?"

"Who am I?" Francesca asked rhetorically as she gestured to herself with cute innocence. "Well, a victim a few years back called me The Torturer as I did some… well, horribly painful things to him. He actually asked me if I was a torturer, but same difference. The Torturer! That name does make me happy. It invoked a feeling of pride on top of the satisfaction of torturing him. So, that nickname is sticking around for a while until I can think of something better, as it isn't the most original. It is self-explanatory, though. Besides, 'stupid bitch' and 'psychotic witch' aren't very nice ones." She shook her head violently and bent the ends of her left fingers. "Damn it! I accidentally rhymed again. That stupid bastard's stupid way of talking is rubbing off on me, and I hate it. Just let me speak normally. Shit!" She laughed and then sighed as she turned her attention back to her victim. "You'll be one of very few to be blessed with such knowledge. My real name, if you *really* must know, is Francesca."

"Oh. It's actually... a nice name," the man said reluctantly. "Not sure if it fits a redhead, but it's whatever."

"Wow. A backhanded compliment? I kind of like you," Francesca commented with a smirk. "My real name, by birth, was Mallory, but I hated my biological mother, and so I changed it once I became an adult. She and I didn't get along entirely." Francesca looked the man straight in the eyes. "Did you know that the word 'unfortunate' is essentially the translation of the name Mallory?" Francesca shook her head in denial as an expression of emotional pain overcame her face. "Why would she name me that? Did she not want me? I've always felt that my birth was unintentional."

"Hey, don't say that," the man replied. "She probably didn't know that when she named you. Not everyone looks into the meaning of names because most people don't even associate meanings with names anymore. It's more of a personal pride thing to know what your name means nowadays. I'm sure any mother would have been proud to have you. You're a beautiful girl who is really smart. You're just mentally unstable, and I think you just need some help. Don't we all need help, sometimes? We can't control how we're born." Francesca turned her gaze away from the man, choosing to move her eyes around from spot to spot on the cement floor. "How come you two didn't get along? I thought you said you got attention from your parents."

"I did, but my mother mostly faked it for my father's sake, as I was his first daughter. I don't know the reason for her disinterest and wariness," Francesca stated quietly. "I think that she knew I wasn't mentally right when I was born. Just from the beginning, somehow, her motherly instincts knew there was something wrong with me as I left the womb and passed through her body into the world. So, she tried her best to fake it, but I ended up being a daddy's girl. That was before the term 'daddy' was overly sexualized, of course. Rotten teenagers and millennials with their fucking sexualization of words. Anyway, my father and I grew really close, but as soon as my mom popped out two more girls... I was out of the picture. *Nobody* cared about me anymore. I mean, my life was great and everything, but I was born like this, and that's just something you can't change."

"Francesca, look at me," the man commanded with a voice of concern. She slowly raised her head and looked at the man, having mistaken him for Damon for a moment. "You have to have hope! There *is* a way to change you, even if you believe that you truly were born a monster. There are medicines and treatments out there. There are doctors and-"

"*Nnnoooo!*" Francesca retorted, her shaky voice echoing coldly throughout the empty room. "I can't be helped," she stated factually as she walked over to where the girl was strung up and choked with her own intestines. "There is no cure for this," she pointed to the body, "or for that," she said with a gesture to where the man was hung up with no skin left on his body. "Do you *see* these horrible acts of *cruelty*? There is *no* cure for whatever dark disease runs through my body. It's a consuming plague that *can't* be medicated. Trust me... I spent years trying to understand both it and myself. I studied psychology, the minds of criminals, and plenty of other stuff. Do you know what I discovered in all of that time? Nothing," she exclaimed coldly. "I discovered no cure except to keep supplying my addiction. The only answer is death. Yet, I don't want to kill myself. Why would I do that? As long as I can sacrifice others to thrive, why should I have to sacrifice myself?"

The man hung his head low. "I see. You and I seem to be in disagreement once again. I believe everyone can be saved, no matter how mentally far they've gone because humanity is something inside of us that can never be destroyed."

Francesca could not help but laugh in disbelief as she shook her head. "You sound just like Damon when you speak. I hate it and love it. He would also call that a paradox. Forget about all of that, though. Now, it's your turn to answer the question. Who are you?"

"I'm William Curran, but everyone calls me Will. The fourth in a generation of names, actually. I honestly thought you knew who I was."

"Why would you think that?"

"I figured you had kidnapped us for a specific reason, and that you knew who we were. I figured you didn't just torture anyone since you do seem to have some morals.

"No, that's Damon's philosophy or whatever. I just like to torture people, and it doesn't matter who they are. Well, I won't torture old people because that would break my heart, or young kids either. Anyway, you were all leaving a bar while drunk, and it was approaching the late hours of the night, so you were all an easy target. Do you seriously not remember what happened? I know I sure would."

"No, I... I don't entirely remember. It's slowly coming back to me, but it might take a while. I've had a few concussions, so you can't blame me. How did you even manage to kidnap us? No offense, but your arms are as thin as a broom handle."

"*Watch* it, Will," Francesca warned as she whipped out a pocket knife from inside her bra and smirked. "You're pushing your limits," she said with a wink as she started twirling the sharp knife around in her hands. "Although, you are my favorite victim out of," Francesca went back to counting on her fingers, "well, I don't have an exact count, but you get the idea. Besides, *I* wasn't the one who kidnapped you if that makes you feel better. That's what Damon is for, and he's good at it."

"You keep mentioning Damon like I'm supposed to know who he is. Is he your partner or something? You've mentioned him a bunch of times."

Francesca laughed and shook her head in playful disbelief. "You must have been seriously wasted if you don't remember who Damon is." She looked at William, expecting him to suddenly realize who Damon was, but all she got was a blank expression in return. "I also knocked you out with drugs, so I guess I can't blame you. He's a large monster of shadows and smoke who rhymed when he spoke?" Francesca instantly cried out in frustration and smacked her forehead. "Damn it! I rhymed again! He likes to be a poet when he attacks people. I have no idea why, but he preaches to his victims and the witnesses of his attacks. Then, he literally writes a whole novel every time he talks. It's charming and brilliant, but it's annoying and irritating as well. That man has got some serious problems. A lot of them actually. Mommy problems, and daddy problems, and society and school and life, and blablabla. I've tried my best, but he's still useful so, I have no choice but to keep him around. I do feel guilty. He'd make any girl's dream come true, but he's not for me. No one is, actually. My own world of madness is mine alone to enjoy."

William cocked his head and thought for a moment, closing his eyes and scrunching his forehead as he thought harder and harder. His mouth fell open, and his face lit up with shock as he realized who Damon was, his whole body trembling. He quickly began to pull against the ropes again as he looked around in panic. "Florida Phantom? Oh, fuck me! That menace in black who attacked the prison and let all of those maniacs free? That demon-like man with the glaring red eyes and black smoke? He's a monster! I know who you're talking about now. I remember. Let me out of here!"

"That's what I just said, silly," Francesca commented playfully as she shook her head and laughed again. "Look at you trying to escape now. And I thought we were just becoming friends. What happened to your calm composure? He's not here, so you don't have to worry. For a while, it'll just be you and me. Isn't that wonderful? He's off on an important mission."

"I saw him in the news a few weeks back." William glanced around the room quickly, fearful that Damon might be lurking in the corner of the room. "They call him Florida Phantom since we basically know nothing about him. He appears and disappears like a phantom, and he makes his attacks randomly, as far as everyone knows. He's a real-life monster and a cold-blooded killer. He's already killed a few people, and the death count has sky-rocketed recently. He's not wanted by the F.B.I. yet, but they'll be coming for him any day now. One more attack and people might actually start paying attention to him as a terroristic figure rather than just some criminal. My neighbors all think that it's some kind of hoax, but I always knew he was real." William tried to break the ropes again, and they were beginning to cry out now from the constant strain. "Please, Francesca, don't let him get me. I'm a good guy."

"Eh, he hates being called Florida Phantom," Francesca said to herself as she paced back and forth, ignoring William's request. "He wants to be called **The Sinful Son**, which makes *no* sense to me. I'm sure he has some kind of five-page explanation he wrote to explain the symbolism of his name and how it illuminates the meaning of his actions as a whole. Florida Phantom makes more sense. Anyway, he's self-trained in stealth and infiltration, so that explains why he seems to appear and disappear to you. Plus, he's fast and quiet. He's also self-trained to blend in anywhere at any time, and he's actually a professional at it. That's without his costume, of course, but with it, he truly is a master of infiltration. Throw in a few shadows, dark clouds, or the night, and he's completely invisible."

"No kidding! We couldn't see him last night. I mean, I wasn't totally aware of everything that was going on, but neither of my friends saw him or anyone around for that fact. His cloak, what is it made of? It was blacker than black. Lethally black. That cloak is *more* than just regular fabric."

"It's called vantablack, sweetie," Francesca answered with a smile and a wink. "Don't exaggerate too much, but you're absolutely correct. Black is insultingly light compared to it. Not many people know about it, but vantablack is basically the darkest material in existence, or at least here on Earth. It absorbs almost ninety-nine percent of light, which is absolutely amazing. So combine that with his already high levels of ninja-like skills, and it's like he's not even there," Francesca whispered threateningly with a proud smile and a gleam of mischief in her eye. "All thanks to me. For the most part, at least. He had an idea of what he wanted **The Sinful Son** to look like, and combining tech and fashion, I made it possible." Francesca leaned close to William. "Between you and me, though," she used her hand to block half of her face and lowered her voice to a whisper, "he's far more terrifying without the costume. Not ugly, but intimidatingly horrific." She winked at him. "One might say he looks like an alien now, thanks to me. Haha!"

"No," William said with a slight shake of his head as he tried to recall what happened. "Stealth alone isn't enough to describe that beast. There's *more* to it. He wasn't just a master of stealth and hiding in the darkness, because he didn't just kidnap us. He was super strong, and I mean in an inhumane kind of way. He jumped high and moved fast. I… I remember now. It was all so terrifying and awful. I thought I must've been dreaming or hallucinating, but now I know that it's, unfortunately, all completely real."

"Oh, so the memories are back, are they? Do tell me what you remember, Willy-boy. I'm interested in finding out myself. Damon and I aren't on the best of terms right now, and he didn't want to get anyone for me to torture last night. He probably just grabbed you three after I screamed at him for long enough. So, what happened?"

"My friends were helping walk me to the car. Everything was kind of blurry, but across the street by my car, a pair of red eyes appeared from out of nowhere. It scared the complete shit out of me. I thought I was seeing things at first, but then my friends saw it too. The Devil's eyes were across the street, and they were slowly approaching us."

"As childish as they sound, I assure you those eyes are terrifying to see. They burn into your soul. In the darkness of his hood, they're frightening, so I can't even imagine how terrifying them just showing up in the darkness would be. It would be Hell and a jump-scare combined into something far worse than death itself. Of course, I made the eyes, so I'm quite impressed by the terror they induce."

"Exactly, and they were looking down at us besides. There was no human life or emotion in them, but they seemed natural. They seemed so angry and full of hatred. Then, I heard a deep and terrifying voice, but I don't remember what he said. I can almost hear the tone… that gut-wrenching, heart-clenching voice of unimaginable terror. My brain can't even reproduce such a horrifying combination of sounds, and I'm glad for that. I never realized that a human voice could have so much power. *Not* just from the filter that I assume he wears but the natural voice behind it as well, along with all of the intense emotions."

"That's also correct! His natural voice is demonic, and when combined with the voice-filtering ability of the mask he wears, it's truly monstrous. Again, I'm a proud creator."

"That alone would have killed the weak-hearted, but it got worse. Far worse. Jason ditched Anna and me like the coward he always was. I don't blame him, though. Unlike Anna, he had a survival instinct and wasn't frozen in place from fear. He sprinted down the street, but that was when…" William's voice trailed off as he gulped in fear. "That was when Damon, as you call him, ripped off a door from my car like it weighed nothing and then threw it down the street, hitting Jason in the back. Then he bolted toward where Jason was and leaped through the air, covering half a block in just a mere few seconds. He threw Jason's body back at us, and it fell limply before us. The ground shook as he thundered on toward us. Anna screamed. That's all I can remember."

Francesca laughed with pride and wickedness. "I could totally imagine him doing something like that. He likes to put on a show and impress people. I don't blame him for it, as his feats of strength are amazing. Usually, he does *way* more impressive things than what you just described. "You're lucky he didn't flip your car or kick it at you."

"How is that even possible? He's not a big beefy guy, as far as I know, and even muscular men and women couldn't hope to achieve such feats. It's quite possible, but to do it so easily and frequently isn't."

"Oh, Will... you are missing out, my friend! Haven't you ever seen videos of those guys who can pull cars with a rope and stuff? Granted, they're usually a lot more stocky compared to Damon, to say the least, but he is strong nonetheless. Trust me, you can look up the world's strongest skinny men and find some incredible people. You see, his strength comes from two places. He is naturally tall and strong, and I assure you he is ripped underneath that cloak," Francesca said playfully as she pretended to fan herself. "He's probably one of the strongest men alive, dare I say it. He was always a scrawny underdog, but his hatred and desire for revenge pushed him to the limits of human ability, and he trained like a madman. I personally believe that it's a mind-over-matter thing. It's an interesting phenomenon, and truly possible. He has mentally rewired his brain to believe he is not human. He truly believes he is a monster, and so his body has increased the strength of its muscle fibers while still maintaining their size. Of course, that might just be horseshit, but I don't know. He didn't even mean to do it. Also, his body is constantly pumping adrenaline, which has taken a great physical toll on him, but his heart rate and blood pressure are constantly peaking because of how enraged he is. His ability to maintain constant anger at such an outstanding level, as well as to permanently engrave grudges into his heart... it's absolutely astounding. Bad? Maybe, but it's impressive. His power grows exponentially with his negative emotions, and I've seen him go beyond the limits set for those who go beyond limits."

"I... guess it is. As fictional as that sounds, I believe it, and I'm impressed. People do seem physically different when they're passionate or emotional. What's got him so angry, though?"

Francesca had a wide mouth and tried not to laugh as she raised one hand up in a gesture to stop. "Sweetie, that is not a question you should *ever* ask him. He has journal entries explaining why from every day of his life, and each of them are multiple, *multiple*, pages long. Trust me, I've heard them all. I've basically been forced to, actually. I don't blame him one bit for being constantly enraged. I think part of his ability to always be angry is that he has so many bad memories that are on loop in his head. As soon as he is done reflecting on one, another one takes its place, keeping the anger going. Then another one, and another one, and another one," she stated while making a circle through the air with her right pointer finger. "It's never-ending because they form a giant loop, and they consist of so many bad memories that by the time he gets back to the beginning, he can relive them as if they are new. It's crazy and unhealthy, but again, remarkable. I think he said he has an iron spine or something. Not physically, but literally. Or was it iron veins? Then, of course, the memories sometimes stack on top of each other, and he gets even angrier. It's a whole thing of its own."

"Sorry I asked, I guess. Maybe he just needs help too, but it seems like writing and venting to people isn't enough to erase his anger, so I don't know what *is* good enough. What's the second part to his strength, though?"

"Oh, well, that part is all thanks to me. He requested it, but it was mostly my idea, I believe. See, I created an exosuit that increases his strength by four times his natural strength. Or is it exoskeleton? I've never been sure of which is which. Exoskeletons are like bugs and crabs, but it's whatever. He's not in a robot suit, but rather it's like a skin-tight layer of metal that has intricate parts that function together on a complex level. It's probably the most efficient and functional exosuit in the *entire* world. Not bragging. It's true. Then, in the back of the suit, he has the thin tanks he uses for his chemicals."

"Chemicals? What kind of chemicals? He really is a terroristic figure. What does he need those for?"

"Well, the two flattened-cylinder tanks are stored in a relatively thin rectangular box. One of them is for the black smoke, which is for his 'presentation' and such, and the other is for his depressive-spray or whatever he calls it."

"Oh, right. The black smoke. I think I know what you're talking about. Depressive-spray, though? What's that?"

"He must not have used it on you," Francesca replied as she began to play with the knife. "It's a spray that destroys the microbiomes in a person's stomach and intestines. It turns out that gut bacteria affect us a lot more than we thought. When the spray kills them off, people become nauseous, experience inflammation in the intestines, become temporarily depressed, and they experience anxiety. Those are just a few effects. There are actually more, and you can read about it all online. All of the negative effects are good at crippling his prey, though. Not that he needs to, but it helps. He has a retractable tube going down each arm to emit the spray when he wants. That was all he had in the beginning before the cloak and the black smoke. Now he mostly just uses the black smoke, but it's more than enough to get the job done."

"So... is Damon your husband, a weapon, or a criminal partner? I've been getting a lot of mixed messages."

Francesca let out a laugh that seemed almost fake as she cackled like a witch. "Is Damon... my husband? Now that would certainly be something. No, it's... a complicated relationship."

"Oh? Interesting."

"You see, I found him after he had tried to kill himself. Well, he actually *did* kill himself, but that's a story of its own. After that, I took him in, and we worked and lived together for a while. He was a few years younger than me, but we started to... fall in love, dare I say it. We were both broken souls, and we didn't know what love was, but we loved each other as best we could. Honestly, we thought that broken pieces would fit together, but that's not true if the shapes, edges, and cracks aren't fitting for each other. Years went by, and I grew more and more sadistic. My brain releases dopamine when I inflict pain on other creatures, or at least I think that's true. So, I created a way for me to get victims to torture and a way for him to let out all of that anger bottled up inside of him. It was a perfect system, or at least we both thought it was at first. Things have slowly begun to fall apart, but it's suddenly crumbling all at once." She rubbed her stomach and gazed at it with a bittersweet look. "Things have gone farther than I would've ever thought, but it doesn't matter anymore. We have a toxic relationship, and I've hurt him a lot, both physically and emotionally. Either way, my feelings for him are long gone. It's not because he's **The Sinful Son** or Damon, but it's because *I'm* The Torturer, and my addiction is all I have and will ever care about. I can't love. I can only cause pain," Francesca whispered as she took to looking at the ground.

"You shouldn't think that way or blame yourself. Maybe I'm the crazy one for feeling this way, but honestly, I'm sorry for you."

Francesca looked up, ghastly tears in her eyes. She clenched her left hand into a fist, her right hand tightening its grip on the knife. "What did you say?"

"I said that I'm sorry for you."

Francesca looked at William, her face distorted with denial and disbelief with a hint of anger. "How could you say that? You're not lying or trying to deceive me. I would know if you were. How could you say something so caring and kind as that to a person like me? A person who has done this to your friends," she said as she gestured to the two tortured corpses.

"Because I forgive you," William replied. "I mean, I don't forgive you for killing my friends, but I don't blame you or hate you for it."

Francesca wiped away the tears, which were now truly escaping from her eyes. "This morning, I spent a long time talking with Damon. I was fake and lying for the most part, but this time the question that I also asked him is real." She studied William's face for a moment. "How could you forgive me for what I've done?"

"Again, I don't forgive you entirely. Still, I'm not mad. It's not just pity, but it's also sympathy and empathy. It's the way that I've always been. Seeing the good in everyone, including people like Hitler and you, has always been a specialty of mine. Some people think it's foolish, but I don't think so. You said you never chose to be like this. It was either this or a mental collapse due to an uncontrollable addiction. That's beyond your power to control. So, I'm sorry that you have to live like this with no one to help you. I believe that you can be helped and that once you're fixed, you would be an amazing asset to the world. You've invented all cool stuff, haven't you?"

Her whole body trembling, Francesca's face warped between several emotions. She could not believe what she had heard. Deep down, part of her knew that Damon had said the same things to her time and again, just worded differently, but this felt completely different.

William closed his eyes and braced himself as Francesca suddenly ran at him, screaming inaudibly and flailing her arms around. He winced as the blade of the knife skimmed right past his neck. William's body swayed forward, and then he cried out in pain as his body collapsed onto the ground with a hard thump, his chin getting scraped open. A surge of terror overcame William as he felt his legs, which had still been tied up, fall to the ground. He opened his eyes and looked up at the animalistic expressions fighting each other across Francesca's unstable face.

"You crazy son of a bitch! I can tell the difference between liars and honest people, and you're lucky because if I thought you were lying just to appease me, I would've killed you." Francesca used her left arm to wipe away a few tears, the discolored scars on her arm glistening with the salty water on them. "You're telling the truth, though. I've never let anyone go before." She whipped out a pen from her bra. She pressed the button, but an ink-dipped tip for writing did not come out. Instead, a thin metal blade came out. She had designed the pen for carving into human flesh. "That said, then use your pure heart to find others like me and help them," she commanded William as she carved the first four letters of her name into the top of his left arm, facing him so he could read it every time he looked at his arm.

William cried out in pain, but he did his best to keep quiet. The thin blade cut smoothly through flesh.

"Now get the fuck out of here! Go! This is a one-time thing in my life. Get out while you still can," Francesca yelled firmly with a sharp point of the pen to the door through her aggressive tears. William was still frozen as he looked at the sanity and insanity fighting in Francesca's eyes as her whole body shook. "*Gooooo!*" she yelled louder as her voice echoed throughout the empty room. She put the pen away. "Take the boat northeast and never speak a word again. Get out of here!"

William sprinted as fast as he could, leaping up two steps at a time as he exited the torture chamber, traces of blood flowing from his arm. Francesca watched him leave, using every sane part of her to stop herself from chasing after him. She began to cry again as she fell onto her knees and screamed out manically, beating her knife against the cold cement ground.

CHAPTER 4
INTERNAL INSIGHTS
(Homestead, Florida. The Same Day: April 16, 2022)

The storm raging outside had grown worse, providing the perfect cover for **The Sinful Son** and Lilith to drive to the boat with his victims for Francesca. Seen by no one, they had taken the chained-up bodies over to the boat. Now, his cloak flapping viciously in the wind and whipping behind him, Damon sped forward on the boat, as it was a bit of a journey to the island. However, once they had left a mile past the coastline, they had escaped the storm. With the waves slightly calmer and the dark sky a quiet grey, Damon slowed the boat down.

"You're not scared, are you?" Damon, his voice filter disabled, asked as he looked down at Lilith, who was tightly clinging to his right leg. The console of the boat had provided shelter from the wind and rain, but she was a little wet from the rough ride. "I understand that the rocking waves, wind, and rain, combined on this unstable vessel while traveling at such a speed, can be frightening for most, and especially for young ones who have never been on a boat before. There's no shame in fear of the unknown or that which is yet to have been experienced."

"It's kind of scary, but I feel safe holding on to you since you rescued me," Lilith replied. "You're really strong."

"Indeed. I won't let you go flying off of the boat. There was once an idea for my body to exude intense heat through the exosuit I wear, but that design was never implemented, so I'm afraid I cannot warm you up. It won't be too long, however, so bear with me through this damp day of hostile weather."

"Okay," Lilith said with a nod of her head as she shivered a bit. She glanced up at Damon, slightly afraid, but her curiosity was stronger than her fear, and she had no choice but to trust Damon. She hesitated a moment, worried about asking the wrong questions or saying something wrong, but she wanted to know more. "What's your name? Are you human?"

"Unfortunately, I *am* a human, but as far as I know, I stand at the pinnacle of all beings. Well, I'm what is left of a human, who is now nothing more than a hollow body, possessed and given up to a calling greater than myself, and used to help prevent the creation of others like me. My name is Damon."

"Demon?" Lilith asked in shock, her eyes wide.

"D*a*mon… not demon, though the two are similar in sound, and my actions are quite demonic. My name is Damon, though very few know that. Those who did are long gone, and there are almost none remaining who know the accursed name that was given to me. Consider it a secret between us. Anyway, I'm glad you're not afraid."

"Oh, well, I've been on boats before. I've been on yachts, cruises, and small private boats too. My parents liked to go on them for fun. I never really liked them. This one is a lot faster and smaller, though, and I feel like I'm going to fall off. I think the ocean is pretty, but it's scary too. There are sharks, and you can drown, and you're really far away from home." She looked out at the rough water, which was slowly becoming gentler. "Is the island far?"

"The island is some distance away, both far and close, but you'll be unable to see it either way. Through various means of manipulating light and camera footage, along with her innovative science and technology, Francesca has hidden the island from all except her and myself, who know how to get to it. Therefore, we can operate in the utmost secrecy, which is vital to our operations and ability to capture people both for rescue and torture, though you're our first actual rescue mission. Before this island was made, Francesca and I were essentially nomadic, and we weren't as active as we are now. Alas, things change, grow, develop, and evolve, which includes both her and I, along with our goals and dreams. I assure you that the island is, indeed, a glorious haven."

"Yay! What is Ms. Francesca like?"

"An understandable question, but the answer is already in your possession, is it not? I thought you met Francesca already. Though she can be a liar and manipulator, it is with all of the remaining fragments of my heart that I believe she met you."

"Oh, well, I did, but she had an umbrella and sunglasses, so I couldn't really tell what she looks like."

"Ah, now, I understand. That makes much more sense, and I understand why you are curious. Unfortunately, she has to cover herself when she goes out in the sun. Francesca is pale, ginger-haired, and has many scars, so I'm afraid that sunlight is one of her greatest weaknesses."

Lilith giggled. "Like a vampire?"

Damon chuckled. "The minds of children make me laugh, but that is, indeed, a reasonable comparison, I suppose. The two beings are quite similar, actually. Don't believe that sunlight kills, her though, and it certainly doesn't weaken her either. The disappointing truth, at least when compared to the fictional consequences that vampires face, is that her skin just burns very easily, so she has to protect herself from the sun. However, she is also a manipulator, like some vampires are, and she hates looking in the mirror since she can't stand her eyes."

"What? Why?"

"Though I speak so intelligently through profound word choice and diction, along with analogies and allusions, I'll try my best to explain it simply for you. Unfortunately, Francesca suffers from a genetic condition called heterochromia. She was born with it, and there's no changing it, though an eye transplant or custom contact lenses could, theoretically, fix the issue. At this point, however, it is far too late for that, as the public embarrassment she has withstood is long over with, and the only individual she sees on friendly terms now is me, so there is no logical sense in fixing the flaw. The condition is one that has always tormented her, but some find beauty in the genetic flaw. I, myself, am a bit bothered by it, but I can find the beauty in it as well. All things are actually both a curse and a blessing, so there's no point in singling out any particular event, gene, ability, idea, or characteristic for existing in such a user-determined state, as it is really just one of many others that exist in the same way. See, her eyes are different colors, which is a rare condition, though it is mainly just an aesthetic problem. Her left eye is a mixture of blue and grey, and her right eye is brown. Combined with her mental issues, she had always seen it as another factor causing her to be an outcast in this cruel world. Some would tell her to celebrate her uniqueness, but, unfortunately, such trends were not around when she was a little girl."

Lilith giggled. "I thought you were going to keep it simple? You talk a lot and think a lot too. I don't know what you said, to be honest. She has special eyes? That's pretty neat, though! I've never met someone with two different eyes. Is Ms. Francesca sad a lot? You made it sound like she's sad a lot," Lilith commented with a pouty face.

"It is an unfortunate truth, but I urge you to feel no pity for her, nor sympathize with her. When you meet her, do not ask her if she is sad, even if she looks like it. I assure you that I have tried to understand her for many years now, but it is an impossible goal. Her emotions are precious secrets that she keeps to herself, and she has been that way for decades. In fact, most of her sadness is caused by her own self. She has accepted her fate, and she knows that there is no helping or changing who she is. It is both admirable and pitiful, but I love her either way."

"You and Ms. Francesca are in love?" Lilith asked in shock, smiling in child-like awe at what she considered a big revelation. "I didn't know all of that!"

Damon was quiet for a moment, his vantablack cloak viciously whipping behind him from the wind as he focused on the dark sea in front of him. His red eyes seemed dim. "No, Lilith. I'm afraid not. I love Francesca and have for many years, but she does not love me back, nor will she ever find it in her heart to view me as anything more than a partner in an unholy business."

"Awww," Lilith said with a pouty face. "That's the simplest I've heard you talk, so I can tell that you're sad. Why doesn't she love you?"

"That exact question has haunted my mind for as long as I have known her, but the answer does not exist, and if it does, Francesca has made it so that no one but her will ever know it. Despite all of my pondering, all of my heart, all of myself... I can find no answer. I have tried countless times, never stopping my quest to find her love, but that journey must have ended long ago without me knowing. If not, today was undoubtedly the conclusion of my search."

"But... you're so strong and brave! You're a hero!"

Damon bitterly smiled to himself inside of his darkness and chuckled very softly, his grunting-laugh masked by the wind. "As exactly as how I imagined it would seem to a young child who has been rescued by me and now journeys across the sea to an island of peace. However, I'm not fearless or brave like you think I am, or as anyone believes me to be. A person who puts everything they have at risk and who values life... *they're* brave. I don't value my own life. I tried to kill myself three times, and on the third attempt, I actually succeeded and died. My unholy resurrection did not change my perspective or cause me to value life even more. Unfortunately, I don't value life, and I don't care if I die or not. I am detached both from life and death, though very attached to the dream-life I long for, but it is impossible to achieve it, and so I have accepted never being able to live normally or happily. I could die right now and be satisfied. I would not care. I have nothing and no one that would be hurt or lonely without me. Therefore, I'm not brave or fearless at all. I'm not reckless or stupid either, as those are types of bravery as well. I just simply value my life as nothing, so I have no fear, and fear is a requisite for bravery."

"Really? But you *are* brave! Just not brave enough to admit that you are," Lilith responded with a giggle.

"The cleverness of that remark far exceeds my expectations for a child's ability to make sense of the world and phrase sentences in powerful ways. Then again, Francesca and I *were* just discussing how children are maturing far faster than in the past. Again, I'm not sure if it's healthy or whether it's beneficial or negative, but it is an undeniable fact about the society that currently exists. Still, you're wrong, in my opinion. Perhaps, you aren't ignorant, and you can see what I cannot, but I know that I'm not brave."

"Liar! You still face death head-on to save people. You might say that you don't care if you die, but that doesn't mean that you're not afraid of the unknown beyond death. There's a difference between the two... I think. You're just trying to act tough for me!"

Damon chuckled softly as he shook his head. *Silly kid. You've got it all wrong, but you're a sweetheart. Thank you. I suppose I do face death all the time, but really, death and I are more than just acquaintances, and we certainly aren't enemies. A hero? Perhaps in the eyes of the broken and my own thoughts, but societies' morals and ethics would most likely mark me a villain or a questionable vigilante. The truth is that morals and ethics are nothing. Honestly, anyone can justify anything. No matter what, there's always a view that proves it right, and there's always a view that proves it wrong. So, in the end, it doesn't matter at all. Sure, the collective social conscience will always generally agree on whether or not one particular thing is good or evil, but there are countless individuals across the globe who have a completely different opinion. I'm not a hero, a villain, a human, or a monster. I'm just an existence, and my purposes aren't necessarily clear, nor are-* Damon's thoughts were interrupted as the boat skimmed over the surface of a rough wave. The whole boat leaped through the air for a brief second. He looked down at Lilith, who had tightened her grip on his leg. "I guess you're right, kid. Thanks."

"So, why do you fight with that big cloak on? It looks cool, but doesn't that make it hard to see and move?"

"That's the point, kid."

"What? Why would you want-"

"Sometimes, when beings are extremely powerful, they use equipment and gear to purposefully restrict their power so that they don't accidentally hurt the people that they care about. It's one of the main reasons I don't use weapons, though I despise the ideas of guns either way. That rare truth stated, know that this cloak is what keeps me human by slowing me down, limiting my peripheral vision, and putting me at a disadvantage during close combat. Without them constraining my unholy power, I would be a far more unstoppable monster, and no one, including me, would want that. It's for the best."

"Woah! I guess that makes sense. You're *that* powerful? What are you like under that cloak then? Why are your eyes red, though? Are those real? How do you do that if they're fake?"

Damon chuckled. "Alas, my isolation has caused me to forget how endless the curiosity of children is. They are full of many questions, and they seek many answers, which is both smart and dangerous, as all things are. My eyes are only red unto my enemies, but my true eyes are green, for I am the embodiment of life, and I shall bring life back to this world once I purge it of the wicked."

"Oh, okay. That's cool. Are my questions bothering you?"

"Nothing you say bothers me. No one can bother me. Children lack the years of experience and education, both standard and self-taught, that we adults have gained. It is only natural for you to seek answers, and we happen to be the most abundant source of them, so ask away until you are temporarily satisfied. Any adult or teenager annoyed by the endless questions of children is no real human, for they severely lack understanding, sympathy, and logical reasoning. I am beyond those wretched false-ones, however. Their existence is unfortunate and undeniable, but I'm sure that will eventually change one day. Either way, I am essentially an open-book. I'll warn you, however, that the story told through the thick volume is one filled with unimaginable horrors, the long sentences written with an albatross feather that was dipped in my own blood from wounds that others had inflicted upon me."

Lilith shivered. "That was really scary sounding. I don't even know what an albatross is, and you wrote a book using your own blood? That's awful."

"I did not write a book using my own blood. That was merely a… fancy way of saying that I had a horrible life as a child. However, that being said, I've granted you permission to ask me whatever you'd like, as I am not a man of secrecy or silence."

"So I can ask you something personal, then?"

"Of course. That permission has been granted to you. No sacred knowledge or epic tales of horror and hope of my past, present, or future are beyond your ability of inquiry, Lilith. By the expression on your face, I can tell that this is about *me* and not **The Sinful Son**. What do you ponder about that worries you so?"

"Well, I was just wondering what your family was like?"

Damon made a subtle growl of perplexity that hummed along his powerful vocal cords of steel, each particle of sound having the texture of broken glass. His black cloak whipped viciously behind him as he stared off at the rough ocean before him, which had grown more unstable. His blazing red eyes burned brightly. "***My… my… family?***"

"Oh, you… don't have to answer if you don't want to. You're a savior, so I assumed that you came from a warm and happy home that's beautiful. And that there, you had a wonderful family that took good care of you. I wanted to know what it was like for you as a child. You've devoted yourself to saving those who are hurt because you know how good life can be, right?"

"I'm afraid that you are terribly mistaken, and I thought through my various words and references, you understood that what you say is the exact opposite of my life. I apologize. As a child, you are still mostly innocent and optimistic, so I understand why you would think that. Unfortunately, and as much as it deeply troubles me to tell you this, reality is not as kind to the good as it should be or is depicted to be. It worships evil and despises good. I know that... more than anyone, and so does every gentleman, prisoner, rich man, slut, priest, soldier, nurse, and every other type of person to have ever existed or ever exist. Pay no attention to that, however, for it shall all change one day. Change, though it is my greatest enemy and one of the things I despise most, is inevitable and unstoppable. The unfortunate truth is that I, myself, am the most broken man to have ever existed, and my past is a never-ending volume of utter tragedy that is unlike any other. Therefore, I am a savior because I wish to prevent others from enduring the unendurable life that I managed to survive. It is not pity, but rather, it is whole-hearted sympathy and empathy. ***The Sinful Son*** is kind of like the man I always wished would come and save me. Now, by becoming ***The Sinful Son*** through the sacrifice of my humanity, I am there for others. The philosophies and my beliefs go far beyond the simplicity of what I have said, but I'd hate to scar your young mind or trouble you any further with complexities that you would be unable to understand."

Lilith was speechless. "That... was a lot. I'm not sure what to say. Honestly, I think I like you more. You know what it's like. You had it worse than us, but instead of living your life now that you escaped your horrible life, you're trying to help us all instead."

"Indeed. I shall tell you about them, so you can understand me more, and so that your question does not go unanswered. It's all a bit blurry, at this point. It's been years, and Francesca tried creating a machine to erase my horrible memories, but the experiment failed. I only lost a few memories at random, and it, unfortunately, included my last name. I was born a twin to a family of many children, but they put my older brother into an orphanage. He was born larger than a watermelon, apparently, but I have no idea what happened to him from there. My existence was chosen over his, and they shoved it in my face all the time. He's lucky he escaped, and he probably ended up being a happy guy living peacefully. My other siblings were each a horror in their own despicable way, but they are nothing compared to those who birthed me. My mother and father stand at the pinnacle of Hell itself."

"They were that terrible?"

"Unfortunately, you know nothing of how awful people can be, to word it so lightly. My father alone seems to be an entity so vile that Satan would be no more than a lowly parasite leeching off of my old man for evil ideas and atrocious actions. Had you ever encountered such an abomination in your life up until now, you would surely have perished internally within an instant of being in his very presence. The monstrous persona I display to the public is nothing but a faint shadow compared to the horror he brought, and what he did and caused was not on purpose or to help anyone but rather it was a natural destruction he emitted without intention. To know that there are beings that just naturally exist as such evil entities is, indeed, a frightening thought that could paralyze even the bravest of people, including those who do not value life. Words and phrases of any language or culture are not sufficient enough to describe his dreadful countenance nor his most vulgar actions. No style of art could ever hope to depict such heinous actions or such a wretched lifeform. He was a being whose very life proves that evil exists in this world, and worst of all, that it continues to persist far past the bottomless black void of death and even further than life itself. My father's existence proved that such unkillable, truly vile unholiness haunts every sinew and trace of the emotional realm and even the mind, seeping its way into even the most pleasant of dreams and lives, forever ruining all living things near it."

Lilith shivered, every ounce of her fragile being trembling just at the mere thought of such a horrid creature existing, and even worse, that the beast had been the father of **The Sinful Son**, the savior of the broken. It horrified her that her savior and the future leader of the world had to suffer at that monster's hand, day after day, for his entire childhood, let alone the unbearable combination of his mother and siblings as well. The very thought, as terrifying as it was, however, also deeply impressed her. It helped her hope grow, for the glorious existence of **The Sinful Son** proved that good people could stay pure even after suffering the worst life imaginable, and that was exactly what she needed to know. "That was really awful, but please don't stop. I have to know what I might one day face while fighting alongside you."

"This life is *not* for you, Lilith. It's true that **The Sinful Son** will need a successor, but I do not wish for it to be you. I don't doubt your power or emotional and mental strength, but it is my goal to see that you have a better life. There is still a chance for you. One day, inevitably, I will save someone who is beyond saving. Though no one could ever hope to match the pain I have endured, I will, unfortunately, meet someone close enough to me, and *they* shall be the next representative of the broken."

"Shouldn't I help people like you do?"

"Your fate is not as concrete as you believe it to be. While you were saved by me, you don't necessarily have to follow in my footsteps. It's quite true that I saved you to prevent you from becoming me, actually. I love myself, but to exist as a being who is constantly enraged and full of hate is not what I wish for anyone else. Only I alone can exist in such a way. If you were not a broken one, you would not have access to the knowledge I have spouted nor the peaceful man with whom you are conversing. Damon and **The Sinful Son** are both exactly the same and exactly the opposite. The relationship between us both is a long-existing one that goes far back, and the complexity of it could not be contained within a short novel or poem like everything else I talk about. It is a piece of ancient and future knowledge that only I have access to, and only I ever will."

"Okay," Lilith said in defeat, trying her best to understand. "I didn't mean to make you angry. I just want to help you since you helped me, and especially since there are others who need our help."

"There's no need to defend yourself or justify your thoughts, for I am a literary genius and philosopher who has explored the darkest places of the universe in both the physical realm as well as the emotional and spiritual. I understand why you want to become like me, but that is not what I want or what you should want if you were old enough to understand why."

"Oh. Okay… I guess."

"However, I shall continue to teach you of the horrors. My father was also a kamikaze of hypocrisy, though his stitched eyes could never open wide enough to see the wounds inflicted upon himself by his own hand, but it mattered not, for the wounds did nothing. Besides, we opened his eyes and cut the lids free, and he was still unable to see because seeing was a choice he had to make. All he saw was whatever monstrous images he conjured forth from the dark depths of the villainous pit inside his skull. Yet that was, by far, the fairest of all his heinous deeds. He didn't see himself a hypocrite, for he truly believed that the rules did not apply to him, as he was king of the world and far superior to all lifeforms. He shot animals right in the head without hesitation or emotions other than pride and joy. People were no different than the animals to him, though he never killed.

"That's awful!"

"It only gets worse and worse, for the list of his foul traits is a long way. Then, the noises that came from his grotesque body and the noises he created were what could drive anyone to insanity and far beyond it. He was an abominable conglomeration of musicians, bands, choruses, singers, performers, and orchestras, whose only instruments and voices were that of his bowels, gut, and his chomping, slurping mouth of vileness, along with odors that could wither the insides of any organic being into a coma. The swamps of death came from his mouth, and the burping was nothing less than inhumane chemical warfare. Then, there was the lying, the judging, the condemning, and the constant dissatisfaction with everything but himself. His laziness was far beyond the deadly sin of sloth… far, far worse. Not only was he a lazy man in ways that punished himself, but he forced his tasks upon others, even when he was the most capable of doing them. Those are just the complaints of a child, however, and I assure you with every ounce of hate, revenge, and rage flowing through me and contained in every quark of my person that he was far worse than anything imaginable, and so were the other members of what was supposed to be a family."

"There's more? I've already heard enough to be really sad and understand why you had a bad life." Lilith looked up at Damon, his blazing red eyes burning like the fiery core of the sun. He seemed bigger and more powerful, and he was beginning to give off a terrifying aura of destruction. "Are you angry? You seem really angry about everything that happened. Not that I blame you, but I've never seen someone so angry before. I'm not afraid, though. Your anger seems... different."

"I seem angry? That's because I am, always have been, and always shall be. After all, I am a soulless being with a heart that was destroyed by the ferocious attacks of unimaginable predators. Therefore, I am lifeless in every aspect, and it is only my endless wrath, anger, rage, hatred, longing for revenge, and immortal grudges that keep me animated and continuing on in this despairing world of anguish. It is this state that one is able to explore and understand a dimension of emotions and thoughts inaccessible to all others. Due to such a life as I have lived and the very source of my unholy powers, I cannot afford to be happy, optimistic, or hopeful. Even if it were possible for me to be powered by such positivity or to exist with both within my being, my past is the true opposition to such a possibility. The present and future can be changed, but the past is permanent. Do you understand? For all of my life in this world and in whatever lies past it, I shall never be anything more or less than I already am. A bitter state of calm thoughts that are composed of harsh realities is as close to peace as I shall ever get. It is the quietest and friendliest I shall ever be. My state of peace is equal to a normal person's anger, but none of it shall be directed toward you ever."

"So, you can't ever be happy? That's really sad," Lilith commented as she looked up with sympathy at the monstrous entity who was taking her to safety.

Damon shook his hooded head somberly with anger. "Happiness would actually be like a poison to me, as unreal as that seems, for it is the opposite of what is keeping me alive and existing, despite how detached from everything I am," he stated firmly. "My heart never stops racing. My blood is always boiling and shooting through my cardiovascular system at top speed. My head is always throbbing, my muscles are always tense. Adrenaline is almost in my system as much as water is. Physically, my body is decaying from the amount of power I wield, for it is too great for any mortal to handle. Yet, I unlocked the secret to it, and I have no attachments to this world, so I am more than fine with my death occurring as a result. I only wish that I had spent more of my life being swapped as I am now than how I had been mentally existing before. I could have done many wonderful things and helped many people, but I was not Damon and **The Sinful Son** combined until just shortly ago, and there is nothing I can do about it now."

"Damon and The Sinful Son combined?" Lilith whispered to herself, afraid to ask Damon what he meant, for she believed it was something only he understood. She did not understand what he meant, but she looked up at him, and that was all it took for her young mind to realize what was going on. The black cloak of the figure before her was whipping in the wind viciously, but it seemed to be doing so in a more calming manner than before as if it were the cape of a superhero perched on a building. His face was still hidden in the eternal darkness of the large hood, and his eyes were still burning red, but the expression behind all of the darkness was almost visible. As Damon looked past the wheel to the dark ocean waves and grey sky in front of them, Lilith was able to see an expression from the lifeless darkness and burning red that no one else could probably see. In his hidden face, which looked off with a pondering mind, she saw that there was great pain and bitterness. Although just a young girl, whose mind still had much growing to do, she could see and understand the moral battles within his broken soul, as his posture and hidden face displayed the casualties and thoughts that resulted from such an internal war. "Okay," she replied. "Just don't go off trying to die on purpose, or die soon, because you just rescued me. And if happiness is a poison... well, you seem like you could fight off poison and live with it."

Damon shook his head. He did not want to deny that fact, for he knew Lilith was trying her best to be optimistic for both herself as well as him, even though he was beyond saving. "Either way, we'll be at the island soon enough. There is still time to kill, however. Do you wish to continue our conversation about my family and past? You have heard some things about my father already, but there are years and people yet to be mentioned, and they are all equally as awful. Talking about it no longer bothers me as it once did. The choice is up to you."

Lilith gulped, but she stayed firm in her resolve. She wanted to be brave, and she wanted to be prepared. "Continue on."

Damon did not look down at Lilith. He stared forward with his artificial red eyes scanning the murky ocean and grey sky. "Lilith, are you sure you can handle it? The decision is yours, but I would deceive you by not warning you multiple times." Lilith nodded her head as she stared at Damon with determination. "Very well, then. I shall tell you all about what created *The Sinful Son*."

Lilith was awe-struck as Damon slowed the boat down and docked it at a creaky wooden pier. Just moments ago, she had seen nothing but the ocean for endless miles that stretched past the horizon. Now, in an instant, an entire island was in front of her, and it made her smile with childish joy. Although she had just been subject to the horrific stories of Damon's past, which were far more unimaginable than he had warned, she was reassured that she would not have to endure such grueling trials, as the beautiful island before her represented more than just joy and peace.

Damon laughed with a hint of pride. "That expression on your face is one that you thought would never happen again, ***right***? Now, you'll no longer suffer each day and ***night***. Calm your anxious ***mind***, for it will, indeed, take some ***time*** to get used to life here, and you might not stay ***forever***. You'll probably depart, once you're ***better***. No matter what, though, I'll make sure you have a safe future. I cannot expect you to forget the horrors or sadness you endured as a young child, because even though you are still young, the human mind has selective memory capabilities beginning at birth far beyond our understanding. Therefore, as unfortunate as it is, a foggy memory of the years up until now created through mental suppression might be as good as close to forgetting as you get, but I truly hope that you'll soon be happy again and not allow your past to become unforgettable chains that burden you to the grave and even beyond it."

"Okay! I want to be happy and forget that I was sad," Lilith said as she walked to the front of the boat. "The island is so pretty!" She giggled. "The sand is so bright and white, and it looks different than regular sand. Aww, and look at all of the trees and flowers! This place really is peaceful and full of joy. I want to build sandcastles!"

"Your observation contains no ounce of false information, and you speak the correct truth. The plant life on this island is, indeed, vibrant and beautiful, as it should be everywhere, existing in an unnatural variety of purposefully picked species. I tend to the plants on this island, ensuring they have everything they could possibly need, and driving away any unwanted wildlife that manages to come to the island. Only the lovely birds are welcome, and they tend to be the only animals that make it to the island, as we are miles out to sea. However, the occasional stowaway manages to slip into the boat and then down the dock and onto the island, as nature always finds a way. The island itself is a few acres large and could easily support animal life, but there's no need for them to live here, as it would be troublesome to Francesca and I. Landscaping, however, is a feeble task that requires no effort on my part, and I have an immunity to the heat of the sun. I love the heat and the power of the sun. It can get hot on this island, but we do have air conditioning in the building, so you'll always be comfortable," Damon stated as he grabbed the chained-up victims, who had been uncomfortably stored near the back of the boat. Throwing them onto the dock, he dragged their bodies along the wooden pier toward the sands of the island.

Lilith skipped in front of Damon happily, jumping into the sand once they had crossed the length of the wooden pier. She grabbed handfuls of it and threw the pearly grains of sand into the air as if she had no care in the world anymore. She waved at a few sandpipers, who were hopping along the edge of the shoreline.

"I'm afraid that you unintentionally torment them, Lilith, as you signal to them to approach you, but you have nothing to feed them. You'll find that the birds here are unnaturally friendly to humans. For quite some time, I have fed their ancestors, their descendants, and now the new generation of young birds, which are quickly growing up. Therefore, having been a reliable source of food for so long and for so many, they know that there is no need to fear harm from me, and they have eaten out of the very palm of my deadly hand." As if on cue, a few of the small and adorable birds landed on Damon, perching on the head and shoulders of the large and ominous figure.

"Ahhhhhhhaahhaha! They like you! That's so cute!" Lilith held out her hand as a sandpiper approached her. It pecked her bare hand a few times before realizing that she had no food. "Aw, sorry, little guy. I don't have any food to give you!" A shower of seeds flew through the air at Lilith, and the sandpipers rushed to get the grains from the sand in front of her. She looked up at Damon, who was chuckling slightly.

"Luckily for you, I had an emergency supply in my pocket underneath this cloak," Damon said as he crouched down and emptied the seed in his hand into hers. The birds perched on him flew off and to the sand, pecking the seeds out of Lilith's hand.

"Haha! That tickles. They're so cute. Thank you, Damon!" Lilith laughed and smiled joyfully as she watched the birds eat in front of her and out of her palm.

His dark and unholy garments slightly drifting in the subtle breeze around him, Damon looked down at the scene before him with a calm state of mind as he stood up tall. "I'm glad that you enjoy tending to the birds so much. Soon, you shall care for these creatures as well if you would not mind the task and could find the peace and joy that I manage to find in it. While you're here, you're more than welcome to take over caring for them. However, we mustn't drag our feet returning. Francesca needs these victims, and I need to show you around."

"Oh, okay! Byyyyye," Lilith said to the little sandpipers as she waved before turning around and following Damon.

Damon led the way to a building, which was the only one on the island, and it was partially hidden by palm trees, shrubs, and the other various types of plants on the island that Damon had grown and maintained. The building was only one story tall, comprised of bland concrete blocks, and it was relatively large. The building had three bedrooms, one kitchen, two bathrooms, a workshop for Francesca, a torture room for Francesca, a rage room for Damon, a large training room for both of them, and a junk-filled basement. Behind the building was a long strip of pavement that featured two experimental jets that Francesca had been working on to make traveling to locations other than Florida efficient and possible.

Damon opened the door to the building after quickly putting in a few passcodes. The door led to a hallway whose walls, floors, lights, and ceilings were not entirely hospitable.

Lilith shivered. "This is your home? It's kind of scary."

Turning around and lowering himself to one knee, Damon faced Lilith. "I sincerely apologize for the condition of this building. I'm afraid that existing for a long time, just as it happens to all living beings, has worn it down to the point of decay and eventual death. So preoccupied with our missions and personal goals, Francesca and I have failed to restore the building to a youthful state that could easily support anyone or maintain it so that it does not deteriorate so quickly. The island itself has also been subject to the natural wrath of a few hurricanes, which has damaged and eroded the outside of the building, but I assure you that the structure is still sturdy and safe. However, I have maintained one bedroom, which is neither Francesca's or mine, in the hopes that I might have a child in there one day. Again, I am more human than anyone else, and if not for Francesca's mental insanity and lack of human emotion, I would have been a father quite a while ago.

Though you are not of my flesh and blood, we are connected through the similar experiences and emotions of those who have been broken. Therefore, the neat room is yours and shall be until further notice. Unfortunately, the rest of the building is rather unsightly, but I assure you that there is no need to be fearful."

"Okay. I trust you, but can I hold your hand?"

"If it would ease your fearful and troubled mind, I will gladly allow it." They heard a woman's screams and sobbing from inside of the building, and Lilith shivered even more. "In fact," Damon grabbed her small hand with his large metal-covered one, "it would seem that Francesca might not be in a hospitable mood right now. Therefore, you'll be safer the closer you are to me. I sincerely apologize, though I do not know what is wrong. Something is not right, and an unfortunate series of unexpected events must have occurred while I was gone."

"Is Ms. Francesca hurt?"

"We'll soon find out, though it's hard for any normal human to inflict damage to her, as she is rather skilled in fighting and possesses an unholy arsenal of tools and weaponry. As I've warned you before, she is not entirely sane. Between her own experiments and the defects of her birth, followed by years of social deprivation and judgment, along with the fact that she started down an unholy path at a young age, her mind has deteriorated rather quickly, and it is most unfortunate. She does have a sweet side, but it's extremely difficult to ever get to it. Lilith, I shall take you to your room, and I want you to lock yourself in there while I talk to Francesca. When she is no longer upset, I shall introduce you two to each other, and I hope that you'll form a lovely bond, even if it is temporary. Unfortunately, right now doesn't seem to be a good time."

"That's sad. She seemed nice the other day, so I hope she feels better," Lilith said unsurely, not understanding what was going on. She squeezed Damon's hand tighter, trusting that everything would be alright.

Dragging the bodies in one hand and guiding Lilith in the other, Damon entered the building, more cautious and paranoid than usual. He constantly glanced behind them, and he checked every crevice of the wall as if it might be able to cause his death. Every corner they turned was scouted first to ensure that death was not right around the corner and waiting for them. The cries of Francesca echoed eerily throughout the building, and they were coming from her room.

After passing through several hallways, and throwing the chained-up victims into the torture chamber, which Damon did not allow Lilith to peek into, they slowed down when they entered a hall that seemed to be a dead-end just beyond a patch of darkness. To the left, there was a door that led to the rage room, where Damon used a variety of objects to smash an even greater variety of objects in a futile effort to expel some of his endless rage. To the right, under the patch of darkness in the hallway where the light overhead had died, was a door that led into a pitch-black and windowless room.

Damon gestured to the door as they passed through the darkness of the hallway. "That room is mine. It lacks windows, but I have no need for them, and I keep the light off to save energy. Of course, we pay no bills for electricity, since Francesca has set the island up using solar panels from R.O.M.A.B.A. Industries, and their designs are flawless and create more electricity than standard solar panels, but I still feel that there is no need to waste power. So, my room is usually dark when I'm not in it and actually doing something. I'm afraid I haven't gotten around to fixing the light that died in the hallway, so it seems rather frightening, but there's no need to be afraid. You're room is at the end of the hallway, so let's continue on."

After they had walked halfway down, Lilith stopped in the middle of the hallway. She was staring at a door that had a tinted glass window, making looking into the room impossible. She stopped partially from curiosity, but the strange sight in the creepy building was also frightening to her, and she had almost stopped involuntarily with anxiety upon passing the metal door, which seemed to have been closed for a long time. "What's in that room?" Lilith asked as she tugged on Damon's cloak. He stopped and turned toward the door. "I can't see through the glass, and it looks like no one goes there anymore."

"What you suggest and have ascertained from the small details of the door are indeed true facts and observations. It has been a while since anyone has entered that forgotten dream, and I doubt that it will ever be revisited. Just like a true dream had by one during their most precious slumber, that dream has faded away and is nothing more than a memory of a fictitious idea that will never repeat itself again in this world or the imagination. It is seldom that we go back to sleep and continue a dream or repeat one, even if it is our deepest desire to do so. I hope that one day, we'll be able to explore our minds and dreams in an entirely different way."

"So… that room has a dream in it?"

"Not a literal one, but the forgotten remnants lurking in that hollow chamber are the parts of a dream I once held in my heart and wished to make true, as the theoretical possibilities and existence of such an idea were not impossible nor illogical. I'm no scientist. My intelligence is frightening, but it merely rots insides of my skull, unable to live without its crutch. My genius seems to only work when I am enraged, which is always, but due to its emotional influence, my intelligence only works in ways that serve me best or inflict the greatest revenge upon others. I'm a monster and a bringer of death. Perhaps that is what motivated me to try and create such an idea. It's quite possible that the unholy truth is that I merely wished to create others like me, but it is not unreasonable to assume that I, the ultimate lifeform, also wanted to help others strive toward perfection in a manner that was efficient and pleasing. After all, the body is the vessel and the incubator of all things to come."

"I'm sorry, but I don't understand anything you're saying. What are you talking about?"

Damon sighed, but it was not an exhale of rage or sorrow. All that came out of him was bitterness and acceptance of the fact that he had moved on from his abandoned project. "I could stand here ominously in this hallway in front of this unholy door all day and night long, preaching and teaching you about all the ideas regarding the human mind and dreams. It is a tale of all I have discovered and learn, and all that I fear, love, and believe. Therefore, I'm afraid that I cannot properly explain this whole project to you, for we lack such time, and there is no doubt that a child has not the patience, experience, or intelligence to understand such complex matters, realities, and fictions. However, you do not need to know all about dreams to understand what this machine would do. Humans don't give dreams the proper respect or attention that they deserve. Occasionally, every human thinks to themselves that, perhaps, their dreams mean something, and they'll search online for an answer, but after that, they move on with their lives. To me, dreams are much more than that. There are countless questions that we all ask in regard to such ideas, and it may be all the way to the end of eternity that we continue searching for them. What are dreams? Why do we have them? Do all beings have dreams? I know that dogs do, for my wretched mother was a torturer of those innocent and occasionally foul creatures. That's not the point, however, and my words go far beyond all of this as they always do. Lilith, do you understand what I'm getting at?"

"I think I do. You think that dreams are mysterious and powerful, and that they probably mean more than we think."

Damon chuckled deeply. "Young child, you are far from the vast power that I preach about, but I shall accept that answer as a correct one. I believe that the mind has power over the body. There's no doubt about that. There are scientific studies about it, but it makes sense even if you are a criticizer of science or religion. Forget about that room and abandoned project, however. It is not in my life that it shall be completed, nor by my hand will it ever become a reality." Damon ushered the girl forward, and she reluctantly turned away from the abandoned chamber, wondering what it was originally meant to be one day. "I apologize about that, actually, for that hollow room of darkness that has been sealed away is right next to your room," Damon stated as he gestured to a door to their left just beyond the darkness.

Lilith followed Damon into the room, and she was relieved to see that, just as he had told her, the room was neat and clean. "Yay! It's not as big as my old room, but I like it." The room was no different than any regular bedroom, and it was neutrally colored. There were a few books and toys, but other than that, the room was lacking everything except for furniture. "Will we be able to go shopping and get some stuff? It's kind of empty."

"Of course, and I know why you ask such a question. After all, this room lacks all that a young girl needs and the toys and books here are for children far younger than yourself. I understand that it is disappointing, but as soon as I can, I shall get you everything you need to be satisfied living here." Damon turned as he heard another sorrowful cry echo throughout the building. "For now, however, I'm afraid that as a man of love and protectiveness, I must go and do my best to comfort Francesca. She has not cried in a long time, and the source of her terrible sorrow might be one that will, unfortunately, affect us all. As I commanded before, lock the door and do not answer unless it is I that knocks and speaks. Once she is calmed down, you shall meet Francesca, and, hopefully, I suppose we'll all have dinner tonight. Perhaps lobster."

"Okay. I understand," Lilith said as she dove onto the soft and clean bed. "Thanks for everything. Just make sure you come back, okay?"

Damon nodded his head before swiftly turning around and disappearing down the hallway. *Such aggravating irony! So few rooms, yet so many hallways. You were never quite the architect, Francesca, and now it is delaying me from helping you. I'm coming. Something isn't right. I can sense unholiness lurking about that is neither mine nor yours. You were supposed to be torturing a man while I was gone. What unhappiness plagues you? Have you realized that I am right and that you are wrong?* He raced toward Francesca's room and arrived there after navigating the hallways of the building. Stopping, he beheld Francesca hunched up against the headboard of her bed, sobbing. She looked up at him, her face a wreck.

Carefully, Damon took a step forward, ducking underneath the doorway as Francesca stared at him, lifeless and unstable. "There is no longer a need to shed a **tear** or experience sorrow or **fear**, for I have arrived, and I am *here*. Your cries echo throughout the *halls*, and your somber screams hit deaf *walls*. Now, my ears do receive such sounds, and I shall respond to all that must be *said*, even if I have to listen until I am *dead*. Francesca, if I dare to say your *name*, why are you not at all the *same*? I left just a few hours *ago*, and now it seems that you are *sorrowful*. It's not like you to cry or *whine*, and not expressing emotions is *fine*, but I must talk with you, for life here is about to change drastically for us both. It has been a long time since I last saw you like this. Is everything alright?"

Francesca, not even angered by Damon's poetic rhyming, flashed back to earlier in the day, and she heard every word of her conversation with William. She thought about some of the people she had killed and her abnormal childhood. She thought about everything Damon had said to her earlier in the morning. "Everything's alright. I just… have a lot on my mind. Don't feel guilty, though. It's not just about what you said to me this morning. I'm thinking about a lot of things."

Damon's heart almost stopped for a moment as shock exploded throughout his indestructible being. "To hear you speak so plainly is quite shocking for me to experience, and I'm glad that you're being more open. However, such pondering is not typical of your *mind*, and it's not like you to be so open and *kind*. What plagues your heart that you cry as *such* and causes you to reflect so *much*?" I am here to hear everything you *say*, just as I have been since that unholy and fateful *day*."

"I know, and I hate it, but I'm feeling a little bit sane," Francesca replied softly as she spun a small buzzsaw blade in her one hand. "It's a clarity that I haven't felt in a long time, but from this clarity, everything is collapsing apart now, and I'll probably end up more unstable than before, because that's the best way to deal with it all. Still, you want to help as always. Th… thank you, Damon," she said softly. She moved a ginger strand away from her grey eye. "It's nothing serious, though. My stomach hurts, and I had a bad experience with that guy I was supposed to torture. He said some things that no one else really has, except for maybe you, and I'm just reflecting over it all."

"Based on the past, which so frequently occurs, I suppose you would rather be alone? If that is the truth, I shall inquire no further, but know that the victims for you to torture are here," Damon said as he turned to leave.

Francesca grabbed the edge of the vantablack cloak that Damon wore. He stopped instantly. "Actually, today you can stay. At least for a little bit. I honestly don't want to be alone. I don't want to talk, but… I don't want to be so isolated, either. Come lie down next to me." Damon did as she commanded, and going to the right of her, he went flat on his back and stared at the cracked ceiling overhead. The artificial red eyes of hate turned off, and he seemed to be no more than a lifeless pile of darkness. Opening up the left side of his cloak, Francesca curled up on top of it next to Damon before pulling it over herself like a blanket. "This world is messed up, and so are we. Still, I don't blame either of us, and I guess that's okay."

"I suppose it is," Damon said quietly without emotion.

Eventually, they both fell asleep.

CHAPTER 5

A DEMONIC DREAM

(Homestead, Florida. The Same Day: April 16, 2022)

Pushing his way through a raging storm of sand that could have easily consumed the entire Dust Bowl, Damon stopped when he bumped into the back of something solid. It was a bench, the two sides consisting of concrete, three boards making the back, and four boards making the sitting part. They had, at one point in time, been a fresh green that could have brought to mind a scene of bright summer fields, but the wood had begun to splinter and crack in small pieces, and the green was fading and peeling off at spots, revealing white and brown.

Damon could barely see through the raging sandstorm, although he was able to note that the sky was blue and free of even the smallest wisp of a cloud. There was the constant sound of low thunder in the distance despite the absence of clouds, and the echoing roars seemed to have no rhythm.

With no other clear option besides pointless resistance against the sandstorm, Damon walked around the bench, hugging a tight curve and veering straight in front of it before taking a seat on it in the center. The bench, although seemingly old and fragile, was denser than steel, and the wooden boards did not whisper the faintest sound despite the weight of Damon's muscles, exosuit, and dark memories.

In an instant, the devastating storm of sand grains stopped. Every grain quickly fell to the ground, vanishing entirely rather than stacking on the ground. Damon felt a powerful shiver travel down his body, his flesh and heart burning as the shiver traveled throughout his whole person both internally and externally. With dread and competitive instinct, he slowly looked up to see the cause of the feeling. A figure loomed before him, about ten feet away. It was a physical shadow of a hooded man, seeming to be three-dimensional yet two-dimensional at the same time, a paradox that Damon had never experienced, though it reminded him of the visual illusion caused by his vantablack cloak.

"Do you know where we are?" the shadow asked in a deep voice that sounded like it belonged to an old man, made wise and bitter by time and experience, although it was still powerful and full of contempt.

Damon looked to his right and left, noticing for the first time that he was at a beach, the water only thirty-six meters in front of him, beyond the shadow-man. To his left was a boardwalk in the far distance, although the air around it was covered by a yellow haze that was visible and seemed to radiate heat. To his right lay nothing but a long stretch of barren sand until there was eventually a worn-down wooden fence with wide gaps between each vertical post, it too shielded by the yellow haze and barely visible. Large sand dunes sat behind him on either side, trapping him on the beach, although there seemed to have been a path of grey boards cutting through them long ago. Damon turned his artificial eyes, which were yellow instead of red, back toward the shadowy figure.

"You seem sentient, yet unresponsive and lacking the usual poetry and profound thoughts," the figure commented, staying where they were.

"Forgive me. It has taken a moment for my senses to come to me, and now that the raging sands have disappeared, I can see clearly where we are. Such a place could never escape my memory, even beyond death and horrific diseases that destroy the mind. I shall always remember and recognize this place, for this is the spot where I killed myself. Well, it was many years ago. The place has not seen any life since, as far as I can tell, but this is, indeed, the place where all life left my face and my blood merged with the Earth as my skin grew pale and grey. There is no denying where I am or what happened here so long ago. This is where I killed myself."

"Where *we* killed ourselves," the shadowy figure corrected as he limped forward, leaving only two feet between him and Damon when he stopped moving. The shadow formed into a solid humanoid and revealed itself to be **The Sinful Son**, except that it was not Damon. This man was taller by four inches and much larger in general. The right side of his cloak and hood were torn and tattered, especially at the ends. Instead of a metal glove on the right hand, it was bare human flesh, burnt and scarred, holding a sizeable indescribable staff made of dark wood whose shape seemed to represent something, although Damon did not know what. The exosuit was visible in some parts where the cloak had holes and tears. It was bigger than Damon's and seemed capable of more strength, except it seemed rusted and tarnished, riddled with dents and uneven holes. The hood of the cloak rested higher up on the head of the man, allowing the high-tech grey sunglasses to be visible. The left lens was cracked and flickering on and off while the right one was black and lifeless. There was no mask around the bottom half of his face. Instead, there was a grey beard growing on the man's chin, the right side partially mutilated. Across his back and underneath his cloak was strapped a pitchfork and a shovel in an x-shape formation. A steady wind from the North continually blew his cloak, and a few long hairs of his chin flowed with it as well.

"I am not shocked, to say the ***least***, for only I could exist as such a ***beast*** as the one before ***me*** standing in front of the ***sea***. I ask that you provide me with an answer to the question I shall ***ask***, and I hope that you'll respond rather ***fast***," Damon said as he looked up at the figure towering before him, his voice natural as he spoke, his mask disabled beneath his cloak. "It's clear that you're not the version of me from the present, and I assume you have not come to threaten me with death or praise my choices. It's quite possible, as my experience and self-education have taught me to expect, that you might not even be real. This could all be a hallucination, though I fear the truth resides within your heart alone. Are you me from the future, hardened by the struggles of the world, both external and internal?"

"An expected question with theories that do not stray from what most would think or guess. Of course, I shall answer your question, for I mean you no harm. I am not from the future in the physical sense of time or reality, which is what you were asking, as disappointing as such a statement might be. The truth is that I am just a vicious conjuring of your subconscious during your resting time of the midnight hours as you recharge your unholy powers to continue on with your work, and both you and I already know that, so asking was just out of politeness or hope. Your mind is far different than any other. Wherever you are, your mind works while your body does rest, and using your experiences and predictions, combined with your vivid imagination, I have been created, though my purpose will always be unclear. This is not the first time, correct?"

"What you speak is, indeed, true, at least based on what I already know. First time? With you, perhaps, but my dreams do not always remain in my *mind*, for some disappear with *time*, and my dreams are as inconsistent as my choice to *rhyme*. There is no rhythm or pattern as far as I know, but then again, it would be so complicated and perplexing that it would most likely take years to figure out such truths. Why imagine you of all people? I have much on my mind, and although I am in universal debates that shake the cosmos of my mind, why summon you if you actually have no knowledge of the future? Usually, I see Francesca, a family member who has been dead for decades, or someone else, but never myself. I am always me, so why are you me now?"

"Who better to help you with such a *task* than a man who has learned from his *past*? It's true that I have no wisdom of the days to come that would have passed for me should I actually be an entity of the future of your true reality. I lack such information, but by every sinister spark of the synapses within your system, through the boiling blood of your burning body, and the monstrous memories of your mind, I am comprised of every prediction and outcome bound to form within your future days. I am what you think the future will be but *more* than just subconscious thoughts and glimpses of memories. I, too, am you, and I am **The Sinful Son** of the years to come."

"You are him as well?"

"I was, and I am."

"What then, foul being, has been done to you to twist you into an even more horrid image than what I already am?"

"The world has been just as unkind to me as it was to you, and even more so, though there has been some success. The broken worshiped me, criminals admired me, the privileged feared me, and so on and so forth as the world was and is meant to be. But society and the government hated me. They despised the very monster that they had created through their failures, just as it is with most creators. They thought me a false savior and a manipulator, and they set out to destroy me as everyone always has."

"A perfect, most vile truth, undoubtedly unholy in its content yet fitting in all that is. *They* shall always be against us. Not just them but the others. It's only the ones we save and us, although they too are unworthy and reckless. Alone is the endless state of such a being, yet it goes both ways upon the altar of all things in morality. Except for yourself and me, almost all are *unappreciative* of what we do, including those we fight for. That is the greatest sacrifice and burden. What has the artificial law done in an attempt to tame the truth with lies and destroy you while calling it life? What now of the problematic parents, the savage siblings, and the punishing privileged?"

"If given an endless sheet of paper with an infinite inkwell and an immortal feather, along with all the time in the universe, I would never be able to finish such a list, just as you have stated yourself. My hatred, rage, anger, desire for revenge, and all my other negative emotions that fuel my unholy body have grown exponentially, but they flatten off, for there comes a point where nothing can be satisfied, and I will die at my own hand. The end came close just once, and it was barely an end, to say the least. Yet I was not afraid as I have never been fearful of anything organic or inanimate. The heart of an exploding star is no more powerful than a grain of sand in the abyss of a black hole. They thought that they could stop me with one of nature's most savage powers: fire. It was not a trap nor an ambush, just a prediction unformed within the vastness of my grand mind, as I had much else going on that needed my full attention. The wicked blaze raged like the anger and hate in my heart and the molten magma of a volcano beneath the Earth upon its core, but it was no match for me. It's true that I escaped barely *alive*, but *The Sinful Son* will always *survive*."

"What you speak is, indeed and undoubtedly, the truth so far as I can tell or know. You have suffered even more than I could have fathomed but gone much further than we had ever plotted when we first began. To be here is an honor greater than any other."

"I have suffered, and you will no matter what path you choose or what choices you *make*. It is what we were born and then *made*. However, I traveled the path with such tormenting knowledge in *mind* with determination and *despise*. So long as the verbally, socially, spiritually, mentally, and emotionally abused continue to suffer, *The Sinful Son* will continue on against all the odds of both life and *death*. By the bonds of my mentality and indestructible determination, my broken bones, decaying *flesh*, and rotting muscles hold on together, my heart pumping with a surging anger that keeps it from cementing with death. My quest has no end in *sight*, yet each sunrise I wake up and *fight*. And with each sunset, I grow wearier as my days come to a close, but what I have done in my life is immortalized in time for *all*. I have made countless wicked *fall*. Families, friends, enemies, all people... they will continue to break one another with physical punishments, demonic depictions, wicked words, and emotional engagements, to name a few of the unholy occurrences of this putrid planet. Our quest has no end, for it is infinite until all are dead or rest in a peaceful utopia made either by us or some other. Such a possibility looms in so far a *distance* that I could never calculate its *existence*. That time is not yet, and it may never be. That stated by my old *tongue* to the *young*, we both know that the ones we represent and fight for are more important than any entity or goal. *The Sinful Son* must become so much more before time runs out. I regret not being me long *ago*, but alas, it is *so*."

After a moment of powerful silence except for the thunder in the distance, Damon stood up and bowed before Elder Damon in a sign of utter respect. "More righteous words have never been *spoken* on behalf of all the *broken*. You truly are a future entity of all knowledge and power in this world and perhaps beyond it. The mentally *destroyed* and the emotionally *toyed*, they all thank us for what we *do*. They are unappreciative, yes, but there is gratitude, *too*, and there always will be." Damon paused for a moment as he looked up. "I wish to stay and converse with you for a long time to follow, but it is merely a dream inside the *bone-hollow*. Time has gone by so fast and so *slow*, and, unfortunately, I *know* that it is soon your time to *go*. One last question shall escape my *mind* before we run out of *time*: why the pitchfork and shovel upon your beaten back?"

Elder Damon licked his dry lips and swallowed a small glob of spit. "I am unsure of it myself, though I believe I do know the general concept behind it."

"Please, teach me."

"Well, the pitchfork is probably a physical representation to what I do as *The Sinful Son*, for I harvest the sinful as a farmer harvests his crops, though I am not the creator of the sinful as he is the creator of his crops. The shovel is for burying those who are wrong, as I am the judge of those who are wicked, and I have cleansed this world of many terrible people and saved the lives of those who would have suffered at their hands and words."

"There must be more to it, as well as more to *The Sinful Son*."

Elder Damon looked away to his right and stared out into the distant land of sand as the wind gently blew what was left of his vantablack cloak as if he were in a cinematic shot. He turned back to Damon as he leaned into his staff. "*The Sinful Son*? He's always been a part of us. Perhaps, at one point, he and we existed as two different personalities, but that changed long ago. We are undoubtedly *The Sinful Son* and always will be," he looked out again before turning back, "but the truth is that I am simply Damon. *We* are simply Damon, and we should give it all up. I know we can't, but Damon is important too. He is who we tried to be, and who we can be. We are really just a boy who may have been born evil, but who was mostly turned into a villain through the mental and emotional abuse he suffered. Others did this to us, and so that is why it is others who must pay. If we were truly evil by heart, no force in this universe, whether God or other, would have allowed us to be saved that day we committed suicide. *I survived*. But you must do more than that. You must thrive and find a *greater* purpose than what I have completed. Our mission is the greatest honor and task there is, but there will always be something greater out there: the life you and I never had, and the one we wish we could have. It calls me every waking second of my life in a tormenting manner that is unbearable. But it's still possible for you to have it."

"I don't understand how you can say this to me, old man. You contradict your own existence, as well as our beliefs. I doubt not your wisdom nor your words, but what you speak of can never *be*, for it was taken away from *me*."

"Then take it back!" Elder Damon boomed, shaking the whole fictional landscape. "They cannot stop you *now*, for to the grave they all do *bow*! Damon, you *must* find in your *heart* the strength to rebuild it part by *part*. The same with your mind, although it's shattered *glass*, build it back without the *past*. Though I speak in perplexing riddles like *so*, the answer is one that you already *know*."

The wind picked up into a powerful northern blast, and a raging wave of sand grains separated the two men. Damon shielded his face with his hand for a moment until the sand storm weakened. The grains all fell and vanished once again. Elder Damon was gone, the remains of his tattered cloak drifting to the ground.

CHAPTER 6

THE ILLUSIONS OF TIME

(Granite Falls, Minnesota. Earlier That Same Day: April 16, 2022)

Having finished an excellent breakfast prepared by the flawless teamwork of Sir Thomas and Laura Godwin, everyone began the preparations for their trip to Florida. Though their sleep had been insufficient due to the deafening flow of theories throughout their minds, the men were rested up and ready to go. Before that, however, Timothy wanted to show off his technology and science, and so Kronos and Sir Thomas followed him into his personal dojo, admiring the large room.

Kronos laughed mischievously to himself. "You impress me even more, Timothy. While your semi-mansion is rather impressive, I'm afraid it falls short in comparison to the glory of my castle. However, you have my respect, as my castle, unfortunately, lacks a training room. Such an addition would certainly boost my unstoppable ego, but there's really no need for me to have one added to my home-empire. My arsenal of custom-made inventions, crafted through the use of my unlimited genius, means that I don't have to train like you do."

"I personally prefer close combat and melee weapons, as any jerk can use a gun," Timothy commented as he gestured to the various types of weapons he had displayed on the wall. "I understand the whole idea of evening out the playing field, but there's no training, really. Sure, it's a skill that is taught and perfected, but it's not like getting ripped or increasing your endurance to fight successfully during melee confrontations. People think it's unfair, since some people are naturally stronger than others, but overcoming the areas you fall short in is part of what makes a person more than human. It boosts their spirit and mind, and it helps them understand the harsh realities of this world better. Well, that's my opinion, anyway. Even if we banned all guns and destroyed them, people would find a way to make them again. It's crazy. No offense to your arsenal of weapons or anything."

"To word it in your world of comic references, I have a personal magical ability known as Wall of the Egomaniac. It's a passive ability that causes the deflection of any and all insults. I believe I am indestructible and unbeatable, and that nothing can harm me. It automatically bends everyone's words so that they praise me or insult the person who spoke. Even the most heartfelt truth can't get past my pride, for I have made it indestructible. So, there's no need to apologize, because I wasn't offended at all. What I heard was that I'm far superior and that you prefer primitive fighting techniques. Besides, I actually have several melee weapons that I crafted with my ability to manipulate atoms."

"Really?" Timothy asked, shaking with excitement. "No way! That's awesome! I forgot how much you can do with your atomic science."

"Unfortunately, he's not lying," Sir Thomas said half-jokingly. "I've seen some of the things he's made, I honestly don't know where gets the ideas for such rubbish. I think he might secretly be a bigger nerd than you are when it comes to comic books and entertainment. Or geek, if you prefer that term. Those words have changed a few times since I was a young lad."

"See, I believe in both quality and quantity, Timothy, and a proper collection of inventions would include both ranged and close combat weapons," Kronos stated factually. "Especially when it comes to profit, but the weapons are all prototypes for me and the future, as of now, so that doesn't even matter. It has nothing to do with an admiration for heroes or villains at all. It's only logical that the most powerful person in the world, which is me, would have an abundant collection of weapons that includes a variety of different types."

"Right. I totally understand, man. Makes total sense, and even if you didn't use your scientific discoveries to create weapons, humans were bound to do it. So, better you than them, in my opinion. Your morals seem loose, but you're a good guy. I can tell. Let me in on a few weapons real quick before I show off my stuff, though. I'm really interested in what you've created. As a hero, I've actually been thinking of all the ways your science could be used to make hero costumes and weapons."

"There are far too many, so I'll just give you a few of the latest ones that are the most practical. There's the Atomic Gauntlet, which I actually have with me in my car, to give one example."

"Sounds wicked cool, Kronos. I love it."

Kronos laughed pridefully. "*Correct*. I also have a project I was working on, which I had been calling the Atomic Knight Project. However, I'm scrapping that name because it's copyrighted, and despite the fact that I'm not publishing anything, I believe in true originality when it comes to my creations. Also, it's a bit cliche, to be honest. I want something cooler, so think about it for me, because *apparently*, I'm not good at naming individuals," Kronos said with a half-playful look of accusation at Timothy and Sir Thomas.

"*Correct*" Sir Thomas replied with a laugh. "I love you, but you're naming skills are rather horrible. I don't even have to give an example, because they're all horrible. The only ones that are acceptable are the ones you've nicknamed yourself, which seems to be on purpose. It's as if you saved the good names for yourself so that you would appear better than everyone, even in name. Never mind that, however, as I'm interested in this Atomic Knight Project. It wouldn't happen to be related to that suit of armor you painted white, would it?"

"Correct, old man. You're observant as ever. The armor was nothing special, and the armor I painted white was just me messing around with some aesthetic design. The real project was focused on the sword and shield. It was a sword that would slice through anything on an atomic level, using the current I created. It's the D.O.O.M. Shooter but as a sword, which is a bit cliche, but you won't be calling it cliche when it slices through all of your vital organs. Then, there was the shield, which applied the current in reverse so that all of the atoms in its structure were drawn closer together and bonded extremely tightly."

Timothy smiled wide, his eyes shaking with excitement even more than his body was. "Nooooo waaaaay! That's actually so cool! An indestructible shield that's compacted atomically? I've heard of similar designs, but that's so unique and useful."

"Correct and incorrect. While it's certainly useful, the shield isn't indestructible, unfortunately. It's probably stronger than almost anything else in the world, but I haven't done enough experimenting with it yet. While I could theoretically compact atoms with any material, the effects are a bit different with different types of materials, and I want to use whatever will create the strongest shield, as one would expect. I have theoretically run through every variable and material, but I haven't tested it out in person yet. A lot of the strongest materials in the world are thin and flexible, which is useful, but they're not the kinds of properties that I'm looking for with this shield."

"Since the sword and the shield are exact opposites in the ways that they manipulate atoms, would a collision between the two objects cause an atomic reaction? Not a nuclear explosion or anything, but what would be the result? The force generated between the two currents trying to pull each other apart could have catastrophic consequences," Timothy assumed.

"As great as your intellect is, Timothy, I'm afraid that you wouldn't be able to grasp the science behind such a collision and the resulting reactions. I have no intention of insulting you, and it is merely the truth of it all. Such theoretical science is far more complicated than one might think."

"No offense taken," Timothy said with a dismissive wave of his hand. "I don't have Wall of the Egomaniac as my passive magical ability, but I'm not sensitive to stuff like that either. I'm sure the science is really complicated, but no one ever said that anything theoretical would be easy. Also, I don't believe in magic or fairies, just to make that clear. Hot mermaids are certainly a dream, though. Anyway, is that lab coat you made special?"

"Correct, although it's nothing compared to the new one I made."

"Right. I assume it's in the car?"

"Incorrect, as the new one isn't-" Kronos stopped himself. He was accidentally going to say that the new lab coat was not for him, but then Sir Thomas would have been more than just suspicious. He would have inquired who it was for, and that would have revealed secrets that Kronos could not afford to have anyone know. Aware that Sir Thomas was already suspicious since he had stopped short, Kronos pretended to cough and clear his throat. "Excuse me. Morning phlegm, I suppose. Anyway, as I was saying, it isn't with me. I left it home because I want to use this old one while I have it, and the new one is a prototype that requires more testing, as it will be far better than the one I already have. The new one can wait for my grand debut as the new world leader."

"World leader, huh? It makes sense to have the smartest person to ever exist in charge, but make sure you're not too cocky and prideful while leading us all," Timothy said with a laugh. "The reason I called you here is actually that I wanted to show you some of the things I've made, along with what you've made. Follow me," he commanded as he passed through a semi-hidden door in the one wall and entered into a small room. "Of course, they'll probably seem lame compared to the stuff you've made, but I love them all. I'm still a hero without them, but they help a lot."

Sir Thomas and Kronos entered behind Timothy, noticing the small room was bare, and it only contained a few items. To their left, there was a sizeable high-tech bike, which was extremely unique, and Kronos recognized it as the one he had designed. To their right, there was a pair of rollerblades. In the back was a single glass display class, and Timothy gently pulled a weapon out of it, holding it out across his two hands for the men to admire.

"Well, I'm gobsmacked, Mr. Godwin! What is that?" Sir Thomas asked in shock as he studied the weapon.

Timothy laughed. "Well, you didn't think I fought people with just my fists and nothing else, did you? Of course, I don't really have a need for this, but I like it, and it goes along with my costume and theme pretty well. I told you earlier that you'd like it! This baby was hand-crafted by me, and it can definitely punish criminals."

Kronos smirked, and an evil look surfaced in his eye for a second before crawling back into his skull. "I like the way you think, Timothy! Now, that is a true weapon, and I'd very much enjoy seeing it in action one day. It's nothing like the D.O.O.M. Shooter in terms of power, but it's certainly just as unique. I've never even thought of a weapon like this, and I suppose atomic manipulation could always be applied to it."

"Right! I call it the Whip-Watch. It's based on chain knives and other weapons from some video games I played during my childhood. Hopefully, you both know what those are."

Sir Thomas stared at the weapon with a mixture of curiosity and distaste. It was a long and sturdy golden chain. At the one end was a small sphere that served as a handle grip so that the weapon would not slip through the user's hands. At the other end of the chain was a hand-sized stopwatch. It was also golden, with a skull engraved onto the back of it. It actually functioned and displayed the time using Roman numerals. It had spikes sticking out of the sides and at the ends, all facing up.

"See those spikes? Those are actually retractable, so I can use this as a normal pocket watch when I'm out in public. Well, one with a really long chain that is. Oh, and the clock is like twice the size of regular pocket watches. No one even uses those anymore since they're outdated, so who would know?" Timothy laughed, but Sir Thomas, a gentleman who still used a pocket watch just to maintain his status and appearance, was offended. "That way, I'm never without a weapon, and it also keeps track of time in case all phones ever go out or something. If you want to take a quick look at the digital blueprint I made, it's on the wall right there," Timothy said as he pointed to a paper taped to the wall above the glass case that the Whip-Watch had been displayed in.

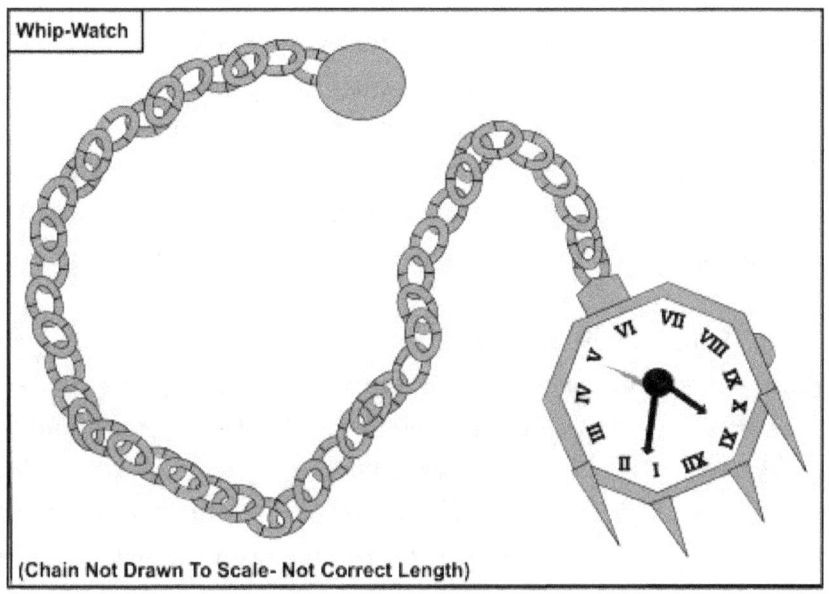

Sir Thomas kept a sharp eye on Timothy. He still did not entirely trust him, especially now that they were alone with him in the room while he was armed and dangerous. "Do tell me, Mr. Godwin, what about your green lightning trail?" Sir Thomas asked. "We heard about it on the news and then saw it in person yesterday. It's very eye-appealing and certainly remarkable. How do you generate that?"

"Right. Good question! I won't go into the actual science, but I generate the trails using a particle suit attachment. Here, it's right over there." Timothy turned around and gestured to the back corner of the room where there was a mannequin displaying a strange metal-framed piece of equipment on it. The suit-piece consisted of a connectable strap that wrapped around the torso. On each of the four corners of the back, a small thin metal arm stretched out of it with a hook at the end. "These hooks attach onto my outfit and then this here," Timothy pointed to a small barnacle-like structure on the hook facing outwards from the back of the wearer, "shoots out a stream of green particles. It gives the appearance of speed and makes me look *way* cooler. They're totally safe for the environment, so don't worry about that, and breathing them in won't harm you either. My steampunk goggles also have a small streamer on each side. The particles are self-forming or self-replacing to give you an idea of how I constantly generate them. Too much science to explain right now." He handed Sir Thomas a laminated paper. "Here's the latest blueprint if you want to see it. Not the best, as I made it on the computer, but it's a basic concept. I'm more like the guy who just builds it without drawing it first if that makes sense. It's just the way my brain works."

Sir Thomas studied the blueprint carefully. *This blueprint is awful and confusing, but I understand it. A neat accessory, although it is unnecessary. It makes the speedster concept more believable, but it draws too much attention. It's part of the reason why Timothy is so noticeable. Otherwise, he could save people undetected. Then again, he wants the spotlight and to be a hero.* Sir Thomas looked at the blueprint again before handing it to Kronos.

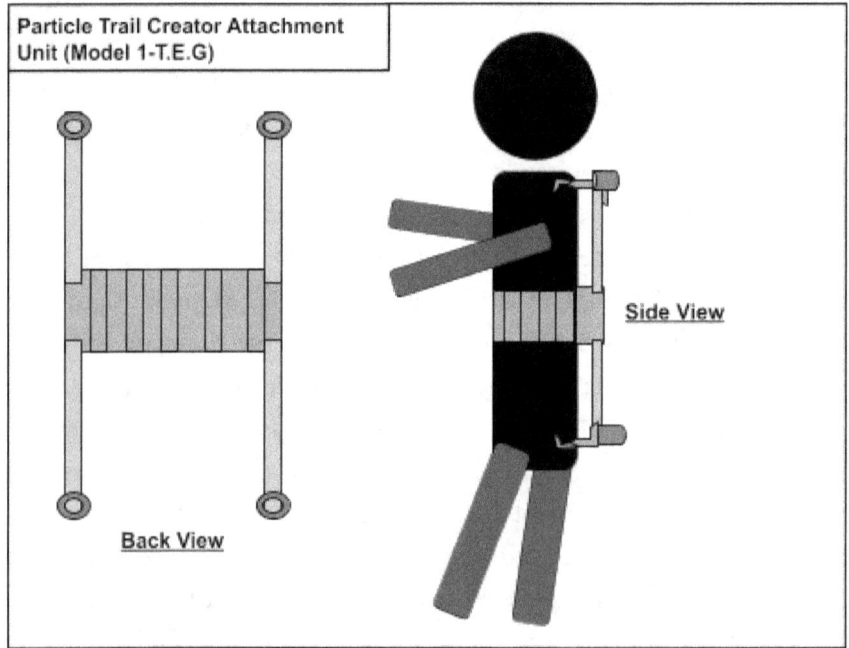

Kronos studied the blueprint quickly before handing it back to Timothy. "You weren't lying about this blueprint, but there's no need to be ashamed. Some people require drafts, sketches, and outlines in order to create, but some do not. It's just the way it is. I'm the same way with my blueprints, or at least the ones I show to others. If it's not for anyone else, why complicate it? After all, I already know how it works. I see that my bike and rollerblades are here as well. How fast can you go on them?"

Timothy laughed. "Well, I'm glad you asked. Those are risky because the speed is almost uncontrollable. Even with a faster mind and improved reflexes, going *that* fast is dangerous. I can go up to 185 miles per hour when I'm wearing the rollerblades you made, and they work perfectly. If I need to go fast, I usually use those over the bike if it's not a far distance or flat area, as I have better control with them than on the bike. On the bike, however, I can go basically double my running speed, so I've calculated a speed of 280 miles per hour for just a guestimate. I can probably go slightly faster, but that's my max speed, and I'm getting slower the older I get, and I'm aging each time I use my powers."

Licking his lips, Kronos smiled greedily with mischief in every tooth. "Such speed is undeniably on a whole other level compared to everyone else. Given the dangers, I understand why you do not use these means of transportation often, but that is still absolutely impressive. Of course, it's also thanks to my genius since I made the rollerblades and the bike, but I have to credit you with even thinking of combining your powers with them. Most people would just run and be satisfied, but you realized that you could apply your powers to anything that requires human energy and is durable enough to withstand your superhuman input. I respect you for that. You truly are one of us, and if we make it through this all, I would be more than glad to have you work with us at R.O.M.A.B.A. Industries."

"Sounds great, Kronos! Let's get going then. I just have to finish packing and then we're good to go. Are we taking your car?"

"I'm afraid not, even though it does stand at the pinnacle of all vehicles. We're leaving it here, and I ask that you trust my plan. We'll be taking you're Jeep Grand Cherokee, despite its age. I actually went to the store and bought a few parts. After tweaking everything early this morning, your car should run better than ever. Now, let's not waste any more time. Thomas, I'm off to fetch some gear from my car. Say goodbye to Laura and then meet me on the front porch, and Timothy, you meet me there once you're done packing."

As the three men drove off, they waved goodbye to Laura, who stood teary-eyed on the front porch of the house, the baby in her arms. Even the young infant Spencer seemed to be crying, although his face was dry, despite the sad expression across it. He looked after them, almost seeming to wonder if they would ever come back. His young and feeble mind had no answer, however, and so his tiny lungs just began to wail as their car drove off into the unknown, his future in their hands.

"It'll take about one day at minimum to get there," Sir Thomas stated as he pulled onto the highway. "That's if we drive through the night as well, which we will. Brace yourselves, as this will probably be the longest car ride any of us have been on, and it'll feel much longer than that besides."

"I could definitely get us there in half that amount of time if you wanted," Kronos grumbled from the passenger seat.

"And get us all into a bloody accident," Sir Thomas stated. "You're driving skills are certainly remarkable. You'd be an ace in the world of car racing, but you're also dangerous. We can't afford to arrive there in less than one piece if we hope to succeed. That, and I value my life and health. I'll let you drive when the roads are open or empty, as I certainly can't stand driving for so many hours straight. Speaking of our destination, why are we heading to Homestead, Florida, Mr. Godwin?"

"That's where I last saw them," Timothy answered from the middle seat behind them. "That's the latest clue we have to go off of, so we might as well follow it. I had been visiting my mother since she has a house there, and that's when I encountered them just as I told you last night."

"I understand that, but you believe that The Dark Depressor and this kidnapper are *still* there and haven't moved on to a different location? It's been some time since that incident, hasn't it?"

"Right, but I don't think they're a traveling villain, and they have no reason to leave since no one can challenge them. Besides, Florida is a gold mine for kidnapping. Sure, there are college kids down there, but it's also full of old people who have money and spend their time relaxing. They're the best to capture and rob." Kronos laughed at Sir Thomas, who turned around and stared at Timothy with a look of disbelief. "No offense. I mean, I don't know *exactly* why they're there. It probably has *nothing* to do with old people! I love the elderly!"

Sir Thomas chuckled. "Hmm. Don't make yourself sound too believable, Mr. Godwin. I certainly don't love the elderly, and I'm almost one of them. Regardless of why they are there, we're assuming that they're still in Florida."

"Right, but their actual base of operations isn't there, though. At least I don't think so. That's not how villains work in the comics. Using an old pair of rollerblades that my mom had, I scouted the closest local towns and found nothing suspicious or that could help us pinpoint a location. I completely destroyed them and hurt my feet, but I healed up fast. Anyway, I believe that they're stationed on a private island off the coast of Florida, because that's the only possibility that makes sense. That brings up the questions of why no one knows about this island or why they haven't been caught yet, and those leave the answers that it's either off the grid, an artificial island, or the government is actually behind all of this."

Kronos stroked his chin as he stared out at the other vehicles on the highway, judging each one of them. "That last option is highly possible. I'm sure that the government could be behind all of this, but it wouldn't make sense to kill your own people in such small numbers. As far as we know, there seems to be no pattern among the victims or the attacks either. Unless The Dark Depressor is a rogue experiment gone wrong. That certainly makes everything more intriguing."

"A classic plot twist that wouldn't shock me at all, and I don't doubt that it's likely the case, but I actually have a feeling that the government isn't involved in this. If anything, it'd be a branch that got cut off from the government or an organization that they tried to shut down." Timothy thought for a moment. "Of course, there's also the possibility that their base is underwater and hidden from us land-folk. I can swim super fast, but I don't have a special lung capacity or anything, nor do I own a submarine. Scouting underwater isn't my specialty."

"I have to say, that's definitely the first time I've ever been called a land-dweller," Sir Thomas commented with a chuckle. "An underwater base, you say? Given recent events, I can understand why such an idea may seem feasible, but that's overstepping the boundaries of reality. Just a little bit. I'm sure that one day there'll be an underwater city, but not quite yet. Kronos has actually spent years planning to build one, but it's never going to happen."

"Don't forget about Drunk Diver, Thomas," Kronos said, disregarding Timothy. "If they privately contracted him, he may have built something for them. Of course, that's if he's managed to get any of his inventions or ideas to work."

"I highly doubt that, Kronos," Sir Thomas replied.

"It honestly doesn't matter where they're hiding because we're three of the smartest people in the world, and I'm actually the smartest in the world, so we'll find them either way," Kronos stated. "Don't worry about it so much, Timothy. I understand how important this is to you, and I trust you more than anyone to know where a villain might be, given the fact that you've spent your entire life studying this kind of stuff and have brought the world of comics into reality. The D.O.O.M. Shooter should be an easy match for The Dark Depressor, and we'll-"

"Let me make this clear," Timothy said, his tone warning and stronger than his usual goofy and fast-talking self. "We are *not*, and I will not say it again, killing The Dark Depressor."

"I beg your pardon, Mr. Godwin?"

"My curiosity is the same as Thomas' is," Kronos stated as he turned around and looked at Timothy.

"*Look*, I don't know where your morals stand, but I've spent my whole life trying to be pure-hearted and good. Otherwise, I wouldn't be the kind of hero that I aspire to be. I mean, I'm all for killing the bad guy, but this person could just be a tool for the actual kidnapper! We don't actually know what's going on, and to take people down based on assumptions would go against everything I stand for. For all we know, this villain is being forced to do their heinous deeds. There could be mind control or hypnosis involved. We *don't* know everything, and so I don't think we should be hasty in our actions. I say it's best that we just follow them back to their base of operations and find out more before we make a decision. Whether you agree or not, that's our course of action. I appreciate your help, but if you guys can't agree, then I'm going solo."

Kronos said nothing.

Sir Thomas heard the warning words of Laura in his head. "I actually agree with Mr. Godwin. I've tried my best to be a gentleman as well, and I wouldn't be one if I killed The Dark Depressor without solid evidence of their crimes. For all we know, this kidnapper might have several henchmen with the same equipment and costume."

"Thank you, Sir Thomas. That's exactly what I'm saying," Timothy stated. "Our best bet is to follow them after they appear. If they are just a henchman, well, people are expendable, and another person will just replace the one we kill. We'll have to shut down the whole operation if we really want to stop this."

"You're awfully quiet, Kronos," Sir Thomas said as he glanced over at Kronos, who was staring through the window still. "What are you thinking?"

"Nothing extraordinary," Kronos replied. "Well, everything I think is automatically grand, but I'm not thinking too hard or really focusing on the current conversation. I may be in charge and the leader of this team, but it's a group mission. If you two believe we require more evidence of their crimes, then we'll have to follow them. That said, I will not hesitate to defend myself or any of us, and if push comes to shove, I will kill without mercy. I admire your spirit and heart, Timothy, but don't be too forgiving or optimistic. You can never forget that villains are human too, and they will do everything they can to survive. Never let your guard down, even with allies too. That's all I have to say regarding the matter. Either way, the mission stays the same. The Dark Depressor may seem like a regular person compared to some of the individuals on the list of scientific rivals, but he's just as powerful if not more dangerous than the others."

Timothy nodded his head, his tone still cold and serious. "Right. I'm well aware of that, Kronos, and making hard choices is part of being a hero. Probably one of the most important parts, actually. I understand the situation we're in, but without knowing the motivation, I can't deem them a villain, because, honestly, we're all heroes and villains. How people look at us and what they deem us certainly influences which of the two most people think we are, but it's our motivations and justifications that truly determine where on the spectrum of good and bad we end up. Just because we haven't figured out a pattern, that doesn't mean that the victims are being chosen at random. The victims might actually be the criminals here, but I don't know that. So, I'm sorry, Kronos, but I can't bring myself to hate The Dark Depressor or villainize them just yet. Rest assured, however, that I won't let such hope or optimism hurt either you or Sir Thomas."

"Correct, because such foolishness would be unforgivable. Since we're on the topic, it looks like you have something to say, Thomas. I can tell by the look on your face that something is bothering you. Given how fast you're driving and the relatively light traffic, I assume it has to do with our mission."

"It's my fault," Timothy said apologetically. He lightened his tone and slowly returned to his fast-talking, goofy self. "I kind of made everything all serious and depressing. Sorry about that. I just wanted to set a few rules and principles before we set out on this mission, just to ensure that everything goes smoothly and there aren't as many problems. Besides, I want everyone's opinion, and I hope to better understand all of our personalities. Well, your personalities, since I already know myself. It's important for a hero to know himself. Anyway, we're in this together, and it's only going to get more and more complicated. At least that's what I think. So, if something is bothering you, Sir Thomas, you can let us know. We're a team, and like my one ex-girlfriend told me, communication is very important. Just wish I hadn't found that out the hard way."

"Very well, then, Mr. Godwin. I apologize ahead of time, but I don't consider you a hero, and that's because everyone has their own idea of what a hero is and what makes a person a hero."

"Wow," Timothy said in shock and a bit of emotional pain. "I wasn't expecting that at all. Still, I think I understand what you mean, and I suppose heroism is subjective, so go on."

"To me, *personally*, you're just a vigilante until you have positive publicity. I'm not discrediting your actions or beliefs, and I admire them, but the truth is that you are not on good terms with the government or even social media. Once you are known and liked, you're a hero in my eyes. Vigilante is a term that some find offensive, like that one man you fought. Some people believe they are reckless or breaking the law. As for where I stand on such behavior, I'll stay neutral. I won't judge your actions, as the justification of your actions and the implementation of your beliefs through those actions can be argued from both sides of right and wrong. Measuring the exact balance of right and wrong regarding you is not my place. That said, I'm curious to know not only what motivates your questionable actions, but also what you hope to achieve through what you've done. Why has your whole life been leading up to becoming a hero? What is your end goal?"

Timothy smiled and laughed softly. "Right. I guess I never explained that part, and now I understand what you were trying to get at. Well, it's rather simple, really." He let out a warm breath of awe as he pictured the future he hoped to create. "It's too late for me, Sir Thomas. I wanted to be a hero growing up, and I still do, but that's not realistic. We don't live in a superhuman society or a world where the government works with vigilantes instead of the police. Still, my father and I believed that reality and society could be changed, and that they have already been changed throughout time. Whether it be someone else who was inspired by my actions or my own words and fame, I hope to bring about a hero-society for everyone else. Sure, I won't be able to enjoy it like I want to, but everyone else who is like me will be able to, and that's the ultimate sacrifice and choice that I've made as a hero."

Kronos smirked with a hint of admiration and pride. He quickly wiped a tear away from his right eye before anyone could notice. "It seems like more and more individuals are willing to sacrifice and devote their lives to creating a future for others that they wished they had. It's quite inspiring."

"I beg your pardon, Mr. Godwin, but did you say a hero-society? I think I get a general idea, but what exactly do you mean by that?"

"I suppose that everyone has their own ideal version of society," Timothy replied. "In fact, I think everyone does because... no one will ever be truly content with society until a utopia is made, and that's a difficult society to make and probably impossible. The very thing that makes this world and humans so great is ironically also the very same thing that prevents it from being perfect: we're all unique individuals. Yet... we don't... we don't need a utopia for the majority of us or everyone to be mostly happy," Timothy explained as he put his scattered thoughts together. "What would make *me* happiest? What do *I* believe would benefit everyone else besides myself? I can answer that, but I can't say what everyone else wants. In *my* opinion, a hero-society would be best not just for me but for everyone else as well, as fictional as that seems. Yet, *we* are living proof that fiction is possible. Fiction is not fantasy. See, fantasy can never happen, but fiction is just yet to be made real."

"Correct and correct," Kronos remarked as he rested with his eyes closed. "What you said is in exact alignment with my beliefs, Timothy. Not regarding the idea of a utopia or a hero-society, but the last few ideas. Fiction *is* possible and believing that is exactly what separates the successful from those who fail. Some people call it hope or optimism, but the reality of it is that it's actually just an understanding of achievement and the fact that impossibilities and boundaries are mental chains placed on us by society and ourselves, easily severed through the tools of determination."

Sir Thomas was shocked, and his jaw almost fell open. "By the grace of God, I've never heard you so confident and composed, Kronos, and you're a bloody egocentric-maniac. This isn't just rubbish that you're spitting out, but this is brilliant wisdom that you truly believe."

"It's because he's enlightened, just as I am," Timothy stated. "He doesn't believe it *because* he's already achieved the impossible and created the fictional. He was *able* to do those things because he already knew those ideas were the undeniable truths of this world."

"That's also correct," Kronos stated as he slid his high-tech sunglass onto his face before going back to resting. "You're a hero for a reason, Timothy, and I hope others will be able to understand that."

"Right. Thanks, man. Anyway, back to my ideal future. Of course, we all have different definitions and ideas of what a hero-society is, so allow me to explain my version, which is probably similar to most people's imagination. The truth is that vigilantes don't do enough to be recognized. Especially since the authorities are always trying to stop them. So, what we really need is a politician who will take the bold stance of trying to create a hero-society. People would be reluctant to understand or join his campaign at first, but it would quickly catch on. There are already a ton of people who would support that idea, or at least in the younger generations. **Vigilantes save lives, but politicians change laws**," Timothy stated with emphasis as he moved his hands in front of him as if he had just created a title for a newspaper. "They have influence over people, and they have money. We need that to help establish the base of the hero-society. After that, rules, laws, and processes would need to be made. For-"

"Pardon my interruption, Mr. Godwin. I don't think you're spouting rubbish, and it sounds reasonable so far, but I *am* concerned about a major detail regarding this society. What about the existing law-enforcing agencies on all levels? Would you abolish those?"

"That would ultimately be up to the people," Timothy replied. "I mean, almost everything will be left up to the people because that's the idea behind America. It's not as vibrant or as powerful as it once was, but that idea is still there. The roles would have to be established. For example, people might want the police to continue to deal with small matters, medical emergencies, and domestic disputes, while heroes dealt with bigger criminals and cases. Or, people might say that they want no cops and heroes would do everything, but the F.B.I. would still exist for more special cases. It's really all a matter of political discussion. *Everything* is a matter of political discussion."

"Correct, but the problem is that the politicians wouldn't agree, and they would drag out the matter for years," Kronos pointed out contemptuously. "They would use it for selfish political gain, never actually delivering the changes they promised. Of course, existing heroes, such as yourself, would be a big influence and help regarding the discussions."

Timothy nodded his head. "Unfortunately, that truth is one of my greatest fears, but it's quite possible that the new political ideas could also help change the political environment, especially if the politicians are backed by vigilantes and celebrities. Don't even get me started on celebrities and vigilantes competing for popularity or how the entertainment world would change, because that's a side tangent that could probably fill a whole chapter if I decided to write a book on hero-society and our world."

"Actually, I agree with that," Sir Thomas said. "Movie stars and singers would suddenly be competing with heroes for fame and popularity. Morning and night shows would be interviewing heroes instead of them, for one example. It would cause a lot of jealousy to stir about. Plus, heroes would start using their fame to create their own workout series and such, which would hurt the current stars of fitness. Of course, I hope that everyone could all get along, and heroes shouldn't care about fame, but it would undoubtedly cause a surge of conflicts in the world of celebrities."

"Right. That's on the less important spectrum of everything, though. There's a lot to creating this hero-society, but celebrities arguing isn't that serious, as of now. There *is* a major part to creating this hero-society that is crucial to whether or not heroes would be allowed. Are the heroes being trained in an academy, or are they lone vigilantes? If they are lone vigilantes applying for a hero license or an official position, how do we know that they are qualified to wield a firearm or are morally and mentally stable? That's what you're thinking, right?"

"I've actually thought over every possible situation and variable already, if that answers your question," Kronos stated.

"Well, I'm not ashamed to admit that the thought hadn't crossed my mind, though I suppose that *is* important," Sir Thomas said as he switched lanes and sped up. "I assume that they'll have to pass intense tests and psychological evaluations. The mental tests will have to be very thorough, however, due to the amount of responsibility and potential danger the future hero has. Mental tests aren't possible, however, because people can easily lie on those. Either way, it's a lot of muck the politicians will be treading through. Having a standard for the physical tests could anger a lot of people. They want to believe that any bloke can be a hero, and I don't blame them for that. Either way, there should be a test, in my opinion. You can't just have a bunch of people lollygagging on the job or jumping around without being able to actually help."

"Right, and most people would agree with that," Timothy replied. "So, I feel like there shouldn't be any set standard when it comes to who can be a hero, but I understand that having anyone be a hero does pose a security threat to a lot of people. Really, I, personally, like the idea of lone heroes doing their own thing, but being trained at an official hero academy wouldn't be so bad either. Again, it'd be up to-"

"Hmph," Kronos sounded as he scratched the back of his neck.

"What is it, Kronos?" Timothy asked.

"I disagree with the idea of having a hero academy, and I greatly dislike it," Kronos stated. "I've never been one for group organizations like that, being a man of individuality who stands above everyone else. Sure, I understand why society would be for the idea, but I feel like it ruins the idea of a hero."

Sir Thomas was as puzzled as Timothy was by the reply. "Kronos, what in bloody Hell are you talking about?"

"You know that I'm a *firm* believer in individuality, Thomas. It's the point of existence. Uniqueness is the key to furthering progression, and that's only one factor of success, but it's a vital one nonetheless. A hero trains on his own. He endures hardships and trains on his own. They might have friends or family that are rooting for them, but they don't train in a class full of heroes. They are made through the trials they endure alone because that is when a person is truly tested, both physically and mentally. That's how it works, and there's a reason for that. I'm usually a man of logic and facts, but that's my personal opinion. Although, you could have every person in the world argue against it and I would still prove that my opinion is actually a fact. I understand that many would be for a hero academy, but lone heroes are far superior, and they always will be."

Timothy slowly nodded his head as he thought over what Kronos said, tapping his foot up and down as he sat hunched over, his elbows on his knees. "Those are some bold statements, and they're some of the most interesting ones I've heard. Do you believe that people are weakest when they are alone?"

"The answer is a paradox, Timothy, and we all know that," Kronos stated.

"Right. I think I understand what you're saying, and it's definitely true. People are at their strongest *and* their weakest when they're alone. I agree with that. You've got it all wrong, though, Kronos. The hero academy wouldn't train a bunch of people the same way and make them all heroes. That's one option, but I think more people would vote for lone vigilantes joining the academy and training in their own way while making sure that they meet the basic standards if that makes sense. We wouldn't create an army of repeats and copies, but we would allow uniqueness and diversity amongst the heroes and what they do and how they act. You get what I'm saying? It's all daydreaming and planning for the conflicts that will come, so it's not perfect, but we, as a country and as a people, *could* make this work."

"I admire your hope, Mr. Godwin. Your ideal society is indeed one that would seem like tosh to most, but you're certainly an ace in the world of planning and have thought about this for a long time. I don't think it'll happen, or rather I hope it doesn't happen, but your dream has my utmost respect. I can see how much it means to you. Since you've thought about it so much, there's no doubt you'll be able to answer some more of my questions. After all, I'm intrigued by how much thought you've put into it all, and I'm curious about how the world would change if such a society existed."

"Fire away," Timothy said with a smirk, gladly accepting the challenge that Sir Thomas was implying. "I'm prepared for anything you throw at me because that's who heroes are. Even villains too, if not more so."

"Well, here's a prime example: why would politicians want to create this hero-society? Sure, they're supposed to represent the people, but there are a lot of selfish politicians out there. Wankers for sure, but they're corrupted by power, bribes, and threats, so I don't blame them all. How would it benefit them, though? Besides publicity and money, that is. What would make them support such a radical concept that might ruin their entire career?"

"A fair question, but, really, money and publicity are the main things a politician wants, or any selfish person, for the most part. Although, some politicians actually want publicity and money to help make changes. However, I understand your point, Sir Thomas, and I've thought about it a lot. Think about it economically."

"Economically?"

Kronos smirked, his eyes closed as he relaxed.

"There are plenty of shows and lores where wars have turned out to be an arranged battle for economic reasons. I say that so you'll understand just how far people are willing to go to sustain a prosperous economy. A hero-society would have major economic impacts. You'll need people to produce clothing, for one thing, and the costumes aren't simple, either. They consist of multiple parts, most of the time. Then, there are weapons. Someone has to make the weapons. If there's a hero academy, there will be a need for trainers, cooks, cleaning people, engineers and construction workers, and people to handle the paperwork. I could go on and on, but the point is that it would create more job opportunities, which is always important. Then, there's the *whole* field of marketing and deals, including hero-backed sponsorships and endorsements, along with limited-edition beverages or toys at businesses. How about merchandise? There's a whole industry for that. Biographies, movies, shows, and interviews! These new businesses and industries might open up to stocks. The list goes on and on! We're not just adding celebrities who save lives to the world. We are adding an entirely new system to our society, and I can't stress that enough! We'd almost be adding a new culture, in fact. I could rant about the economic impacts alone for the rest of the ride, honestly."

"Interesting. I agree with you, Timothy. Not entirely, but I enjoy theorizing about it all and imagining such a world. Now, pretend that I'm a person who is physically fit as well as mentally stable, and I'm interested in trying to become a hero. What are my options?"

"Well, Kronos, you have many options available to you, because my goal as the leader of the hero society is to make everything convenient for you and the people who need us. You can be a hero either full-time or part-time. There is the option to become a military hero and go overseas, or you can have your choice of state and town size. If you just want to do midnight patrols, then I would recommend a small town. In fact, you can choose whether or not you want to work at night or during the day. I suggest choosing what best suits both you mentally, as well as your hero identity and abilities. That also goes for what kind of hero you would like to be. The options range from fire control to intelligence, just like how the military has all kinds of jobs. There are also two main options when it comes to being a hero. You can get certified and just sit around home, only going out when you hear an alarm or police scanner in your local town. That's more of the celebrity-hero lifestyle, but it's still just as dangerous and important. The other option is for you to work for an organization, the government, or a hero's union. Full details are available to anyone trying to become a hero, and what I've listed are just the main basics. As you can see, everything is essentially customizable so that both you and society benefit the most."

"Correct. That was almost as good as the microwave situations I made up on the spot," Kronos complimented.

"I told you that I'm ready to justify my future society! I've been dreaming of it since I was a kid. I've been training to be a hero since I was a kid. I've been mentally preparing myself since I was a kid. I'm not saying that the age you start at matters because it's almost never too late in life to start something, but I want you to understand how much time I've put into this. It's awesome! Even though Sir Thomas is being a critic, it's still nice to have people to talk to about it. It's not something that gets brought up in regular conversation, and most people would look at you funny if you did bring it up. With you guys, I can talk about it all I want! Trust me, there's more and more to it!"

"Such energetic enthusiasm intrigues me," Kronos commented without emotion. "We are both passionate men, but I'm afraid that I am a relatively quiet man who does not get excited or loud. Occasionally, I get caught up in my ideas and rant to myself, but not like this. You're on a whole other level of passion, and it's quite astounding. You *really* want this society to happen, don't you?"

"More than anything. Not just for me, though. I know that sounds false, and I probably seem really selfish, but I truly believe that the hero-society I hope to create will benefit everyone. I won't deny that it'll be a lot of work creating it. Setting new laws and rules alone will take forever, and it might even cause an increase in protests or criminal activity, but anything political does. Every new idea starts out rough like a boulder, but the water of progress will eventually smooth it out into something worth collecting."

"A poor analogy, Timothy, but I agree with you. We do have hours upon hours to waste, so tell us all about this hero-society. If you manage to completely win me over with your ideas, I'll help you create this society once we finish our missions."

"Have you gone bloody mad, Kronos?" Sir Thomas almost lost control of the wheel in his shock. "Now you're just being a wanker, making false promises like that! Not only would you never do something like that, but we couldn't do it if we actually wanted to. Don't you dare fill this boy's head with any more rubbish! Apologize for getting his hopes up."

Kronos sat up straight in his chair and looked over in annoyance at Sir Thomas. "I only lie when it is to protect others or prevent the enemy from understanding my plans, or at least attempting to understand such complicated ideas. I mean what I said. R.O.M.A.B.A. Industries is the most influential and powerful company in the world. We're an unstoppable empire, and we could easily get politicians on our side. The news is currently interested in the Minnesota Speedster and what his goal is. If we support and vouch for Timothy, everyone will listen to what he has to say. He'll be both a politician and a hero, creating the hero-society he has dreamt of for everyone to enjoy. The best part is, we'd get credit and even more fame," Kronos said as he went back to resting. "Now, go on with what you were saying, Timothy. Tell me everything about this society, as I have important theories to think about. Your society might help me prevent the world from doom."

It had been about 9:30 a.m. when the three men left for Florida. After listening to Timothy describe every detail of his hero-society for the next hour and a half, the men finally stopped for their first break. They enjoyed a few snacks that Laura had packed, and then Sir Thomas and Kronos switched seats, Timothy choosing to stay where he was. They drove off at double the speed that Sir Thomas had been driving at, Kronos weaving in and out of lanes as if he were a runner in a desperate sprint in the deciding-seconds of the race. The conversation had died out after their break, and they drove speedily and in silence for the next two hours. It was a little past 1:00 p.m. when Sir Thomas grew restless, his patience declining with each minute, his mind no longer forced to focus on the road.

Kronos glanced over at Sir Thomas, noticing that he was moving more and more in his seat. "Everything alright there, old man? You're starting to annoy me a bit. We've been driving for quite a while, so my blood sugar is low, and that means I'm even more irritable than usual, which is already a lot, so I suggest you stop."

"*Are we there yet?*" Sir Thomas asked jokingly as he imitated a young child crying out. "I'm a man of patience, but my bladder is not, and that's not even the problem! I don't have to use the men's room. The silence isn't all that bad, but the lack of movement is causing half of my body to be numb, and my joints don't like it either. Luckily, I don't have arthritis. If only I had packed a great novel with me to read, and one of great length written by a brilliant teenager. I find those ones to be the best, believe it or not! Anything to distract my mind, actually. This car ride seems to be taking forever. They say that time goes by faster as you get older, but this day is really dragging by, and I'll admit that I'm no spring chicken."

"Ah, a good ol' illusion of time," Timothy said philosophically from the back, where he was dangerously sprawled out across the three seats. "It's more like your mind is the thing that's dragging."

"I beg your pardon, Mr. Godwin, who is resting comfortably in the back? I hope that wasn't a joke about my age. I have a sharp mind for an old guy, with an even sharper left hook for disrespectful punks. You'll find that the slums of London were not nice to a young gentleman such as myself back in the day."

Timothy laughed at the retort, Kronos finding it funnier than anyone. "My apologies, Sir Thomas. I'm sure your mind is sharp, and I meant no joke at your age. I honestly meant that remark to all people, and even animals, I guess. You see, I have a very unique belief regarding the whole concept of time and space. Well, at least I think it's unique. I won't bore you with it, though."

"Quite honestly, theories regarding time and space are a bit of hogwash and rubbish mixed together with some theoretical science, but I'm interested in hearing your view, Mr. Godwin. I'm honestly still trying to recover from the amount of hero-society information you dumped on us, but I'm afraid we don't have anything else to do right now, so tell us all about it. I'm at your mercy."

"Right. Well, the way I see it is that there are two forces in the world. Then there are the minds of living beings. This is going to be hard to describe, honestly, but I'll try my best. It's interesting and easy enough to understand once all of the pieces are put together."

"Hard to describe? Now that's intriguing. You've got my attention as well, Timothy," Kronos stated as he changed lanes three times within a few seconds.

"That's good to know. Now, start by picturing a black void and nothing but that complete darkness. There's a green cylinder flowing through it in the middle, a pink one above it, and a yellow one below the green one. Put some darkness between them so that they're not touching. Everyone with me so far?"

"Correct. Of course, I am."

"Roger that, Mr. Godwin."

"The green one is time. The pink one is space and life, which is nothing more than the movement of atoms. The yellow one is the human mind. They all move at different speeds. Time is merely there to help the yellow mind understand how the pink life is moving. Now connect the pink and yellow one so that the green one seems to pull the pink along with the yellow one, attached to the two others at fixed points. The pink one never changes speed. The green one moves at whatever speed the yellow one is moving at, which changes speeds. When the yellow one slows down, the green one, time, seems to be moving faster than normal. It's not faster, though. The pink is pulling it so that rather than be vertical between the pink and yellow, the green is angled forward. Time is moving forward quicker in contrast to our slower-moving mind. When we concentrate our minds on a task or are having fun, the yellow cylinder is spread out, which causes a reduction in speed and power, in the sense that I'm describing it. Then time seems to move slower, as now it is being pulled back by the pink so that it is not vertical between the two others, as now the yellow is moving faster than the pink. It also happens when we are bored or whenever our mind is moving faster than the pink cylinder. This is especially noticeable after pointless standardized testing in school or when clothes shopping with your girlfriend. Time is always the same, and any change of it is merely caused by our minds moving at a different speed than it. Time is a measurement used to help describe the current location, movement, and actions of all atoms in existence, as that is what the progression of life and time is."

"Well, *bloody* Hell, Mr. Godwin. That certainly *was* a lot to take in! Even Kronos hasn't perplexed me with such philosophies, but I do understand and agree a bit. Especially with that last part about the atoms. I'm sure Kronos also loved that part. He is The Atomic Alchemist, after all," Sir Thomas said with sarcastic praise. He looked through the window at the sky, thinking about what Timothy said in an attempt to truly understand it. "I've never thought of life in that kind of way before, but it's certainly worth considering. I'm sure some would chalk it up to hogwash spoken by a drunk bloke, but what you said is quite sophisticated, and it does make sense."

"What makes sense and what is actually true are two different things, Thomas," Kronos commented. "Never confuse or mistake the two, as their difference means more than you could ever imagine. However, I do agree with you, Timothy. Somewhat, anyway. Do you believe in time travel or manipulating this force of time in any way? I would guess no."

"I would shout 'correct' like you always do, but it's not the same. My answer *would* be no because the green one doesn't actually exist. There is no physical form of time, and time having a physical form makes no sense. The green cylinder of time is just a human-made one to connect the yellow one to the pink one and kind of mimic it. The pink one is nothing more than the current state of atoms, and atoms only move forward. To time travel, a person would have to force atoms to go backward and retrace every change and movement that's ever occurred with them or to them. That's *impossible*, because atoms don't have a memory that would allow them to go backward and slowly reset everything, and they wouldn't naturally go back either. Plus, even if that were possible, a person hoping to time travel would have to reverse all atoms except their own to stay the way they are. They'll never be able to undo the changes, either. Even if they could then move all atoms forward, after immediately regretting their traveling, his atoms from the 'future' already changed the movements and direction of the 'past' atoms, so everything would be different no matter what. Also, let's not forget that, theoretically, such power would only affect Earth at maximum potential, meaning that the time of day and everything in space would stay the same, which would also drastically impact the 'past' atoms. It's completely impractical!"

"Holy crap and by the grace of God!" Sir Thomas exclaimed. "Forget being bored, because now I'm gobsmacked! I've never heard a person rant so quickly and thoroughly about time and atoms like that besides Kronos. Mr. Godwin, you are undeniably a man who is extremely passionate about everything you enjoy learning about or theorizing. You almost rival Kronos when it comes to theories and views on stuff like that. The amount of explanation and knowledge is almost enough to knock me out, but I understood every word. You're bloody brilliant! A true ace when it comes to one view on the universe. You've earned some respect."

"Well, as a man with a terrifying fear of growing up and a man who is quickly advancing in age, I've spent a lot of *time*- get it?- thinking about time and manipulating it. It's also part of being a speedster, as it's part of how I create my illusions of time, in a way. I drastically change the speed of both my mind and others to change the way the green cylinder is connected to the pink cylinder and the yellow cylinders."

Kronos sped up, going far faster than anyone would even dare on an empty road in the desert. "Congratulations, Timothy," Kronos said non-sarcastically, though he lacked enthusiasm. "Those are higher-level thoughts than most could ever create or handle, so you have my respect. I agree with most of that, believe it or not."

Timothy cocked his head. "Really? As the world's best scientist to have ever existed, I figured you believed in wormholes and space tunnels and different dimensions mixed with the physical fabrics of this universe or whatever. There are tons and tons of scientific theories regarding time and space, aren't there?"

"Correct, and I assure you that I've studied them all. At the end of the day, however, it doesn't really matter, so I don't care. Whether time is physical or not, and whether the universe loops around or is infinite, I'm still the most powerful being alive. I'm still living my life. Unless something extremely drastic happens, I couldn't care less about how time and space work. As long as they work and manipulating them is far beyond possible, why should I care? Does that make sense? I understand that it juxtaposes my vast intellect and personality, but it's actually logical."

"I actually agree, Kronos. Let's just live our lives! To be honest, I question whether outer space exists or not. We never leave Earth, and how do we know that spaceships and astronauts actually do? It could all be fake. Mars, Saturn, Jupiter... they could all be fake, and we would never know, but it doesn't affect us either way. Fossils could have been man-made creations meant to astound and trick people because other than that, we have no proof that dinosaurs were real. Whether they did exist or didn't exist doesn't matter, though. The same goes for aliens and mermaids. Unless something major happens, it doesn't make a difference. I'm still me, and life moves forward the same. Anyway, my belief in time and the three cylinders is what I believe, and my point is that it doesn't really matter. They're just my version of time and a way to understand it differently from one who manipulates it. The three cylinders are actually a concept I first created back when I was a teenager."

"Good for you," Kronos remarked earnestly. "I agree with it, for the most part. Animals have a natural clock that responds to outside stimuli from the force of life. All molecules and matter cannot be destroyed or created, only transferred or transformed. Time is just a measurement represented by numbers that are used for counting and keeping track of these particles as they change. Specifically, time is a measurement split into two categories, which are time regarding the measurement of every atomic movement ever, and time on any given day, which measures atoms for a period of twenty-four hours. To explain it simply, anything equivalent to the measure of a day or more refers to the current state of all atoms at a given moment that a person chooses. Anything less than a day, which are measurements such as seconds, minutes, and hours, refer to the current state of atoms within a specific day, and a day is twenty-four hours because that is a measurement that resets once the atoms of the Earth complete a movement that is part of a repetitive pattern."

"I think I preferred when it was silent," Sir Thomas mumbled to himself. "Not only do my legs and buttocks hurt, but now my head is pounding."

Timothy laughed. "Hang in there, Sir Thomas! You took what I said and analyzed it in an odd way, Kronos, but I understand what you were trying to say. That was really complicated, but by breaking it down into what I think you meant and applying it to my three cylinders theory, it makes sense. I'm sure it could be explained better than that, but as long as we three understand, there's no need to break it down any further. No matter how you put it, the pink cylinder consists of forward-moving atoms, so nothing can be done."

"Not necessarily true, Mr. Godwin," Sir Thomas said through a yawn. "I might as well jump in on the conversation now that we're all talking. That, and I was wondering if you've ever studied tachyons?"

"Good point, old man," Kronos stated as he changed lanes a few more times. "At this rate, we'll probably be able to hit the same speed as tachyons with my professional driving."

"You're not wrong about that, Kronos! You speed like crazy, and I've never gone this fast in any car before today. I know that Sir Thomas isn't particularly fond of your driving, but I frickin' love it! As a speedster, the feeling of intense speed is what I thrive off of, no matter how it's accomplished or how temporary it is. When I was a little kid, swing and amusement park rides were the best way to go really fast, and I loved it. Anyway, I don't believe in tachyons. I'm sure they might possibly exist, but it doesn't make sense to me. How would traveling faster than the speed of light allow anything to travel backward in time? That doesn't make *any* sense at all! Look, even if they do exist, I doubt discovering them or manipulating them will happen while I'm still alive."

"If they are found and proven to travel backward in time during our lifetimes, however, we could, theoretically, achieve time travel by using our technology at R.O.M.A.B.A. Industries," Kronos stated as he slowed the car down a bit, thinking over the properties of tachyons and atoms.

"We've seen and discussed all sorts of theoretical rubbish and some true ideas, but now I'm actually gobsmacked, beyond a shadow of a doubt" Sir Thomas said as he straightened up in his seat and looked over at Kronos. "I trust you since you're an ace in everything you do and think about, but do you really mean that Kronos? It's possible?"

"Let me first emphasize that it's all theoretical. Look, if tachyons can travel backward in time, we could use our technology to bond a tachyon to every atom in a human being, and if faster-than-light speed is still possible with the additional weight, then science theorizes that a person would, indeed, travel backward in time. However, there are a lot, and I mean a whole multitude of problems with that. Even if, and I mean *if*, tachyons do travel backward in time, where do they stop? Or rather, *when* do they stop? Why do they stop."

"Right!" Timothy sat up, scooching over to the middle seat again so he could talk more easily to the two men. "We don't know, and there's probably no way to control it. For all we know, they go on forever! You'd be stuck, traveling backward through time for all eternity, and you might still be conscious besides, which is even worse! Man, that's awful."

"Incorrect, Timothy. Think about the laws of science. If something traveled forever, then the world wouldn't work, or perpetual energy machines would be possible. There are two possible explanations that I can think of, but they're only theories. I haven't spent much time studying tachyons. The first is that tachyons stop traveling upon collision or when they experience a certain amount of friction. The second is that they travel backward in time proportionate to the amount of energy they have. Either way, think about it for a moment. Even if attaching tachyons to atoms worked, and time travel was achieved, it would be a one-way ticket. Not only are you forced to travel backward, but you *can't* get back. Unless, of course, by moving backward, you go back to the day you traveled from, but it's all theoretical madness."

"Right! Because if I traveled back in time yesterday, then traveling back in time again to yesterday would technically reset everything… I think? Hold on a second."

"My headache is officially far worse than it was just a moment ago, and all of this time travel tosh is making me feel terribly ill. You're speaking about theories about theories about theories and justifying them with other theories. I hate it!" Sir Thomas shook his head and sighed, laughing ever so slightly. "I also have a theory that uses atoms, though. We could essentially make a reset-machine. It would transfer and transform all matter in an area back to a prior stage, just as you had mentioned before, Mr. Godwin. However, as you also mentioned, there is no specific memory for each atom that remembers where in the world it has gone or everything that it has been a part of. So, time travel would only be possible in areas watched by a machine that traces the movement of all atoms and then, when activated, uses our science and the movements it has traced to force everything backward. A machine of such power and abilities would be impossible to make. The energy it would require is on a whole other level."

Kronos smirked. "Not bad at all, Thomas. An idea worthy of my attention, to say the least. I'll give it some thought one day. To think that an old man came up with such a young and brilliant idea. Then again, I suppose that old people want to reset time more than anyone."

"Forget time travel," Timothy said in defeat. "You guys are way smarter than I am, and I think that all of our theories just keep proving that time travel is impossible, and they're only providing small concepts that are kind of similar. What I think would be cooler than that is using those ideas to freeze time."

"Now you also have my attention," Kronos commented as he sped up, no longer focused on tachyons and atoms. "Freeze time?"

"Well, life itself, actually. If the currents you use can rip apart the bonds of atoms and molecules, then perhaps it could hold them in place. Im suggesting a machine that you could place down, and it would emit a wave of this unique electricity constantly. Then the person using it wears a suit that produces a current around them that is immune to the freezing current. Everything in that specific area is frozen in place, but the suit-wearer is not. Or something along the lines of that, if you get what I'm trying to create. I don't know, though, that's also an unimaginable idea."

"Apparently not, since you just thought of it, and for the first time ever pondering such science," Kronos pointed out. "The only problem is that it's possibly harmful, Timothy, and I mean *extremely* dangerous to those you freeze. While it wouldn't be dangerous to freeze the molecules and atomic structures of non-living things, organ functionality stopping like that would probably be fatal in a living organism. Not just their organs, but stopping any progress in the body can be lethal. Theoretically, anyway. Your concept is, indeed, astounding, but it's, unfortunately, like all new theories, not flawless."

"Right. I agree with that, but besides actually testing it out, there isn't really an exact answer. I feel that what you say is true, but only to a degree. See if we stopped the functions and movement of a few organs than yes, death would occur, but if we suspend all of them at the same time, then maybe not. If everything is stopped to the nitty-gritty details, then I think it won't harm people. There is no between, basically. You either have to stop everything or nothing. Then again, that could be completely false. Freezing everything could cause death, but all of your atoms being frozen in place at once is a bit like a coma."

"Mr. Godwin, I appreciate your optimism, but I'm afraid there's no way around it: freezing every atom in a living organism will kill it. I don't disagree with the idea that perhaps nothing will be harmful, but it's a chance I'd rather not take. One day, I'm sure someone will try and attempt such an experiment, but I've been a part of too many scientific tests gone wrong, and I'm done with them."

Timothy nodded his head in defeat. "I know. It's such a cool idea, though. Honestly, I'm perfectly happy with the scientific discoveries I've made already, and there's no need for me to delve into time travel or freezing time. I'm a hero, and I'm on my way to forging a road that will lead to the construction of a hero-society. Whether time can be manipulated or not, I don't regret my choices. I bear one sin of lust that constantly weighs heavy in my heart, but besides that, I'm content, and I wouldn't ask for anything more."

"Good for you. I'm glad," Kronos said earnestly. "Enjoy it as much as you can, and never underappreciate it or take it for granted. I'm afraid such joy is not meant for me. I've reached a point of intellect where I know things that will never allow me to be happy. Before we throw time-talk away, I do have one last question. Have you ever studied theories about speeding up the atoms in your body so that you'll be faster than almost everything? The world would be moving in slow motion or almost not at all, depending on how fast your atoms are moving."

"Right. I've heard of such theories before," Timothy replied. "I've never really researched it or read about it, but I think that it would be a death sentence and a torturous one. Again, I'm not The Atomic Alchemist, but I do know a bit about atomic science. Based on my own consequences resulting from my powers, I predict that you would age a whole lot faster if all of your atoms were sped up. I don't know if that's true, but that's my hypothesis. Plus, you would be stuck that way if you were ever to achieve it. You would be alone and unable to live for the rest of your life. If this is invented, it needs to be made as a biological and chemical switch. On and off. Not all science is like that, though. Still, I assume if you can speed them up, then you can slow them down. If you were even able to survive moving at such speeds, that is. Then, there are also the factors of heat and energy, which both pose major issues. So, it seems like an awesome idea that has awful consequences, just like most things nowadays. Between the other rival scientists and my own life, it's almost a trend."

"Unfortunately so, Mr. Godwin. That's enough talk about time and speed for the day. I'm tired from our theorizing," Sir Thomas said with a sigh. "Kronos, pull into the next rest stop. It's about time for a bathroom break, and then I'll drive for a while. My bladder doesn't work like it used to, and kidney-stimulating tea doesn't help me either."

The three men agreed, and after quickly driving a few more miles, they stopped and rested for a bit. It was approaching 2:30 p.m. They each attempted to take a short nap, trying their best to fall asleep despite the buzzing noise of the unanswerable questions that flew around their head. They managed to sleep for about an hour, but they were all woken up by a strange sound in the car.

"What's wrong, Kronos?" Timothy asked through a yawn as he sat straight up.

Sir Thomas, who had been in the trunk resting, quickly got out and hopped into the driver's seat. He turned to Kronos, who was in the passenger's seat, listening to something from a unique earpiece he had put into his left ear. "I didn't even know you had that in your ear? How long have you had it?"

"I put it in this morning before we got on the road so I could be alerted when I was driving and didn't have my phone," Kronos answered half-attentively as he paid attention to the earpiece.

"Alerted about what?" Timothy asked in concern. "Is everything alright?"

Kronos, agitated by their questions, paused the earpiece and turned to face the two men. "I understand you're all worrying, but it's nothing that will affect us right now. Using my coding skills and vast intellect, I designed a program on the private and unbreachable network that I created for my personal use as well as for everything done for R.O.M.A.B.A. Industries. I programmed it to search and scan the entire public internet and all social media platforms, which are constantly updated, for anything related to *any* of the rival scientists, including the lesser-known ones, by searching for specific words that I manually inputted. The words all relate to the rival scientists, but a certain amount of them have to be present in order for the program to deem it important and related. After doing a major scan, the system put together a bunch of matching information from multiple sources, such as news websites and social media, and created a report that it is now reading to me. I'm trying to listen to it. The global web was inundated with multiple verified sources that all published articles or posts containing not only the specific words but matching phrases and information."

Timothy gulped and tensed up. "In other words, you're saying that one of the rival scientists just made a move, right? Like a major one?"

"*Correct*, and not just any rival scientist, Timothy." Instantly, the air in the car grew dark and somber. Everyone knew what Kronos meant. "It was The Dark Depressor. They've made a major move, which is good news and bad news. The bad news is what happened, but the good news is that you were right, Timothy. Homestead, Florida is exactly where we're going." He allowed the earpiece to resume with its message. After allowing Kronos to listen to the remainder of the report, the two men turned toward him, eager to know what had happened. "Well, there was an attack on a building called the Hall of Homestead. Just a few hours ago, actually. There was a private brunch being hosted there earlier today for a club whose members are all rich."

"So, their goal *is* money!" Timothy pointed out. "I had a feeling it was. That's a common goal for villains to have, but also a weak and stupid one. At least if it's just because of pure greed and not justified."

"Incorrect! While money may seem to be the motivation, they say that the humanoid-monster was summoned or hired by a young girl. He didn't go there on his own accord."

"My God," Sir Thomas commented. "Bloody Hell... this is all messed up now. You're saying that The Dark Depressor is a mercenary for hire? That would explain why none of his victims seem connected. They're just the targets of other people that pay him to kill."

"Also incorrect! Formerly deemed Florida Phantom by news organizations and local papers, the humanoid-monster, which we know as The Dark Depressor, now has a new name. At the brunch, he announced that he was **The Sinful Son** and represented the broken ones or something. As stupid as it may sound, that name might be a clue, and his claim might be what connects all of his targets together. The reports came from witnesses who were attending the brunch, but they were all panicking and attempting to escape. However, the only casualties were the guards, and he kidnapped the Siolla family. Apparently, there was also a dead alligator on the premise. A few witnesses all said that the daughter of the host-family, Lilith Siolla, is the one who summoned **The Sinful Son** to the brunch in the first place and that she should be blamed. Think about it for a moment. There's a brunch hosted by the Siolla's. Their daughter hires or requests **The Sinful Son** to show up and kidnap her family and no one else?"

"It's quite puzzling, isn't it?" Sir Thomas remarked as he thought over the basic summary of the incident. "It's certainly a weird twist of dark fate. I understand, Kronos. You're trying to say that something doesn't add up here, and I have to agree. He said he represents the broken? What does that mean?"

Timothy clenched his right hand into a tight fist. *Represents the broken? No! No, no, no, no, no! That means he might be a hero. If he's a hero, then he's not a villain, and if he's not a villain, then I can't make my grand debut as an official hero. This ruins everything! It ruins everything, everything, everything! Of course, I'm glad he's a hero. No. I'm not glad. We don't have any proof that he's a hero. He's still a villain and a killer, or at least his leader is, for all we know.* His eyes closed, Timothy took a deep breath to calm himself and gather his thoughts. "It's possible that he's keeping them all as hostages. People do that all the time for ransoms."

"An understandable thought, but incorrect," Kronos replied. "If he wanted money, he would have robbed the people there and taken more hostages. He specifically took one family and the person who supposedly summoned him. It doesn't make sense. We don't know enough to connect all of the pieces together, and he hasn't been seen since this morning. Get driving, Thomas. We have to get to Homestead, Florida, and that's not possible while we sit here. It's time for us to get some answers."

"Well, this is bloody fantastic!" Sir Thomas could not help but smile as he drove off. "I mean, if it turns out that they're actually good, we won't have to fight them. That's what we all want, right? They could even become one of our allies or a partner for scientific discussion. When I first heard you say **The Sinful Son**, I was rather gutted, but now I'm rather cheerful. Again, representing the broken may still be a villain's motivation, as Mr. Godwin would word it, but things are certainly looking better. Off to Florida!"

Timothy, however, was not cheerful as one would expect a hero to be, or anyone, for that matter. Lying down across the three back seats, he closed his eyes in defeat, spite, anger, and frustration, deciding that sleep would be the only way to revive his good nature and joyful spirit.

CHAPTER 7

MR. MONATOMIC

(Traveling Across North America. Later That Same Day: April 16, 2022)

A few more hours on the road and two stops went by after the trio of travelers had received the report regarding **The Sinful Son**. The conversations flowed in and out as they talked about the various aspects of life once Timothy had woken up. After sleeping, he was in a better mood, and they sang along to some songs on the radio every now and then, Kronos immediately turning it off every time a commercial came on.

Once the sky darkened to 8:00 p.m., Timothy asked Sir Thomas to tune in to Maggie's Midnight Station, which was a channel that aired from eight until ten during the night. His father had often played it when they were traveling at night, and Timothy still listened to it. The channel was hosted by Maggie, who had a soothing voice that was beautiful and comforting even through the machine as if it had been created solely for reading aloud and speaking. She would occasionally talk to people, but for the most part, she would take song requests from people who had special reasons to request a song. She had been inspired to create the channel after staying up until midnight reading a book to some friends who encouraged her to do something with her soft and narrative voice.

Kronos listened to the channel without really paying attention, for he had never been in a genuine relationship and so the sappy conversations between Maggie and her listeners meant nothing to him. In fact, it only served as a painful reminder of how lonely he had always been and still was, and he always tried his best to avoid such reminders. In his mind, he felt that he had missed out on a lot in life, and that was his sacrifice for the world, but nevertheless, it upset him. So, he subtly began to listen with jealousy and bitter regret, coated with anger and spite.

A woman had been calling Maggie's radio station, trying to request a song. Finally, she got through to the station. "Maggie, thank you so much for finally answering. It is so amazing to be talking to you on the radio! I am such a big fan. I *can't* believe this is happening."

"Well, the pleasure is mine. What's your name?"

"Christina. I listen to your station every evening during my night shift at work, and it's always enjoyable."

"Well, I'm glad I'm there for you, Christina. What a beautiful name, by the way. Absolutely love that. Now, why are you calling tonight, and what song would you like to play?"

"I was hoping you could play the song *Reality Made From Dreams* by Charlie Salicet for my fiancé, Adam. He just proposed to me yesterday, and of course, I said yes! The song is an old one, but I feel like it perfectly describes how we both feel, and I wanted to do this for him in return for all that he's done to me. He is such a great guy."

"Well, isn't that just lovely! Congratulations on that, sweetie. What an exciting thing to happen, and we're all happy for you. Here is the song as requested by Christina for her fiancé, Adam."

The song, which Charlie had written for a talent show in middle school, was all about how his soulmate made his life perfect, and how it was ironic that a girl who seemed like a dream was what made his life a reality. It was the song that had kickstarted his career as a singer.

The three men listened to the song for the duration of it, and then the channel went back to Maggie. "Well, there you have it, folks. What a lovely song. Congratulations to Christina and Adam on getting engaged." She began talking to a man named Zack, who was guest hosting, about what had just happened. "Not a hit song, but I'll tell ya, it *is* a good one. I have not heard that one for a long time. It was first released in 2006, but it seems to be making a comeback, and that's one of the things I love about the music industry. Some songs are timeless, and there's nothing better than that. Although, it does makes me feel old when I realize how long ago some of these songs were produced. I can't believe it."

"I completely agree with you, and I'm sure that most of America is with me on that," Zack replied. "I feel like that is what we *need* right now. What we *always* need, actually, and that's more songs about real, personal stuff. Deep philosophical thoughts or cheesy romanticism. Enough of all the songs about sex, love, and drugs. We have enough of those, and they're crude. A large percent of modern music is like that nowadays, and it's absolutely ridiculous. You feel me on that, Maggie?"

"Exactly my thoughts, Zack. I agree. I'm not discrediting the talent of today's music artists. They do have amazing voices and talents, but their lyricism is awful. I understand that some of the younger generations like this kind of music, but unnecessary cursing, drug use, and sexual activity is not what creates good music."

Maggie and Zack continued talking about music and other related topics. Sir Thomas slowly turned the radio down a bit before eventually turning it off.

It was silent for a short while afterward before Timothy broke the silence. "Well, that was a nice story. Romantic enough, although a bit too cheesy for my liking. It reminds me of what I had meant to ask you guys before. If it's too personal, you can decline, but I was just interested in your romantic lives. After all, you both met my wife and know about her sister. Do you have a lady-friend, Kronos? A wife?"

It was again silent for a moment. The highway ahead of the three men was dark and ominous, with only a few people scattered across its vast length. It seemed that the closer they got to Florida, the more somber the atmosphere became.

Kronos answered, staring out through the car window from where he sat in the passenger's seat. "An understandable question that I won't decline to answer since I have no shame regarding anything, but I'm afraid such a question has a simple answer. Although, I'm sure you'll inquire for more details. Despite the fact that I could have any girl I wanted, between my fortune, intellect, and charms, I am far too busy to have time for love. Always have been, always will be. I've chosen helping the world over love, and just as you've made sacrifices as a hero, I have made mine as the future leader of our world."

Timothy shook his head in disappointment and disbelief. "Too busy for love? Kronos, what's the point of having everything if you're alone? I mean, that message is basically in every show nowadays. Why save the world if you won't be able to enjoy it?"

"The same reason why you hope to create a hero-society that you won't be able to enjoy."

As if physically stabbed by the retort, Timothy flinched. "You've got me there. Honestly, that really puts it into perspective for me. I'll admit that, but Kronos... everyone needs a little love in life. That's one of the major parts of life. Everyone needs just a little bit of it once before they die. You're telling me you've never felt anything for anyone?"

"Regardless of whether or not it's a major part of life, I've sacrificed it. I can't afford to be chained down by anyone, and I live a dangerous life that would only put them in harm's way. Are you telling me love is worth losing the person you care about? That seems ironic and almost paradoxical. Besides discovering scientific breakthroughs, I also create inventions and products on a daily basis while running the world's most powerful and useful company, and now I hunt self-made heroes and villains. So, besides the fact that I've chosen to not love, I would say that I *am* too busy. No offense to your kind and hopeful heart, but I've always been called Mr. Monatomic. It's a reference to a single atom that is by itself and does not need anything but itself."

"Well, that's sad. Mr. Monatomic sounds like a cool name, but I don't think it's a positive one. I'm sorry to hear that, Kronos. I respect your decision, but you should really reconsider your choice. Love is one of the greatest things in the world, and that's in every book, comic book, show, movie, and anything else, honestly. You're the most powerful man in the world, so you shouldn't be worried, because if anyone could keep their love safe, it'd be you."

Sir Thomas kept his eyes on the dark road ahead as he drove, but he shook his head in disagreement. "My turn to join the conversation. You are *far* too kind to him, Mr. Godwin. Also, you shouldn't believe everything he says. Kronos is just in denial. For example, you should ask him about Elizabeth."

"That's no one's business except mine, Thomas, and I don't know if it's love. Quite honestly, I don't entirely trust her, and trust is a key element when it comes to love," Kronos stated. "Besides, you're not supposed to know about that, but I knew that damn woman wouldn't be able to hide it from you, nor could I hope to keep something like that from you when it was within the walls of our castle."

"Woah, okay," Timothy said with his hands up in innocence and defense. "Let's settle down now. Sir Thomas, if he doesn't want to talk about it, then that's fine by me. I was just curious. There's no need for us to delve into his personal life. He's made his choices."

"Mr. Godwin, you are still being too kind. I think I'm actually enjoying this," Sir Thomas said with a smirk at Kronos, who knew that his caretaker was finally getting some revenge. To hide it from Timothy, however, Sir Thomas spoke innocently and with concern. "Delving into the life choices of Mr. Monatomic over there is what we're here for, right? I'm his caretaker and you're one of his only friends out of two people, so why not? We should help him while we're trapped in this vehicle together for the next few hours. He needs us to be there for him, because he has trouble with his emotions."

"It's okay, Kronos," Timothy said reassuringly and earnestly, tricked by Sir Thomas into believing that Kronos actually wanted to talk. "We all have trouble handling our emotions, and we all deal with them differently. After all, our emotions are all different and have different levels of power. Some people are actually less capable of emotions than others. Still, talking always seems to be the best way of dealing with them."

"Exactly my thought, Mr. Godwin! We should talk about everything," Sir Thomas said with a mischievous grin at Kronos, who rolled his eyes. "Too busy for love? Always Mr. Monatomic? Well, those aren't too far from the truth, but back in high school, Kronos did like a girl once. Well, the British version of high school, I suppose. Her name was Annabelle."

"Oh? Is that so?" Timothy laughed. "What a lovely name. That alone makes her sound so interesting. I love name culture and the whole idea of names and what they mean. I've even read articles about how your name can determine your life or at least certain aspects of it. Back in high school, you say? That's awesome. That was long before I was hanging out around the halls of high school, so I wonder what that must've been like. I remember those days. A roller coaster ride of ups and downs in life. That's good that you had her, though. Everyone should make room for love in their life. Even if it only be short and sweet, love must be experienced before death. So, what's the story with Anabelle?"

Now, Kronos was growing impatient with their talk. "That's quite enough, everyone," he stated coldly. "Timothy, I don't blame you for your curiosity, especially since Thomas is encouraging you, but I'm afraid there is nothing to tell. It never happened."

Sir Thomas objected to this with a hearty laugh. "Of course, there is! I'll tell the story since Mr. Monatomic here is refusing to. It's a wonderful story, after all, and would go quite well with tea and biscuits, to be honest. The muck I had to go through for young Kronos. Oh, those were the days of headaches that were far less complicated than the ones nowadays."

"No, Thomas. I'd rather not talk about it," Kronos protested coldly. "If you make me repeat myself again, I assure you that everyone in this car will receive a scathing verbal thrashing that is unlike any other. I will verbally destroy you, your pets, your neighbors, your family, your friends, your careers, and even your rotten houseplants. There is no need to discuss the past. Nothing really happened, and it was over three decades ago."

Timothy laughed. "You're going to make fun of my houseplants?"

"Well, something did happen because you've been counting every day since," Sir Thomas pointed out. "For *three decades,* apparently. Besides, it'll be good for you to open up. Timothy might as well listen since we don't have anything better to do."

"There's no denying that, as we do have about twelve or more hours of traveling left," Timothy said as he checked the time on his Whip-Watch. "Plus, I'm really interested in hearing more, but I'm sorry for upsetting you, man. Still, it's not good to bottle up emotions. Every man who does that says to themselves, 'Oh, it won't bother me to do so like it does to others.' Nah, man. That's not how it works, and they're always wrong. If I kept my emotions bottled, I probably wouldn't have ended up with Laura. Being scared of judgment is stupid because everyone judges everyone. There's no avoiding it."

Kronos went back to staring out through the car window and looked at the cities in the distance. The lit windows that were scattered across the darkened sky almost blended in with the stars that spread out across the black atmosphere above. He looked up at the sky and saw a shooting star. He took it as a representation of his fallen dream of love with Annabelle. He turned his attention back to Timothy. "If you insist, I suppose I'll talk. There's nothing to be ashamed of, as I was the clear victor, in a way."

"Right. I'm all ears, Kronos. Tell me everything." Timothy leaned closer to the front of the car so he could hear better. "Trust me, man, I had my fair share of drama and rejection back in the day. Almost everyone has or will."

"It was back in high school, which seems like a lifetime ago as well as yesterday. It happened over the course of two years. Freshman year and sophomore year. The important years of high school that either make or break you for the remaining years to follow. Anyway, the first time that I had met her was in Algebra class. I sat in the back of the class, and she sat at the desk in front of me. I was, of course, a genius, but I didn't purposefully try to stand out. School was never for me. I was simply too intelligent. What caught my attention was her hair. It was a huge bun of brown hair, enough to host a mother bird and her chicks. I found it distasteful, but it made her stand out. A little bit too much, sometimes. The damn thing blocked half of the board. I couldn't see anything, and I would be missing notes. With time, however, I grew to like her hair. It was a brown mixture of dark and light shades. There's no other way to describe it, really."

"Ah, so hair is your weakness. Noted. That's a bit unusual, but I won't judge."

"Well, she had a lovely chest and nice eyes to if you want me to go into detail. Actually, her eyes were gorgeous. They were a light blue color that was almost grey. You could look into them and see many things. There was a caring look behind those eyes, but at the same time, there was a coldness. It was a chilling evil that only grew each year of high school, but it wasn't there at first. They say that eyes are the window to the soul. Well, in her one eye, I saw her soul, and in the other, I saw mine. Not at first, but with time as we grew to know each other."

"Oh, wow. We're getting farther than I thought, That's pretty deep, Kronos. I wasn't expecting you to be so poetic. You really liked her. Tell me more."

"She did mean a lot to me. She was my favorite girl throughout high school. No matter who I talked to, she was my favorite. Even after all of the problems that had happened. I hated everyone. I was cold and always alone by choice, and the more bitter I grew, the more confident I got. The only reason I stayed neutral was for her sake. If not for her kindness or my desire to impress her, I would have verbally destroyed everyone and struck fear into the hearts of all the staff and students. I've never been too fond of anyone, but she was different."

"Wow, so she was that special? The kind of person you still like after all Hell breaks loose? This is way more than I had expected, and she sounds awesome. What was she like, Kronos?"

"Annabelle was amazing, Timothy. Her intelligence was the perfect level, in my opinion- not too smart, nor was she stupid. One of the things I loved the most about her was her attitude, though. She was very sassy, but in a fun, playful way." Kronos smiled for a brief second, and it was not filled with evil or bitterness as usual. He seemed glad in a way that showed he had traveled back to the past and was reliving some happy memories with her. "She was always joking and teasing people, but she was a little different when it came to me, and it made me feel special. She would threaten to punch me in the head or would make angry cat noises at me, which she then laughed at realizing how crazy she seemed. I loved it, especially when she would do it while arguing with her friends."

Timothy laughed. "Not necessarily my idea of romance, but you do you, man. I'm honestly glad, because she helped you stay human, and that's what we all need."

"Well, I found it cute and funny. I think every girl needs a hint of crazy, or everyone for that matter. If this world has too much logic and sane people, it'll erode and die. Annabelle was so sincere and kind to me. It wasn't an act that she put on, which was the best part. She was actually real. I could tell, having met many liars in my life. I despise fake people. They tried to take advantage of me and use me for my brain, but I knew better. I-"

Sir Thomas interrupted him. "He only knew better because I taught him how to know the difference between real and fake. He can thank me for that! Along with everything else about his life."

"I do, Thomas, but that's not the point I'm trying to make. Really, my point is that Annabelle was just fun to be around, and I enjoyed every moment with her. Two years and four classes in total. That was the highlight of school. She was smart and funny. What more could a guy want? She never overdid it, though, when it came to her sass or flirting.

Same with her makeup, in fact. She was just slightly above a simple girl. A natural beauty, but that's my personal preference."

Timothy agreed with this statement. "Me too, Kronos. It's one of the things I love about Laura." Sir Thomas grew envious and tense, but he forced himself to relax his grip on the steering wheel. "They say there is a balance for everything in the universe. That *especially* includes makeup!" Everyone broke out laughing. None of them even knew why they all found it so funny. "I'm sorry, but I just don't like girls looking like clowns or a piece of abstract art!"

"You sound a bit misogynistic, Mr. Godwin," Sir Thomas pointed out. "That's not very hero-like, nor is it respectful when in the presence of a gentleman such as myself."

"My apologies, Sir Thomas. I assure you that I respect women, as well as all races and cultures. It's part of being a hero, as you said before, and I am a hero, so I abide by good morals. I just can't stand artificial things when it comes to the human body. Plastic surgeries, for example. Nothing is worse than nail polish, though. I mean, it looks beautiful and people are free to use it, but the smell is absolutely cancerous. I mean, not literally, but figuratively, it's cancerous. Is it just me, or does nail polish actually reek of artificial death?"

Sir Thomas shook his head, laughing. "Unless you're my sister. She loved the smell of nail polish. I never understood it. She's dead now," he added. "However, rest assured that the smell is only that: a smell. It's not harmful, and I trust beauty companies to provide us with products that are safe to inhale."

"I'm sorry, but are we listening to my story, or are we just going to discuss women's products that none of us use?" Kronos asked angrily, his patience almost gone. "The point is that Anabelle was perfect." He sighed a breath of angry complaint. "At least... she *was*."

"Sorry, Kronos," Timothy said after he took a sip of water from a thermos he had. "So, what exactly happened?"

Kronos did not respond.

Realizing that Kronos was lost in bitter memories of his past, which he had not discussed aloud for decades, Sir Thomas figured he would tell the story for now. "Well, the two of them got along very well during freshman year and for half of sophomore year. They were flirty with each other, and it was clear that Kronos had feelings for her. Though, we were unsure as to whether or not she was aware of that. If she did know and also returned those feelings remained undeterminable, and it's still unclear to this day. Some girls are naturally flirtatious. Kronos was waiting to ask her out because he did not want to rush things and scare her way. I applaud him for that, yet such was not the best for this case. It was during that time that *he* came into the love story."

Timothy gasped. He had seen enough dramatic romance movies to know that it was about to get even more interesting. "*He*? Who's he? A father, a brother, or a boyfriend? Oh my God, is he an ex?" Timothy asked, throwing his arms around with each guess. He was almost shaking.

"*Mark*," Kronos hissed. "His name was Mark. He came in and stole her from me like an eagle sweeping up a dead mouse!" Kronos' voice was now tense with hate and anger. He held onto the inside of the car door tightly. Revenge served as an underlying tone as he continued the rest of the story. "Fearing that he was going to steal her away, I told Annabelle everything that I felt. She said she was flattered, but she wasn't looking to date anyone in high school. We stayed as just friends. She would poke me in the back for fun, and we would flirt, but we never dated. It was tormenting because I wanted to be angry and hold a grudge, but to do so would mean getting rid of the only person I cared about."

"I understand, but who is Mark? Did they meet that spring?"

"Nowadays, he's her husband and correct. It was the spring of sophomore year. Actually, using my vast intellect and internet capabilities, I managed to see that she posted a picture of them recently. High school sweethearts, I suppose, but he seems just as rotten as he was then, if not worse. I despise him more than any other inferior human."

"Well, was he actually that bad, or is this jealousy speaking? I don't know him, so I don't want to hear a biased opinion. What did he do? Well, besides stealing Annabelle away."

"Well, for one thing, he was an adult dating a minor. That minor being the girl I liked. Disgusting," Kronos spat out with contempt. "I don't care that much, since age does not matter at all when it comes to love, but he made me hate the idea of age gaps during high school. So, yes, I am biased about it since I wouldn't have cared if it was anyone other than me, but that man stole what I was told was not meant to be for anyone."

Timothy's eyes almost popped out of his head in shock. "No way! I figured Mark was a fellow classmate or at least a high schooler. Well, with God above me as a witness to such evil, how old was this Mark guy?"

"You can calm down, Timothy. He wasn't *that* old. Although, I suppose how old is 'too old' is up to personal interpretation. He was only twenty, or maybe he was twenty-two, but that was too old to be dating a girl who had just turned sixteen and was still in high school. Inappropriate and immoral. I hate those filthy grubbing men tryin' taking advantage of high school students. I know not all of them are bad, nor their intentions, but not everyone is an exception like those few."

"Right. I agree. It was only a four-year difference, and that's not bad at all, but only *after* high school. The age gap is different when in school than when you are graduated. Especially when it is minors and adults. But that's just my opinion. I can't say I haven't felt my heart stutter for an older woman before. I'm sure there are plenty of people who think it's acceptable. Everyone thinks their own thing, and that's how the world functions, and it's part of its beauty."

"Exactly, and I let Annabelle know this. She had lied to me about not wanting to date, or perhaps she had changed her mind, but either way, she had broken her belief of not dating in high school, and it was with a piece of garbage! A man who was not worth bending her morals for was what had caused her to cast aside her promise to herself, and to me as well, in a way. Unfortunately, she wasn't pleased with what I said, but no one ever is when their true nature or new flaws are confronted. I was just a concerned friend for her. I don't know why she couldn't ever see that, but it had hurt me deeply. It still hurts my heart now. It wasn't just the age that troubled me. That would have been a bit of an overreaction. If she had loved him and he treated her right, then twenty would have been fine. Her parents were fine with it. It was the... *other* things about him that I didn't like. What she saw in him is far beyond my comprehension, and I have taught myself all things that one could ever hope to learn."

"Other things besides his age?" Timothy asked with concern and curiosity. "Tell me all about him. It gets worse?"

"Unfortunately, it does get worse, and I swear to you that I am not exaggerating. On their own or even in regard to others, they are not terrible things, but combined with his personality, along with what I knew about him, they shed some warning on the future that was to come."

"Foreshadowing in the real world? I love it."

"Correct. For one thing, he was covered in tattoos. Not that people who have tattoos are evil people or anything, but he most certainly was. I have nothing against tattoos, but his tattoos were vicious and covered everything. Distasteful language decorated his knuckles, and there was an eyeball that had the artistic illusion of coming out of his neck. Those were just the few I managed to see, though I'm sure there were more, for I heard about him from many other people who had grown up with him."

"Kronos, you swore to Mr. Godwin that you wouldn't exaggerate anything," Sir Thomas interrupted, recognizing that Kronos was getting emotional, though his demeanor had not changed at all except for a few octaves of anger in his voice. "He only had a *few* tattoos, but they were, indeed, wicked. That man was a wanker and a troublemaker, as much as I hate to say it. The knuckles tattoos and the eyeball one that

Kronos just mentioned were there, however, and based on the post we saw, he's gotten even more since high school."

"Pfft. Well, that's his burden of regret to carry. I've thought about getting tattoos before, but I probably won't. They don't make you a bad person at all, but I trust your judgment regarding his tattoos. What exactly was this post that you guys saw?"

"I assure you that I'm not big on social media or anything, but from what Kronos showed me, it was a photo of them at the mall shopping together. Quite honestly, I didn't think people in their forties used social media like that, but I don't know too much about it. Mark was wearing a custom-made leather jacket. It was white leather with the initials G.C. on the back. I was so preoccupied with trying to figure out what those letters stood for, that I didn't even bother really looking at him. The sight of him makes me sick, as he caused Kronos and I a great deal of trouble, as you'll soon find out. I try not to judge anyone without truly knowing them, but he is awful. My pet peeve was the gauge earrings he had back in the day, and he's still wearing them. Perhaps it's because I was born a long time before him, but those I found… disturbing, to say the least. I don't like them on anyone, but it's just my opinion. Even earings disturb me a bit, as do all piercings on the body. His were the *worst*, though. They were big enough for a bird to perch on one and peck food out of his ear."

Everyone laughed. "And you have the nerve to say that I'm exaggerating?" Kronos asked rhetorically, poking fun at Sir Thomas. He continued to tell the story, feeling a little bit better now. This was the first time he had talked about it in a long time, let alone to someone other than Sir Thomas. "It's true, though. The gages were distasteful, but only on him. Again, I have nothing against people with gauged earrings. Anyway, besides that, he was just an eyesore overall. His hair was always messy, and it was unevenly cut. It was an untamed garden of brown poison ivy. Then, he was always smirking in a greedy and mischievous way that reminded me of a bandit spotting a score in public as he schemed what he would do later on when no one was around. His face read juvenile trouble like a graffitied wall in a dark alleyway. His eyes were almost always bloodshot as well, and the cause remained unknown, though I'm sure we can all imagine a few reasons behind that."

Timothy nodded his head. "There's no need for you to describe him physically anymore. I understand the kind of character you're trying to describe, and I've met many people like him in my lifetime. However, looks alone are not enough for me to condemn Mark. What were his goals and motives? How did he treat Anabelle? Was he actually trouble?"

"Indeed, he was, Timothy, and it was long before he entered my life that he had made mischief and torment his hobby. He got into a lot of trouble, actually, and that's no exaggeration. A few classmates of mine had warned me. I was never quite able to figure out exactly what kind of trouble it was that he got into, but he was with the police numerous times. I heard it from several people, and he had been in juvenile detention for some time, though I do not know for how long. After I told Annabelle how I felt about her and Mark, it all went downhill. She couldn't understand how I felt or why I was concerned. To her, Mark was the perfect guy. She claimed that he had changed and that he was sweet and caring, or whatever it was that she saw in him. To her, I became nothing and meaningless in the great shadow of him. *He* was everything."

"I understand, for that is often the case, Kronos. People in love often can't see the faults of their partner, or they cling onto what their partners had been like or who they hoped their partner was like or would be like. They say that love is blind, but the closer truth is that love is blinding. I know what you mean, as I was once in a similar situation when confronting one of my best friends, who had strayed far from the path of cleanliness. I'm very sorry to hear about that."

"Don't be sorry for him just yet, Mr. Godwin, as there's still plenty more of the story to tell," Sir Thomas pointed out. "We're only halfway through it all if even that far in. Do you remember Hurricane AW-1?"

"Of course, I remember it! Who wouldn't? Well, I've heard the stories about it at least. It started in the Gulf of Mexico, traveled along the east coast of America, and then made it all the way to England. The biggest hurricane in all of history! That's what I've been told. It destroyed my parents' house when I was just born less than a year before. It's what caused them to move. So, I technically lived through it."

"As you just mentioned, that powerful hurricane hit England, and that's an important part of the story," Kronos stated. "Even now, after so much time has passed, I remember everything exactly as it happened. I'll admit that I've forgotten countless facts and pointless memories since my brain is overflowing with knowledge, but I have *never* forgotten this."

"Neither have I," Sir Thomas added.

"Woah, guys!" Timothy laughed and shook with excitement and anticipation. "You're giving me goosebumps. I'm literally on the edge of this car seat. Something major is about to go down, right?"

"Correct. Before the hurricane hit, I contacted Annabelle out of concern for her safety. Thomas has always been fond of staying updated on the news and weather, so I knew how bad the hurricane was going to be when it hit us. So, I offered for her and her family to stay at my castle during the duration of the storm. She accepted, as her family wished to be safe. This conversation was all on the phone, by the way. The old flip phones that were around during that time. I was rich, so I had one, and I had gotten her one for her birthday. After she agreed to come over, I sent her a text saying that I would be glad to see her, and I listed what amenities my castle had."

"That always wins the ladies over," Timothy said jokingly. "Even back then, you were a prideful show-off, huh? Were you considered an amenity of the castle?" They all laughed, and Kronos shook his head. "No, but seriously, I'm getting anxious. I have a bad feeling about this. Using my years of comic book experience and entertainment industry cliches, combined with the patterns of life amongst teenagers, I'm guessing that *she* didn't open that message, did she?"

"You impress me more and more each time we talk. You're quite smart, Timothy, and correct in what you say. Well, not about me being an amenity of the castle," Kronos said with a laugh. He got more serious, however, and his tone shifted back to contempt. "She didn't open it. Her boyfriend did. *Mark* opened it, and he was not at all thrilled about what he read. He mistook my message for romance. Annabelle knew that I was just being myself and watching out for her, but Mark, he didn't know me. He didn't know what I meant or who I was. He just assumed that I liked her, and that automatically made me his enemy."

Timothy shook his head, relating to the pain Kronos felt over this simple misunderstanding that had changed his entire life. "Pfft. That's unbelievable. I'm actually sorry to hear that. Just another consequence of the inevitable force of assumption that lurks in us all." Sir Thomas and Kronos looked back at Timothy. "My bad. Just a habit I have from reading so many books that ponder the concepts of time, space, and humanity, along with everything else in this universe. Anyway, what happened?"

The car stopped moving as Sir Thomas parked at a rest stop. "I'm afraid you'll have to wait a moment, Mr. Godwin. Let's take an actual break and get dinner. It's late, and we've been driving almost all day. Is that alright with everyone? Not that I'll change my mind, but I should ask first."

"Even though I'm dying to know what happens next, I won't disagree with that," Timothy replied. "I'm constantly hungry, and I could use some stretching and open space. Being a speedster and an active person, sitting in the car for an hour is torturous, let alone several hours at a time like this."

The three men hopped out of the car and went into the rest-stop building. They stood waiting in line at an area called Dr. Finch's Fast Food, which only had one employee working at the moment. The line was the longest out of all the eateries in the building, which only had two or three people waiting. The building itself was eerily quiet, however, as it was an odd day to be traveling, and the time of night was not a busy travel time either. They slowly moved down the line.

Sir Thomas, who was worried about Kronos' patience, began to wonder why the trio of travelers had not just gone to one of the other eateries with a short line. He glanced around. "Mr. Godwin, what exactly is this Dr. Finch's Fast Food? Why were you insistent on going here rather than any of the other places that have shorter lines?"

Timothy quickly turned around to face Sir Thomas, shocked by his questions. "There's a reason that the line for this place is longer than any other, and that's because it truly is the finest food around. I suppose you don't have any over in England? Otherwise, you would've never asked such questions. What a shame."

"My apologies, Mr. Godwin," Sir Thomas replied half-heartedly. "I'm afraid that I've never seen one in all of my time living in England, nor any of the time I've spent in America."

"Correct, for I have never seen one in America or England, and I'm observant of everything," Kronos stated. "What exactly makes this food so much better than any of these other places? You seem to be a big fan of the franchise."

"I am. My dad used to get me this a lot, and since I was close with him, it was one of my favorite places." Timothy thought for a moment while he skimmed the menu displayed above on a glowing panel. "Well, I guess I should give you a brief history of the franchise. It all started back in the early 2000s from what I know, or perhaps it was the late 1990s, but it doesn't make a difference. Dr. Finch created the first restaurant around that time. He's actually a scientist, just like us!"

"Really?" Kronos asked in disbelief and disappointment. "Clearly not if he ended up being a restaurant franchise owner."

"No, it's true. Dr. Finch has an actual Ph.D. You shouldn't discredit his abilities and intelligence just because he chose to apply his scientific skills to the food industry." Timothy glanced around before leaning in close to Kronos and Sir Thomas, lowering his voice. "There are theories that his food is so good because he uses some kind of secret serums from his lab when he's cooking."

Kronos smirked. "He applies his scientific skills to cooking? That's disappointing but rather intriguing, and the idea of chemistry makes logical sense, though it could be biological science as well. An entire list of theories far beyond the comprehension of most people has already gone through my mind, Timothy. Genetic modification to the animals and plants that make up the foods would certainly be controversial, but that's not grand enough. It has to be some kind of even darker secret," Kronos said with an evil chuckle. There was a tone in his voice that made it seem like he wanted to join this business, or even take it over.

Timothy laughed at how Kronos thought of himself as an unstoppable evil genius. "Easy there, Kronos! He may be taking over the food industry, but he's not taking over the world. You sound like you want him to, so long as you're in charge of the operation. I'm not too sure what it is, and the rumors are kind of crappy. Genetic modification? I don't know about that. I was told that the truth is he uses some kind of special egg sauce, but I'm not entirely sure. It's mostly just drama to help people have something to talk about."

"Egg sauce?" Kronos rolled his eyes and sighed in disappointment and anger. "You've wasted my intelligence by getting my hopes up. I thought that there might be potential in the rumors and that Dr. Finch might even be a rival scientist. A modification to the food industry would fit in perfectly, given Birch Willow's discovery regarding cellulose and cellulase. Why even spread rumors if egg sauce is the truth? If he is as smart as everyone believes him to be, I'm afraid that he is just a waste of scientific talent."

"Let's calm ourselves now, Kronos," Sir Thomas said. "It's not at all our place to judge his life choices or what he chose to use his intellect for, and there's really no reason for you to be upset." They moved up the line a bit. "Mr. Godwin, what's he like, this Dr. Finch fellow?"

"Well, I've never met him, and no one has seen him in over a year, which is odd, but I had seen him on the news before he disappeared. He's a really short fellow. He almost looks Korean, actually, but he has informed everyone that he's not, as he spent his high school years trying to convince everyone he was Italian, and he's tired of it. He's actually an immigrant from Italy, so maybe he moved back there, and that's why no one has seen him. He's got dark hair and wears glasses.

Seems like a pleasant enough guy, although a suspicious and shady figure. Moved here from Italy back when he was a child. Began practicing science once he could speak English and has experimented ever since then. I believe he majored in chemistry and culinary classes. That about sums it up. They were supposed to be making a movie about him and his franchise, but I'm not sure what happened to that."

"What was he on the news for?"

"An interview of some sort. They were opening a new location up in New York City, and it was the biggest one yet. He was well-mannered and educated with his responses, although he did dodge a few questions. Apparently, everything he does is organic and eco-friendly, though, so I'm not sure what the problem is. It was probably related to the rumors about him experimenting with his food and customers."

Kronos smiled proudly with greed and power. "Is that so? I honestly wouldn't be surprised if he uses our eco-friendly technology, seeing as we've basically reinvented that part of society, and will continue to do so. Between our graphene-based solar panels, sun-following panels, our bladeless turbines, our water-powered machines, our lunar panels, and our kinetic energy engines- to name just a small handful of our inventions- he probably uses our technology like most businesses are starting to."

"Oh, sweet! Good for you guys, and I'm glad you're helping out the environment. I'd love to hear more about R.O.M.A.B.A. Industries sometime," Timothy stated. "I feel like there is *so* much more to it than anyone knows or would believe."

The three of them finally reached the register. All of them ordered the same thing from the menu. Timothy had suggested they all just get what he usually orders. It was a massive burger, tenderly cooked with the special sauce, covered in an assortment of condiments, and then topped with a toasted bun.

"Actually, let me get another one of those," Timothy added. "Oh, and two large fries, if you can. I'm quite hungry, and I actually burn through *a lot* of calories. I'm a runner if you couldn't tell, and like professionally. I have a big competition soon, so I'm already starting to carb-load. Also, can I get a toy with mine, please? They just released a new series, from what I understand." The cashier rolled her eyes at Timothy but threw a toy onto his tray, not wanting to argue. "Thanks! I'm going to go grab napkins and stuff," he told Sir Thomas and Kronos as he walked away, moving speedily as always.

Sir Thomas pulled out his wallet, which was almost as thick as a brick. "I apologize for him. He's got a lot more energy than most people do." He pulled out more than enough cash to cover the bill and told her to keep the change. "That should cover it, and enjoy your evening." She fountained with gratitude, happy for the extra money.

The tray of food ready and grabbed by Kronos, they made their way over to a table and sat down, Timothy sitting across from Kronos and Sir Thomas. He grabbed the toy from the tray. It was a shirtless man with insect wings coming out of his back. The man had four arms and large eyes. They assumed that it was a dragonfly-man or something from a fantasy video game, as even Timothy did not recognize it from any comic lore. The plastic bag had said something about genetics or fighting on it, but Timothy had ripped the plastic to the point that it was unreadable. Timothy waved his arm around with the toy in his hand and made buzzing noises. It was actually a sad sight to see, for it reminded Sir Thomas and Kronos that Timothy was actually a young man. Perhaps not so young that he should be playing with toys, but it did remind them of his sacrifice. He had lost his days of youth, the prime time of his life, to help others.

After he grew bored of it, Timothy placed the toy standing up on the table. "Sorry about that. I suppose I'm a child at heart. We should probably get drinks before we eat. I was so excited about hearing the rest of the story that I forgot about them." Timothy gestured over to a machine that was over by the Dr. Finch's Fast Food area. "That machine is our drinkable water in our desert. Best part is that we can just put the money in the machine to unlock a cup and then fill it up as many times as we want. Can't beat that deal!"

Sir Thomas looked over at the machine and laughed. "Between my health choices and the rumors about this shady fellow, there's no way I'm getting a drink from that! You Americans make fun of us for drinking tea, but bollocks, would you look at that."

Kronos looked over at what they were talking about. It seemed like a standard soda fountain machine, but he read the bright neon flashing sign above it aloud. "Dr. Finch's Fizzy Fountain?"

"See, Mr. Godwin? Even Kronos seems wary of it."

Kronos nodded his head. "I fear nothing, but your irrational fear actually seems justified, Thomas. Fizzy Fountain sounds even more acidic than soda already is. It's certainly a texture that will burn and tear apart your internal organs after eradicating your esophagus and eroding your teeth."

Timothy laughed heartily and for quite a while. "You two are hilarious. I don't think I've laughed so hard in quite a while. My childhood restaurant is being torn apart by you two, but the soda *is* really fizzy. So, I don't blame you for being skeptical. After all, not everyone can handle drinking such fizzy soda," Timothy said challengingly to the egomaniac across from him.

"You would dare suggest that I could not drink from the fountain of fizziness? I assure you that Thomas and I are more than capable of handling extra fizzy soda, Timothy. More than anyone, in fact, or at least I can, considering that my internal organs are far superior to all other functioning ones. I'll have whatever flavor is closest to Birch Willow Beer, and just get Thomas something that seems British. Tell me, are there rumors about these beverages as well?"

"Nothing too different from the rumors regarding food. I've just heard that Dr. Finch began to experiment on customers without consent by using his restaurant as a public front for his research. He would create serums and chemical formulas, and then secretly administer them to the public through his soda machines, just like how he would put stuff in the food. It's all just fake news, honestly, which is almost all news, nowadays. At least that's what I think since I've never experienced any weird side effects. Anyway, it's just extra-fizzy soda. Probably not healthy for anyone, but it does taste delicious. The flavors are unlike any others." Before anything else could be said, Timothy had quickly gone and gotten them each a soda.

Kronos and Sir Thomas each took a sip after some hesitation.

"Perhaps it's because I'm old, but this is *powerful*." Sir Thomas winced in pretend pain. "Blimey, that's strong. How are we supposed to sleep after drinking this?"

"This is actually quite a flavorful beverage," Kronos stated.

Timothy nodded his head in agreement. "I'm glad you guys like it. Again, it's not for everyone. Trust me, though, the food is even better," he said as he started biting into one of his burgers. "Anyway, Kronos, please finish the story. You left off with Mark opening the message." He dumped his individual containers of french fries into one mountainous pile.

"Correct. One of the most unfortunate parts of my life, to be honest. *Mark* opened the message. He took it the wrong way, and so there was a problem because of that. It's a perfect example of what kind of conflicts will happen when people assume things that aren't true, just as you said earlier. *Especially* when they don't know everything that's going on, or what has been going on for over a year before he was even a part of Anabelle's life."

"No kidding. He shouldn't have read it, though!" Timothy cried out in frustration and anger. "Ugh! I hate people who share their phones like that. That doesn't put your relationship on a whole other level above everyone else. It's just as much a lack of trust as it is more trusting. It gets rid of the privacy between them and their contacts. The fact that you don't know whether you're texting your friend or your friend's boyfriend, it shouldn't have to be like that! The only type of people worse than that are those who have you on speaker phone the whole time and don't tell you until the end or until you say something stupid."

"Words of wisdom, Timothy. You know what's right in life, and if I were religious, I would tell you to preach. Well, the first part of the conflict was him arguing with Annabelle and getting mad at her. He assumed that she was cheating on him with me, but that wasn't at all the case. They argued over that for some time, but he eventually believed her. Even though he believed her, however, he knew that I had feelings for her, or at least he assumed so. Suspicious and filled with a desire to eliminate me, he followed her to my castle."

Timothy gasped. "No way! Are you kidding me? He *actually* followed her to your castle, and right when a hurricane was supposed to be hitting? I can't believe it. That's going too far. I hate this guy."

"Not as much as I do, Timothy. It's all true, though. He *followed* her to my castle. In fact, rather than drive, he pulled the old trick of holding the back of a car while skateboarding. It suited him well, that trick. Dark grey clouds covered the sky above, and the wind blew dangerously as the storm approached us with an uncertainty of the future. She came in with her family, and Thomas took care of them. I was closing the main gate to the castle when I looked out at the storm in front of us. In front of me was an expansive field with a dirt road heading away from the castle. To my left, one great oak tree stood as the only plant that had been there for many, many years before I had even arrived at the castle. Behind that tree, I saw a figure step out, and I saw the face of one man. A face I had despised and seen pictures of, many times before."

Timothy grinned cockily as if he was ready to fight Mark himself, as he finished his first burger and got ready to eat his second one. The other two men had barely started theirs. "It was Mark! There's no doubt about it. Who else would have been out there? This could be a good movie flashback. I'm actually so into this."

Kronos started talking faster, his body tensing, and his veins pulsing. He tried to maintain his composure. "Correct, it was *him*. It was the enemy that I had been secretly fighting within my heart, and now, he was there to fight me for real. The battle was no longer internal, but external in a way that I had not predicted. It almost struck fear in me, but I wasn't afraid of him because I knew that he had traveled all that way, only to be disappointed. My genetically mutated bones and my rough skin alone would be more than enough to defeat him, but he did not realize how much I hated him. If I were a good man like you, Timothy, I would have gone back into the castle. Mark wouldn't have been able to get in, and he would've been forced to go home due to the hurricane. Yet, I knew that would not end it. All that would've done was postpone events that were almost inevitable."

Sir Thomas smiled a bit, glad that Kronos' feelings of hatred toward Mark and his need to verbally thrash him to other people caused him to open up to others. It had been a long time since he had heard Kronos mention any of these names. They all laughed at it now, including Kronos, but the events he was retelling had been serious problems at the time. In fact, Sir Thomas' exact words of advice to Kronos after the events that occurred, which Kronos was just about to tell Timothy, had been to go back into the castle instead of doing what he had chosen to.

Timothy was chomping down like a maniac on the second burger, his eyes filled with an anxious look of anticipation and desire to know what was going to happen next. "You shouldn't even think like that. If a conflict between a hero and a villain is bound to happen, postponing it will only allow the conflict to grow more. You did the right thing. I may be a good man, but there are times when you have to fight your enemies and make choices. There's no doubt that he would've just fought you on a different day. I assume you didn't go back in?" Timothy already knew the answer to his question, but he knew that if he asked, Kronow would answer it dramatically.

Kronos had a smug look on his face as he shook his head. "*Nope*. I walked out to that great oak tree, and I confronted the man who wished to eliminate me from Anabelle's life, even though I had been there long before him. We stood within *inches* of each other. We looked at each other in the eye, and we knew that it would not end well. It was a connection understood between us as rivals. We knew right then and there that we were enemies. Of course, there was uncertainty, because he asked me if I was Kronos."

It went silent.

Timothy almost jumped out of his seat. "Don't leave me hanging like that! What did you say?"

It was silent for a moment as Kronos set a tense mood into the air, letting the anxiety grow inside of his audience. "*Nothing*," Kronos hissed smugly with a sinister chuckle. "I said nothing and fought dirty. As soon as he asked me that, I hit him with an uppercut to the chin and neck using my right arm. My fists were like iron. He stumbled backward, and I jabbed him directly in the face with my left arm. **Pow**! It was a direct shot that broke his nose. After that, I gave him a right and a left hook. The rain began to pour with such a force that it almost seemed to be raining bullets. I couldn't believe that he was still conscious after receiving those brutal attacks. He was bigger than me, being twenty and all. Using that to his advantage, Mark pushed me to the ground, and we rolled and wrestled in the mud like swine. I got punched once or twice, but he hurt himself more than me with his attempts. Soon I was on top of him, and my fists piled onto him like jackhammers to concrete. You think you're a speedster? Well, you should've seen how fast I destroyed him. He got another hit or two in, but then I pushed him into the great oak tree, and soon he was half unconscious. I began to walk away, back to the castle, but he yelled after me. I turned around and saw that he had gotten up to charge at me. That's when everything took a turn for the worst-"

"Allow me to interject here and switch up the point of view for a moment. First, though, I have to tell you that these burgers are absolutely astounding," Sir Thomas remarked as he finished his burger. "You weren't lying, Mr. Godwin, as these really do hit the bee's knees." Timothy nodded his head with pride as if he had made the burger before digging into his pile of fries. "Anyway, it was by this time that I had grown worried, as Kronos had not returned inside yet. Annabelle asked me where he was, and I answered that I thought he was right behind her. I quickly took to the window, and when I saw them fighting,

I didn't know what to think. My only option was to go outside and intervene, but it would take me a while before I could get to them, and seeing how it was going, I knew I'd be too late. I quickly ran out there with an umbrella. I had only gotten to the gate when *it* happened."

"*It?*" Timothy smiled and was almost hyperventilating. "You guys are really making me anxious. What do you mean *it*? Something worse happened? Weapons were drawn? What happened?"

"Were weapons drawn? Perhaps the sword of God was pulled out and used, but I cannot say that for sure. I'll let Kronos tell you the rest."

Kronos quickly finished his burger, ready to tell the rest of the story as he snatched a few french fries from Timothy's pile. "I shall. To quickly recap, I was walking away from Mark, who I thought was half unconsciousness and slumped against the tree. Well, after yelling something, Mark had gotten up and seemed ready to charge at me when the storm began to take a turn for the worse. As the wind whipped, the hurricane's wrath came down from the sky on that juvenile delinquent, and lightning struck the tree. **Pow**! It burst aflame, and lightning had coursed through it, hitting Mark. His veins scarred where the electricity had flowed through him, and the side of his body that was closest to the tree had been burnt by the flames of it."

Sir Thomas and Kronos almost laughed at the shock that had completely taken over Timothy's face as he dropped a french fry and froze in place. After he managed to close his mouth, which was hanging open, he could utter nothing except the simple phrase, "Holy crap…"

"I would say exactly my thoughts, Mr. Godwin, but back then, my mind was not as filtered as it is now," Sir Thomas said with another laugh. "Being a gentleman took me a few years to achieve, and I wasn't able to maintain it forever, considering the fact that I accompany Kronos through uncleanable muck."

"Are you guys serious right now?" Timothy asked, almost shouting the question. He took a large gulp of his fizzy soda, which was artificially green, through a paper straw. "Mark actually got struck by lightning?"

"Well, technically, the tree got struck by lightning, and it's not hogwash at all, Mr. Godwin. It actually happened, and right before my very eyes. I stopped in place and had no idea what to think, for I was in more shock from watching the lightning bolt hit the tree than Mark was, and he had actually been hit by it." They all laughed, despite the severity of the situation which they were describing. "I witnessed all of this from the gate but could bear it no more. I was just glad that Kronos had not been affected by the lightning. The rain came down so fast and so hard that soon the fire was extinguished. Just like that!" Sir Thomas snapped his fingers. "The hurricane was approaching faster than we had expected, and what we had been experiencing was just the faint outer ring of the natural monstrosity."

"What about Mark, though?" Timothy asked with uncontrolled anxiousness, throwing his hands up. "Was he *dead*? Oh crap! This is awful. What a tragedy. I know that he's your enemy, and I hate the guy, but that's actually horrible. I mean, I know it wasn't your fault, but that's crazy!"

"Indeed," Sir Thomas said with a hesitant sip at his fizzy soda. "It left me gobsmacked for sure. Mark was keeled over on the ground, screaming in pain as his hands covered his face. I've never heard such screams like that in all of my life, except for when Kronos was sick just recently."

"Even my screams of pain are better than everyone else's inferior abilities," Kronos sated proudly with an evil chuckle.

"Anyway, I quickly ran over and got Kronos, who stood there, staring in shock at what had happened. Even he was speechless. Even his anger was calmed by such a freak accident."

"Correct."

"We ran back into the castle, locked the gate, and told Annabelle nothing of what had happened. Luckily, she hadn't seen any of what just occurred, as she was preoccupied."

Timothy had been laughing but now looked concerned and confused. "Woah, wait a minute now. You just left him there? You left

Mark bruised and broken, with his flesh peeling off and heart abnormally beating? That's actually awful."

"Of course, not, Mr. Godwin! I'm no wanker, and if there was any chance of saving him that I didn't take, then I would've been guilty for the rest of my life regardless of whether he survived or died. Kronos probably would have left him, but I couldn't do that. I called a hospital, and they sent an ambulance for him. Due to the weather, it took some time."

"Thank goodness! I feel so much better. I've heard plenty of tales about lightning strikes and even people getting stricken more than once, but you actually had me worried there, Sir Thomas!" Timothy devoured a handful of french fries, finishing the remainder of the pile.

"Don't be so glad just yet. Prepared to be gobsmacked and gutted, mate, for Mark was *gone* when they got there."

A single french fry fell out of Timothy's mouth as it dropped open in shock at the eerie statement. "*Gone*? What...what do you mean?" He glanced around the quiet building. "That's really creepy, man. I don't like that at all."

"Neither did I, nor did Kronos like it at all. We had no clues to where he could have wandered off to, for the powerful rain had washed away any drops of blood that would have left a trail of evidence. We sent them away, seeming like our call was rubbish. Kronos and Annabelle played some games and enjoyed each other's company as friends, while I sat and sipped tea with her parents."

"That night was rather special," Kronos stated, his face and tone unusually emotional for him. "Not in a sexual way, but what I mean to say is that she apologized to me. I suppose she realized how great of a friend I was and had been, and I guess she understood why I was upset. Well, she didn't apologize, but she told me that she could understand why I was upset, and she reassured me that Mark was a great guy and that she hoped he and I would be friends one day. Such stupidity sickens me."

Sir Thomas slowly nodded his head. "In the morning, the hurricane had shifted slightly, and the weather partially cleared by us. It seemed like the storm was over, and we had seen the last of it. After consulting with her parents and checking the weather reports, we waved her goodbye, and-"

"The last wave goodbye I would ever gesture to her," Kronos stated somberly, finishing the story.

Timothy, almost as somber as Kronos was, looked up in pity, a bitter frown on his face. He realized that while Kronos had won the battle, he had lost the war, as they often say. "Why? What happened?"

"As expected, the truth came out despite the slim chance that it might have been knocked out of existence. Thomas can fill you in on the rest of the story, which isn't much at all. That fizzy soda has sent my kidneys into overdrive, and it's about time I take a piss." Kronos left to use the bathroom, which was a short walk across the eating area, his lab coat flying up behind him viciously before slowly drifting back down.

Once Kronos, who walked slower and less confidently than usual, was out of earshot, Timothy turned toward Sir Thomas. "Truth be told, that was a simple story, and undeniably a sad one. Quite honestly, it's not too far beyond the occurrences that most of us experience growing up. I'm not sure what the whole deal was with him and Anabelle since it's hard to get the emotions and memories without all the detail, but I can tell that what happened affected him a lot more than one would think. Am I right about that, Sir Thomas?"

"Right on the money, Mr. Godwin. Blimey," Sir Thomas shook his head in sympathy, "that story gets me feeling gutted every time. Kronos was a changed man from then on. He no longer trusted people, he disliked most, and he pushed people away. He felt that if he got close to people that they would only eventually hurt him or allow others to do so. I homeschooled him from then on, although he mostly taught himself everything. He was bitter over everything, as well as heartbroken. He had truly loved that girl, although she was never his. It changed him in a way that I couldn't understand and never have. Even after decades, I still miss the young Kronos I had known before all of this. He had been a bit of an outcast before everything, but he was mine, and a good kid. High school changes people, and so does love. He had both affect him at the same time, and not for the better. Part of his problem was that he idolized her for more than she was, and he had everything relying on one person. It's important to have people you trust in life, but you need more than one, as relying on one person alone will let you down in the end."

"I understand, and honestly, I can't say that I blame him for being bitter after all of that," Timothy replied. "I think that if I ever see Mark, I'll teach him a lesson myself, but hopefully, I never have to meet him. Yet, you can't give up after just one person or incident. Life moves on, people move on, and *you* have to move on. Everything stays the same yet different, and if we ever meet The Immortalizer, I'm sure he, with all his life experience, would say the same exact thing. Kronos can't hold a grudge against everyone over the mistakes of two people." Timothy took a sip of his fizzy soda. "We aren't all the same. Look, I won't lie and say that not everyone is selfish. I think we all are, and we all also take for granted the people in our lives because we don't realize how much they do for us. Getting past that is part of not only love but also friendships, relationships, and life. I won't get all philosophical on you, but I think Kronos is wrong to allow one thing to ruin the rest of his life. *Especially* when he could be living better than anyone."

"I know Mr. Godwin, but Kronos is stubborn. He hates change, and he doesn't like to take advice from others. I tried telling him that not all was lost, but for him... it was." Sir Thomas sighed. "A day doesn't go by where I wish I had done better with him. Perhaps I could've prevented all of this. Homeschooling isn't the best, but he couldn't go back to school once Annabelle found out what happened. Besides, he had always hated school, and the only reason he could tolerate it was because of her. There was no longer a reason for him to go back."

"Now I know that's wrong for a fact! Sir Thomas, you're a great man, and what happened was inevitable. I can tell that Kronos is a good man. Although buried, I can sense it. I can see the bad in the good and the good in the bad. It's a gift that is not always smiled upon, but it has been useful in life. I hope we can help him. No man can correct himself all alone. You've done well, and I hope that I may do just as good of a job. I'm very sorry to hear all of this. That's part of the reason why I'm traveling alongside you two. Part of being a hero is helping others, and that doesn't always mean rescuing them from fires or fighting criminals. Some heroic deeds go deep into a person's personal life. I've gotten a feel for Kronos' personality, and I think that as soon as we finish this quest he started, he'll finally be satisfied."

"I hope so, for his sake as well as mine. I assure you that the story you just heard was the main factor of the bitterness that now resides in Kronos, but there are plenty of other reasons why he's unfriendly, and a good amount of those details are secret from even me."

"If only he had met someone that could've changed his mind when he was younger. Like a college sweetheart or something."

"A hopeful thought, but it never happened. The rest of his life was spent in either isolation or my company. He never went to college."

"*What*? You're telling me that the smartest person to ever exist didn't go to college?"

"Of course, he didn't go. He hates school and views the whole system as a flawed scam that could never work unless it underwent heavy reform. Plus, he believes that self-education is the most valuable skill and ability anyone could have, and it's the ultimate key to success, along with being able to use the education you give yourself. After all, he calls himself Emperor Empirical for a good reason. That name means that he relies on his own experience and observations alone. Most people think that he has more degrees than a thermometer, as some say in clever word-play, but that's not true at all. He believes that he doesn't need to sacrifice years of his life, along with spending a fortune, to earn a simple piece of paper that tells him he's considered smart by others. He knows he's a genius, and while I hate his pride, I do admire all of those ideas. Some judge such opinions, but that's unavoidable. Instead of wasting his life, he forged his own path that was untraditional, but that led him to success far greater than anyone who had done what society wanted."

"I know exactly what you mean," Timothy said bitterly with a hint of nostalgia. "Quite honestly, I talked to Kronos about this the other night for a little bit. You know, he's not the only one who made that choice. Only a rare few are brave enough to think it, and even fewer actually act on the hope of achieving such a dream. I was one of those few people. I'm sure people will discredit me since I won the lottery, but taking the chance I took is enough on its own to prove me better, and to prove that I was right and not suicidal. I assure you that I was ready to work my ass off to go beyond everyone else as I forged my own untraditional path, and investing in the lottery counts as part of the hard work I put in. I used a game of chance to succeed in the bigger game of chance I was playing with life. So, there's no need to try and defend Kronos. His choices don't surprise me, and I respect and admire them, more than anyone who takes a traditional path in life. I respect them as well, though. They're trained and taught to go to college, trade school, or the military, and I'm thankful for all of them. However, they aren't our equals at all, and they could never match the spirit we have within us. In fact," Timothy stopped short as he saw Kronos coming. He stuck out his hand for Kronos to hit it.

"Are you trying to high-five me in an attempt to congratulate me for going to the bathroom?" Kronos sneered as he sat down. "How childish and impudent! I may require two hands to hold everything to take a simple piss, but the boiling acid that leaves my bladder is not a threat at all."

"*What?*" Timothy laughed. "Not at all. What are you even talking about. It was supposed to be a reference to relay races, like passing the baton or tagging a teammate in. I have to go to the bathroom, so as you returned, I was going to have you tag me in to go. Nevermind. Just forget it. It made sense in my head. Give me like five to ten minutes. On top of all the snacks we had today, all of this carb-loading has gotten my bowels moving quite a bit."

The two men laughed at Timothy, which confused him.

"Did you say five to ten minutes?" Kronos asked with a laugh that was half playful and half condescending. "I thought you were a real-life speedster. You can't go any faster than that?"

Timothy laughed and pointed at Kronos. "Coming from the guy who took like seven minutes just to piss. I *wish* I could go faster. My life would be so much easier." Walking speedily as always, he left the two men to go use the restroom.

Kronos scooched over a bit, putting more room between him and Sir Thomas so he could turn and talk to him. "Now that you and I are finally alone, I have some questions for you, old man. As caring as you are and as much of a gentleman as you are, it turns out that even you have secrets, and I didn't think you had any," Kronos said with a disapproving shake of his head. "Why didn't you ever tell me about Laura?"

"It was kept secret for several reasons. Quite honestly, as gutted as I was, I knew that talking about it wouldn't have changed anything. There was no winning her back, and telling you about it would have served no purpose at all. All it would've done was cause you to feel guilty for no reason, and you would have constantly been blaming yourself or your parents for dying. The guilt would have been understandable, but it was my choice. You want the truth? Laura Godwin was once my fiancè, and I did throw her away for you. But, as I said, it was my choice. It wasn't up to you, and it wasn't your fault."

"Correct, yet I still feel horrible. I've caused you nothing but trouble and sorrow for all these years on top of the choice you made. Even though you'll probably thank me for it one day, it still hurts. It hurts me more than you would ever believe. You really loved her, didn't you? I saw the emotion between the two of you back in Minnesota. Sure, it was clearly tainted by time and certainly chaotic, given the surprise meeting, but there was an unspoken romance that I could sense."

Sir Thomas smiled with a cup of bitter nostalgia, a pinch of regret, and a spoonful of acceptance. "Of course, I loved her. She was absolutely wonderful. We had been together for quite a while, and we were as close as two people can ever get."

"Then why are you so okay with the fact that you let her go? Don't give me that fucking crap where you say you loved her so much that you knew letting her go would be best for her, and so that makes you happy because I hate that bullshit. It doesn't actually work like that."

"There's no need for foul language, Kronos. After all, if anyone should be unhappy and cursing, it should be me. I'm fine with it because I'm a gentleman, and that includes making hard choices. No. Scrap that, because I'd hate to lie. The truth is that I blame her, and so it's easy for me not to be angry at myself or you. We could have worked things out, but she forced me to choose between you and her. She created the choice that I had to make. It was either raise a child of our own or raise you. I argued that we could do both, as that was the truth and a possibility, but she didn't want that. You weren't hers, and you weren't mine, so she felt unobliged to care for you despite the tragic death of your parents and the fortune that we would receive upon taking you in. After that, I never saw her again. I was told that she moved over to America to find a new life, and it turns out that she did. At least Timothy is a good guy. I still don't trust him entirely, but he's not that bad."

"Should we tell Timothy about you and Laura? He could just be pretending to be oblivious, or perhaps he's being respectful, but I'm pretty sure that he doesn't know about you two."

Sir Thomas cocked his head in confusion. "Why would you even suggest that? You tend to keep a lot of secrets yourself, so it's odd that you'd want to tell him. Either way, I don't see telling him about that as doing anything for any of us except making things awkward and more complicated."

"I'm saying that it's suspicious. Thomas. Don't you find it odd that out of every single man in North America, Laura just so happens to be with The Chronological Changer? The exact man who we were hunting down? That doesn't seem suspicious in any way to you?"

"Not at all," Sir Thomas replied seriously. "You act as if someone planned that or that it's a trap by someone, and perhaps set by Timothy himself. Kronos, you're paranoid and untrusting. What you suggest is actually why I believe in God," he said with a point toward the sky.

"What do you mean?"

"Well, I'm a man of faith naturally, but it's stuff like this that reinforces my beliefs. I always love the evidential icing upon the cake of faith. A lot of times in my life, things have connected in ways that I never imagined possible. Things that seemed awful have worked out to be better than I would have expected and resulted in blessings that were double that of my troubles. I don't know why God separate her from my life, but it's possible that Laura was never meant to be with me because she was meant to be with Timothy, who then became The Chronological Changer. Without her in his life, Timothy may have never become a speedster in the first place. That alone is all I need to know to be satisfied. Secondly, we may have never created R.O.M.A.B.A. Industries if Laura had been my wife. You would've been raised in a completely different manner, and, in fact, you may have never become smart at all. Lastly, what if someone else had answered the door when we arrived at the Godwins' house? Hmm? Our meeting with Timothy may have taken a very different course."

"So, *what*? It's all part of God's master plan for us all? You're basing your religion off of what-if questions."

"That's all life is, Kronos! What if I had done this? What if I had done that rather than that? What if I do this? What if I don't do this? Life is just a bunch of what-if questions. I don't concern myself with them because I know that God has a reason behind all of them. It's about trust and recognizing that everything works out later. Isn't that what your science and theories are? What if I do this, and how will it affect that? Well, if I do this, then that will happen. The only difference is that you actually know what all of the variables are, or you can at least figure them out. In my case with God, I might never find out what the variables are, but He knows what they are and how they affect each other. I'm okay with that because not knowing the variables doesn't bother me."

Kronos took another sip of his fizzy soda. "That does put it into perspective a bit, but I don't know, Thomas. I still find it rather odd that Laura, your ex-fiancè, is married to the Minnesota Speedster that we were hunting down."

"Kronos, you need to stop looking at life as a strategic battle map or equation and start looking at it like it's a planned puzzle. All the pieces already line up, and they already serve as parts of the bigger picture."

"I prefer to think that we make our own pieces. That's part of what makes humanity the greatest species of all time."

Timothy finished using the bathroom and speedily walked over to rejoin the two men. They poked fun, breaking out in laughter at the trail of toilet paper that was stuck to Timothy's foot. He was quite embarrassed and scraped it off against the floor before sitting back down with them.

Kronos looked at Timothy as he sat down, studying the small grey hairs that were scattered across his head, out of place for his age. Then Kronos looked at Sir Thomas, who appeared healthy but seemed weary and overworked. Kronos thought about himself. After studying each of them externally and internally, he thought about the future and what he believed was going to happen.

Timothy yawned. "I'm surprised I can even yawn after drinking half of that soda. Plus, I'm definitely going to finish it." He checked the time on his Whip-Watch. "Let's get to sleep, though. We'll rest for a few hours and then start driving early in the morning. If everything goes well, we should be able to arrive before nightfall tomorrow, and we can have dinner at a real place."

Everyone agreed on this, and they toasted their fizzy sodas together. They chugged down the soda, their throats burning from its acidic composition, as they stood up from the table and left, throwing their garbage on the way out. As they walked away, the toy dragonfly-man fell over, forgotten about, and left behind.

The men all went back to the car, dreading the idea of sleeping in the vehicle. It was the dark hours of the night.

Kronos reclined his chair back as far as the car would allow it. He could not help but ponder on both the past and the future.

Sir Thomas slept in the trunk of the vehicle, which was spacious except for their luggage. He looked up at the stars through the back windshield. He thought about all that the men had talked about. There was a sincere feeling of regret in his heart about what had happened between him and Laura. The truth was that he could not help but blame himself as well. He had buried that romantic past, but seeing her had resurfaced it. He did not let the past bother him, however, nor did he fear the uncertain future. His life was complete, as he had done and accomplished most of the dreams that all people had. He had found friends, family, money, love, and on a deeper level, himself. He needed nothing more from the world. He was satisfied and doubted that the world needed or would need him for anything else now, but he would stay and help it for as long as he could.

Timothy slept across the three middle seats, a few tears leaking from his eyes. He also looked at the stars of the night sky through the window across from him, and it made him both nostalgic and sorrowful. Life had not turned out as he had expected. Whether it was for the better or for the worse, he could argue an answer for both sides. *What have I done to myself? What am I asking these men to do? Can I defeat The Dark Depressor, or will this be my final battle? More importantly, how many years of my life am I going to lose over this? Will we be able to find a cure? A hero-society. I'll make it for sure.* Timothy let out a long sigh of emotional neutrality.

Soon, the three of them, despite their complicated hearts and grand minds, could think no more. They eventually closed their eyes and embraced the darkness of sleep.

CHAPTER 8

FUTURE AND PAST DECISIONS

(Chatham, Cape Cod, Massachusetts. The Next Day: April 17, 2022)

Ava awoke to a barren bedroom, and she shivered as she slipped into an old robe that John had purchased years ago. It was far too large for her, but that was exactly how she liked her clothes, and the fact that it was John's made her like it even more.

Upon arriving in the living room, Ava was stunned, and her heart broke a bit. She had spent yesterday watching John pack everything away that she would not need once he was gone. She tried to tell him to stop, but he was intent on going, and he believed that some of the items in his house should be buried with him when he was gone. So, he went around the living room, getting rid of anything related to The Immortal Man and the legacy he would have left behind.

Ava had no choice but to watch, powerless to stop John. She had watched as he carefully removed the Japanese painting of his rescue mission from the wall and wrapped it up before packing it away in a cardboard box. She watched as he reluctantly swiped all of the puzzle pieces off of the dresser and into the blood-stained box before he winced in pain as he closed the box and taped it shut, adding it to the cardboard box with the painting. Seeing the sorrow on his face for just those two objects had been painful enough for Ava, but it got worse.

She felt as if she had been stabbed through her heart, her hope diminishing, as she had watched John viciously tear down and rip all of the papers off of the board across from the couch. The only thing he did not destroy in his haste was the picture of Kyle. Gathering the papers from the floor, he threw them into the box, burying the painting and puzzle set. Then, from his bedroom, he had grabbed a framed picture of him and Carly. Ava jealously watched as he looked at it for a while, a single tear escaping from each eye. He gently placed the picture and frame on top of the papers, and then he sealed the cardboard box shut. Carly's glowing smile almost seemed to shine through the enclosed darkness at him.

Now, the room was empty and cold except for the couch and the dresser, as John figured he would leave those for Ava, who was meant to inherit all that he had once he successfully died. Across from the couch, the board still desperately clung to the wall, but it was lifeless now. The legendary life of John Leach was now nothing more than a seemingly fictional tale that very few knew.

Entering the kitchen, Ava noticed that the falcon was gone, though its cage was still there. She made herself a cup of pine needle tea before going back to the living room and taking a seat on the couch. She wrapped herself up tightly in the large robe, sipping at the tea. She wondered where John was, hoping that he would come back happy from wherever he was, and everything could go back to regular, as he realized that life was not as bad as it had been for him so far and that it could get better. The tension over him leaving had made the place unsettling and cold for the past few days now, and she longed for the days she had first spent with John.

A few minutes later, John entered the living room through the sliding glass doors at the back of the room, wearing the same outfit he wore every day. His pet falcon was perched on his left arm. "Morning, kiddo. You're up early for a Sunday."

"Couldn't sleep," Ava said softly in a somber tone, trying her best to sound happy.

"I figured that, but you look nice, and I see you made yourself some tea. That's good."

"Went for a morning walk around the backyard?" Ava asked more enthusiastically than her reply before, trying to avoid the fact that John was leaving by acting like it was just a regular day.

"Yep. I let 'im stretch his wings for a bit while I reflected to myself about all kinds of terrible things. I even thought about setting him free, but I'm actually attached to this bird. He'll be in good hands, though, so I'm happy about that, and I'm never happy, so good job, kid." John glanced around the room and let out a long exhale of nostalgia through the mask, even though he was glad to finally be moving on. "I'm guessing you're a bit bummed-out from seeing the place like this." Ava slowly nodded her head, barely moving it. "It doesn't seem as warm and cozy as it's always been. I'll admit that. This place was one of the few things that kept me going, or at least surviving. It's been my own little bubble for a long time now, and I hate to say goodbye to her, but we must part ways. *When* I die, though, you can spruce it up however you want. Just take care of her for me, Ava."

"You mean *if* you die," Ava corrected in a quiet voice.

"Right. *If* I die," John replied half-heartedly, realizing that Ava actually believed he would be returning. They had talked about it a few times now, but John was never able to get through to her, nor was she able to get through to him. He had tried telling her not to idolize him or grow attached, but there was nothing he could do. She was determined to believe that John would return, and he knew that he could not convince her otherwise. "Sorry... kid. All that's left now is to throw this board away," he stated with a gesture to the board. "After years of it tormenting me with the papers and pictures of my past, it'll be a relief to get rid of it."

"Don't get rid of it."

"Oh... why not?" John looked over at the board. "Do you want it for some reason? It's not really practical for a teenage girl to have it."

"Pack it away with the other boxes."

"It won't fit, though, and I'd rather not have it loose and separate from the boxes. There won't be too much room where I'm storing them, and so that's why I only have a few boxes, besides the fact that I don't own many personal possessions. Thank God that I'm not a hoarder, because, after over a hundred years of collecting junk, this place would've been unliveable and so disgusting."

"So break it, then."

"What?"

"Break the board into pieces and pack it away in a box. That way, when you return as a normal human without the suit and mask, we can put it back together and hang it up. You'll start keeping track of the memories and dates of your new life on the new board made from the broken pieces of the past."

John sighed. He quickly put the falcon away in the kitchen before sitting next to Ava on the couch. He waited a moment as he tried to think of the best way to confront her. "Ava... I know how upsetting all of this is, and I'm glad that you have hope, but I thought we talked about this? You *have* to move on. I saved you, and that's what's important, right? I can't be with you any longer because I have to move on in life. My whole purpose in life has been to find death, as ironic as that sounds. Depression and suicidal thoughts are powerful forces of corruption, and they've been growing inside of me for decades. My isolation and traumatic memories only fuel them, and I told you that they're not gone. For the past few days, you've been seeing me at my best, because I'm trying to put on a strong persona for you. Usually, I mope about, cry, whine, complain, or sleep. I'm trying to stay strong for you, but I need to do what's best for me. At least understand that the most important part of meeting me was being rescued and set free from your old life of pain and that living with me was just a bonus feature. Our lives were meant to intersect, not connect."

"I... understand," Ava whispered, so softly that it was almost inaudible. She did not have the strength to look at John, and her gaze was focused on the remaining tea in the cup she held. "Where are you going today, though?"

"Well… guess I can't hide anything from you, kid. Although, I'm surprised you knew I had plans for today. Then again, I usually have no plans at all, so it's easy to tell when I'm actually going to do something. Right now, I'm debating between heading to Florida or England. Based on what I know, R.O.M.A.B.A. Industries has its largest building in England, and that's their main operation of business. Most likely, Kronos would be there, and I need him specifically, but I have a feeling he's heading to Florida first to investigate a man called *The Sinful Son*. Well, I guess they could be a woman, but witnesses stated that they believe it was a man."

"*The Sinful Son*? That sounds pretty serious, but I haven't seen the news lately. What are you talking about?"

"Remember how the news had nicknamed a guy, who was stirring up some trouble, Florida Phantom? We talked about it a bit the other day."

"I remember. I know who you're talking about."

"Basically, he attacked a rich-people's brunch and made a big scene in Homestead, Florida, announcing that he's *The Sinful Son*. Given the evidence I have and the theories I've crafted, it's highly likely that Kronos is going there next to check it out. Again, I don't know what his motives are, but there's no doubt that he's interested in *The Sinful Son* since he investigated me, Birch Willow, and probably the speedster in Minnesota. Either way, I have no quick and easy way to get to Florida or England if I did pick a destination. So today, I'm going to meet someone who can help me get to where I need to be."

"Oh, right. You can't go on planes since you have the mask and no medical proof regarding why you have or need it. At least you could drive to Florida, but he'd probably be gone by then. So, I'm guessing this person you're meeting owns a private plane that you're hoping to use?"

"Yes and no. It's complicated. Her name is Morgan, and she's the granddaughter of Kyle, the doctor who had been my only friend."

"I thought he was a bachelor for life," Ava stated, shocked at the revelation. "He had a family? Why didn't you ever mention this?"

"Kyle's wife died young while giving birth, but they had one son who married an immigrant from Puerto Rico. They then gave birth to one child, and that's Morgan. She had been a charming girl when she was young, but I haven't seen her in years. Now people fear her blunt and insincere personality. They say she's vicious and unfriendly, but no one knows why. Of course, those are just the rumors that I've heard around town, and I have no proof. After Kyle's death, I stopped visiting the family. His wife and son were nice people, but it was too painful for me, and I couldn't be a part of his son's life any longer. I need a favor now, though, so I have no choice but to visit her. Life tends to work that way."

Ava hesitated a moment. She turned and looked at John, who was pondering deeply about something. "Do... do you want me to go with you?"

"No, but thank you." John stood up. *Sorry, kid, but I can't trust ya anymore. You care about me, and you'll try to convince her to stop me someway or another. For all I know, you're going to try and find her later today to talk to her behind my back.* John slowly headed toward the front door. "Unfortunately, this is a part of my past that I'll have to face alone. I cut myself away from the family tree that Kyle was a part of and helped create, and returning to it will be frowned upon, to say the least. She might be overjoyed to see me and understand the choice I made, but I have a feeling it won't go that way. I owe her and her family an apology, though I did nothing wrong, and it'll be hard convincing her to let me fly over to England. Take care of the place for me. I'll be back in less than two hours."

Ava bitterly attempted a smile as she waved him goodbye, but John's back was turned, and he was gone in an instant.

Morgan lived alone in a small bungalow across town from John, and it was just as secluded as his own home was. He slowly drove over there, trying to figure out how the meeting would go. As he arrived, he decided that there was no point in being prepared, and he would just have to go with whatever happened. He parked halfway up the driveway, which was made out of crushed-up shells. Getting out of the car, he looked around.

John's arrival had stirred awake a Golden Retriever that was tied up to a flag pole in the front yard. The dog lunged forward as far as its leash would allow, barking defensively at the intruder. John walked over to the dog and glared it down with an inhuman look in his dark eyes. The dog stopped barking at once, backing up a few steps. John took a powerful step forward, an ominous aura exuding out of every microscopic pore of the suit as he towered over the dog, who then went into a submissive position and whimpered in fear. Somehow, the dog could tell he was an ancient being, and it was intimidated by the face covered by the black handkerchief, and the sullen eyes that were just above it.

John walked up to the house with a resolute stride, and after a moment's hesitation, he rang the doorbell. He stood waiting, unsure of what to expect. He had never actually met Morgan, and she had never met John. She never even knew Kyle or her grandmother, as they had died before she was born. Morgan's father was nowhere to be found, and her mother worked two jobs, so she rarely saw her own mother either, who should have been retired by now. It was a complicated family, and John did not want to enter into their lives again, but he needed the favor. Worst of all, John feared that they had always blamed him for Kyle's death.

John, always alert though never fearful, caught a glimpse of a person to his left, subtly peering at him through the window blinds before they disappeared.

After a moment and some noise inside the house, Morgan opened the door with a shotgun in her hands. "Who are you, and what do you want? This is private property, and no one ever comes around here. So, for you to show up here wearing the handkerchief for no reason, it's really suspicious, and I tend to shoot first."

Nodding his head, John walked straight up to Morgan, placing his chest against the end of the shotgun barrels. "Then go ahead and shoot me, but I assure you that it won't do anything against a man such as myself," John said as he pulled the handkerchief down to his neck, revealing the mask. "I mean you no trouble, and I come here in peace."

Morgan gulped, turning pale and stumbling backward a step, her arms shaking. "No. It ca-ca-can't be true. You're... y-y-you're the immortal man that my grandfather knew!" She fired the shotgun out of fear.

As soon as he heard the noise of the gun, John flexed his chest for extra protection. The shells hit his chest with robust power, but they fell to the floor, dented. John looked down at his grey shirt, which was now ruined. "That's the *second* grey shirt to be ruined by a gun in just one week," John muttered to himself. "At least you didn't ruin the leather jacket. That would've pissed me off." He shook his head and sighed. "Was that really necessary, Morgan? If you were wrong about who I was, you would have just killed a man for no reason. Telling the judge in court that you killed a man because you mistook him for an immortal man wouldn't go over well for you."

"You know my name? You're actually *real*? I never believed the tales to be true. I've only ever heard a few stories and seen pictures, but I thought it was all fabricated. This can't be happening!"

"Well, surprise then," John replied. "Do you mind if I come in? I'd like to talk to you for a bit."

"I... I guess." Morgan gestured to the living room, and he walked in as she scanned her yard suspiciously before closing the door.

John sat on a couch and watched as Morgan put the shotgun back into a bucket of umbrellas. She walked into the living room and sat on a white couch across from him. He looked over at the wall behind Morgan. There was an old picture of John and Kyle on a fishing boat. He remembered that day, which had been decades ago. It had been a fun time that fishing trip. John shook his head loose of the memory, as he knew he had to stay focused, and he turned his attention back to Morgan. "I'm sorry to disturb you on such short notice, but some things have come up that I need to take care of."

Morgan sighed in frustration. She was a woman who preferred not to be disturbed. "What kind of things, and why am *I* involved? My life has never been connected to yours, as far as I'm concerned, and I don't want to be dragged into some ancient problem or modern mess."

"Unfortunately, problems like this bring back old connections, so you're connected even though this is our first time meeting. I'm afraid that they're supernatural things, in a way, and I'm involved. Trust me, I'd rather live my quiet life of mental agony, but this is actually important. They're not werewolves or fairies, but something is happening across the country if not the whole world, involving several humanoid figures who are of great concern." John noticed Morgan was tapping her one leg up and down rapidly, and her opposite hand seemed to be shaking. *Is she holding back from attacking me, or is she scared of me? I'll have to be cautious with her. The rumors I've heard are quite disturbing and mysterious.* John adjusted himself on the couch. "Anyway, I'll get to the point. Have you ever heard of R.O.M.A.B.A. Industries?"

"Of course, I have," Morgan replied aggressively as if John had questioned her intelligence. "They basically rule the world economically, and we're all lucky that the company is on our side and run by peaceful people who understand the world and how it should function. They're the company that made my Automatic Pet Watcher."

"What's that?"

"What do you think it is?" Morgan asked rhetorically as she threw her hands up, annoyed.

"There's no need for such aggression. I apologize, but regarding this situation, every detail must be accounted for that has to do with that company and the man I'm searching for, so it may be self-explanatory, but I still require an explanation."

Morgan rolled her eyes and exhaled a gust of hot air through her nostrils. "It's a machine that's controlled by an app on my phone. I use the app to tell the machine to pour water or food into bowls for my dog when I'm not around. It works out since I'm away from home a lot, and I'm sure a lot of people use it since it's user-friendly and efficient. I can also set a specific time or times for the machine to automatically fill the bowls in case I'm too busy or forgetful. What does R.O.M.A.B.A. Industries have to do with this, though?"

"I know that it seems unrelated to me, but I assure you that everything is connected. There was a man named Kronos, who I believe works for R.O.M.A.B.A. Industries, going from house to house asking about me. I'm unsure what his motives were, but he was investigating me, and that's a concern. In fact, it's likely that he's investigating these other humanoids that I mentioned earlier. Steven, who is a local acquaintance of mine, watched Kronos teleport away with some sort of advanced technology. He let me know about it right away, and I've been doing some research since then."

"John, are you *kidding* me?" Morgan asked violently. "You came to me after never being a part of my life just because some dude saw a guy teleport? I know R.O.M.A.B.A. Industries is pretty advanced. I saw their store in person when I was stationed in England once, and it blew my mind, but *teleportation*? Are you for *real*?" Morgan thought for a moment. "However, I did just shoot you in the chest, and I've been told that you're immortal and old, so I'll be a bit more lenient with my beliefs on what is possible and impossible. Even if what you're saying is true, there's still the question you haven't answered, which is *why* you're here. Why am *I* involved with any of this?" Her eyes were getting more towards a glare, and her face was growing tenser with impatience. "I'll be blunt: I don't want to be involved. I like my life just as it is."

"I understand all of that, and I don't mean to ruin your life or anything. Quite honestly, you're not involved that much. You won't get in trouble, nothing will change, and after tomorrow, your life will go back to the way it was. I'm not asking you to tag along as my sidekick and fight crime. Cape Cod Crusader is a name that is long gone. But, I *have* to get to England to investigate these matters, and I need to get their *fast*. A normal airline company won't let me on-"

"*Noooo!*" Morgan yelled as she abruptly stood off of the couch, throwing her arms out to each side. "You haven't visited our family for *years*. Ever since my grandfather died, you stopped talking to us. When my father disappeared, and my mother needed help, you weren't there for us. Now, you're just gonna show up here and ask me for *favors*? Not a chance at all."

"I know. It's not right for me to just show up here after all those years of silence that haunted you. There's a reason for my actions, and that's the fact that my best friend, your grandfather Kyle, *died* right in front of me. I was right there! No one from your family knows the truth about what happened that day, or the guilt I carry with me. Even though it wasn't my fault, I've blamed myself for his death for a *long* time, and I figured you did too. I have the jacket of the man who killed him! Life isn't peachy, okay? Do you have any idea how old I am? Do you know how many horrible things I've seen? I fought in both World Wars! Vietnam! I've watched as men and women have destroyed themselves, as the world has changed, as technology has become more dangerous, and much, much more. Didn't you see the news? That attack on Charleston has to be Kronos. Molecular-deconstructive weaponry explains what happened perfectly. It has to be him. The world is heading for a major change, and from what I know about these humanoid figures, it's going to be absolute chaos. Please, Morgan. I need your help."

"Need my help with *what*? Saving the world from mankind and then humans from themselves? What are you going to do to help us? Lead us into the light of God with your countless years of wisdom?"

"I told you that Cape Cod Crusader is no more. That's not what I need you for. I couldn't care *less* about the world or where it's heading. I may be indestructible on the outside, but I'm certainly not on the inside. The world has done nothing for me, so why should I help it? I'm here for myself! That man is the only one capable of killing me, and that's what I've spent decades searching for. All I'm asking you to do is get me to England, so I can find him. I would drop everything to help Kyle, and as his descendant, it's only fair that you do the same for me."

"I don't owe you *anything*! I could lose everything over what you're asking me to do, and it's all for a *stupid* reason. You're selfish, but it figures you would be since most people who gain immortality in movies are. After all, greed is what drove them to get immortality. Now, you regret getting it? That's not my problem at all. Kyle may have been your friend, but I'm *not*! You mean *nothing* to me, and you never will." There was a slight flicker of regret and disappointment in herself when Morgan said that, but it was gone in an instant. "Now get out of here! I don't want to see you again," she said with a violent gesture to the front door.

"Look, you need to *calm* down. I heard rumors that you were an angry bitch, and it shames me to think that they're true. Finding Kronos is more important than you think, and there's a lot going on, and that has happened that you don't know about. So, please, let me explain everything. All I'm asking for is a one-way trip to England, and you're a fighter pilot for a military organization, from what I've heard. I know you have the resources to get me to England, and I'll even compensate you if necessary. I'm sorry for abandoning the descendants of Kyle, but being a part of your life wouldn't have changed anything, Morgan. In fact, I probably would've only made things worse."

"That's the one thing we agree upon, so stick to that and get out of here before I get you in trouble."

John got up from the couch and looked at Morgan, his dark eyes cold and lifeless. "Get me in trouble? You wouldn't dare threaten me, would you? Because that would be extremely foolish and suicidal on your part, as well as a death sentence to anyone who would try to stop me. I can easily get to England if I really wanted to, but I'd rather not have any blood spilled for my own cause. I only spill blood for others or during wars when I'm bored. Please, it's a simple favor."

"My answer is still no, and I'm not going to change my mind. You can't guilt me into helping you. I don't owe you anything, and whatever you do from here… whoever you kill or whatever you destroy, well, that's not my fault. That's on *you*. Now leave me in peace," Morgan demanded as she walked over to the front door and opened it.

John looked at the fishing picture. *She's right. I've failed you and your descendants, Kyle. Turns out that I'm an even worse friend than I thought. Then again, I never really had any friends except for you. She's not that much of a bitch, and it's my fault she turned out this way. In a way, she reminds me of Ava. I had the chance to be Morgan's father-figure, but I didn't take it, and now I'm turning down that chance with Ava. Sorry, Kyle. Still, it's about time I die, right? I'll leave her alone regarding this, as I do respect and care for her since she is your granddaughter.* Turning away from the picture, John reluctantly exited the house. Morgan slammed the door shut as he walked back to his car. The dog had been running freely on its leash, but it began to whimper again as John passed it. He kicked at her driveway of crushed-up seashells before speeding off, realizing that he could not achieve his death peacefully. Now, it was time for the world to see the other side of The Immortal Man and what he was capable of.

CHAPTER 9

THE DARK FUTURE AHEAD

(Traveling Across North America. Later That Same Day: April 17, 2022)

The morning had been passed by with conversations, the radio, and a few car-games, but by noon, Sir Thomas, Kronos, and Timothy just sat in silence, seeming more dead than alive. They drove all day, Kronos behind the wheel, and breaking as many laws as he could. When the men finally arrived in Florida, they were exhausted from the long ride. Their legs were still stiff and sore, and their backs ached with pain. Their eyes were half-closed, and they were all sleep-deprived.

Halfway through Florida, Kronos pulled the car over. "Alright, gentlemen, we're almost at Homestead now. It's been a terrible journey, especially for me, since I hate wasting time like this, but I *have* enjoyed being the king of the road compared to all of these other lame drivers. Obviously, the road is mine anytime I drive since I'm **King Kronos**, but these past two days were special. Before we go any further, I think we should plan out what we're going to do, and I figured we better do so now since it would be risky to do so at Timothy's mom's house. It's been fun and games up until now, but this is where things are going to get serious and dangerous."

"Thank you, Kronos," Timothy said with a nod of his head. "Now, you guys don't know all of the details, and you probably won't, but I want to explain the situation before we head in. After all, it wouldn't be fair not to. It won't affect you two that much, and my mom said we're all welcome to stay for a bit, but, it's important that you guys know that I still hate my mom, and she most likely hates me despite the fact that she denies it. I won the lottery, and while that provided me with the safe and stable future she 'wanted' me to have, it's only fueled her disapproval of me. She believes I merely got lucky, but she doesn't know or understand anything about me at all. Anyway, it's been years since we had our last argument because we've 'moved' on in life. Maybe she has forgiven me for whatever she believes I did wrong or for being born, but I haven't forgiven her and never will. So, I can act all friendly just because she's my mother and we're supposed to love each other, but-"

"I assure you that we understand, Mr. Godwin," Sir Thomas interrupted. He remembered everything that Laura had told him about Timothy and his past. "There's no need to go into detail, and we won't judge or inquire about it, as it's your personal life and whatever happened between your mother and you is your business alone. Either way, we'll be generous to her and thankful for her hospitality. I assume that she doesn't know about your heroic actions?"

Timothy shook his head. "Nope. Not yet, and maybe not ever. I don't know when or if I'll tell her, but she doesn't need to know right now, and I'd appreciate it if no one said anything about any of this or our mission to find The Dark Depressor."

"Correct. I pulled over for that very reason, Timothy. So, enough about your mommy-problems. We need a thorough plan for tomorrow. Today isn't a good option. I understand that there's a greater chance of encountering The Dark Depressor at night, but I think we can all agree that we're exhausted. After all, objects at rest tend to stay at rest, and we've been stuck in this care for the past two days, or at least yesterday and most of today. We'll rest up tonight, and then first thing tomorrow morning, after breakfast, we'll go out and begin our mission."

"I suppose we can't fight crime on an empty stomach, but make sure that you two don't eat too much and get cramps. That could be the difference between life and death. Unlike you two, my metabolism is through the roof, and my powers burn and require a lot of carbs and such," Timothy pointed out.

"Ah, now calm yourself, Mr. Godwin. It would seem that you're getting anxious and worried about confronting The Dark Depressor. We'll be fine. Kronos already fought The Ruthless Root, and we all know he was holding back. While I haven't had my fair share of fighting a rival scientist, I assure you that I can handle myself. This is your grand debut, and you don't want to mess it up. We all know that because we know how much your dream of creating a hero-society means to you. So, rest assured that we've got your back, Mr. Godwin."

Timothy nodded his head, smiling bitterly. "I'm aware of that, and I'm really thankful for your help. It means a lot." He was still shaking with anxiety, however.

"Correct, and it should. Any person is thankful just for being able to breathe the same air as me, so you should be eternally grateful for my assistance," Kronos stated. "However, there *is* one variable that has not been accounted for, Timothy. It's something that's been bothering me a bit. Your mother is unaware of your actions as a vigilante or your powers, and Thomas and I won't say a word about it, but she might not need our help in discovering your secret."

Sir Thomas nodded his head. "Kronos, I believe you're thinking about the same thing I just was, and it's definitely a concern."

"Wait, what are you guys talking about?" Timothy quickly glanced around and then hunched over more in his seat, lowering his voice to just above a whisper. "Is there something giving away my hero-identity?"

"Not necessarily, Mr. Godwin. You're completely safe from the public. It's something that only someone close to you would be able to pick up on and make the indirect connection to your powers. While you may not be close to your mother, she's actually more likely to notice than anyone. Of course, to be able to guess the side effects of your speedster powers would require great intelligence, but she'll definitely be suspicious that something rather fishy is going on and perhaps that it's unnatural. Of course, she might assume that it has to do with something entirely separate from your scientific breakthroughs, but I can't say for sure."

"Stop *dragging* it out," Timothy cried out in anxiety. "What are you guys talking about? You're really worrying me."

"Your *age*, Mr. Godwin! Surely, your mother will be suspicious and shocked when she sees you, as your appearance has altered quite a bit, has it not? As a result of speeding up your body's natural processes and nervous system, along with your heart when necessary, you've advanced in age at a rate faster than normal. I mean, you have a few specks of grey throughout your hair, and you're only supposed to be thirty or so, from what I understand. Now, you look like you're approaching forty or older. There's no doubt that she'll suspect something. Perhaps, she'll assume it's some regular disease or cancer, but there's a chance that she'll make a connection between you and the speedster of your *hometown*. A mother's natural instincts and intuition can go further than you think."

"I did have one neighbor tell me that I looked unwell, and they asked if everything was alright. As far as my mom goes, though, I'm not entirely sure. Last time I saw her, she made no comment regarding my appearance or the age I seem to physically be, but it wasn't as bad as it is now. It's been a few weeks or months, or however long it's been, since I last saw her, so it might seem natural for me to look older. Either way, just don't bring it up or anything that might make her double-guess my age. If she says something, I'll improv an excuse or tell her that she's just getting old, and I'll make sure that she's not suspicious."

"Again, as Thomas said before, it's your personal business, and we won't get involved. However, I *will* warn you that if anything serious happens with The Dark Depressor during our confrontation, there's a high probability that she'll find out about your powers and your hero-identity," Kronos pointed out. "Even if it goes successfully, she'll find out one day. I understand that you hate your mother, but whether she loves you or hates you, she'll disapprove of your actions. Any parent or guardian would, as you're doing something extremely risky, both legally and physically. So, understand that you cannot avoid talking to her about it, and the fact that you're traveling around with two older gentlemen will certainly arouse suspicion as well, though it might be a different kind of suspicion. That's all."

Timothy sat straight up. "I know. The truth always escapes, even if it's just on the last dying breath of a person who can't speak. Now," Timothy got out of the car and opened the driver's door, switching places with Kronos, "it's time that we finally got to where we need to be. I can drive us from here. Off to my mom's house!"

After Timothy drove for the rest of the way, the three travelers arrived at his mother's house. It was a small house that was illuminated by only a downstairs light, the rest of the house dark and lifeless. When they pulled into the driveway, a motion light turned on, alerting Timothy's mother that the three men were here. She looked through a front window before opening the door. She stood in the doorway, waiting for the men to come over.

"I *hate* this already," Timothy grumbled as he got out of the car.

For the first time since they had entered the state, Sir Thomas stepped out of the car into the humid Florida air. He took a deep breath and coughed a bit. "Blimey, Mr. Godwin! The air quality here is absolutely atrocious!" They all laughed, just happy to be breathing air outside of the vehicle. "I'm afraid Kronos and I have never been in such a climate as this, and for a good reason. At least I haven't. No one knows where Kronos has or hasn't gone." Sir Thomas took a deeper breath. "My God, I honestly don't know how anyone could live here."

"With the air conditioning on, Sir Thomas," Timothy replied with a laugh and smile. "Trust me, you'll get used to it soon enough. Until then, let's get in. I hate the air here just as much as you do since it's not the best for running."

"What inferior respiratory system you all have. Air is air, and your body should adapt and process it no matter what. Although, it does make my lab coat and black pants seem out of place. At least I'm not wearing a suit like Thomas."

"You two do stand out like a sore thumb, but it shouldn't be a problem. Now, follow me," Timothy said as he led the way to the house, the two men following him up the porch. He did not hug or kiss his mother, but he simply followed her into the house and then gestured for Kronos and Sir Thomas to enter after him.

Sir Thomas gently closed the door behind him and locked it for the night. He allowed the cooling air of the house to flow over him. "Ah, much better! This cold air hits the bee's knees as I like to say." He turned toward Timothy's mother. "Ms. Godwin, I am Sir Thomas of England. It's a pleasure, and I thank you for your hospitality as well as allowing us to stay with you." He grabbed her hand and softly kissed the top of it before bowing halfway with one arm.

Shocked by Sir Thomas' formality, Ms. Godwin was flustered and even blushed a bit. "Well, the pleasure is mine, and please, there's no need for the etiquette. I appreciate the proper manners, but you can just call me Stella."

"As you wish," Sir Thomas replied.

Stella smiled before she turned toward Kronos. "That aside, then I assume you must be Kronos?"

"The one and only," Kronos replied half-coldly.

"You've all had a long ride. Would any of you care for something to eat or drink?"

"Not to be a stereotypical British man, but I'll have some tea if you have any," Sir Thomas answered. "Preferably, the kind to help me sleep at night." He removed his expensive shoes at the doorway and then walked over to the open doorway of the living room, which was right across from the front door. "Is this room fine for us to relax a moment?"

"Now I know why Timothy referred to you as Sir Thomas over the phone. Such a gentleman. If only everyone were like you. That room is fine, and feel free to make yourself at home." Stella turned to Kronos. "What about you? Anything to eat or drink?"

"Thank you for the offer, but I don't require anything," Kronos answered as he walked into the living room and sat next to Sir Thomas on a sofa.

"Water is fine for me," Timothy said before sitting on the couch next to Kronos. He watched as Stella left for the kitchen, which was on the other side of the house. "As much as I hate it here, it is nice to be sitting on something soft instead of a car seat." He turned to face Kronos. "I know that I hate my mom, but that doesn't mean that you have to. You can be nicer to her."

"Incorrect. The enemy of my friend is also my enemy, especially when that woman is one who does not appreciate creativity. I don't like her, Timothy, and there's no changing my mind. She may be the host of our visit, but I don't plan on being here for long. After tonight and then tomorrow morning, I'm hoping to be gone from this place. I'm not here to bond with your family or listen to your tales of woe. The cold truth is that I'm here to fight The Dark Depressor on behalf of our deal in exchange for your help later on when we encounter The Immortalizer and The Ruthless Root. Don't mistake this with a vacation, Timothy."

"In my opinion, she seems friendly enough to us," Sir Thomas remarked. "Of course, I can't speak for her relationship with you or how she treated you in the past, Mr. Godwin, but I'll be respectful and kind. It's only fair. I hope you understand." Stella walked into the room with a water bottle and a warm cup of tea. "You seem pretty handy with those drinks, Ms. Godwin. Were you ever a waitress, by any chance?"

"Why, thank you, Sir Thomas, and I told you to call me Stella. I was a waitress for fifteen years, actually. I'm surprised that you noticed because I didn't think it was noticeable. I guess after so many years of working in the service industry, you just naturally treat home like the restaurant."

"It's probably just noticeable to me," Sir Thomas said. "You see, when we first got our two servants at our castle, I had to train them a little bit. They were rather skilled and attentive, but I had to adjust them to our style of living, and I'm a stickler for specific etiquette since I try to be a gentleman and I was a server myself at one point, so I taught them a thing or two about delivering drinks and food. So, I happen to have an eye for that sort of stuff."

"Oh, how wonderful! Timothy mentioned that you work for a big company and that you're all working together on a project?"

"Correct," Kronos answered. "Not just any company, actually. We happen to be the owners and founders of R.O.M.A.B.A. Industries, the number one company in the world."

"Well, shit!" Stella put a hand to her mouth. "Pardon my language, but you're the owners and founders of R.O.M.A.B.A. Industries? That's incredible! That company is *huge*, which explains why you have a castle and servants. Holy crap! I would've tidied up the house a lot more if I knew I was going to have such high-ranking people here. What *are* you doing here? What could you possibly want from my son? I mean, he's a wonderful kid, but your company is top-notch, and he has no education except for a high school diploma."

"What does that matter?" Kronos barked. Stella flinched and was taken aback by the response. Timothy was shocked at first, but he smiled as he realized that Kronos was going to defend him. Sir Thomas sighed internally. "Your son, regardless of his choice to continue his education or not, is a brilliant genius, and he's now an official member of our board of all company affairs, making him one of the most powerful and influential people in the world as of right now. Using the money he won from the lottery, Timothy chose a life of work over relaxation, and he used the funds to help his research about human biology and anatomy, and it's tremendous work. That's why he's now a part of our team. He's one of very few people to ever catch my eye."

Stella gulped. "Oh, um… I… I didn't know about any of that." She quickly turned to Timothy, a harsher expression on her face. "Why didn't you tell me you were a big-shot board member or that you were doing all of this scientific research? You're embarrassing me!"

"Don't be angry at him," Kronos commanded. "*No one* knew about his private research, and it was by fate or coincidence that Thomas and I found out about it. See, Thomas is an old friend of Laura Godwin, who happens to be Timothy's wife. Well, Laura's friend needed to purchase an Automatic Pet Watcher since her new job has her traveling a lot. It's one of our most popular items, though its simplicity satisfies me. Anyway, Laura contacted Thomas asking if he could deliver it himself so that he could also visit her while he was here, and she also wanted us to meet Timothy, as she figured we'd get along with him. Then, we met him and started talking about science and technology, and we began working together on a few projects. We always work a lot, especially me, but lately, it's been extra taxing, so Timothy suggested we go to Florida for a break that would allow him to see his mother and allow us to relax. His work has been kept a secret on purpose."

"Oh, my! Well, I suppose that is fate, then. What are the chances of all of that? It's such a small world! Well, I'm sure you all deserve a break, and I'm glad to know that everything is going well. Why didn't you take a plane, though? It's such a long drive from Minnesota."

"Well, quite simply, and unfortunately, Kronos here is afraid of heights and flying, for some reason," Sir Thomas lied, poking fun at Kronos, who had a vein bulge on his forehead as he tried not to blow their cover. Timothy could not help but laugh.

"That's not a laughing matter, Timothy," Stella scolded, assuming that he was laughing at Kronos for being afraid of heights and flying, when, in actuality, he was laughing because he knew that Kronos hated the lie. "The fears of other people may seem bizarre to us, but that doesn't give us a right to make fun of them or laugh at such fears. Some fears may be irrational, but that doesn't take away from how much they can affect a person." She turned to face Kronos. "I suffer from arachnophobia if it makes you feel better. Then again, almost everyone does."

"Thank you for correcting your son, Stella. I really appreciate that," Kronos said mischievously with a smirk at Timothy. "It's quite a grueling backstory, actually. See, I slipped from my mother's hands as a young child and fell from a great height, which is why I'm afraid of heights and flying. The fall broke twelve bones in my body! It's rude of him to laugh at it, as I did receive quite the concussion from that fall besides the broken bones. For a long time, being in high places scared me, and then, during a confrontation with some bullies at school while on a field trip, I got pushed off of the side of a mountain, receiving more injuries from falling."

"That's terrible! I'm so sorry to hear that," Stell said, sympathizing with Kronos as she shook her head at Timothy, shaming him.

"It's tragic, and not a day goes by where I wish I could climb great heights without my knees trembling and my heart racing. There's nothing I can do about it, though, as it's a permanent biological instinct formed from memory. At least, now Timothy knows to never laugh at people's fears again," Kronos said, heartily laughing on the inside at Timothy, the tables now turned.

"Well, we all live and learn." Stella looked over at a clock that was hung up on the wall. "Oh my, look at the time. It's getting late, and you all had a long ride here. I'll show you to the rooms we have available, but you'll have to sleep on the couch, Timmy."

"Mom, you know I hate it when you call me that. Everyone calls me by my full name, and that's how I like it. Also, we're going to stay and hang out here for a bit if you don't mind. We have some work to finish up real quick before we can start relaxing."

"Alright," Stella replied. "Anyway, if you two gentlemen need anything, just let me know. I'll be in the other room."

Once Stella was gone, Timothy turned to Kronos. "I guess we ended up just about even during that verbal battle," he said with a laugh. His face grew hard with determination and focus. "But like you said, it's no longer fun and games now. We don't know when The Dark Depressor will show up, and sitting around and waiting until he does isn't a good option. It could take forever."

"Correct. You have an idea?"

"It's a bit of a long-shot, but it'll increase our chances of actually encountering The Dark Depressor by giving him a reason to attack. There's a social media fan page dedicated to my hero-identity. I'm not sure who made it or why, but I want you to anonymously tip them that Minnesota Speedster is going to be in Homestead, Florida, on a heroic mission to fight **The Sinful Son** and end his criminal activities, while also drastically increasing their publicity. Since we don't know his motives, finding him will be hard, but by challenging him like this, it'll give him a reason to come fight us."

Kronos thought it over. "I suppose that's an option. We might as well try it. I'll have it done right before I go to bed, which is now. It's been a long journey, so let's all get some rest, couch-boy. Then, we'll wake up early and fight The Dark Depressor."

CHAPTER 10

DEPARTURE: CAPE COD KILLER

(Chatham, Cape Cod, Massachusetts. The Next Day: April 18, 2020)

Ava woke up early, and while she was getting ready for school, she heard John moving around the house a lot more than usual. She left the bathroom in a midnight-blue tank-top and walked into the living room, already upset, sensing that something was not right. After coming home from Morgan's yesterday, John had not been the same. He had sat on the couch in silence and solitude for a long time, and now that he was active again, Ava was worried that it was not for the right reasons.

John, a lifeless expression on his pale face and lurking in his dark eyes, was walking over to the kitchen, and he stopped when he saw Ava enter the living room, a worried look on her face. "Oh, morning, kid. Why do you look so sad? Shouldn't you be getting ready for school?"

"You're going somewhere again, aren't you?"

Sighing, John slowly nodded his head. "Yep." He paused a moment as he studied the emotions in Ava's face, none of which were positive. "I'm going over to Morgan's place, and then I'm heading to England."

"I thought it didn't work out? You said that you and her argued, and that-"

"All of that is true, Ava, but I'm going to talk to her again. She works at some kind of private military branch, and there's a protected and secluded station for it just a few miles away from here. She'll be heading there for work today because I'm pretty sure today was her last day of leave. She's shipping out somewhere, but I'm not sure where. I stopped by Carol's restaurant and talked to her. Morgan was there just a few days ago and told Carol that she was leaving soon, and that day happens to be today. I think, at least. What's today's date? To me, there is only today, tomorrow, and yesterday, so dates don't really mean anything, but I want to confirm that today is the right day."

"Today is April eighteenth."

John froze in place, not even his fingers moving, and his chest did not rise with a single breath. His eyes seemed to receive no light from the world.

Concerned, Ava quickly rushed over to John, stopping just a foot away from him. "What's wrong, John? You're frozen in place like you've seen a ghost or something." She thought for a moment. "The date! Is that what did it?"

John nodded his head very slowly as he closed his eyes for a moment that lingered longer than a blink. "Today," he whispered, "is the anniversary of Kyle's death. It's been over half of a century, now, I think. I lost count, which is a disgrace to him, but you can't blame me for that. All the days of my life blend together into nothing but a single day of eternity."

"Oh... well, sorry... John. I know how upsetting those memories are to you, so hearing that date must have made you feel so awful, and-" Ava suddenly looked up. "Wait! Doesn't that also mean-"

"Yes. I know what you're going to say, and it's correct. Today is also my birthday. I'm officially twenty-two years older than an entire century, although only appearing to be in my thirties or forties. That's impressive, but... it's not what *I* want. No offense to everyone who doesn't make it to their next birthday."

Ava hesitated a moment. John remained quiet, and he was staring beyond her into the past. She brought her feet closer to each other. "If you don't want to, and we don't have to, but maybe you could celebrate it this year now that you're not alone anymore."

"You're mistaken, Ava. I'm always alone, and always will be. Still, I'm thankful for the offer, and I appreciate it, kid," John said with an attempt to seem happy as he ruffled the hair on top of her head. "I haven't celebrated my birthday since I was twelve or thirteen. Once I hit that age, my parents said that I was too old for birthday celebrations or parties. Then, when they passed away, I was alone, and Carly died before I could ever celebrate with her. The only time I would celebrate was with Kyle, and that was just me watching him drink and eat, and of course, that was the very thing that led to his death."

"I figured you'd say that, and I understand..." Ava said somberly, her voice trailing off as she lowered her head. "Are you *really* leaving today?"

John pulled Ava close to him and hugged her tightly, for her sake, as well as for a bit of human comfort before he left to achieve his death. "I *am* leaving, and that's why I'm hugging you and saying goodbye. Look, Ava, I don't know what I can say that'll make you feel better. I'm not a parent or a guardian. I'm a washed-up fighter who happened to rescue you because your former jerk-of-a-boyfriend picked a fight with me. In the past few days, however, I have been a bit happier. You're a good girl, Ava, and I hope that you don't let your former upbringing or my disappearance ruin your future, because I can see you doing great things. Whether you become an artist or a public speaker, or whatever your heart ends up desiring, I know you'll succeed in life, kid."

"John, I-"

"And I truly hope you do, because this world has progressed and regressed a lot during these past few decades, and it could use some powerful figures causing change. I know you'll say I should be one of those people, but I'll pass on that. It's time for me to leave this world like everyone else does," John said as he turned and looked toward the sky with longing-for and hope. "Ava, I know my death upsets you, but we all have to die. We're all *meant* to die. For almost my whole life, I have been punished for cheating the system of life and death. It's time that I die, just like everyone else has and will. Understand?"

Ava did not reply, but she just hugged John more tightly, sobbing, and almost crying.

"Now, get to school, kiddo, and learn as much as you can. Make sure to teach yourself some stuff about the world too." John lowered himself to one knee, so that they were almost face-to-face, as he was much taller than Ava. "I *promise* you that if I do survive, I'll come back to you, okay? I'm seeking death, but should I find life, then I *will* return."

"Sounds like a deal, The Immortal Man." Ava tried her best to sound hopeful and happy, but she struggled. She had to use her arm to wipe a tear away from her face. "I'll wait for you, and I'll keep on living and thriving. Every morning, I'll open this front door and look to see if you're coming down the path, and when I finally do see you, I'll call you The Mortal Man," Ava said through tears, which she could no longer hold back. John wanted to tell Ava that she would spend the rest of her life waiting and that she should not do that, but he did not have the heart to do so. In fact, he began to cry, as well, though his voice and sobs were silent. "Either way, thank you, John... for everything." Ava hugged him tightly one last time, pecked a kiss on his cheek, the soft emotion blocked by the suit, and then took off for school without any of her belongings, unable to bear it any longer.

John watched Ava as she left and ran away from the house. After a moment, he walked into his former bedroom, his face now cold and harsh as he entered the room with determination and death. "Ava, I'm sorry, but I'm not coming home," he said to himself through a sob as he glanced over at the unmade bed, which she had been using. "This feeling of guilt... it's worse than when he died, but I'm not going to come back. I *wish* I had the strength to tell you that with a smack across the face so you would come back to reality and understand that I'm going to die as I must, but I don't. I hope that you'll be able to forgive me one day. Although, I'll be dead, so who cares? I honestly don't know what you see in me or how you feel, Ava, but you deserve a role model who is *way* better than me."

After making the bed for her, John turned toward one corner of the room and looked at a small stack of five cardboard boxes. The bottom one contained the extra copies of the suit and mask that he had. The second one had the Japanese painting, the puzzle box, the papers of his life, the picture of Kyle, and the framed picture of John and Carly. The larger box above it contained pieces of the board, which John had ended up breaking, feeling guilty for abandoning Ava. On top of that box was one that contained the jacket John had taken from the bar fight the night that Kyle died. Then, on top of that, was the final box, which John grabbed and placed down on the bed.

"Can't believe I'm opening this box back up," John mumbled to himself. "I literally just packed it. Never thought I'd be using those ever again, but it has to end just like it started. The sunset will be there, and so will I, the once-mortal man." John glanced over at the stack of remaining cardboard boxes. "Might as well take care of the other ones first."

John pushed the bed across the room, revealing an ordinary wooden floor. Pulling out a knife from the inside of his leather jacket, John used it to open up one of the floorboards, which was purposefully loose. He then moved the adjacent floorboards away until a trapdoor was revealed. John opened the door and then slid the stack of the remaining cardboard boxes over the hole, and they fell through for a bit before hitting the cold ground below with a dull thud. John climbed down a ladder, and when he got low enough, he jumped off to avoid landing on the stack of boxes.

"Haven't been here in ages, and honestly never thought that I'd be coming back. Then again, I do need a place to bury my washed-up past before I'm buried myself." Using a lighter, John lit fire to a torch that was supported on the wall. "Easier than installing wires, that's for sure. Let's see now. This place is smaller than I remember." John looked around at the stone-wall basement, which he had made himself a few years ago. It was only several feet by several feet, perhaps big enough to install a small bathroom.

Grabbing each box individually, John placed them all next to each other, and the four boxes took up the whole space of one wall. He opened the lighter up again, the flickering flame coming back to life. He stared into the fiendish soul of the flame and then stared at the lifeless cardboard boxes across from him. He looked back and forth between the two, thinking to himself. *Over a hundred years of life and my only possessions take up no more space than five boxes, and only four are here. Besides that, the board was only broken at Ava's request. Still, it was a major part of my life. Actually, all of these objects represent major parts of my life. Love. Pride. Honor. Sacrifice. Survival. Friendship. Revenge. Success. Victory. Determination. Honestly, it hasn't been all that bad. Do I really want to burn it all? Do I really want to destroy it all and die?* John took a small step backward. *The truth is that it hasn't been all that bad, but the evil greatly outweighs the good. Did I do it to myself? Some of it, perhaps, but mostly it was others and life. Wars. Loneliness. Fits of insanity. Death. Despair. Horror. Heartbreak. Friends come and gone. Generations come and gone. Allies shot down in battle. Buildings destroyed. Businesses destroyed. Those I couldn't save. Depression. Suicide. The tormenting agony of others and myself. I can't back down now. Not after all these years.* He took a small step forward.

John looked at all of the boxes one more time before he swung his arm out, the lighter open and the flame lit. Right before it flew out of his hands, John abruptly closed the lighter. "Not today," John said, almost laughing in disbelief. "Not ever. I guess some unlucky son of a bitch'll find this someday. I feel sorry for them, but the punishment of those cursed objects is a well-deserved lesson if they have the nerve to come here and take them. I was taught that long ago," John muttered as he blew out the torch and then climbed back up the ladder.

"I probably should've made a lock and key for this," John said as he closed the trapdoor. "That's their problem, I guess. The floorboards and bed should be enough. That girl better not go looking for that suit and mask." After replacing the floorboards and placing them back tightly, John moved the bed back into place and then cut the box on top of it open. Behind the darkness of the mask, he smirked the same way he did when he first put on the suit and mask. "Time to return to action. I'm getting to England, whether you like it or not, Morgan, and you're taking me there."

❊ ❊ ❊

John planned on leaving Ava his car, so he ran all the way to Morgan's home at speeds that only Birch Willow and Timothy Edward Godwin could beat, all while he was carrying a small bag containing the objects from the box he had cut open. Stopping amongst some trees, John scanned the yard. Morgan had not left yet, which was what John had hoped and planned for. It was early in the morning, and the house was dark, so he assumed that she was either sleeping or getting ready to leave. Luckily for him, her dog was not outside on guard duty, and he was able to go undetected.

Nodding his head in suicidal satisfaction, John smirked behind the darkness of the mask when he confirmed that the rumors were true. He had heard that Morgan liked to speed around in a jeep with oversized tires, and in the driveway, he saw it, assuming that she had it inside a garage yesterday or somewhere else, for he had not seen it.

Due to the suit, John could do a lot of things that most people could not, and unlike the past few decades, he planned on actually taking advantage of the powers of the suit. John stealthily made his way over to the jeep, and then he dropped to the ground and rolled underneath it, staring at the cold metallic underside. The vehicle had enough space between it and the ground underneath it for John to enact his plan. So, grabbing onto the underside of the car with his bag between the vehicle and himself, John clung like a spider to a ceiling. He intended to tag along for an uninvited ride to the station when Morgan drove there.

It was a task that few could do if any could do it. Gripping on to the underside of the vehicle would require intense strength to hold on for such a prolonged amount of time on unstable terrains at high speeds, and most people would not have the strength to do it. Besides that, the air quality underneath the vehicle was not as pleasant, and not everyone had a mask as John did. In addition to that, despite the space between the ground and the vehicle, the flesh on their backs would most likely be scraped off into a bloody mixture in the street. However, since John wore the suit, the damage would simply brush off it when he did occasionally make contact with the ground at high speeds. Still, he wanted to make sure that he rarely hit the ground, though. A possible build-up of friction between his body and the ground could create sparks, consequently causing the car to explode, which John did not want to happen for everyone's sake. He also did not want the force of the contact with the ground to travel through his arms and onto the underside of the car. He had seen one car crash too many.

A few minutes later, John heard the front door close. He could not see anything except for approaching feet. He clung as tightly as he could to the underside of the jeep, pressing everything against it until Morgan got in. Once she was inside, he allowed there to be some room between the bag on his stomach and the underside of the vehicle to avoid any possible problems with heat.

Morgan drove for over an hour, and it was a bumpy ride for John, who had not realized how far away the base was, as the location was kept secret from the public. He had to make sure that he held onto the vehicle firmly and did not slip off by accident. John almost lost his grip and fell off a few times when the jeep hit some potholes that had torn up the road. He made sure to hold himself as close to the vehicle as possible, without directly pressing against the underside, to prevent contact with the ground. Unfortunately, John did brush against the ground several times, but it was not enough to cause any trouble. Part of the problem was that Morgan drove fast and violently, just as John had heard, and there was no doubt that she was still upset and angry over their meeting yesterday.

Eventually, Morgan slowed down as they came upon a dirt road that was bordered by woods on either side. After a few minutes of traveling along the private road, John knew that they must be approaching the base soon. He let go of the vehicle, figuring that he would be caught if they scanned and inspected the jeep before Morgan was allowed in. Either way, the confrontation today was going to be huge and unavoidable, but if he were to be caught underneath the vehicle, he would not have the opportunity to use what he had packed. Falling straight down, John waited a few minutes before he rolled over to the side of the road. He brushed himself off as he stood up and looked down the road, the jeep far down it already. Towering in the distance was the station, heavily guarded.

Having been underneath the car and facing the underside of it, John had been unable to see much of anything, even when he craned his neck, so he had no idea where they were. Dense forests surrounded the area, concealing it from most of the public or anyone who happened to wander by the place. The number of trees and their size seemed to be unnatural, but John had no way of determining how or when the woods on each side of the street had grown. They were still in Cape Cod, as far as he knew, but it was not marked on the map or by any of the popular tourist destinations.

John retreated into the concealment of the trees. Currently, he was naked, the dark and bulkier areas of the suit covering his private parts. He opened the bag and held up the change of clothes, a tornado of various emotions swelling up inside of him. Shining in a few rays of sunlight that passed through the trees, it was John's World War I uniform. He had kept it in perfect condition since he wore it back then, looking at it every few months when he thought back to the beginning of his immortality. The uniform was old, but it seemed as if he had just gotten it. There were still a few stains of blood on it from when he had experienced combat, but those only served to make it all the more authentic.

John did not bring the hat or gas mask, as he did not like the way those looked and felt that only the uniform was necessary for him to end his tormenting life of immortality the same way he had started it. He felt it was only fitting that he should finally die in the same uniform he had had been wearing when he found the suit and mask. It would bring everything around full-circle, which was something he had always found pleasing in literature. Besides the uniform, John pulled out the rifle he had used during his battles to kill the men who stood against him and his country. The bayonet glistened in the sunlight, awakened from its long slumber. The weapon was also in prime condition, as he had taken good care of it as well. Now adequately equipped for the siege, John set off for the station.

A large stone wall with barbed wire at the top surrounded the military base. At each corner of this wall stood a tower with rapid-fire turrets on them. Armed guards patrolled the premise as well. Besides the towers at each corner, there was a tower on either side of the entrance into the base. Those guards were equipped with rapid-fire turrets as well.

"Oh, man," John muttered to himself as he walked down the road toward the base, noticing its unusual security measures. "This place is different than just a U.S. military base. What's going on here? I'm in for a lot more trouble than I thought."

A female guard on the left tower at the gate entrance spotted John and quickly alerted the others. She pulled out a walkie-talkie. "Sir, an unidentified individual is approaching the base, armed with a bayonet and what appears to be an old war uniform." She nodded her head, even though she was talking to just a voice. "Yes, sir, he is wearing a mask... wait, *what?* Sir, with all due respect, shouldn't we give him a verbal warning first and question his motives?" There was loud yelling from the other end of the walkie-talkie. "Understood, sir. I apologize. We'll engage as soon as he is within range."

As soon as John was within the range of the gate entrance weapons, which had extremely far reaches, the two rapid-fire turrets began to shoot at John with advanced speeds that had not yet been used by even the military. "I knew this place was special," John spat out through clenched teeth as he crossed his arms in an x-shape across his chest. The bullets were deflected off of John, their force traveling down his legs. Deciding to use this to his advantage, John sprinted forward, having the redirected forces propel him as he ran at the front gate, cracking the ground and leaving a hole where he stepped. He flashed forward at superhuman speeds. When he came within fifty feet of the entrance, the two front corner towers began firing at John as well.

John had to stop running, and he stood his ground, shielding himself with his arms and hands. The impact of so many bullets was starting to push him back a little bit as he began to bend his knees. *Even the suit is having a hard time redirecting the forces from this relentless sandstorm of bullets*, John thought to himself. *Interesting. I've never experienced so much firepower at once from four different angles, even if it's just frequent doses of small but lethal impacts. Still, this is nothing compared to the suit and mask. They can handle almost anything!* Smirking, John planted his feet firmly on the ground and stopped shielding himself with his arms. Taking the stance of a powerful being and forming a divine image, John extended his arms to either side of them while he flexed his legs. He looked upward at an angle with total pride and divine power. The curses placed upon him over a century ago were now blessings that would help him achieve death, and he was ready to unleash their full power.

In his leg-focused defensive position, the forces of the bullets were then channeled primarily down John's legs, and straight into the ground. Individually, the force from the bullets would not have done much, but there were so many bullets hitting John at such great speed that the total force was starting to dig into the ground. John was sturdy enough that he did not get launched into the air by the force between the ground and his feet. In fact, the suit was redirecting the opposite reaction from the ground and sending it back down, generating even more force and energy in a powerful cycle that was growing stronger each second. A crater was beginning to form where he was standing, and around his feet, the ground was being torn up and destroyed. He started sinking into the ground.

The guards stopped firing when John vanished from sight, having fallen into a hole with a width and depth made it appear as though a small meteor had struck the planet and pulverized John into the ground. The guards could not believe the unnatural sight. Everything was put on red-alert as sirens started to sound around the base, signifying they were under attack.

Jumping up, John grabbed the edge of the hole and then pulled up with immense strength, launching himself out of it before spinning once as he landed gracefully on the road. He brushed himself off as he stood up, his eyes growing darker as he looked at his uniform, which was almost entirely destroyed from the relentless shower of bullets he had endured. The ragged and shredded uniform clung to him hopelessly. While that did upset him, John could not help but laugh at the situation. He could only imagine what the guards must be reporting to their officers, trying to explain that an unknown humanoid was attempting to enter the base and that their advanced weapons had failed to stop it.

Walking forward unstoppably, John sighed. He thought about trying to explain that he just needed a plane, but he doubted they would believe him. Most likely, they all thought he was a terrorist, or perhaps, Morgan was explaining to her boss how The Immortal Man was an old friend of her grandfather, Kyle, and that he wanted to find a teleporting man who was researching supernatural occurrences. Either way, John knew he had to get into the base, and unfortunately, some of the soldiers would have to die for that to happen. He felt it was ironic that they would have to die so that he could die, but all he cared about was himself and death.

John's rifle was almost as old as him, but it still fired, and it still killed. It was powerful enough to reach and kill the guards at the two closest towers, which were within John's range as he quickly approached the front gate. He watched as they stumbled backward or forward, falling to their death on top of the injury he had given them with his rusty shooting skills.

Before John could inspect the front gate, he was alerted by noise that two perimeter guards were rushing him on either side. He stabbed the closest one with his bayonet, shot the person behind that guard as he sliced through the man, and then he turned around and shot a woman before stabbing a man behind her. In an instant, four perimeter guards lay injured and heading toward death at John's feet. He grabbed a pistol from two guards, stashing one on each side of his hips for later.

Safe for now, as the two corner towers had seized firing at him, John inspected the front gate to the base. It was large and heavy ironclad metal that was reinforced. *Even if those two tower guards were to start shooting me again and I redirected the forces, all I could do at most is possibly dent this gate. I need a better way in.* John looked up at the sky. *God, please help me open this gate. I need to atone for my sins in Hell or come into Heaven and party with you. Either way, this gate will need to be broken open, and-* John stopped praying and laughed maniacally as he turned around upon hearing a heavy rumble approaching behind him. "Thanks, God," John shouted as he looked at an armored tank approaching at high speeds down the dirt road before it slowed down to a stop, seventy feet away from John.

The hatch opened, and a man stuck the upper part of his body out of the tank compartment. He retrieved a megaphone from somewhere on his person. "This is your last chance to surrender now." John recognized the tank's design as being similar to an M1 Tank design, though it seemed to be a bit superior to that. Assuming that it operated under a four-person crew, John knew that the man speaking had to be the driver. That reassured John of his safety, as that meant the tank could not move forward, and John feared that if the tank did run him over, he might not make it out alive. He did not want to die except for on his own terms. "Do you understand me? Desist your criminal behavior and surrender at once, or we will be forced to take lethal action."

John looked around and then pointed to himself. "Wait, are you talking to me?" He laughed at his own question, figuring he may as well have some fun. "Criminal behavior? I was just on my way to ask if I could borrow a plane when your soldiers started shooting at me. I find all of this violent behavior to be reckless endangerment of civilian lives, as I *am* a civilian. I've been a civilian for longer than any of you, actually. So, *really*, all of you seem to be the only criminals here."

The man kept a professionally stern face, but he was clearly angered by the comment. It was an attack on his pride. "I've heard that you're bulletproof somehow." He spat over the side of the tank. "Let's see if you're tank-proof."

"Hold on a minute!" John threw his hands up as if surrendering, though his hands stopped at his shoulders. "Now, that really *is* reckless endangerment! If you shoot at me, you'll blow up this whole gate, and you might hurt some of these people on the ground who are still alive and can be saved," John pointed out as he lifted up one of the guards he had stabbed. "You wouldn't do that, would you?"

"I'm aware of that, but I've been given a direct order from the boss, who's been given an even more direct order from the ultimate man himself. All of the land you see for the surrounding few miles were purchased by him with permission from the federal government. There's no denying what must happen, and we shall properly honor the sacrifices of these brave men and women once I kill you." The man sunk back into the tank compartment.

Knowing that he would be fired at in just seconds, John quickly pressed the one button on the side of the mask. The mask sucked in the air around him more powerfully, still filtering out everything except for what was necessary. John, being filled with a purer and greater amount of oxygen than usual, now had a slightly sharpened mind. The tank fired at John, and his reaction time, combined with his almost superhuman body, was fast enough that it skimmed right past him, barely missing him as he turned. It crashed through and exploded the front gate.

John was launched back by the force of the explosion. When he got up unscathed, he looked through the broken gate. Beyond it was a large area with several buildings. The soldiers were all running around, some panicking, and some preparing. John had a feeling that soon they would call in an airstrike if they did not care about friendly fire just as the man in the tank did not. Men and women were running inside the base, equipping themselves with heavy-duty guns and advanced weapons. Some of them even looked experimental. *Who's supplying this operation? The ultimate man? Well, it doesn't matter. I can't be bothered with who he is or what he'll do in the future because I won't be there for it.* John quickly ran through the hole in the gate before the tank could fire again.

As soon as John had walked past the gate, the real fighting began, as some of the soldiers decided to hold the frontline. He was greatly outnumbered.

One woman managed to jump onto John's back and put him in a chokehold, but he quickly disposed of her by throwing his arms back, the bayonet stabbing her in the face. As she fell off of him, John used the butt-end of the gun to powerfully smash in the face of a guy in front of him, the old rifle cracking. John tossed the gun aside and quickly whipped out the pistol, shooting five soldiers rushing at him, giving them a bullet each. He was then rushed at from behind by two more soldiers. Both attempted to taser him, but John held out his arms and redirected the electricity at two soldiers in front of them. He had never done it before, but his plan worked, and the two soldiers in front of him were zapped down with a small current of electricity that shot out of his hands. After all, there was no direct path to his body for the current to take. He then turned around and grabbed the wires before yanking the tasers out of the soldiers' hands and tossing them behind him. The two soldiers, still conscious charged at John, and both fiercely attacked him, but he blocked and countered all of their attacks, leaving them both unconscious.

John turned around and winced his eyes shut in response to a wave of bright light before slowly reopening them. Everything was suddenly orange, red, and yellow, but John quickly realized what was going on. John ran through the fire toward its source, and circling around the soldier with the flamethrower, John crushed the canister on his back with his bare hands. The tank exploded, taking two more soldiers on their way to help to a fiery death instead.

John was soon surrounded by twenty soldiers. They hesitated, unsure of what to do. One woman fired a single shot at John's head, and he headbutted the bullet into the ground. Rather than gulp or be terrified, the trained soldiers all began firing their weapons. Without hesitation, John quickly charged forward at the nearest soldier, but the firing did not stop, despite the fact that the soldiers might shoot their own allies. The shower of bullets was simply a shower to John, and he cleansed his years of laziness off of himself as he quickly injured, knocked-out, and killed everyone in his way. He was unstoppable, and the bodies were beginning to pile up as he grew more powerful and merciless with each second.

"It's time to end this," a woman shouted from across the base, her voice indicating that she was swiftly approaching.

John turned, recognizing the voice. In the distance, Morgan was running at him, armed with a gun and screaming a plethora of vulgar words. He nodded his head as he stared at her, his eyes almost black. "I agree. It's time to end my life after decades of torment and suffering. You wouldn't help me, but all who stand in the way of death and I shall die, including myself." A direct shot to her forehead left blood spilling from the middle of Morgan's head as she collapsed to the ground and died.

With an unstoppable and powerful stride, fueled by his desire to finally die, John walked over to Morgan and grabbed her lanyard and keys, ripping them from her dead body. He had gotten sidetracked, but now it was time to get what he came for. John read what the lanyard had listed on it. Aircraft CF-13. The plane was the one she piloted for them, and it was just what he needed to get to England. Heavily armed guards covered in gear and equipped with heavy-duty firearms were now flooding the base like an infestation of ants defending their queen. John quickly ran over to the hangar building, fighting soldiers along the way.

Getting into the plane, John forced his thoughts back to a book on flying that he had read. With all the time in the world and as slow as his aging was, John had read enough books to fill a few libraries. He was perhaps one of the most educated people in the world, but certainly not the wisest. After a moment of thinking, John powered everything up and was out of there before anyone could even think to stop him.

The highest-ranked general of the base was steaming with anger as he watched John fly away, his lift-off a bit messy. Medics ran around the base frantically as they attended to the injured and inspected the dead. He was yelling on the phone at someone. "That's right... shoot him down! I don't care how you do it, but we *cannot* afford to allow him to escape."

"Cancel that order, General," a feminine voice commanded. "Him escaping is not a problem at all, and there's no need to shoot him down. Besides, that would draw a lot of unwanted attention."

The general turned around and saw who was speaking. Realizing who it was, he quickly put the phone back to his ear. "Forget what I just said! Cancel that order, and switch your attention to the restoration and security of the base!" He hung up with an angry press of his thumb against the screen. He jammed the phone into his pocket before turning his attention to the woman, still enraged. "No need for that!" He threw his hands up in disbelief. "We have a rouge cargo jet flying across the Atlantic with unknown intentions, and it's being piloted by a human who is immune to most weaponry, as far as we can tell. I bet you he's one of those damn scientists, isn't he?"

The woman to whom the general was speaking to was dressed in a black skirt and suit top over a white dress shirt, and she wore solid black shades to match the outfit. "That's correct, General. While he's technically not a scientist, John Leach is among those people. The first, if you *really* must know. A small-minded man like you hates not knowing everything, don't you? Everything is set into motion already for today, and the man who hijacked that plane is a major part of the plan and critical to our success. Let it go, General. In case you get hard feelings, I've been authorized to give you an additional bonus for your services." The agent pulled out a thick wad of money and handed it to him. "I bid you adieu, and *don't* do anything stupid, or *he'll* have your head for it." She saluted him with a smug expression and then walked away.

"You mean to tell me that you knew he was coming here?" The general asked in outrage. "You could've told us! I would've evacuated my soldiers, and nobody would've had to die today! At the very least, we could've been more prepared." The general looked at the money. It was more than enough. Then, he looked around at the fallen soldiers. Half of him felt they had died for a crucial step toward the future, but the other half, that side of him knew they had been killed in vain for sacrifices that were unnecessary and avoidable.

The woman stopped, frustrated as she turned around and looked at the general. "Of course, we knew he was coming. We know *everything*. He couldn't show up to an empty base, though. In order to lower John's suspicions, the base had to be occupied and unprepared for him."

"That's bullshit, you substitute! Where's Abraham? He's the real man in charge of this weapons-operation here, not you, and I demand to speak to him."

"Abraham is currently in Charleston, West Virginia, finishing the preparations needed to escort Birch Willow to England so that he will be there at the right time. You don't know anything about that, and quite honestly, you've gotten on my nerves too much." The woman pulled out a gun and shot the general directly in the heart. She walked over and looked down at him as he clutched his bleeding chest. "Don't worry, at all. A cleanup crew is on the way. It's a shame that John Leach shot you in the chest while raiding this place. I'll be taking that bonus, while I'm at." The agent turned around and slid Morgan's body aside with a kick of her foot before leaving the base.

CHAPTER 11

THE DARKNESS WITHIN ALL

(Homestead, Florida. That Same Day: April 18, 2022.)

Two hours after the sun had risen, Sir Thomas, Kronos, and Timothy woke up to the smell of bacon and eggs being cooked. Stella had awoken before all of them and decided to prepare some breakfast for her guests, who she assumed had big plans for the day.

Sir Thomas was the first of the three men to get out of bed, and he got changed into his suit, quickly freshened up, and then grabbed a recent newspaper from the bathroom before yawning his way down the stairs, making sure to cover his yawn. "Good morning, Stella. Everything smells wonderful, as expected. However, there's certainly no need for you to do all of this for us. It's already more than enough that you're allowing us to stay here."

"You're way too kind. It's no trouble at all. I'm just making bacon and eggs, plus I'll be making pancakes in a minute. Timothy has always been a bottomless pit, and besides that, I figured you boys must be hungry after the long drive, and that you probably haven't had any real food in a while now. Granola bars don't count," she added with a laugh. She continued to attend to the food as Sir Thomas sat down at the kitchen table behind her.

"You're certainly right about that. Yesterday and the day before weren't the English feasts of scones and biscuits I usually enjoy at my castle, nor were they a platter of shrimp, lobster, and caviar, but I can't complain when there are others with no food to eat at all. Of course, I frequently donate to charities to help starving children, but there's only so much that money can do. Granola bars aren't that bad, so long as you get a variety. Although your son did introduce us to Dr. Finch's Fast Food. As upsetting to my guts as it was, the food there was actually quite enjoyable. The fizzy soda, on the other hand, was not my cup of tea… literally. It's a franchise we don't have over in England, so it was nice to try something different. Unlike Kronos, I don't mind a bit of change every now and then."

While Kronos stayed upstairs scheming and working on his laptop and phone simultaneously, Timothy joined the downstairs group, dressed in an old pair of black pajamas with green lightning bolts on them that did not fit him entirely. His mother looked over at him, judgingly. "What are you wearing, Timothy? I planned on donating your old clothes or saving them for Spencer, and now you're stretching them out. Oh, and I thought I told you not to eat at Dr. Finch's Fast Food! I don't trust that man or his business, and the food isn't healthy at all."

"Yeah, well, so is almost *every* food in the American diet, so who gives a crap?" Timothy retorted. He was not smiling or energetic as usual. He was stern and intent on verbally destroying anyone he deemed wrong. It was a different side of him, and he did not even notice Sir Thomas. "I'll eat wherever I want. Life is too valuable and short to worry about how many days a *fucking* french fry will take off of your life because the days that are being taken off are days that you *won't* even be able to walk or dance, so why sacrifice good food for worthless days? Does that make *any* sense to you? Why extend life if you can't enjoy the extended days? Just so that *other people* can enjoy your company or the fact that you're still alive? That's so stupid! You're always saying that I'll get fat or that I should eat healthier, well, I'm perfectly healthy and have been for the past forty years!"

"You're only thirty, Tim! To think you would be so rude to your mother and start arguing first thing in the morning. I can't believe that you would curse at your own mother."

"That's *Timothy* to you, and I'm not the one who started it. The first two things you had to say to me when I came downstairs were complaints and critiques, as usual. And *who* cares if Dr. Finch is shady? Have you ever watched any documentaries on restaurants or companies? Like, every single person who owns or created a business is shady. It's how business has always worked, and it's how business will always work. If you actually believed in avoiding companies with shady owners or employees, you wouldn't be able to enjoy a majority of the places you already do."

Sir Thomas hesitated and held back his tongue. As a gentleman, he wanted to correct Timothy for talking so rudely to his mother, but he knew how much hatred was in Timothy's heart toward his mother, as well as why it existed. He was caught between choosing a side, and he would rather not choose at all. "Look, I-"

"You're arguing is annoying me, and it's disturbed my work, which is the most important kind in the world," Kronos stated coldly from the other room as he descended the staircase slowly, each footstep sounding like impending doom. "To think that there would be so much commotion and noise this early in the morning is inconceivable and pitiful. After all, I am a guest, and I expect my stay to be enjoyable and rewarding. Yet, I feel like I have paid for a beautiful hotel room but ended up being underneath a room packed with several children who do not understand the concept of floors and ceilings, and they continue to jump around and shout during the late hours of the night while I'm trying to sleep," Kronos said emotionlessly but with power as he made his way over to the kitchen. "Now, continue your family drama later when I'm not around. I hate being disturbed and annoyed no matter who it is or what it concerns. It's such a shame. I, myself, have always lacked a mother, but considering the amount of verbal battling taking place here, I might have to admit that I'm relieved. Upon my arrival, I demand either silence or applause," Kronos stated as he stopped in the open doorway between the kitchen and front area of the house. "Now, what's for breakfast?"

Timothy smirked and laughed internally.

Sir Thomas shook his head in shame and disappointment as he brought the newspaper up to act like he was not associated with Kronos and his rude behavior.

Stella slowly gulped and took a step back, bumping into the countertop, intimidated and terrified by the commanding tone of irrefutable intellect and power that Kronos had spoken with, almost shaking as she looked at him. "W-w-well I was just making pancakes, eggs, and bacon for everyone." Looking at Kronos and dreadfully struggling to shift her eyes away from his ominous and petrifying gaze, Stella turned to Sir Thomas, who was the only one treating her nicely. "How do you like your eggs cooked?"

"I'm afraid that dippy egg and soldiers is a popular style of eating eggs in England that I took a liking too, so just make it in whatever way is easiest for you. To me, an egg is an egg, and I'll eat it any way that it is cooked. For Kronos, I suggest you scramble them up and make scrambled eggs for him, as he likes his eggs like his brain cells," Sir Thomas said with a smirk and a held-back chuckle.

Timothy smiled before he broke out laughing heartily at the mediocre joke. "Scrambled like his brain," he said in a light voice through laughs. "Not bad, Sir Thomas. That was a good one."

"Quiet down, Timothy. Kronos needs to concentrate, and it wasn't *that* funny," Stella remarked. "And I'm not making any eggs for you since you complained about them last time."

"For your information, it was more of an inside joke if you really feel the need to comment about it, and secondly, that's fine by me. I'm not eating anything because we have a big day today, and I want to be light on my feet. Plus, I already ate earlier this morning when I woke up before I went back to sleep. I'm only here to talk with them."

"Are you sure you don't want to eat, Mr. Godwin?"

"Leave the boy alone, Thomas," Kronos said as he sat down at the kitchen table next to Sir Thomas and across from Timothy as if he were sitting down in a throne. "His unhealthy and troubled relationship with his mother is none of your business. He's old enough to know when he needs to eat and to be able to feed himself. Let's not forget that he ate double what we ate yesterday, and there's no doubt that he already ate this morning. In fact, he stated that he did just that. He'll be fine."

"Blimey! Stella, are you alright?" Sir Thomas asked worriedly as he saw how upset she was out of nowhere. "What's wrong? You seem to be on the verge of tears."

"I'm fine," Stella replied, fanning herself with her hand. "I just happened to see the headline on that newspaper you're reading. That devastating attack on Charleston was so awful. Did you hear about it? I almost cried when I saw it on the news. That Birch Willow guy, whew, he's hot, but more importantly, I hope he's okay. What bad luck he has. He's so nice and helpful, and this is the thanks he gets? He always donated to charity, isn't that sweet?"

"Correct. It was rather sweet of him to donate to charity. What a shame that his gym had to be destroyed. Now, serve breakfast, as it's getting late fast, and we have a big day ahead of us, Stella. Your son plans on showing us around the town a bit. In fact, for treating us so kindly, I think I'll add thirty dollars to his hourly salary. Not that it matters since he's already being paid a couple thousand every day, but more money is undoubtedly more money. I would know, since I'm the richest person alive, as far as I know."

Stella almost fainted, letting the eggs burn due to her lack of attention to the food. "Timothy, you're making thousands every day?"

"Oh, so now you want to talk? How unsurprising. I am, and you know what, I think I'll use it to fund a political campaign to support and promote vigilantism and the idea of a hero-society. In fact, you could be a part of it, *Mom*."

"How dare y-"

"That's enough from both of you! I'm hungry, and given the fact that I'm the greatest human to have ever existed, my appetite comes before your arguments," Kronos pointed out. "I get irritable when my blood sugar is low or when I have not eaten. Also, you're burning the eggs, Stella, and that appalls me."

"Lord, please help me through divine intervention. It's going to be a very long day at this rate," Sir Thomas mumbled to himself before sighing and shaking his head.

After finishing a rather awkward and unpleasant breakfast, Sir Thomas stayed behind to help Stella with the dishes while Timothy and Kronos went upstairs to work on planning out the day.

"I sincerely apologize for that breakfast, Stella," Sir Thomas said as he washed the dishes, passing them to Stella for her to dry them with a towel. "The way Kronos talked to you was most displeasing, and I can't believe that he's behaving like this. I'm afraid he's a man of solitude who does not go out often, nor does he really like people that much, and I understand that you and Timothy have a troubled relationship."

"Unfortunately, we do," Stella said with a sigh. "I assume he said all terrible things about me on your ride here and made me out to be the villain? Wouldn't be the first time he's done that, and his father always did the same once we started arguing over little Tim. He probably already plans on telling Spencer that his grandmother is a wretched old woman who hates her own son because what I want for him doesn't match his dreams, which happen to be bad. I just want what's best for him, but his slander says otherwise."

"Actually, he didn't say anything too awful. At least not to me, anyway. He has a closer relationship with Kronos."

"Well, they are closer in age."

"Indeed. As far as what I know goes, it was actually Laura who told me all about you two, as well as Mr. Godwin's father, and about that tragic crash. She, just as I assume you are, is concerned for Timothy, fearing that his childlike values, beliefs, and ideas, combined with his optimism and nostalgic person, will be his downfall, or hurt him one day, as well as their family. She asked me to take care of him while we're all traveling together."

"Figures. She's always looking out for him, but he gets upset over it just like when I worry about him. I think he mistakes concern for criticism and condescension, but that's not what's going on."

"Laura, for as long as I've known her, has always been a loving and caring woman, and I know that her concern comes from a love for both Timothy and their child. Similarly, I know that as a mother, your anger and disapproval comes from concern which comes from love. He knows that, but his love for his dream is greater than his love for you, so he chooses that over you if that makes sense. It's not just him, though, and understand that a lot of children do that. Honestly, he probably thinks that there's no way to recover your relationship with him, and so that's why he's just chosen to stay on bad terms with you. He still has ties with you, and he's chosen not to sever them, so that must mean something. Then again, I have no idea what Mr. Godwin thinks or believes. All I know is that he is a good-hearted person with an honorable and admirable dream. He hopes to change the world, just as we all do, but he actually plans on trying, and that makes him a lot better than most of us."

"Thanks, Sir Thomas. What you said means a lot, and it makes me feel a bit better. Honestly, though, I don't care what anyone else thinks or if anyone else understands. I just want Timothy to realize and understand everything that you just said because the approval of other people means nothing if my own son hates me. He always has, and I think that he always will. All that I've done has been to help him. I know the heartbreak of reality that I caused him was horrible, but when he fails to accomplish his dream after sacrificing everything for it, well, that'd be a whole lot worse, and as a mother, I didn't want to see him suffer like that. It's not even the fact that he'll face a lot of hardship on his path to creating a hero-society, whether he's an activist on social media or an actual politician. In the end, we'll always face difficulties and enemies on any path we choose in life. The difference with his is that the end goal is impossible to reach. If it was about green energy or rights for minorities, I wouldn't be so concerned, but what he's trying to fight for is unpopular, irrational, and impossible. On top of all of that, it's something we don't need."

"Is that the truth, though? See, throughout my years of service to this world, I've grown to know that society and the world don't often know what they need or don't need. The world works by trial and error. So does math and science and art and literature and music. The final product is perfect, but the path to it isn't. You should be concerned about how he'll respond to rejection rather than fearing rejection. We never know how a person or society will react to something new, but that doesn't mean that there's no need for it."

Stella started drying the dishes more slowly. "I guess you're right, but still…"

Timothy came speedily walking into the kitchen, Kronos trailing behind him. "If you're done flirting with my mom, Sir Thomas, me and Kronos are ready for you. Let's get going. We don't have much time to waste, as they're forecasting rain for this afternoon with a high chance of it hitting us earlier than that."

"Well, anyhow, think about what I said." Sir Thomas turned off the sink. "I bid you adieu, Stella," Sir Thomas said as he joined Timothy and Kronos, following them into the garage, where Timothy had moved the car to so that they could get their gear. Sir Thomas closed the door behind them, making sure it was closed as tightly as possible. "So, what's our plan, gentlemen?"

Kronos opened up the trunk to the vehicle. "We're gearing up and walking toward the ocean, hoping that he'll show up. Three individuals, such as ourselves, are bound to draw attention, especially with me walking amongst the streets of peasants. In addition to that, the social media post I made about the fight got a lot of forced attention. One comment stood out from the others, which were all relatively useless, and it was from a poetry account called Damon of Darkness. It had underscores between the words, of course, but I wasn't going to say the word underscore. Anyway, I think it was The Dark Depressor's account, based on the poems I analyzed from the account, as well as the comment, which wasn't entirely suspicious, but it was enough for me to understand what it meant."

"Right," Timothy said with a nod of his head, in a much better mood than before. "Enough talking. He'll confront us, and that's all that matters. We need to start preparing mentally, and we need to quickly gear up." Timothy grabbed his suit and then went over to the other side of the vehicle so he could strip down to put his suit on. His costume was all grey with a green lightning bolt on each of his upper arms. Steampunk goggles protected his eyes, and a green bandanna masked his mouth and nose. Over his left shoulder, looping down around his torso diagonally before wrapping around to connect its two ends, a black strap stood out against the grey. Attached to this strap were three round black spheres, the chemical and light grenades he used to make his time illusions. From his wrist to his elbow were black elbow guards, and from his ankles to his knees were black shin guards. His shoes were indescribable.

Timothy went back to the trunk and opened a small bag. He grabbed a few medical needles that contained his speed drug. Carefully, he stashed them into hidden pockets deep within his pants. They lasted for about half an hour each, and he did not think that he would need too many. However, he wanted them in case. The other set of needles was for his heart. Then, for the final touch, Timothy attached the particle suit accessory to his back, connecting the strap around his lower stomach, and he was ready for action.

"Well, guys, what do you think?" Timothy threw some punches into the air before pulling out the Whip-Watch, swinging and spinning it around with professional skill. Everything he did, even without the drugs, was super fast. His punches were untrackable. "Now, you're officially seeing me in my hero costume. I don't think you guys got too good of a look the other day when you recklessly endangered the lives of innocent civilians."

"My plan was practically flawless, and it's exactly how we were able to find you," Kronos replied. "Regarding your homemade outfit and gear, if it's truly necessary for boosting your heroic confidence, you have my approval, Timothy. Your costume is actually relatively eye-appealing without being too flashy or hindering your ability to perform."

"Coming from the man who basically wears the same outfit every day, and has for the past few years," Sir Thomas pointed out. "Still, you're not wrong. I have to agree with him, Mr. Godwin. It's a good start for now, and you're free to keep it. Just know that if you do become famous, a fashion company might try to partner up with you."

"True," Timothy agreed, quickly jogging in place and stretching. "I actually like the way Kronos is dressed. No homo, but it's a good look. I mean, the black cargo pants are supposed to match the R.N.T. Suit, right? Plus, the lab coat makes sense. Then the grey shirt matches the D.O.O.M Shooter and the Atomic Gauntlet, so it works out perfectly. Oh, and you have the black shades with the fiery lenses. It's almost like you were born to look like a hero or a cool guy who uses advanced technology to get what he wants. We make a great team. Unfortunately, what are we going to do about you, Sir Thomas?"

"I'm also a member of Kronos' scientific empire, so I assure you that I have a few gadgets as well. They aren't as powerful as a gauntlet meant for fighting or a gun that destroys everything, but they can kill and defend." Sir Thomas whipped out a custom-made knife and slashed it through the air. He stabbed at the space in front of him and twirled the blade around in his hand like a trained assassin. Timothy looked over at it in awe. The design was flawless and beautiful.

"Right. I should've guessed as much. That's awesome! Mind if I take a look at it?" Sir Thomas handed the knife over to Timothy, who studied it carefully. It was ten inches long. Engraved down the middle of the blade was the company name, R.O.M.A.B.A. Industries, etched into the metal. It had a black handle with several indents in it for gripping. There was a button on one side. Timothy pressed down on it and jumped back, gasping, as the blade sparked with an electrical current around it. He quickly took his finger off of the button. "What was that?"

Sir Thomas quickly took the blade away from Timothy. "Ah, my apologies, Mr. Godwin. I should've warned you about that, but it slipped my mind. We call the series it's from the Deconstructor Blades. Kronos made them similar to the D.O.O.M. Shooter. The current will destroy everything it touches as you slice through your enemies with it. Both he and I have one, and those are the only ones we have on us. Otherwise, I would offer you one." Sir Thomas placed the blade down in the trunk. "It's a simple use for the ability to manipulate atoms, but the knife gives the wielder a greater advantage, as it is far more fatal than a regular blade, and it can also be used in countless ways with the terrain and such."

Kronos dug into in the trunk for a second bag he had brought, and from it, he pulled out a dark grey business suit. He held it up for everyone to see. "Nevermind the fancy weapons. What would a proper caretaker be without the appropriate outfit?" He threw it to Sir Thomas, who looked at it as he rubbed his hand over the strange fibers. "I custom-made it for such a predicament as this," Kronos explained. "It's resistant against most things, but it's not invincible. It was the best I could do with such material. It's bulletproof, however, and that was the most important aspect I needed to include. You're in excellent health and shape for a man your age, so I don't doubt your ability to run, jump, and fight, but you can't dodge bullets. It has an inside sheath for the knife and a gun holster." Kronos pulled out an expensive pistol and handed it to Sir Thomas. "I was creating the knight's armor for you. It was meant to be satirical on how you're a white knight, as they say. Unfortunately, it came out brilliantly, but it would have been too much for you to handle. The weight of the armor alone is quite a bit."

"This is more than enough, Kronos. Thank you," Sir Thomas said as he went around to the other side of the vehicle to change.

Kronos slipped the R.N.T. Suit over his back and strapped it on, equipped his left hand with the Atomic Gauntlet, placed the unique earpiece into his right ear, and stashed the D.O.O.M. Shooter into the satchel on his left side. He dramatically slid the high-tech sunglasses onto his face.

Sir Thomas came around from the other side of the vehicle, now dressed in the grey suit. "Well, it would appear that we're all ready to go. Now then, you two hide in the trunk while I drive. That way, we can get away from here without your mother seeing us."

Timothy and Kronos agreed, hopping into the trunk with the tinted windows before Sir Thomas drove off, as he was the only one dressed like a normal person. He drove a few blocks toward the southeast, parking four blocks away from the beach in a quiet area with no one around.

The three men hopped out of the car and then walked over to the main road. From there, they started heading toward the beach. As they walked, a few people on the street and in the buildings gasped in confusion and awe at the sight of the three men. Some people panicked, thinking it an attack or protest, while others thought it was some kind of comic-con parade. A few people recognized Timothy as the vigilante from Minnesota, and they loved it. Others ran away. Regardless of their emotions, every bystander was taking pictures or recording videos, which would help increase their chances of encountering The Dark Depressor, as they had planned.

"It's alright! We're the good guys here," Timothy shouted with a friendly wave at an elderly couple, who were afraid of the three men. "I'm a helpful hero from Minnesota who has come to free you all from the horrible reign of *The Sinful Son*, also known as The Dark Depressor." The couple backed away after giving a slight wave. Timothy turned toward his two allies. "You know, guys, I'm starting to think that maybe we didn't think this all the way through when we made the plan. It makes sense, and I love the attention, but I'm pretty sure people are going to end up calling the cops on us."

"Blimey, Mr. Godwin! Make up your mind! That was my fear this whole time, but you two insisted, and we don't have many other options. What makes you worried now, though? No one has any reason to believe we're terrorists or anything. Except for Kronos, who looks like he has a bomb strapped to his back. Some of these people seem to be fans, however. Like that guy over there," Sir Thomas said as he gestured to a shirtless man with scruffy black and grey hair, who was cleaning a window on the side of a building.

"Hey, how are ya?" the man asked from up where he was cleaning the window. "What are y'all doing dressed like that, walking down the middle of the street? Is this one of those Japanese anime conventions or something?"

"Hello, innocent civilian," Timothy said with an enthusiastic wave and a bright smile, forgetting that he was wearing the thick bandanna around the lower half of his face. "I'm more than happy to assist you in any way and answer all of your questions. I'm a vigilante and a speedster from Minnesota, known as The Chronological Changer. My allies and I are here to fight the evil voodoo man who has recently been terrorizing Florida and kidnapping people as **The Sinful Son**."

"Oh, nice, I guess. We appreciate it. You might want to work on that name, though," the man suggested. "Looks like you have a bigger problem to deal with first, and I best be getting out of here given my history," the man said as he pointed down the street behind them.

"Bollocks," Sir Thomas muttered as the three men turned around to see what the man was pointing at. "They didn't use their sirens so they could catch us off guard. It's the coppers of Florida."

"No shit, Thomas. We can clearly see that. It's not a problem at all, as I can easily pop all of their tires from here," Kronos stated as he whipped out the D.O.O.M. Shooter. "However, that wouldn't be quite as fun as what's to come," Kronos hissed, not attacking the police, which surprised Sir Thomas, who chose to trust Kronos. "This will be a test for him," Kronos whispered indiscreetly to Sir Thomas, referring to the fact that Timothy would most likely have to deal with situations like this in the future.

Timothy was already injecting himself with a drug to speed up his body and nervous system. However, he did not yet speed up his heart, as he preferred to save that for when he truly needed it.

Blue and red flashes of light took turns coating the air as the police cars parked and barricaded the road. The three men were surrounded by the police, two vehicles on each side, forming a diamond around them. The cops all jumped out of their vehicles in an instant, gun in hand, surrounding the men on all sides. There were eight officers in total. None of them dared to venture closer except for one police officer who approached them, shouting at them the warning they probably gave all criminals.

Kronos looked at the man and rolled his eyes, forgetting that he had the high-tech glasses on, even though they were busy scanning and monitoring everything in front of him, relaying information about all of the officers, weapons, and vehicles to Kronos. As always, he spoke harshly with absolute power and intimidation. "How impudent of you to treat us like we're criminals after we drove for over a day just to get here in order to save your sorry asses from a terroristic figure of advanced science and technology that you couldn't possibly hope to injure, let alone actually defeat. I understand that both of your corneas have suffered mild scratches from a small feline species, but can't you see that we're the good guys?"

"H-h-how did you know about Mr. Muffintops and my eyes? Are you some kind of stalker? Just surrender now. Resisting will only end in bloodshed or death, given the fact that you seemed to be armed with actual weapons. You have no permit, authorization, or reason to be here. Besides, heroes don't exist. They're fiction. You're just a bunch of guys in costumes."

"Is that so? Then why send so many police officers? It's because this whole town is on edge ever since The Dark Depressor showed up and proved that beings beyond regular humans *do* exist. Fearful after seeing his power, the appearance of three individuals claiming to be his rivals scared the crap out of everyone." Kronos took a step forward. "Heroes and villains do exist, and I exist above them all. I am **King Kronos**, and you shall all know my name one day and praise it with a thousand bows of gratitude. However, if you insist on more proof, then brace yourself."

"I said don't mo-"

Sprinting forward like a bullet train, Timothy charged at the cop, the green particle trail following him. The gun went flying from his hand as Timothy knocked it away without anyone following the movement before he pushed the cop backward into a police car, moving the whole vehicle back an inch. He seized the cop by the neck and held him against the car. "Really? Heroes *don't* exist?" All of the officers were shocked, and they all took a step backward. Timothy waved his arm in the air as he turned and looked at everyone, still keeping a firm grip on the officer who was trying to pry Timothy's hand from his throat. "Then how do you explain *this*? Well? Just try to defeat me! Who said that vigilantes and heroes don't exist? Who decided that?" He pushed the cop harder into the car. "I had a firefighter back in Minnesota say the same thing. I respect all of you and your profession, and I'm a good-hearted man, but I will not tolerate anyone mocking our profession. Just let us do our job."

Sir Thomas gulped. *My God! He isn't speaking or acting out of a passion for the idea of being a hero. This is... obsession and delusion. His mother and Laura were right. He wants to be a hero so badly that he's willing to temporarily be a villain. Whether it's from the pressure he feels or just selfish desire, he's become mentally unstable!* He turned toward Kronos, who watched the scene silently with an emotionless face, hoping to be reassured that he was wrong.

"Wait, I believe you!" Timothy turned to see a female cop taking a step forward. She kept her gun pointed down, although she was ready to draw it at any time. Her eyes glanced over at Kronos. "I saw you on the news the other day. I thought it was a hoax or something, but I can see with my own eyes that you're real." Timothy loosened his grip on the cop and then threw him to the ground. "You're Minnesota Speedster, aren't you? That's your hero name?"

"More or less, though The Chronological Changer is a temporary name that I also go by. We mean no harm, and we hope to work with you peacefully regarding this situation." The cop Timothy had thrown to the ground angled his gun upward at Timothy's head. After a moment of hesitation and with shaky hands, the cop shot at Timothy. Everyone flinched, except for Kronos. With heroic and quick reflexes, Timothy dodged the bullet, then grabbed the police officer before speedily running down the block with him to a four-way intersection. He then threw the cop away from himself before he quickly returned to the scene, all within a few seconds. "That guy was annoying, and officers and bystanders who get in the way of heroes are essentially criminals who should be charged with the obstruction of justice. Besides that, attempted assault or murder on any hero is punishable."

Bloody Hell, Sir Thomas thought to himself. *What is he even talking about? The way he's acting makes it seem like he believes that the hero-society already exists and that he's a popular hero in it. Obstruction of justice? Coppers and bystanders are criminals if they get in the way? This is madness.* Sir Thomas gulped, but he did not know what to do.

The female cop slowly readjusted the grip on her gun as she looked at Timothy, who was cacking his neck. Every movement he made, from the fidgeting of his fingers to the slightest tilt of his head, was far faster than even the fastest humans could hope to achieve, and he seemed like a glitched character in a video game. She gulped in anxiety, but she wanted to settle everything before anyone else got hurt, and it seemed like talking would be more effective than shooting. "What are you doing here in Florida, though? I-"

Out of nowhere, a heavy toll echoed throughout Homestead as a metal fist struck a giant bell of the open tower of a church down the street by the body of the officer that Timothy had thrown. "**They've traveled all the way to the nearby sea in the hopes that they could defeat me!**" a monstrous voice boomed like thunder. The voice was followed by sinister laughter that shattered the air, and each deep note was filled with unstoppable power. The church bell tolled ominously again, loudly echoing throughout the town as if to alert everyone of incoming death and destruction.

Everyone instinctively looked up toward the church steeple, feezing in place as they spotted a tall figure with burning red eyes looming next to the large bell under the open tower. The monstrous man was encompassed in black smoke, his cloak whipping viciously in the harsh wind, which was bringing in dark clouds from the sky behind him. The figure thrust the giant bell away from him so that it would toll on its own as he jumped down from the tower, cracking and destroying the pavement below him. The bell tolled every six seconds as the ominous figure walked toward the group of officers and heroes, bringing with him not only a storm of black smoke but a petrifying aura of death and fear. As he approached, he appeared to be larger and larger. It started to rain, and the storm clouds in the sky above seemed to be following the humanoid as the wild wind flowed toward the group from behind the tall man approaching them.

The cops immediately turned their attention and guns toward the figure, no longer concerned about the heroes. Some of their legs and knees shook, but they all held their ground. One officer attempted to shine a flashlight into the increasing black smoke that was filling the street, but it had no effect. All that they could see was the living silhouette approaching, slowly, but dangerously, creating a feeling of crippling dread. The ground shook with the force of a tank rolling by with each powerful step the looming humanoid made.

"I am Damon, also known as The Sinful Son and the universe's unholy chosen one. My person you did dare to seek, and now you're all frozen and cannot speak. Heroes, where are you words of encouragement and salvation to prove that you're all the best of this nation? I cannot blame you for your frozen silence, as it's only natural when fearing such violence. You mistake me for a villain, but I am not one at all, and I hope that none of you will have to fall. Peacefully, this can all be resolved without blood if you heroes are truly about justice and love. I have nothing against any of you but negotiate or capture, that I must do. My boss has taken an interest in your power to run at such speeds, as it's something she thinks she needs."

Sir Thomas slowly glanced around before whispering to Timothy and Kronos. "On our way here, Mr. Godwin, you lectured us about his innocence and how we should find out more before making a final decision. I was hesitant, but I agree with you. He's working for someone else, just as you predicted. Here's our chance to talk and find out-"

"No," Timothy replied coldly. "We can't take that chance."

"Don't speak to me so coldly as if I'm any old bloke," Sir Thomas retorted. "I won't allow you to do something foolish in your desperate desire to put on a show and be recognized as a hero. This isn't the time for being a hero and thinking with your heart. The wisest decision right now would be to think rationally and negotiate with this man. We'll save a lot more lives that way, and that's the goal of a hero: to save lives. It's not to fight villains in order to gain popularity so you can change the world using your fame. That'd be selfish!"

"I see my mom poisoned your mind, old man. Forgot the idea of him being innocent. There's no doubt that he's trying to trick us or something. His stance and movements are relaxed yet lethal, and he's completely open yet seems to be defended in every way. We have to quickly take him down before he hurts anyone else," Timothy stated as he ran off even faster than before. His burst forward expelled all air around him as he took off like the bullet of a sniper rifle.

Damon, who was just passing a four-way intersection, saw the green flash of light rushing toward him. With an explosive burst of speed and strength, he side-jumped over to the closest corner and ripped a stop sign out of the ground, pole and all, before swinging it like a baseball bat, smashing Timothy with the giant octagon, sending him flying across the street. He had just narrowly avoided being slammed by the charging speedster, who had been unable to avoid the dark fiend's attack.

Resting the stop sign over his shoulder like it truly were a baseball bat, despite how heavy it was, Damon lumbered toward Timothy, who was on the ground, trying to understand what had just happened. "*I suggested a peaceful solution to our current conflict, and instead, you rushed toward me like a cop toward an escaping convict. Now, unfortunately, to the ground, you did drop, for I had to force you to stop. I was once more human than any other being alive, and because of that, I barely did survive. I am now a monster from what others have done, and I did not choose to create The Sinful Son. My goal now is to be a savior for those who have been in my shoes, for that is the only thing I have left to do.*" Damon continued to menacingly stomp toward Timothy, who had just rolled over to get onto his knees.

Kronos shook his head in disappointment as he and Sir Thomas looked on at the scene down the street with concern. "Unlike me, he should have listened to you, Thomas. The truth hurts, but you're right about how he is acting and thinking. Ever since we've been here, he's been a different man. Foolishness results in hindrance and harm." Damon raised the stop sign sideways high above his head to bring it down on Timothy in a manner that would slice his torso open. "Now I have to save his sorry ass. It's just within its range," Kronos muttered as he swiftly fired the D.O.O.M. Shooter.

The yellow beam ripped through the air and then followed the path that Kronos traced, slicing a street light at its base. The pole slipped and then quickly fell toward the fighting men, and Damon threw the stop sign away as he caught the pole from crushing them both.

"Quick, get out of there, Mr. Godwin!" Sir Thomas shouted.

While Damon was distracted with throwing the metal pole of the street light off of him in outrage, Timothy speedily ran over to Kronos and Sir Thomas, barely escaping death. He skidded past them a foot as he came to a stop. "He's a lot stronger than I thought," Timothy coughed out. "That stop sign he smashed me with did a lot of damage. More than I imagined it would have. He swung it so fast and hard that I didn't have a chance to dodge it. I don't think anything is broken, though."

"You're fortunate, Timothy," Kronos stated harshly. "A few seconds later, and the black smoke would have been covering both of you, and

I probably wouldn't have been able to make the shot. Quit acting recklessly. You're going to get yourself killed, and if that happens, I'm bailing out, along with Thomas. We signed up to help you, not to save this town. If you die, we're leaving, and your legacy will be nothing but a tragic tale. We agreed to help you be a hero, not a villain, or a selfish man who endangers others. Understand? Now we can't even see him," Kronos stated as he pointed down the road at Damon. Between the dark clouds above them and the exponentially growing black smoke clouding the street, almost nothing was visible. The rain was coming down harder with each second. "Besides that, he's wearing vantablack material. Half of the time, he looks two-dimensional, and when he isn't, you can barely see him at all. Be on high alert. Old man, you better get out of here."

"I appreciate your concern, Kronos, but this old man can handle himself, and I'm certainly not abandoning you or Mr. Godwin. Although our lack of a plan is making me feel rather gutted. Due to the black smoke and the number of people and objects encompassed in it, it'll be too risky for Mr. Godwin to use his speed powers without colliding into something. And a sharpshooter like yourself can't shoot what he can't see. Unless, of course, those sunglasses of yours have a few tricks of their own, which wouldn't leave me gobsmacked at all by now."

Kronos smirked.

Once again, Damon spoke louder and more violent than thunder, both with unstoppable power and intimidating death in each demonic word. "*I am always in a constant state of anger, rage, vengeance, and hate! Your rude behavior has made me feel even worse, and the next time you ride in a vehicle, it'll be a hearse.*" He roared more monstrously than the most brutal animal sounds conglomerated together into a fearsome creation that could shatter a person's hope with a single fiendish note. "*No one had to be hurt or die, but you've waved my generous mercy goodbye. Now, every one of your bones shall break, and I'll laugh maniacally at the cracking sounds they make. As an unholy being, I can always sense fear, and you all completely reek of it here! Every step I take is another step upon the path toward emptying the burdens upon my back. Do you think the yellow and green light shall be able to pierce through darkness far worse than the blackness of night?"* Damon had reached the first two police cars, though nothing was visible except for a wall of black smoke taller than him. The sound of shattering glass was heard as the lights on the two cars were smashed, the red and blue vanishing.

Instinctively, the cops closest to the smashed vehicles started shooting into the black smoke, but it was a useless effort. The three cops screamed as a pair of red eyes burning worse than the flames of the deepest layer of Hell appeared above them, looking down at them with condescension and a condemning glare that sentenced them to an instant death. They turned around and ran over to the other side of the diamond, joining the other cops and two vehicles.

Kronos, Timothy, and Sir Thomas had all backed up past the vehicles and cops, trying to get into the clear air. They watched in horror as, without warning, the officers fell over sick, some of them throwing up. They moaned and groaned in pain or as if depressed, and some of them began to suffer from extreme anxiety. The female officer, who was the furthest away from Damon, called in backup and explained the situation before falling to the ground, hugging herself and crying.

Quickly noticing what was happening, Kronos and Sir Thomas covered their nose and mouth, trying not to breathe in the chemicals of depression and damnation. While the officers screamed and fired shots at the figure in their futile effort to combat **The Sinful Son**, the three men began to come up with a plan. Before they could discuss anything, however, Timothy told Kronos and Sir Thomas to close their eyes as he threw out one of the time flash-grenades that were strapped to him. It seemed as if they were in the middle of a hurricane, as his grenade sent a flash of light rippling throughout the darkness that was beginning to consume everything and everyone.

A few of the cops who had been able to resist the depression-gas that was mixed within the black smoke now slowed down, affected by the illusion Timothy had just sent out. They moved in slow motion, desperately shooting their guns and swinging their fists through the darkness. Damon, however, seemed unaffected as he continued to massacre the cops as more arrived on the other side of the black wall of smoke in an attempt to help out. The remaining blue and red flashes of light faintly pierced the darkness before they were smashed by the unstoppable overlord.

Timothy went to throw another sphere out, but Kronos stopped him. "That won't work. His mouth and eyes are most likely covered, as his voice is being filtered, and you said he wore goggles or something."

"Right. That sucks-"

Kronos shoulder-checked Timothy out of the way as Damon jumped out of the darkness from behind Timothy in an attempted surprise attack. Using the Atomic Gauntlet, Kronos countered the lethal blow from Damon's right hand, directly connecting with the punch. The two metal fists colliding powerfully as the metal bang echoed above the wind and rain, expelling the black smoke in the area away for a second. The two fists pushed against each other, but Kronos was outmatched, and he jerked back as Damon broke through, ending up punching the ground and smashing the pavement apart.

"*You are just like me in terms of advancement above humanity, and I can tell by your outfit that your just as equal when it comes to sanity. You have my respect!*" The black smoke continued to flow out of Damon's cloak, and soon, Kronos and Timothy were encompassed in the darkness as well as it took over the area they were in. "*There are only two of you left standing before myself, and I'll deal with you two before anyone else. A fight like this only happens once in one's entire life, for this is far greater than the death granted by a gun or knife. My only order is to bring back Timothy alive, but I can't control whether he'll live or die. You with the metal upon your fist and spine, I'll allow you to escape this one single time.*" Damon disappeared amongst the raging sea of darkness with a maniacal laugh of demonic joy.

Unlike Timothy, Kronos could track movement in the smoke using his high-tech sunglasses, but fighting **The Sinful Son** was not his priority any longer. Sir Thomas had gone missing, and he assumed that his caretaker had breathed in the chemical that attacked the gut microbiome, and that concerned him. So, Kronos left to find Sir Thomas, also knowing that this battle was a personal conflict that Timothy had to deal with himself. Kronos had the ability to manipulate atoms, and he could easily use it to destroy **The Sinful Son** if he wanted, but he knew that Timothy needed to fight this villain himself to change his life and feel like a true hero.

Noticing that both Kronos and Sir Thomas were gone, Timothy started to panic a bit. He thought back to his conversation with Kronos about whether or not people were strongest or weakest when completely alone, and he assumed a fighting stance as he braced himself to find out the answer. He clenched his hands into fists, and at superhuman speed, he bounced up-and-down and left-to-right like a boxer warming up. He knew that **The Sinful Son** was lurking amongst the darkness and that the raging storm above, which was growing worse with each passing second, would work to his enemy's advantage. With the odds so stacked against them, Timothy knew that it was the perfect time for a hero to shine, and that helped his hope and determination grow.

A bright strike of lightning branched out across the sky in the distance as the rain began to pour down more viciously. Everyone was drenched. As the powerful lightning illuminated the area, through the smoke, Timothy saw **The Sinful Son**. He towered above everyone else, over seven feet tall. His red eyes burned through the black smoke with indescribable rage and hatred. The illuminated outline of the overlord was holding a defeated cop in one hand, their head bent unnaturally. The lightning disappeared as quickly as it had been birthed in the sky. With the death of the lightning, the silhouette of the unstoppable humanoid also disappeared. The red illumination of Damon's artificial eyes faded away with him as he vanished in the darkness, laughing maniacally in a way that would make anyone's knees cave in, collapsing the person to the ground.

Using his incredible speed and willing to risk possibly colliding with something, Timothy began to quickly run all throughout the street, zig-zagging through all of the black smoke, leaving a temporary trail of green light. Along with the light, the black smoke was blown away wherever Timothy sped by, though it made little difference.

Damon laughed monstrously from somewhere within the unholy darkness. "*Trying to create some green light so you might actually survive this fight? A clever idea that deserves applause, but I'm afraid you're trail quickly falls. You'll never find me, for I am too quick, and a single wrong breath will leave you sick. I've been playing around quite too much today, but I've never gotten my way, so I might as well enjoy it while it lasts, but unfortunately, I should probably end this all fast. After all, it's rather hard to suppress my undying wrath and my desire to destroy everything in my path,*" Damon bellowed as he watched the green trails of light speedily zipping across here and there as Timothy continued to run around the raging sea of black smoke. He ran away from where he had just spoken, as he knew Timothy would run past there soon enough in an attempt to find him.

"Then consider me indestructible," Timothy said confidently as he continued to run. "Kronos nicknamed you The Dark Depressor. That's exactly what you are, and I'm going to stop your reign of terror. You won't be killing me so easily. You may be quick, but I've spent my whole life training and researching how to become faster than anyone who has ever existed, and that includes you!"

"*Undoubtedly, you are faster, indeed, but you're not at all as powerful as me. I am fueled by emotions that go beyond all humanity, as well as beyond the combinations of saneness and insanity,*" Damon boomed before moving to a different spot. "*The Dark Depressor is the name you have chosen to bestow upon me, but The Darkest Depressor is who I shall soon be! You haven't even seen half of my true power, and with each day, I grow stronger every hour. When it comes to speed and running, you may be the best, but even speedsters can't outrun death!*"

Timothy laughed at the condemning threat. "Well, I don't plan on trying to run away from you! I'm The Chronological Changer! The very first hero in our world, and the founder of the future hero-society that generations will benefit from. Just like you, I've been holding back on my power as well. I didn't want to accidentally hurt any of the officers or my allies, but now that they're out of the way, I can let loose." Timothy pulled out his Whip-Watch and swung it all around him before swinging it in a small circle at his side while he waited for the right opportunity. He pressed the button on the weapon, and the spikes came popping out, ready to fight for the sake of justice.

Chuckling deeply, Damon continued to jump from spot to spot in the darkness, cracking the ground wherever he landed, invigorated with power by Timothy's threat.

Lightning flashed across the sky again, and Timothy saw Damon, who happened to be close by. "Now, I know where you are," Timothy shouted as he charged at full speed toward Damon. "Let's see how you like my ultimate move: Time-Tornado!" Just as he was about to reach Damon, Timothy gripped the end of the Whip-Watch chain tightly, and he spun in a circle at remarkably insane speeds, creating a green tornado of particles and power. The amount of physical strain it put on his body was gruesome, but he had trained for it. Despite his training, the ultimate move left Timothy's mind spiraling around without any thoughts to get his bearings, but it was almost impossible to stop, and getting hit by it was either paralyzing or fatal. He spun and spun and spun, forming a tornado of green light with an outer ring of death that was formed by the head of the watch. "You're *finished* for, The Dark Depressor, because this will stop *any* enemy! Now, die!"

All of Timothy's bubbling hope and confidence instantly drained away, replaced by utter fear and dread as the Whip-Watch stopped moving, and Timothy got wrapped up in the chain, his spinning body continuing to spin for a moment after the Whip-Watch had stopped moving.

Another vicious lightning strike in the sky behind the monstrous figure of **The Sinful Son** showed that he had caught the weapon. His rage-filled red eyes flickered back on, and using his thumb, Damon cracked the glass on the clock. "*Speechless, without a word to say, because your ultimate move was nothing more than a small obstacle in my way! I am truly disappointed by how weak that attack was, and it barely cracked my metal gloves. My strength goes far beyond what your speed could generate, for it is powered by undying hate,*" Damon yelled as he took a menacing step forward.

Timothy's head was still whirling around and spinning. His sight was warped, and his breathing was all over the place. On top of that all, his spirit had shattered. "Impossible," he coughed out as he untangled himself from the golden chain that was wrapped around him.

Damon lumbered toward the panicking Timothy, who was in complete shock from what happened. With each monstrous step, the ground shook mildly within in the area, and directly beneath his foot, the ground cracked more and more as he stepped more forcefully to intimidate Timothy, leaving craters in his wake. "*Without a doubt, I can admit that you are very brave, but there is no chance that you could ever be a hero who does save. You're not a hero but rather something far worse than a zero. You're a failure whose actions have resulted in the deaths of innocent lives, and now these men have left behind their children and wives. It all started when you attacked me first without warning, and now you won't live to see another morning.*"

"Not good," Timothy coughed out. "I have to do something." He struggled to keep his balance, and he held on to the chain for his life, suffering from the consequences of using the Time-Tornado. Timothy focused as best as he could as he glanced at the approaching feet, noticing that Damon was wearing advanced, heavy-duty metal boots. The left boot came down on the head of an officer who was half-dead on the ground. His head caved in, the skull crushed flat with snapping sounds, dark blood coating the asphalt which was barely visible.

Damon was now close enough to Timothy that the outline of his horrifying figure could be seen against the black smoke, which had now stopped pouring out of his cloak. The slanted red diamond eyes beamed inches away from Timothy's face. Still a little messed up from spinning so fast, this image blurred and warped in Timothy's mind creating an even worse nightmare than ***The Sinful Son*** already was. Damon's voice seemed to crawl all along Timothy's skin as he came even closer to the defeated hero. He yanked the Whip-Watch right out of Timothy's hand and threw it behind himself into the darkness. "***I won't ask you what your last words are as of now, for to Francesca's will, you'll have to bow. Tell me, though, before we all go: are you afraid? Hmm, that sounds cliche.***"

"Are... are you rhyming?" Timothy asked as he stood up straight, making a fist in each hand.

"***This entire time, I have spoken only in rhyme!***" Damon boomed in outrage as thunder shook the sky above. "***How dare you insult my literary genius like that, and for it, I think I'll break your back! It's the most rhyming I've ever done in my life before, and that's the question you've chosen to ask at Death's door?***" Enraged, Damon clenched a fatal fist and raised it back in the air behind him, ready to kill Timothy with a single punch. "***DIE***," he almost whispered harshly as his fist flew through the air like a nuclear missile and smashed into Timothy's face.

The force was so powerful that Timothy actually flew backward through the air for a few feet, his body airless for a few seconds before it crashed back onto the ground.

Blood came spurting out of Timothy's nose, and his head was even fuzzier than before. Struggling, he managed to get up to his feet.

Damon thundered forward, taking his time as he walked through the darkness. "***Such a devastating blow directly to the head would have left any regular human being dead. Your body is far superior to most, but the party's not over, and I'm the host. You have my respect for managing to survive, but that doesn't change the fact that you'll die.***" He stopped just a foot away from Timothy, looming over him like the merciless judgment of God.

His body aching, Timothy slowly looked up at the demonic figure that towered unstoppably above and before him, staring into the red eyes that were condemning him. His mind stopped spinning, and he took a deep breath as he gathered his senses together, knowing that he could not give up just yet. His hope and willpower began to grow as he forced himself to remember why he was there. "I may be at Death's door, but I came here for a ding-dong-ditch. In fact, I'm going to light a bag of steaming dog crap on fire just so you stain your shoes, you bastard. You asked me if I was afraid before, and the truth is that I'm not because I'm the world's first and greatest hero, and you're nothing but a coward! You're hiding in black smoke because you're afraid and know that you need every advantage in order to win a-"

Not seeing the attack, Timothy was sent back to the ground by a powerful kick to the chest from **The Sinful Son** that knocked all of the air from his lungs, along with a few teaspoons of blood. Somehow, Timothy's sternum and ribs were still intact.

"*That is unforgivable blasphemy that will result in your death after I rip off your head! I'm surprised that you're still not dead. How dare you call me a coward as you fight against me this hour! I went to death and came back to life after slitting my own wrists with a knife. Fueled by emotions that allowed me think for myself, I moved on to a level above everyone else. My humanity was torn from me and The Sinful Son did emerge, and you're insult has only made my power surge.*" Damon grabbed Timothy by his neck and lifted him up into the air with one arm, bringing the pair of steampunk goggles face to face with the burning red eyes, which seemed to burn more violently than before.

Timothy was helpless as he tried to kick Damon, but he was unable to reach his body. In a desperate attempt, Timothy kicked both of his legs as fast as he could, creating a shaking force unlike any other. It was a move he had used to break wood and even cement blocks, but Damon's grip around Timothy's neck only tightened as thunder shook the sky again. He tried to pry the fingers away from his neck, but that too was a futile effort. "You're quite the first villain for me to face. What," Timothy coughed, gasping for air, "what are you?"

Damon's demonic voice was louder than ever as he spoke, just inches away from Timothy's face as he moved his victim closer. "***Even I do not quite understand what I was, though I am still a man. The Sinful Son is the universe's unholy chosen one. I'm an unstoppable force of revenge that will lead all I hate to their end. I am the darkness of destructive depression, and the greatest teacher of your final lesson!***" He threw Timothy through the dark air, who fell to the ground in excruciating pain, skidding across the asphalt. Damon then ran forward, and picking up Timothy, charged him forcefully into the wall of a building. Timothy fell to the ground, his back bruised and almost broken as blood shot out of his mouth.

"Oh, fuck," Timothy coughed out. Using all of his strength, he stood up, assuming a fighting stance. "Bring it on, you-" A devastating blow struck Timothy across the face as Damon punched him with a right hook. Despite his enhanced reflexes and speed, Timothy had been unable to avoid the powerful right hook that came soaring through the darkness, and it sent him flying to his right. He slumped against the wall behind him in pain. He put his hand to the lower half of his face, the green bandanna around it mutilated, feeling that he was heavily bleeding from his left cheek. The left side of his steampunk goggles had been torn up and scratched, which made it even harder to see through the darkness, but Timothy managed to see the small spikes on the top edge of Damon's knuckles, which must have scraped him due to the angle of the punch. "I guess this is it," Timothy whispered to himself. "So much for being a hero, let alone the world's greatest hero. I ended up being the biggest failure of all time." Then, beyond the menacing outline of ***The Sinful Son***, Timothy saw a light coming. At first, he thought it was the famous light of death's tunnel, but he quickly ducked down as the devastating yellow beam went flying toward him.

The yellow beam of power skimmed past ***The Sinful Son***, who swiftly evaded the attack at the last second like a phantom. The beam hit into the wall of the building behind Timothy, forming a gaping hole in it. A few chunks of brick fell down and hit Timothy, who covered his head to protect himself. He looked out past the monster in front of him to see where the beam had come from, and he half-laughed.

Kronos came running out of the darkness and through the rain toward them. He fired again, but ***The Sinful Son*** turned his body and dodged the beam with swiftness, the sparkling energy outlining his horrid figure. Turning around, he charged forward at Kronos and lept over him with a powerful jump, landing behind Kronos and cracking the ground. Before Kronos could turn around, Damon grabbed either side of him and threw him away, as he wanted to deal with Timothy alone.

Menacingly, ***The Sinful Son*** slowly walked back over to Timothy, who was slowly standing up. Thunder boomed again as a merciless lightning strike lit up the sky. Timothy looked up at the towering figure, assuming another fighting stance. "Although he failed to fight you, Kronos gave me all the time I needed to get back on my feet. You said you're the teacher of my final lesson? Well, I'm dropping out of your class," Timothy yelled as he quickly ripped a time-grenade off of his sash and threw it at Damon. The sphere flew through the air, its timer automatically counting down. Instinctively, Damon caught it, and before he could throw it away, the grenade exploded. Although the illusions did not affect him, the small explosion and shock were enough to send Damon stumbling back a few steps. "There's your end of the year gift, bitch! Class dismissed!"

The rain was slowing down, and the weather went from a storm back down to a drizzle, though the sky overhead remained dark. Using the opportunity, Timothy speedily ran away from ***The Sinful Son***, who was momentarily distracted. Looking around for anyone to help him, Timothy spotted no one alive or nearby. Kronos had disappeared again, and Sir Thomas was still missing. Then, almost as if they were angels answering a pray, two helicopters flew in, shining a bright light on the scene below. The wind caused by the rotating blades of the helicopters started to blow most of the gas and smoke away, clearing the air, making it visible once more. The only darkness that remained was from the storm clouds overhead, and even they were beginning to lighten up.

Pumping a fist into the air, Timothy laughed. "I didn't do as much as I wanted, but either way, your reign of terror on Florida and its people ends here, *The Sinful Son*! No matter how powerful you are, your death is now inevitable."

The Sinful Son turned and glared at Timothy, petrifying him with his demonic gaze and monstrous laugh of power. "*Is that truly what you believe? Then you are undoubtedly naive. Only I can defeat my horrific self, and I shall not die because of someone else. Besides that, not a gun, a knife, or any kind of machine would ever be able to destroy me. The helicopters that provided you with such joy are nothing more to me than a child's toy. Now, from the sky, they shall fall, for I am the one whole judges all!*" Opening up his vantablack cloak, which was parted down the middle, Damon whipped out a large knife that was attached to the inside of the drawl. Squatting down and drawing his arm with the knife back, Damon launched himself eight feet into the air with an explosive jump. At his highest point, with tremendous force, he threw the knife at the helicopter, aiming for the tail rotor. The knife was powerfully magnetic, and following the path Damon had set for it, the blade collided with the tail rotor, which then malfunctioned and exploded. Landing dramatically with one fist on the ground between his two legs, Damon broke all of the asphalt below him apart, and he stood up ominously before turning around at Timothy and laughing menacingly. "*It would appear that my power has grown, even more than I had expected or known.*"

"*Impossible*. This can't be happening," Timothy cried out as he watched the scene above, powerless to do anything about it.

The helicopter went spiraling through the air, spinning in fatal circles as the pilots tried to control the aircraft. The uncontrollable helicopter collided into the second one, which attempted to veer clear of its path, the two helicopters heading down dangerously and at high speeds. Fires were blazing throughout the hunks of metal as they crashed into the ground behind Damon, across the street from Timothy.

"His power level is only growing stronger with each passing second, and he's definitely getting angrier," Timothy speedily muttered to himself. "I thought he was exaggerating, but he really has been holding back. This guy is more powerful than we thought. I guess I should've just tried talking to him first. Well, being a hero is sometimes trial and error, I guess." In dread, Timothy watched as the menacing figure stormed over to one of the crashed helicopters, and ripping the door off, found a survivor. He threw the man out of the aircraft and onto the pavement behind him. "I got you," Timothy yelled as he quickly sprinted over at incredible speeds and grabbed the man before returning to the other side of the street from the crashed helicopters. Without hesitation, Timothy quickly ran to the helicopters and back four times, rescuing four survivors in a matter of a few seconds, forced to leave one dead pilot behind.

Damon turned around, looking over at Timothy and the survivors he had rescued. "***You have my respect as The Sinful Son, as a good job is what you have done. That was the quickest I've seen you move yet, and you seem more calm than upset. I am honored to be your first official rival, even though this has barely been a test of survival. This battle has dragged out for far too long, and soon the sirens of the government shall play a song. I need to end this now before there gathers a spectating crowd. Unfortunately, it's time to take you back to my base after knocking you unconscious with a punch to the face.***" Damon took a powerful step forward, cracking his neck and forming a fist in each hand.

"You're not wrong about that! It's time we end this. The rain has stopped falling, the clouds are grey, and your black smoke is gone. Now, you're nothing more than a man in a costume, just as I am. That is why, for the sake of humanity, I swear that I, The Chronological Changer, will defeat you, right here and now." On top of his speed drug, Timothy injected himself with his heart-formula, drastically increasing his heart rate. Speeding off in a flash of green, he ran down the street and retrieved his damaged Whip-Watch, which he had spotted once the black smoke cleared, before quickly running in a large circle around *The Sinful Son* randomly smashing him with the Whip-Watch.

"*Keeping your distance so you can hit me without getting smacked away, now that's the best strategy you've had all day. Your blows, however, are barely doing any damage at all, and I felt more pain when I once stubbed my toe against a wall.*" Damon shielded his chest and face with his arms and hands, understanding that his face was most vulnerable. To escape the circle of attacks, Damon squatted down and jumped up to leap over Timothy.

"Nice try, but you're not getting away that easily," Timothy yelled with a bright smile as he launched the Whip-Watch through the air and wrapped it around Damon's right arm. "Take this!" He pulled down with all of his strength, and Damon was pulled backward and slammed into the ground. "After seeing you jump so powerfully before, I knew you were going to try and jump over me."

"*Of course you saw through such a feeble plan, and that is what I expected you to predict and understand,*" Damon stated as he menacingly stood up, the Whip-Watch still wrapped around his arm. His prideful smirk was hidden in his own darkness. He stared down at Timothy, who was starting to worry but still kept a stern face and grip on the chain. "*I knew you would use this yo-yo to try and drag me down, though, I figured you'd wrap it around my leg then slam me to the ground. This works out even better, with my arm wrapped up like this, as now I can reel you in, you worthless fish,*" Damon boomed as he began to pull the golden chain, hand over hand, toward himself.

"Oh, crap," Timothy muttered through clench teeth as he pulled back on the chain with all of his strength, being dragged closer toward Damon. The sturdy chain had been designed not to break, and so it became a tug-of-war. "You're a lot stronger than I am, so you planned this perfectly, but you didn't take into account my speed," Timothy exclaimed as he tried to walk backward, still pulling on the chain. "Small forces in fast enough doses can quickly match your strength!" Timothy dug his feet into the ground as best as he could before stomping them up and down, trying to run backward. His legs were powerful, and they moved in a blur as his legs became jackhammers against the pavement. He managed to win the tug-of-war for a few seconds, pulling Damon's arms forward a few inches.

"*That's enough of this foolish, childish play! I cannot afford to waste the time left in this day. You've made me a lot angrier than I already am, and now I'll destroy you with the force of water breaking a dam,*" Damon bellowed as he yanked on the chain robustly, pulling Timothy forward through the air. He let go, however, as he heard a gunshot before collapsing to his knees and then falling forward onto the ground. "*This unforeseen shot has pierced my abs, far worse than the wretched words of my former dad! A bullet, but I do not know how it could be, for all the cops died after encountering me. I undoubtedly took care-*" Damon coughed and gagged before two more shots hit him, causing him to scream monstrously in agony before growing quiet.

"Except you forgot to take care of the *care*taker," Sir Thomas said as he helped Timothy to his feet, who was shocked to see him. "Your chemical formula certainly did a number on my old guts, but I managed to get away and recover before I could breathe in too much of it. I waited until the moment your guard was lowered to make my surprise attack. It turns out that you're human after all, and a few bullets were all that was needed to end you. Unlike Mr. Godwin I don't care about the pride of training and using melee weapons. I'll shoot my enemies if I have to."

The clouds began to drift away, and a few rays of sunlight managed to slip through every now and then. The humidity increased as it got hotter and hotter.

"I can't believe it. You crazy son of a bitch," Timothy said with a laugh as he slapped Sir Thomas on the back. "I love old people!"

"You have a *long* way to go until you become a hero, Mr. Godwin, but you weren't too shabby out there today," Sir Thomas remarked as he clapped Timothy on the shoulder. He turned and looked at him, gasping as he did. "Blimey. Why… you've grown a mustache, and some chin hair as well! You have a few more patches of grey hair as well, but not bad at all, considering the battle. I suppose you didn't have your body sped up for too long, but you best shave Mr. Godwin. You're a man who does not look good with facial hair."

"I'll keep that in mind, and… I'm sorry about before. I got so caught up in wanting to be a hero that I didn't act like one at all. This is all my fault, and it's a sin and a burden that I'll carry with me for the rest of my life. I barely did anything today, other than getting my ass kicked. I'll grow from this for sure, though." Sir Thomas eyed The Dark Depressor cautiously as Timothy put away the damaged Whip-Watch. "Thank you for everything, Sir Thomas. Ugh, it hurts to talk." Timothy held his left cheek in pain, but it had already begun to heal. "My speed is about to wear off, but we still have to look for Kronos. Anyway, you saved me. You saved us all." He nodded his head at Sir Thomas in a sign of gratitude as he did a mini-salute.

Sir Thomas nodded his head back and smiled. "Just doing my job as a caretaker and a gentleman. That's all." His smile quickly faded as he saw Damon's body stir with a slight movement.

"How ignorant of you to believe that I would die after merely being shot by a guy. I told you that only I can kill myself, and now your hands will be soaked with the blood of someone else!"

The speed-drug in his system now diminished, Timothy was slower than ever as his nervous system reverted back to its normal state, his body and mind tired and sluggish. As quickly as he could, however, Timothy spun around and saw the incoming figure of **The Sinful Son** charging at him. He felt his body get slammed, but it was not Damon who had hit him. The slam had come from his side. Sir Thomas, with the promise he had made to Laura Godwin echoing in his head, had pushed Timothy out of the way. Timothy fell to the ground in shock, his head ringing. Black smoke spilled out of a small smoke-bomb before his eyes. As he stood up, he was all alone. ***The Sinful Son*** had instantly disappeared, taking Sir Thomas along with him.

www.ingramcontent.com/pod-product-compliance
Lightning Source LLC
LaVergne TN
LVHW012059070526
838200LV00074BA/3734